Tessa dropped her head back, her hair brushing his arm.

The truth was the last thing Ian wanted, or at least the last thing he was willing to give back. "Sure."

"The fact is, I'm wishing for a man."

Now we're talking. At least *she* had some common sense about what was going down here. He threaded his finger into her silky locks, gently turning her face toward his. "Looks like you found one."

"But I want something specific." In her eyes, he could see the flecks of gold…and a hell of a lot more. Goodness. Understanding. *Truth.* All things he could never reciprocate.

"Whatever floats your boat, Tessa. I can do slow and sweet or hard and fast." Her eyes flashed a little. "You can tie me up or take me down."

Another flash, this one more than surprised. Maybe she wasn't quite that adventurous. "I'm yours for the night," he finished, coming closer. "Only the night, though."

He let his lips brush hers, tasting a hint of the ale and something warm and hopeful. Too bad, but he wasn't her hope, not by a long shot.

By the time she figured that out, he'd be long gone.

PRAISE FOR THE
BAREFOOT BAY SERIES

BAREFOOT IN THE SUN

"Fun and engaging...[Readers] will appreciate the resilient heroine and her journey."
—*Publishers Weekly*

"St. Claire's latest novel takes you back to Barefoot Bay, Florida, and the genuine, warm characters who inhabit the coastal town. She explores the bonds of love, friendship, and loyalty, and how far one will go to maintain those bonds. Filled with raw, real emotion, this story will warm your heart as you turn the pages."
—*RT Book Reviews*

"Roxanne St. Claire keeps this series fresh and the characters mesmerizing with stories that are jaw-dropping [and] eye-opening."
—*The Reading Reviewer*
(MaryGramlich.blogspot.com)

BAREFOOT IN THE RAIN

"In a love story with genuinely flawed yet sympathetic characters, set on a picturesque island off the coast of Florida, St. Claire focuses on the complexities of familial relationships, and the past hurts and experiences that can shape them. Honest, genuine, and occasionally gritty, this is a story that will resonate."

—RT Book Reviews

"I'm so glad I found the Barefoot Bay series. Not only are they well-written but [I] love connected books...You'll love it. You'll love it even more if you start with *Barefoot in the Sand*, but each book definitely stands on its own."

—Examiner.com

"[I] really enjoy the Barefoot Bay series and am anxiously awaiting the next in the series. I've come to love and adore these women and the resort they are building together."

—TheBookPushers.com

"This book stayed with me even when I had to put it down. It can challenge the reader and make her think, which is a quality I greatly enjoy in a book...I have to admire Ms. St. Claire for taking risks with this novel. They paid off."

—All About Romance (LikesBooks.com)

BAREFOOT IN THE SAND

"*Barefoot in the Sand*—the first in Roxanne St. Claire's new Barefoot Bay series—is an all-around knockout and soul-satisfying read. I loved everything about this book—the indomitable heroine, the hot hero, the lush tropical setting, and secondary characters I can't wait to read more about. Roxanne St. Claire writes with warmth

and heart, and the community she's built in Barefoot Bay is one I want to revisit again and again and again."
—Mariah Stewart, *New York Times* bestselling author of the Chesapeake Diaries series

"Lovely, lush, and layered—this story took my breath away. Rich, believable characters, multilayered plot, gorgeous setting, and a smokin' hot romance. One of the best books I've read all year."
—Kristan Higgins, *New York Times* bestselling author

"I enjoyed the typical mother/teen relationship Lacey had with Ashley—so comfortable and believable. Lacey is older than Clay, but the difference never matters. The chemistry between them is scorching hot. I adored her friends and I'm looking forward to their stories as well. *Barefoot in the Sand* is a wonderful story with plenty of heat, humor, and heart!"
—*USA Today*'s Happy Ever After blog

"4½ stars! St. Claire, as always, brings a scorching tear-up-the-sheets romance combined with a great story: dealing with real issues starring memorable characters in vivid scenes. Best of all, since this is book one in the Barefoot Bay series, there's more to come."
—*RT Book Reviews*

"Roxanne St. Claire hits a home run with *Barefoot in the Sand*…It is impossible not to be completely enthralled from page one of this outstanding story…You just have to read this beautiful story to find out why I love these characters so much!…Lacey has some really cool chicks as friends and they each have mysterious pasts that I cannot wait to dig into."

—JoyfullyReviewed.com

"There is nothing I didn't love about this book, from the wacky secondary characters to Lacey and Clay themselves…With a cast of zany troubled friends and neighbors, this book will have you dreaming of love all while picturing yourself on a sandy beach with the waves tickling your toes…I cannot wait to return to Barefoot Bay."

—GoodReads.com

"I loved and adored this book…such a fun, lighthearted, and super sexy read…I just know that St. Claire is going to rock the rest of the series, especially if this first book is any indication…Fans of Jill Shalvis, Carly Phillips, and Susan Mallery will definitely want to check out this series! I give *Barefoot in the Sand* an A!"

—TheBookPushers.com

Barefoot by the Sea

roxanne st. claire

FOREVER

NEW YORK   BOSTON

Copyright © 2013 by Roxanne St. Claire
Excerpt from *Barefoot in the Sand* © 2012 by Roxanne St. Claire

Forever
Hachette Book Group
237 Park Avenue
New York, NY 10017

www.HachetteBookGroup.com

Printed in the United States of America

First Edition: October 2013
10 9 8 7 6 5 4 3 2 1

OPM

Forever is an imprint of Grand Central Publishing.
The Forever name and logo are trademarks of Hachette Book Group, Inc.

The Hachette Speakers Bureau provides a wide range of authors for speaking events. To find out more, go to www.hachettespeakersbureau.com or call (866) 376-6591.

The publisher is not responsible for websites (or their content) that are not owned by the publisher.

ATTENTION CORPORATIONS AND ORGANIZATIONS:

Most Hachette Book Group books are available at quantity discounts with bulk purchase for educational, business, or sales promotional use. For information, please call or write:

Special Markets Department, Hachette Book Group
237 Park Avenue, New York, NY 10017
Telephone: 1-800-222-6747 Fax: 1-800-477-5925

For Gena Showalter
My mentor, my friend, my spiritual sister.

Acknowledgments

The team kills it again! Many thanks to all of the people who make this job look so easy and fun, even on the days when it is anything but easy or fun. I have to call a few out for their outstanding contributions:

My partners at Grand Central Publishing/Forever, especially Executive Editor Amy Pierpont, who has proven she can perform magic on a rough draft, along with the entire team who gets the job done every single time (Lauren Plude, Michele Bidelspach, Bob Castillo, Jamie Snider, and Jihan Antoine are standouts!) and the talented folks in art (love this cover!), sales, marketing, and distribution. What an amazing group of dedicated individuals I get to work with every day.

Big love to literary agent Robin Rue of Writers House, who has my back and holds my hand, and assistant Beth Miller for keeping everything running smoothly.

Huge thanks to the awesome Ottawa Romance Writers Association, who showed me true Canadian love and a tour of the city that makes an all-too-brief appearance on these pages. In particular, I'd like to thank Malena Abel, who shared her British intelligence and helped me create a realistic background for the hero.

A very special hug to Elizabeth Brooks, who guided me through the Florida garden, taught me the fine points of harvesting sweet potatoes, and has become my very own Mema. More hugs to Miss Lib's son, awesome Sonny Brooks, who let me drive his tractor and happens to be the finest bro-in-law ever.

My writer friends are the best in the business and I guarantee you wouldn't be reading this without the moral support of a small but mighty group of women who know who they are and why I love them. Kristen, Kresley, Louisa, Laura, Leigh…I'm talking to you. In addition, I'm grounded spiritually by my amazing "quad"—Nina, Megan, and Jill—who aren't writers but know exactly where the story comes from.

I've been overwhelmed by the readers who keep coming back to Barefoot Bay! I'm thrilled to have found such a loyal audience and love connecting with each and every one of you through our small cyber world. Thanks for inspiring me every day and major thanks to my Facebook followers who did the honor of naming Ian/John in this book. You all are amazing!

Of course, I have to acknowledge the home team, who loves me no matter how bad the writing is going, how late the book is, how knotted the plot, how certain I am that "this time I can't do it" even though they know I will. My husband, Rich, our wonderful children, Dante and Mia, and our superdogs, Ginger and Pepper. You make my home and my heart so happy.

Finally, but never last, I thank my Father, the source of all my joy!

Barefoot
by the Sea

Chapter One

⟨ornament⟩

I suppose I could just walk up to a man and *ask* for sperm." Tessa picked up her bottle to punctuate the statement with a sip of cold beer, but froze midway as she took in the reaction around the booth. "Guys, that was a joke."

Her friends weren't laughing. Although the evening out at the local dive was supposed to be a business strategy session, the conversation had, of course, turned personal. After all, the four women might be partners in the Casa Blanca resort, but they were best friends long before that, and no topic was off limits. Not even this one.

"No harm in asking." Next to Tessa, Jocelyn leaned in to make her point over the din of the Toasted Pelican crowd. "They love to give that stuff away."

"Absolutely," Lacey agreed from across the table, her topaz eyes lit with enthusiasm instead of humor. "Knowing your donor takes all the guesswork out of it. What you see is what you get, unlike anonymous sperm."

"Sperrrrrm." Zoe made a disgusted face, her gaze

drifting over the action in the bar. "Couldn't man's life force have a more inviting name? You know, like chocolate or Cabernet?"

"Baby juice?" Jocelyn suggested.

"Liquid gold," Lacey added.

"Nature's protein smoothie," Tessa said dryly.

That made Zoe laugh, but she didn't take her eyes off the crowd. "Says the organic girl."

Tessa waved her beer bottle to prove that she could have plenty of lapses in clean living and to move the conversation along to a more comfortable subject.

"We have bigger issues than my baby needs," she said, looking down at the paper Lacey had printed for them to read, the last line of the brutal review jumping off the page. "Did she really have to call the dining room 'as lively as a morgue'?"

Lacey sighed and pointed to the printout. "We can weather one bitter blogger."

"The Vixen of Vacation Vows is not *one* bitter blogger," Jocelyn said. "Vix is *the* bitter blogger, with thousands of hits a month. No one plans a destination wedding without checking her snark-fest—er, I mean reviews."

And what would those potential guests see when they searched Casa Blanca on Barefoot Bay? The words were still fresh in Tessa's mind. *This sweet homegrown resort might conjure up images of Bogie and Bergman, but brides will be lost in a desert of disaster.*

The review had made them all a little sick and scared. Especially Lacey, who slumped her chin into her palm. "If we don't hire a chef and start getting some positive buzz for Casa Blanca, the resort we spent the last two years of our lives building will never get in the black."

"How long until those wedding consultants can come for a preview?" Tessa asked.

Lacey lifted her head and gave a slow smile. "Eight months until the wedding consultants can get us on their schedule, and by then you can be good and pregnant."

"Or we can be good and out of business."

Lacey closed her eyes at the punch that had to hit her, the resort owner, even harder than the rest of them, who'd just invested and worked there.

Jocelyn waved off Lacey's blues. "Look, with the right chef, a few great events, and some powerful Internet reviews, this winter will have snowbirds flocking to Casa Blanca. When the wedding planners come next summer, we'll be ready to knock their socks off."

She paused long enough for the four of them to share a silent "We hope."

"But your baby dreams are as important as our resort dreams, Tess," Lacey continued. "It took you months to scour all those applications to find a surrogate who meets your exacting standards. What if she gets scooped up by someone else?"

"I hope she doesn't. I've put a deposit down and the clinic has scheduled a house visit and interview. Once they do the psych evaluation…" She paused, knowing that was where the process had fallen apart once before with her ex-husband, and it was the reason she'd never tried again. "I'll meet her and make a final decision. Obviously, I want the perfect surrogate mother as much as I want the perfect sperm donor."

"No one's perfect," Lacey shot back.

"You know what I mean." But did they know? None of these women had any idea how gut-wrenching and grueling infertility had been. "And the baby won't be perfect because these are my eggs, which I harvested already." Defensiveness lifted Tessa's voice as she raised her beer bottle. "Or else I wouldn't be drinking this."

"But you need to line up a donor," Lacey insisted.

"I'm thinking about that. I keep reading these horror stories about donors who lie or have six hundred kids running around and—"

"Didn't I tell you to stay off the Internet on this subject?" Lacey asked.

Tessa ignored the comment and took a sip of beer. "I just haven't made a decision how to handle that when it comes test-tube time."

"Ugh, test tubes are so clinical." Jocelyn groaned. "I still think you should try the old-fashioned way."

Of course they'd all think she should. Her best friends were falling in bed every night with the men they loved. Lacey had a baby, and Zoe's was due in five months. No doubt Jocelyn would be next.

"I tried the old-fashioned way for ten years with my ex-husband." Tessa fought to keep any bitterness out of her tone but might have failed. "And now he's the father of two kids, and I'm…" *Alone*. "Obviously not capable of getting pregnant by traditional methods."

"But Joss is right," Lacey insisted. "Maybe your infertility was Billy's fault."

Tessa angled her head and gave a "Get real" look. "Tell that to his children. *Both* of them."

"I'm only saying maybe you should *try* the traditional way," Jocelyn said. "There is such a thing as being inhospitable to certain sperm. It's an acid and pH-balance thing."

"I know all that." Tessa halted the conversation with a

flat hand. "Billy and I were experts on the subject of fertility." Or futility, as he sarcastically called it. "I think the conversation was the only thing that kept us together so long. Once we gave up trying, our marriage fell apart."

Zoe pulled her gaze from the bar to give a cynical choke. "Yeah, 'cause it had nothing to do with him boning a twenty-two-year-old yoga instructor."

Well, there was that. Tessa studied the moon on her beer label but Jocelyn nudged her arm. "Tess, you need to *make* history, not change it."

"Ah, the life coach speaks."

"The life coach is correct," Lacey said. "When was the last time you had a date? Gave a guy a chance? When was the last time you even thought about getting intimate with a *man* instead of a *test tube*?"

"I'm going to assume that's a rhetorical question."

"How long?" they asked in unison.

"Obviously, I think about sex, since I have a pulse. But a date? No. Not since I found out Billy was doing more than the downward dog with a fertility goddess. So, three years at least."

They shared a suitably pitying look, further irritating Tessa. "Guys, we've been a little busy building a resort and I've started a functioning farmette from nothing."

"None of us has been too busy to fall in love," Jocelyn replied. "And, trust me, some of us did not have it on the to-do list."

Lacey leaned forward, tightening her grip on Tessa's hands. "She's right. Look at the three of us. We're living proof that love can happen when you least expect it."

Tessa looked to the ceiling and breathed a sigh, mining for patience. She didn't begrudge them their happiness, not one single bit. Since they'd met in college and especially since life and love had brought them all together in Barefoot Bay, these women had been sisters to Tessa. Their joy was her joy.

But staring all this *love* in the face every single day wasn't easy. And think if they *did* succeed in making Casa Blanca a premier destination-wedding resort. All the guests would be lovestruck, too. *Oh, kill me now.*

"We want you to be happy," Jocelyn said.

"And pregnant," Lacey added.

The din of Mimosa Key locals blowing off steam competed with an old Fleetwood Mac song on the jukebox, but none of it was loud enough to drown out Tessa's well-meaning friends. Or the truth.

"I don't believe the guy exists who could make me happy *or* pregnant," she finally admitted.

Lacey shook her head. "You don't know that. Someone amazing could be right around the corner."

"Someone amazing *is* right around the corner," Zoe whispered, pointing to the bar. "And I've been studying him for the last twenty minutes. Let me tell you, if that man right there can't make you happy or pregnant, then he can certainly make you scream for mercy. Probably a couple times a night."

Jocelyn swung out of the booth to peer into the crowd. "*Whoa.* Is that a *scorpion* tattooed on his neck?"

"Lovely." Tessa took a deep drink, refusing to look.

Lacey popped up to look over the back of their booth. "You mean that guy with the long hair and…damn. Those are some serious biceps. And triceps. And"—she squinted—"all ceps." She slowly dropped back into her seat. "Speaking of smokin'-hot bad-ass sex gods."

Tessa rolled her eyes again. "Excellent, since 'smokin'-hot bad-ass sex god' was at the top of my donor checklist."

Jocelyn took another look, and then turned back to face the booth, her eyes wide like she'd seen something unspeakable. "He certainly looks like he'd make a potent…protein smoothie."

Zoe's smile wavered. "And, oh wow, I think he's—"

"Enough," Tessa ordered. "I don't care if he looks like Channing Tatum's twin brother."

"He kinda does," Zoe said. "Only hotter. Is that even possible?"

They couldn't help it; they didn't know what it was like to be in her position. "Guys, I was kidding, okay? I'm not going to walk up to some guy and say—"

"You don't have to," Zoe said softly.

Tessa closed her eyes and raised her beer bottle in the air. "Hey, smokin'-hot bad-ass sex god with the long hair and deadly tattoos, can you fill 'er up with some of your potent liquid gold?"

Silence. Dead silence.

Tessa opened her eyes. She felt the presence more than saw it in her peripheral vision. Something smokin' hot, bad ass, and—

"Liquid Gold? Is that a local brew?"

Oh, man. *Sex god* was really kind of an understatement.

In Ian's experience, they didn't usually keep the best-looking one hidden like this. Normally, females used the real beauties as bait. But this girl hadn't even gone out of her way to check him out. And that made the sweet-faced beer drinker begging for action even more appealing.

The blonde who'd been staring at him for the last ten minutes wasn't his type. The one with the wild red curls sported a shiny gold wedding band, and the other one was a little too conservative for his tastes.

But the hottie tucked into the corner was just right, looking at him with wide eyes a shade darker than the amber beer bottle she slowly lowered to the table. She wore barely a hint of makeup, so Ian could see her creamy complexion deepen with a flush as they held eye contact for one heartbeat past casual.

"Beer's a good choice in a place like this," he said, rattling the ice in his rocks glass. "The scotch is watered-down piss."

Surprise flickered in her eyes. Because of the curse word, or had the pisswater been enough to bring out his accent? After all these years, he should know better than to slip and give away his British birth.

"What was that beer called again?" he asked.

"It was…a joke," she said, so softly he almost didn't hear her over the bar ruckus.

"Can I get you something else, then?"

"No, thanks. I'm…fine."

"You sure are."

The other three reacted instantly.

"We need to hit the ladies' room," one of the women said, sliding out to make room for him. "Coming, Zoe?"

The blonde scooted out, too. "We'll refresh the drinks." She turned to the redhead and gave a look with all the subtlety of a baseball bat. "Coming, Lacey?"

"Oh yeah." She nodded and gave an equally transparent raised eyebrow to the woman in the corner. "Hold the booth for us, Tessa. I'm sure we'll be a good long while."

Ian nodded his gratitude. "We'll guard it with our lives." He slid right into the vacated seat next to his doe-eyed target, trapping her in the corner and getting a whiff of something flowery and clean. "Tessa. Pretty. Short for something?"

Finally, she slid him a sideways look, long lashes tapering into the kind of distrustful gaze he'd been eliciting for a few years. If the tattoos, gym time, or total disregard for a haircut didn't scare them, the bike parked out front usually did.

"Just Tessa," she said as her friends disappeared into the bar, leaving laughter and chatter in their wake.

"Just Tessa," he repeated. Not to be funny, but because he'd want to remember the name tomorrow morning when he was rooting around the floor of her flat looking for his jeans. *Apartment, dickhead, not flat.*

"I'm John, by the way."

She hinted at a smile. "Hello, John Bytheway."

Cute. "John Brown."

"That sounds fake."

Because it is. "So tell me something about yourself, Tessa, other than the fact that you like"—he turned the beer bottle and read the label—"Belgian White Wheat Ale." Bloody Americans would buy anything they thought was from Europe.

"Blue Moon's my favorite…" She inched back. "Blue Moon," she said softly, her whole face lighting up in a way that took her from good-looking to gorgeous in the space of a second. "Maybe that's what Aunt Pasha meant."

"Who's Aunt Pasha?"

Her eyes twinkled with a secret. "A late, great fortune-teller."

He inched closer, letting his thigh press against hers and earning another sweet blush. "Did she see trouble in her crystal ball?"

"She saw…something."

"Whatever she saw, I hope it happens tonight." He gave her a slow once-over, enjoying a spark of electricity crackling between them as he admired her toned arms, freckle-dusted skin, and the alluring slope of small but appealing breasts under a simple white T-shirt. This one wasn't trying too hard to get attention, and he liked that. It reminded him of—

Don't go there.

"Are you staying in Mimosa Key?" she asked.

"At the moment." For the past month, since he had to tear-ass out of Singapore, he'd ridden around the state of Florida, finally finding his way over a bridge to this suitably out-of-the-way island. He'd checked in to the first motel he'd found and headed straight out the door for his numbing agents of choice: cheap scotch and a willing woman. He'd found one, and, with a little luck, was looking at the other. "You?"

"I live at the resort up the road in Barefoot Bay."

"You *live* on a resort?"

"I run the gardens."

That explained the sun-kissed skin and shapely shoulders.

"What do you do?" she asked.

"I don't run anything," he admitted. "I just run."

"From what?" She gave him a curious look and he cursed himself again. What was wrong with him tonight? The scotch mustn't be watered down enough.

Instead of answering, he stretched his hand around the back of the booth, letting his fingers graze her shoulder, getting a quick rise of chill bumps on her arm in response.

"You're pretty," he said, happy to note that this time his standard but woefully uncreative line was actually accurate. She was very pretty, in a simple, sweet, genuine way. Another thing that reminded him of—

"You didn't answer my question."

Because I'm still fucked up. "Because you're so pretty I forgot what you asked."

She looked skyward and fought a smile.

"What do you want to know, pretty Tessa?" Not that he'd tell her anything, ever.

"Why do you have a lethal insect tattooed on your neck?"

He angled his head to let her get a real good look, remembering the unspeakably dark night when he'd gotten the ink in some hellhole off Balestier Road.

"Do you have a death wish or something?" she prompted.

"Something." He slugged the rest of his scotch. "What about you?"

"Me?" She laughed softly, with a wry and ironic shake of her head. "Well, I don't wish for death."

He stole a look at her, lost for a second in the honesty in her eyes. Damn it, sometimes the small talk wasn't enough. Maybe this meaningless chatter was a necessary evil before getting a woman on her back, but for one brief instant, Ian ached for…*more.*

More information, more revelation, more than a quick screw to kill the pain for a very short while.

But John Brown couldn't have more. And Ian Browning best not forget that.

"Then what *do* you wish for?" he asked, the question proof that his mouth was ignoring the warnings in his head. *Talk about sex, dumbshit. Not wishes.*

"You want the truth?" She dropped her head back, her hair brushing his arm.

The truth was the last thing he wanted, or at least the last thing he was willing to give back. "Sure."

"The fact is, I'm wishing for a man."

Now we're talking. At least *she* had some common sense about what was going down here. He threaded his finger into her silky locks, gently turning her face toward his. "Looks like you found one."

"But I want something specific." In her eyes, he could see the flecks of gold—and a hell of a lot more. Goodness. Understanding. *Truth.* All things he could never reciprocate.

"Whatever floats your boat, Just Tessa. I can do slow and sweet or hard and fast." Her eyes flashed a little. "You can tie me up or take me down."

Another flash, this one more than surprised. Maybe she wasn't quite that adventurous.

"I'm yours for the night," he finished, coming closer.

He let his lips brush hers, tasting a hint of the ale and something warm and hopeful. Too bad, but he wasn't her hope, not by a long shot.

By the time she figured that out, he'd be long gone.

Chapter Two

Tessa closed her eyes and opened her mouth, certain the silken flick of this alluring stranger's tongue would shock some sense into her. His scotch-flavored kiss shocked a whole lot of things, but *sense* wasn't one of them.

Unless sense resided way, way low in her belly and whipped through her with a snap, crackle, and pop of arousal.

"Wanna get out of here?" he murmured.

She backed up to respond, maybe slow this train down, but he came with her, refusing to let their lips separate. Sense was derailed again.

"Or will your friends have me arrested?" he asked into the next kiss.

"Hard to say." The way they'd been talking, the girls were likely to shove Tessa into his car and say "Call us in the morning" instead of rescuing her from doing something really impulsive and stupid and…and…

His tongue trailed the roof of her mouth, sending an avalanche of chills down her spine.

Amazing.

He finally drew away, still so close that she couldn't focus on anything but the silvery blue of his eyes, the irises rimmed in a smoky charcoal, all fringed with thick black lashes that brushed together as he squinted at her. "I'd prefer they didn't have me arrested."

"I'd prefer not to take off with an ax murderer."

He twirled her hair around one finger, thumbing the nape of her neck with a maddeningly light touch. "I'm not an ax murderer." Though deep and rumbly, his voice had a strange flatness to it when he said that. "I'm a guy passing through town and you just admitted you're looking for a man."

She had, hadn't she?

"Not exactly a man…" She said vaguely, her brain finally engaging into something close to functional since the moment he'd approached the table and decomposed her gray matter.

"Then what exactly?"

"More like the *essence* of a man."

He lifted a brow and fought an amused smile. "What the hell is essence?"

Liquid gold. She tried to scoot back, but she hit the wall and he didn't give an inch.

"Can you do complicated?" she asked.

"No." Still holding her head with fingers tunneled into her hair, he took her chin in his other hand and turned her face away from him, leaning so close his lips grazed her ear. "You want me to tell you what I *can* do?"

She quivered at the warmth of his breath and the heat

of his tone. She managed the slightest nod because, yes, *please*, every nerve in her body tingled in anticipation of what he could do.

"I can kiss you until you can't even remember your name…or mine."

John Brown. She couldn't forget that.

"And…" He dragged a fingertip under her chin and down her throat, a single stroke of fire, stopping right at the dip between her collarbones. With his thumb, he flicked at the neckline of her T-shirt. "I can strip you out of this top without ever taking my tongue out of your mouth."

That was…a good trick. Yep. She'd like to see that.

"And I could…" His finger dropped a few inches, settling on her breastbone. "I could lick a tattoo right across this sweet, sweet skin." He flicked her earlobe in case she hadn't figured out just how talented a tongue he had.

"And I could…" He took a quick pass right over her nipple with one fingertip, making her suck in a surprised breath as she budded like an acorn, her breasts already aching and heavy with need. "Suck on these tasty rose-buds until you melted like chocolate in the sun."

"Mmmm." She closed her eyes. "I like chocolate." And rosebuds. And this. She really liked this.

"Then we'll get some for you. You can eat it off my…body."

Silently, she closed her eyes and dug for composure, coming up with nothing but a helpless shudder.

He blew more warm breath into her ear. "Want to know what else I can do?"

"I'm actually…no, well, yeah. Okay."

He laughed softly. "How 'bout I show instead of tell you?"

The suggestion vibrated through her, tightening every muscle in her body, especially the ones between her legs. She tipped her head to get a look at his smoky eyes, the dark shadows of an unshaved face, the perfect bow of lips she'd already sampled and wanted to taste some more. "You better tell me first."

"Show." He closed in for a ferocious kiss, wild and hot, his tongue sliding right into her mouth as his finger continued straight down her body, between her breasts, over her stomach, and stopped right at the snap of her jeans.

"Um, we're in a bar," she murmured into his mouth.

"That can be changed."

Sense. Common freaking *sense* disappeared at the sight of him. Was this the desperate act of a woman craving sex so badly that she could have it in a bar booth…or was he so unspeakably attractive that she'd let him…

Snap.

Was that the sound of her jeans or the last shreds of her dignity? "I think we should…take a breather here." She backed into the wall and he put his hand on her thigh.

"I'm breathing fine." He scooted his hand a little farther between her legs. And, God help her, she didn't push it away. Even though all she wanted was *a sperm donor.*

Right? Yes…and no. She wanted the sperm, but she also wanted a man. This man. She closed her eyes and tried to take a steadying breath, putting her hand on his but not exactly moving him off the thigh real estate. Damn, girl, talk about giving mixed messages.

She cleared her throat. "Like I said, it's complicated."

"Doesn't have to be."

Actually, it did. There'd be explanations, interviews, legal documents. So not what this hot kisser had in mind. "I have some important issues."

He frowned slightly. "Are you married, Tessa?"

"No."

"Involved?"

"No."

"Psychotic?"

Right now? Debatable. "No."

"Straight?"

"Yes."

Finally, he relaxed into a smile, a sinful affair that made his eyes gleam and hinted at sexy dimples under the shadow of his beard. "Plus you've got bedroom eyes, a delectable mouth, and"—his gaze dropped to her chest—"a sweet rack. Meets all my criteria. What are yours?"

She finally managed to grip his hand and extricate it completely from her leg. "Availability and attraction is all you need to go to bed with someone?"

"Don't forget the sweet rack."

Another soft laugh caught in her throat and she studied him. "Well, you are honest, and I like that."

The faintest, fastest, nearly indecipherable response flickered in his eyes. "What else is on your list for a hookup?"

Someone who didn't want a hookup. But then, maybe a hookup was exactly what the doctor ordered. No, the fertility doctor ordered sperm, not sex. Couldn't she have both? Weren't they supposed to show up at the same party?

"Tessa?" he prompted. "Your list?"

She conjured up the form she'd recently filled out in a clinic. "Blue eyes." She'd always wanted a blue-eyed baby. Magnetic, mercurial, blinding blue with dark-rimmed irises like the ones she was staring into.

He winked. "Check."

"Over six feet." In case she had a boy, she'd want him to have a shot past her own five-foot-four.

"Plus an inch," he assured her. "And maybe another quarter past that."

"Athletic and strong."

He raised his arm and tensed his biceps, letting the bunched muscle wrapped in a tattoo of deep purple thorns speak for itself.

"No illegal drug use, ever."

Rattling his ice, he said, "As long as scotch is legal, we're good."

Things were looking better, so she decided to push her luck. "Highly intelligent with good math skills." Because a child would need that in this world.

He raised a brow. "Seriously?"

"You asked my list. Math skills is on it."

"Fine. You want me to figure Pi to twenty digits?"

"Can you?"

"Without a calculator."

Oh, boy. He might be…perfect. "Okay, then. We need a clean bill of health, no allergies, and absolutely none of those, you know, tight white underwear."

"I don't have a cold, won't get hives, and I don't think I even own underwear."

"You are sounding better every minute. Just one last thing…"

He laughed. "Don't tell me. A quick DNA test?"

"Um, actually, yes."

His smile froze, then faded. "You're kidding."

If only she were. "I'd really like to check for recessive genes that might carry a disease or disorder."

"What?" He backed away, putting a good six inches between them. "You *are* serious."

She swallowed against a bone-dry throat. "I told you it was complicated."

"I'm not marriage material, sweetheart, and by the sound of your list—"

"No, no. I don't want to get married." Well, she did, but admitting that was like inviting him to leave.

He frowned, searching her face as though he could figure this out by a careful inspection. She doubted he could. "Then what *do* you want if not a hookup or a husband?"

"I'm looking for a…" Another failed attempt to swallow nearly choked her. "A sperm donor."

In the two or three seconds it took to register, a symphony of emotions played over his face. Realization, surprise, disbelief, and, finally, rejection.

"Good luck with that." He started to slide out of the booth.

"No strings attached," she added, fighting the urge to reach out and stop him. "Not a father, not a husband, I need your—"

"Sorry, not your man." He sliced her again with that icy blue gaze, one more emotion shimmering in them. Pain. Bone-deep, soul-searing, life-changing pain so real it took her breath away, then disappeared so fast she thought she might have imagined it.

"Nice talking to you," he murmured, getting farther away.

She lost the battle not to grab him, closing her hand over his wrist, the sheer width of it surprising her almost as much as the insane rhythm of his pulse under her thumb. "Wait."

He shook his head and he yanked out of her grip. "Good luck with your list, honey. I'm pretty sure you can find all that in a doctor's office or something. No need to grill the guys who are trying to get laid at the bar."

"I…" Any explanation sounded lame. Any explanation *was* lame. "I'd rather know what I'm getting."

One mighty shoulder lifted in a shrug that tried to convey he didn't care, but something in his expression said differently.

He might look like a bad-ass sex god, but there was more going on in John Brown's head than getting laid. And damn if that didn't make him even more attractive than his dirty talk and smooth tongue.

"Why?" he asked, pausing on his way out of the booth. "Why not do the anonymous thing?"

"Things could go wrong. They could be lying on the application. I don't trust…anyone."

His smile was slow, rueful, and never got anywhere near his eyes. "But you're willing to trust me?"

"I was thinking about it."

"Word of advice," he said, leaning in one more time to a kissably close distance. "Don't."

And with that, he headed to the bar before she could even think of a reply.

In the space of one long sigh, Zoe slid into the booth, directly across from Tessa.

"What'd you do, demand access to his family health history?"

"Shut up, Zoe."

"You did, didn't you?"

"He's not my type." Tessa turned to look at the crowd, hating that her eyes misted over. Now she was going to moon over this tattooed loser who got her all hot and bothered with one wet kiss and a compliment on her rack? *Get a grip, Tess.*

"Really?" Zoe almost crawled across the table. "'Cause he sure looked like your type when he had his tongue down your throat and his hand in your pants."

"Zoe, stop," Lacey said, slipping into the booth with two bottles of water. "Can't you see she's upset?"

"I'm not upset," Tessa denied.

"I would be," Zoe puffed, twisting the top off a water bottle. "Dude was totally digging you."

Jocelyn appeared with two Blue Moons, giving one to Tessa. "What did you say to Channing Tatum's brother?" she asked. "He practically mowed me down trying to get out of here."

Tessa closed her eyes, trying to get her heart rate back to normal. "Well, let's see, first we discussed how he was going to tattoo me with his tongue."

Zoe's bottle froze partway to her mouth. "I knew I liked that guy."

"C'mon, Zoe," Jocelyn said. "She's kidding."

"No I'm not," Tessa said humorlessly. "He claims he could strip my top off without ever taking his tongue out of my mouth."

"Oooh." Zoe dropped her chin on her knuckles. "The guy's got a good tongue."

"You have no idea." Tessa lifted the beer bottle, but the Blue Moon held little interest now. Zoe's recently passed Great-Aunt Pasha may have predicted that Tessa would meet her man "after the next blue moon," but she hadn't meant *this* Blue Moon. She meant the kind that happened about as often as men like John Brown dropped into Tessa's lap.

Which would be just about never, ever.

"So how did it go from mouth all over you to disappearing act?" Lacey asked.

"Well, I..." Tessa nibbled her lip, knowing they'd get the story out of her so trying to soften the truth was a waste of time. "I kind of told him...I mentioned that I...I thought I should be straight and—"

"You didn't." They all said it at the same time, which would have been funny except that, right then, nothing was funny.

"I did."

"Did you actually *say* the five-letter word that starts with s, ends with m, and rhymes with worm?" Zoe demanded.

Tessa took a drink and stared at Zoe, who face-palmed. "Holy, holy, *holy* hell. She did."

"How'd that go for you?" Jocelyn asked, rich with sarcasm.

"Not so great," Tessa admitted. "One minute he was breathing fire down my neck and the next he turned to stone and disappeared."

Lacey put her hand on Tessa's arm. "Maybe you'll see him again around town."

"He said he was passing through and, honestly, if I never see him again it'll be too soon."

Zoe snorted a laugh. "Famous last words."

"Spoken by whom?" Tessa challenged.

"All of us," they answered. In perfect unison, of course.

Chapter Three

A *sperm donor*? What the bloody hell was that all about?

Ian twisted the ignition on his bike and punched the starter, grinding through gravel as he exploded out of the bar parking lot. He revved the Ducati's engine to get her soft lips and impossible words out of his head.

Didn't work.

Just what he needed. Another kid he never saw. Another life that belonged to him raised by a complete stranger. Another fucking mess.

And wouldn't Henry Brooker love that? Ian could only imagine the response of his opinionated, short-tempered liaison when they had their next phone conference.

Bloody fecking hell, mate, you're in the witness protection program, not a blasted sperm bank.

No doubt she'd pay, but offering up his seed to some chick who wanted a baby probably didn't qualify as the "legit labor" his UK Protected Persons Service liaison said Ian had better find if he wanted to stay in the States.

And he did want to stay here, one country away from…

Don't go there.

He took a curve so sharp he practically ate the sidewalk and refused to give a shit. Physical pain was always welcome. It drove away the other kind.

Warm, tropical wind smacked his face as he made his way across the main road of the island town, passed a convenience mart, and drove into the parking lot of the Fourway Motel.

The place wasn't as much of a dive as the name would indicate, but it wouldn't work long term if he decided he wanted to stay for a while. This morning it had seemed like a good idea: sultry weather, off the mainland, and away from crowds, Mimosa Key offered a chance to regroup after the mess in Singapore, a place to wait—and wait and *wait*—for news that might never come.

But if tonight's unfortunate encounter was any indicator what the locals were like, he'd have to get the hell out and find somewhere else to lie low and do his infernal waiting.

He skidded to a parking place, automatically scanning the empty lot for trouble. Damn, he was sick of hiding.

As he pulled the key from the ignition, the motel-office door shot open and a woman walked out, the light behind her highlighting blonde hair and a silhouette that looked…interesting. Except he'd blown his interest wad in that bar. Now all he wanted to do was stuff his head under a pillow and end this day.

"Excuse me," she called. "Are you Mr. Brown?"

He was now. In Singapore, he'd been Sean Bern. Now he was John Brown. Who would he be next week?

The thought turned his already sour stomach. As the quick click of her high heels against the walkway accompanied her approach, he took in sharp features and a predatory smile.

"I'm Grace Hartgrave." She gave him an obvious once-over, and he considered—and instantly discarded—the idea of her as a replacement for the woman he'd been so close to in the bar. "I own the motel."

He frowned as he climbed off the bike. "Something wrong?"

"I have to ask you a question." She reached him, and he could see that she was a few years past forty, the lines of a lot of drinks and a plenty of cigarettes etched on what was a passably attractive face. "My morning desk clerk said you…" She dropped her gaze, lingering on his chest, her brows lifting appreciatively. "And damn, she wasn't kidding."

"About what?" As if he didn't know.

Another lingering glance on his body, then she met his gaze. "You paid in cash."

"You got a problem with that?"

"It's unusual." But her ravenous eyes said she didn't mind at all. Problem was, he wasn't hungry anymore, and even if he was, this one wasn't on his personal menu.

"I paid through the weekend," he said, taking a step away so she got the message. "If I bolt, the money's yours."

She didn't get the message, coming closer. "You a bodybuilder?"

"Not exactly."

"What brings you to our remote little island?" She flipped some blonde strands over her shoulder, an invitation he'd seen a hundred times from a hundred blondes. Too bad he had brunettes on the brain.

"None of your business."

She raised both brows, unfazed by his gruffness. "Everything that happens in this motel is my business. I own it."

"So you said."

She beamed at him. "I think we're getting off on the wrong foot, Mr. Brown." She reached her hand out. "Can we start over? Can I call you John?"

He didn't move a muscle. "No."

"Not very friendly, are you?"

He narrowed his eyes at her. "If you don't have any more questions, ma'am, I'm—"

"Ma'am?" Her laugh was a little too loud. "I might be a year or two older than you, but no need to ma'am-slam me, big guy."

"Gracie!" The office door popped open again, and this time a monster of a man walked out, damn near as wide as he was tall. "Where are you?"

She glanced over her shoulder, then rolled her eyes at Ian. "And that right there," she muttered under her breath, "is my ball and chain." She cleared her throat. "Talkin' to a paying customer, Ron."

The man ambled over, the light casting a sheen on his dome, his dark eyes drilling right through Ian. "You the guy in 301?" he asked.

Ian nodded, a sixth sense for jealous dickhead husbands rising up and forcing him to brace for the trouble he'd been looking to avoid.

The man looked from Ian to his wife, distrust and disgust on plain display. "What's going on out here?"

"I was telling him about the new diner that opened up, since we don't have room service," she said quickly.

Ian shot her a look. Why was she lying? Turning, Ian extended his hand to the man. "John Brown." Maybe the gesture would allay the man's misplaced jealousy.

"This is my husband, Ron Hartgrave," the woman said, shamed into the introduction.

Ron nodded, offering a meaty and damp hand that probably carried a considerable punch. Not that Ian couldn't crush him; he didn't want to. Trouble was the last thing he wanted, especially after Singapore, where trouble had landed him in jail—and right on the radar of the man who wanted him dead.

The Protected Persons board wouldn't be so understanding this time. Ian's plea to at least be on the same continent as his kids would be ignored and Henry Brooker would ship his ass off to Corvo or Tasmania or some other remote section of hell. There were no third chances with Ian's government liaison.

And no second chances with the gang members and bounty hunters scouring any lead for the identity and location of Ian Browning.

"Your mother's looking for you, Gracie," Ron said to his wife. "She wants you to close the store tonight."

She blew out a breath, fluttering her bangs. "Of course she does, because my freaking cousin is still on her honeymoon." She gave him a wide smile. "Duty calls from the Super Min," she said, pointing to the convenience store across the street. "You let us know if you need anything, Mr. Brown." She turned so her husband couldn't see her face and winked at Ian. "Anything at all."

Ian didn't respond except for a nod to the big man behind her, then he headed toward his room, relieved to hear the sound of her heels heading in the opposite direction.

As he reached the door of his room, he glanced to see Ron Hartgrave still standing in the same place, staring at him.

Great. Like he needed this headache.

He turned the key, went inside, and fell onto the bed, not bothering to undress or turn on a light. Staring up into darkness, he tried to let his mind go blank, a trick he'd learned in the early days when the booze didn't do the job and dark memories threatened to swamp him.

But his trick didn't work tonight.

Instead of a blissful blanket of nothing, a pretty face teased his consciousness, eyes so big and brown that he wanted to fall into them, and a kiss that promised—no. They promised problems, that was all.

With a soft grunt, he rubbed his eyes, grit and exhaustion burning behind his lids. That face and those eyes slowly morphed into another…one much more familiar.

Don't go there.

Rolling over, he smashed his face into the pillow, despising the punch of pain in his gut and the squeeze in his throat. No, no. Not tonight.

Think about the pretty girl and her sexy mouth and perky tits. Oh, hell, think about the jealous husband and desperate motel owner. Think about any fucking thing but—

Kate's body on the dining room floor, a pool of blood spilling over the hardwood, the sound of two helpless infants screaming in their cribs.

Don't go there, Ian. Don't go…

Too late. He was there. Smelling the blood, hearing the

cries, breathing in the anguish of a perfectly wonderful life snuffed out by the hand of a coked-up, crazed-out, black-hearted killer named Luther Vane.

"Oh, God." His cry was muffled by the pillow and the fist he slammed into the mattress over and over and over until his shoulder throbbed like his poor, miserable heart.

His wife was dead and nothing would ever bring her back again. Not sex with a stranger, not a bottle of booze, not wind in his face. Nothing. Kate was dead.

Why couldn't he just shove a pistol into his mouth and join her?

Because of Shiloh and Sam. As long as there was a ghost of a chance he'd see them again, he'd do anything...*anything*...to make that happen. Except the chance got slimmer every day.

And Ian fell farther and farther into the depths of his personal hell.

Tessa marched to the compost bin with purpose and anticipation for the next chore.

There was a reason she loved to compost, and it wasn't simply the money they saved creating natural humus to fertilize the farmette grounds that provided so much food for the resort. Ever since she'd walked onto her first collective, fresh out of college with the totally useless degree in sociology, and the farm manager had stuck a pitchfork in her hand and told her to "turn the trash," she'd enjoyed composting.

Of course, there had been a collective member by the name of Billy Fontaine hanging around that compost bin, and maybe he had something to do with her love of creating "black gold" from the unlikely mix of table scraps and dried leaves.

Approaching the side of the bin, Tessa took a deep breath, letting the earthy, natural scent calm her. Wiping the first stings of perspiration from her forehead with her sleeve, she opened the wire door and eyed the breakdown of this batch. The smell told her they were making progress, but it was time to turn and water.

Taking her pitchfork, she stabbed hard, instantly gratified by the strain of her muscles.

She fluffed for a long time, probably more than the pile required, but every poke of the pitchfork was relaxing to her. Each time she lifted a few layers, her mind slipped back to that first farm and that first true love.

She'd loved Billy, yes, but she couldn't give him all the credit for the pleasures she discovered in gardening and farming. Growing something from nothing thrilled her; she loved the systems, the process, the bone-deep satisfaction of doing something a certain way—the only way, the right way—and getting exactly the desired result.

After a month on that farm, she'd known she'd found her calling in life. And after a few months with Billy, she'd thought she'd found the man who'd be the love of that life.

And he had been—for a while. She stabbed the fork into the heap, heaving a full load with a grunt, letting the old failure demons work as if they themselves held that pitchfork. Guess not everything gets the desired result, no matter how much you do things the right way. She'd failed in her marriage, failed at her attempts to be a mother, failed—

"Tessa, here you are!"

She spun at the sound of a man's voice, surprised to see Clay Walker coming around the greenhouse. Lacey's husband, and the resort's main architect, rarely made it out to the gardens.

"Where else would I be?"

"At the resort, with Lacey."

She drew in a soft breath. "Shoot. I was supposed to go over the chef apps with her, wasn't I?"

"I told her I'd look for you on the way to the house. I need to relieve the sitter."

"I thought Lacey had the baby with her today." A little disappointment tugged inside her chest. The only thing she liked more than planting, harvesting, and composting was a chance to hold Elijah, and she'd planned to do just that while they reviewed resumes.

"No, she's interviewing."

"Interviewing?" That wasn't right. "I thought we were going over the new applications first."

"There was a walk-in who blew her away. She didn't even want to leave to get Elijah—that's why I'm going home." He stepped back, obviously anxious to leave. "Better hurry, and so should you."

She looked down at her khaki work shorts and boots and a T-shirt streaked with dirt. She had to interview a potential chef smelling like the compost bin?

Taking only the time she needed to wash her hands, she jogged across the western border of the gardens, past Rockrose, one of the prettiest and most secluded villas at Casa Blanca, and straight to the beach.

As she hustled along the walkway that cut through the property parallel to the shore, she looked out to the Gulf, noticing that the drier winds brought a slight wave to the usually calm swells. That meant the best shell-hunting possible.

Could this be the day she'd find a junonia?

She crossed a quaint bridge to the sand to take a faster route to the resort. Keeping her eyes down, she scanned the shell-laden beach, looking for *the one*. The rarest shell in the Atlantic would be a coup even for a seasoned sheller, but for a freshman hobbyist like Tessa, it would be a stroke of pure luck. And *hope*.

She was a practical and sensible woman who knew her secret game was flat-out silly. Finding a junonia didn't really mean she'd find her lifelong dream. It wasn't some imaginary "sign." What she wanted didn't come from a seashell, for God's sake. But it was fun to play this game even as she bounded down the beach.

She paused at the sight of a chipped giant cockle, the brownish color close to the giraffe-like spots of the junonia, but she wasn't fooled. She looked up to check how close she was to Casa Blanca's picturesque hotel building, taking a minute to admire the view. The resort's khaki-colored barrel-tile roof angled over creamy Moroccan-style archways always reminded her more of a sandcastle built on the shores of northern Africa than a typical Florida resort.

In a couple of minutes, she was close enough to see the upstairs pool deck peppered with a few guests enjoying a late breakfast. *Very few.* She moved a little faster, spurred by how much they really needed a great chef to rebound from the scathing review they'd suffered shortly after the soft opening. For weeks they'd been running ads and reviewing resumes, but the real talent was either out of their price range or had no interest in working or living on the unpretentious barrier island of Mimosa Key.

So who was Lacey interviewing?

As she approached the employee entrance, Tessa took one more glance at the sand, slowing when she caught a glimpse of brown about ten feet away. Was that a jun—

"Tessa!" The back door popped open and Lacey's coppery hair appeared in the sunlight, along with her not-so-thrilled expression. "I thought you'd never get here. Why don't you answer your cell?"

Because it was probably under a pile of seed invoices in the greenhouse.

"Gosh, I'm sorry." Tessa squinted at the shell, then Lacey. "I didn't know we were interviewing anyone."

Lacey didn't say anything in response. Whoa, was she mad? Maybe. She leaned on the door, arms crossed over a pretty white sweater that hung down to her hips and showed off the figure she'd been working so hard to get back to pre-baby weight. Her expression was tight, and strange.

"Sorry," Tessa said again, the dry sand kicking up under her work boots. As she reached Lacey, she took one more look, peering at the tiny brown shell a few inches from an empty chaise. She had to check. "One second, Lace."

Lacey snagged her arm. "Now."

"Lacey, that's a…" How could she explain this silliness? *A shell I think will mean I'm going to have a baby.* "Can I just…"

Lacey shook her head and tugged her inside. "Listen to me."

"I know I'm late, but…" She stole one more look over her shoulder, memorizing the shell's location. Not that there was a chance in hell a junonia wouldn't be snatched up by the first person who saw it. "I need to get—"

"No."

At the harsh syllable, Tessa turned from the sunny beach to look at her friend, a woman who rarely spoke a word that wasn't encouraging, warm, and selfless. "What's the matter, Lace?"

Lacey blinked her brownish-gold eyes, her expression balanced precariously between excitement and dread. "Nothing. Everything. Maybe something."

Tessa laughed softly. "Does not compute, boss."

Lacey let out a slow, exasperated sigh, then gave Tessa a once-over. "You really should answer your cell phone."

"I'm sorry. Am I too filthy to interview a chef?"

"This chef."

Tessa frowned. "Why?"

"Listen, I have good news and I have...*other* news."

"Good news first," Tessa said instantly.

"I found a chef, I mean, I found *the* chef."

"Really?" What a relief that would be. "You're sure?"

"So sure. He's brilliant, talented, fast, creative, cheap, and can start tomorrow."

"That's awesome." She reached out to squeeze Lacey's arm. "What's the other news?"

"Excuse me, Mrs. Walker?"

Tessa turned at the low voice that came from the hall, the sound oddly...familiar. She knew that voice.

"I've got the prosciutto eggs Benedict..." His words faded as their eyes met and locked, his as crazy ice blue as she remembered, hers no doubt widening in speechless shock.

"That would be the other news," Lacey whispered.

Chapter Four

Ian suspected he might run into the sperm-hunting gardener. When the talkative old lady in the convenience store mentioned that the local resort was probably going out of business if they didn't find a chef, he remembered that the dishy woman he'd met in the bar had said she worked at a resort.

And that had almost kept him from making the drive up the beach road to check it out, but he wanted the job too much to let one little encounter stop him. Except that, based on the way she was staring at him like he *was* the ax murderer she'd feared the other night, perhaps staying put might have been smart. No doubt she was still pissed he'd blown her off.

"Prosciutto eggs Benedict?" she asked, finally tearing her gaze from him to Lacey Walker, who'd been interviewing him while he cooked in the kitchen for the last hour. "That's not on our menu."

"It could be. John, this is Tessa Galloway, but...I believe you two have already met." Lacey could barely hide the amusement in her voice, but Tessa didn't look too amused.

"Hello again, Tessa."

"Hi." She gave him a not-too-friendly smile, brushing some hair off her face that revealed a smudge of dirt on her cheekbone. She crossed her arms as if she didn't want to be forced to shake his hand. Or maybe she was covering up more dirt on her shirt.

Woman needed a shower. And just the thought of that made him need one, too. Ice-cold.

"Um, Tess." Lacey gave a quick brush to her own cheek to silently tell her friend about the dirt.

"Oh, oh." Tessa wiped her face, then glanced down self-consciously, giving him a chance to check out her long, tanned legs and clunky work boots. Damn if they weren't cute as hell on her. "I didn't know we were interviewing."

He shrugged. "No big deal."

An unreadable response crossed her face as she took a step closer, the light of the kitchen hall catching the golden threads woven into her chestnut-colored hair and highlighting the rise of color under her sun-warmed complexion.

"No, it's not," she agreed quickly. "Absolutely no big deal."

Except, by the look on her face, it was a huge fucking deal and no doubt his disappearing act in the bar would cost him the job. *Damn* it.

"Tessa runs our on-site farmette," Lacey said quickly, trying to fill the gaping silence between them. "So she's always involved with what goes on in the kitchen."

Which meant she could put a freeze on his hire right this minute. Unless he won her over, which might take some doing, but he needed this job.

Lacey nudged her closer, and he silently thanked this enabler who was on his side.

"So you can consider me a supplier," Tessa said, her color returning to normal and her voice finally finding some volume. "For the kitchen. And food. And…stuff."

More nervous than normal, then, which he'd use to his advantage. As she came closer, he dipped his head slightly. "I love working directly with a supplier."

"Good, that's good." Lacey put a hand on her friend's shoulder and urged her even closer. "That's why I've asked Tessa to be part of this hiring decision."

"I don't remember you saying you were a chef," she said.

"I didn't," he admitted. "But I can cook."

"He's being modest," Lacey said. "He can more than cook and you'll never guess who sent him our way."

Tessa raised an eyebrow that said she had lots of ideas—the devil, perhaps?—but didn't answer.

"Charity Grambling," Lacey said.

"Really?" Tessa seemed surprised, a smile pulling. "Then maybe you're a spy or planning to poison our guests."

He shook his head. "Neither. Is the local shopkeep an enemy of the state?"

"She didn't want me to build this resort," Lacey said as they all walked toward the kitchen. "She thought it was competition for her daughter's motel, the Fourway."

He snorted. "Hardly. And I say that as a paying guest."

"You're at the Fourway?" Tessa asked.

"We'll have to do something about that," Lacey said confidently.

He turned in time to catch Tessa give a wide-eyed "What the hell" look to Lacey, who shook her head quickly.

Screw it, he didn't have time to dick around. If he couldn't work here, he needed to move on. "Excuse me, ladies," he said, pausing at the kitchen door. "But if you're going to kick me to the curb, then let's not waste anyone's time."

"Okay," Tessa said.

"No way," Lacey countered.

After an uncomfortable beat, they all laughed, Lacey and Ian more than Tessa.

"So, which is it?" he asked.

"Let her taste your food," Lacey said.

"I will," Tessa replied. "But first I need to talk to you in your office, Lacey." She gave her friend a gentle push in the opposite direction. "Can you excuse us for a second?"

"Of course." He paused at the kitchen door, watching them walk away. No doubt they'd stroll back in to tell him he was out of the running.

Unless…

"Hey, Tess," he called.

She turned, slowing enough for him to see something in her eyes. Surprise, humor, a hint of hope. He winked and waited for a quick laugh at the unsubtle flirt.

Instead she raised one eyebrow and kept walking. Bol-locks. He'd lost that round.

When they turned into admin area that separated the restaurant from the spa, Tessa steered them into Lacey's office and shut the door. "Seriously, Lacey?"

"I am completely serious. He's a great chef. You should see his resume."

"I'm sure he's an amazing chef. Hell, if he cooks like he kisses, we'll be Zagat rated by next month. But, Lacey, I practically threw myself at him the other night and I'm still stinging from how fast he turned me down."

"You like him, don't you?"

Tessa puffed out a frustrated sigh and dropped into the guest chair, which only gave her a bird's-eye view of her dirty shorts and bare legs. "Look how I'm dressed. I look like a…a…"

"A gardener, which you are. Listen, Tess, give the guy a chance."

"I did."

"No, you asked him to be a sperm donor."

"Well…"

"If you hadn't, you'd probably still be in the bed with him, maybe just now coming up for air."

Tessa let out a grunt and crossed her work boots. "I can't do it. I can't work with him." She shook her head, trying so hard to convince herself that she meant that. "I mean, I guess I could, but he's so…so…" *Frickin' hot it hurts.*

"I guess if he upsets you that much, then we'll find someone else."

Tessa didn't answer, mostly because she knew Lacey well enough to recognize that there was absolutely zero sincerity in that statement. She was ready to make the guy an offer now.

From behind closed eyes, Tessa corralled her thoughts, but the only thing her brain could conjure up were delphinium-blue eyes, hair the color of streaked hickory bark, and that menacing, deadly creature on his neck. Hell, he was a human garden of delights and dangers.

"Does he upset you?"

"Upset…" *Doesn't even begin to describe.* She looked at Lacey and fired up some sarcasm. "Slightly."

Lacey grinned. "I remember that feeling."

"No." She held her hand up to stop the inevitable—and *wrong*—comparisons. "This is different."

Lacey ignored her. "I still have that feeling, to be honest."

"No, no you don't."

"Hell, yeah, I do. Last night, as a matter of fact—"

"Lacey!" She slammed her hands on the armrests. "This isn't like when you met Clay."

"It's not?"

"No, that was real. This is…not."

Lacey laughed. "You don't know that yet. And trust me, I do know what you're feeling." She dropped down into the chair next to Tessa. "Is it so horrible if a guy turns you on, Tess? Would it be the end of the world to get a little wild and crazy with him?"

She blinked at her. "I want to have a baby, not a fling with the tattooed man."

"Have both."

Could she do that? A powerful longing twisted through her whole body. Was that longing for him or just her usual maternal aching?

She sat up, an idea occurring. "Isn't that against the Casa Blanca employee rules?"

Lacey laughed. "I'll check the handbook I haven't had time to create yet. Look, even if I had one, the property owner who fell into bed with her architect would be a hypocrite if she made a rule against fraternization."

Tessa dropped her head back. "I don't think I can do it."

"Sure you could. You damn near *did it* the other night."

"I mean work with him. I'll make a complete fool of myself."

Lacey laughed. "Could be fun."

"Fun for you and Joss and Zoe, maybe. Anyway, he seems to have no problem turning me down. It's one thing to lust after a coworker, but it's another to lust *alone* after a coworker."

"I don't think he'll hold out for long."

Lacey made it sound like fun and games, but the reality of the situation wasn't fun, and getting pregnant wasn't a game, despite her playful musings about seashells.

"I told him I wanted a sperm donor. What's he going to think when he finds out I'm cooking up my eggs and some stranger's sperm in a test tube to be carried in another woman's belly?" She let out a soft groan. "Oh, God, when I spell it out like that, it sounds so horrible, doesn't it?"

"Horrible?" Lacey was up and had her arm around Tessa in an instant, the move as natural as her next breath. "Honey, you want a baby and you're moving heaven and earth to get it. You have to separate the two things. There is nothing horrible about wanting a baby and doing what you can to get one. That's quite understandable. At the same time you met a man who makes your heart skip and your toes curl and the entire lower half of your body wake up and want to play. That's understandable, too."

Tessa relaxed into a grin. "You *do* know how it feels."

"I do, and it's awesome."

"With the right guy," Tessa shot back. "Not a long-haired…"

Lacey raised a brow.

"Okay, tattooed…"

And she smiled.

Tessa had to laugh. "He does have a lot in common with your husband."

"Listen to me," Lacey said softly. "I know that feeling, but I also know how it feels to hold your child. All I'm trying to say is there's no law that you can't try to have your baby and date the new chef. They aren't mutually exclusive."

Except that dating and babies generally *did* have something to do with each other. Then Lacey's words hit her brain. *The new chef.* "You've already hired him."

"I want to, assuming his references check out and he passes the physical." Lacey gave a bad Groucho Marx eyebrow wag. "Which of course would give you all the info you need to know about his potential for *all* the jobs available at Casa Blanca…including sperm donor."

Oh, brother. "You're not listening, Lace. He couldn't have run away faster. He's not—"

"Hey, are you in there?"

"Come on in, Joss," Lacey called. "Tessa's here, too."

"Did you see who is in the kitchen?" Jocelyn practically leaped into the room. "Scorpion Man!"

Tessa dropped her head into her hands. "Could this get any worse?"

"I already texted Zoe and told her," Jocelyn added.

"In other words, yes, it can get worse." Tessa threw her hands up in surrender. "Look, if you hire him, Lacey, you all have to stop acting like we're in middle school and I have a crush. I have to work with the guy, plus he's not my type, and he couldn't have been less interested in me in the bar the other night."

"He turned down your request to father a child," Jocelyn said. "Prior to that, he was majorly interested."

"Interested in getting laid."

"Semantics," Zoe said, stepping through the open door and giving Tessa a once-over. "Ugh. Couldn't you have lost the boots and filthy shirt for his interview?"

"I didn't know he…" She waved her hand to shut them all up. "Listen, this is crazy. He's just a guy."

Zoe choked. "And Godiva's just a chocolate. Didn't you tell him you worked here?"

Tessa frowned, replaying their conversation. "I think I told him I was the gardener at a resort."

"There's only one resort on Mimosa Key," Jocelyn said, obviously picking up Zoe's train of thought. "I bet he's here on purpose. Trying to pick up where he stupidly left off."

Tessa silently cursed the little butterfly of hope that pirouetted around her chest, remembering the wink.

"He said he heard about the job from Charity," Lacey said, verbally swiping at the butterfly. "Who's trying to tell every island visitor that we're going out of business."

They shared a quick moment of silence, the possibility so unspeakable that no one could really say a word.

"That is so not going to happen." Tessa slapped her hands on her legs to stand. "If he's a great chef, available, affordable, and his references check out, let's hire him."

Nobody responded as they looked at each other, surprised by her change of heart.

"Guys," Tessa whispered. "Do you really think I would let my pride or insecurities stand in the way of Casa Blanca's success? Of course I'm going to work with him.

I'll do whatever I have to even if it means I have to be right next to him all day…and night."

Lacey smiled, reached for her. "Thank you."

"That's really unselfish of you," Joss added, circling her arm around Tessa's waist.

Zoe grinned. "Way to take one for the team, kiddo."

Tessa pointed at her. "Don't you have a balloon you have to fly?"

Lacey's cell phone rang and she grabbed it, reading a text. "Front desk says there's someone here to see me about a group booking. You handle the new hire, Tess."

"Me?"

Lacey nodded. "Finish the interview, seal the deal, and call his references for me."

"You might have to interview him over dinner," Jocelyn suggested.

"And overnight," Zoe added. "You know, for the good of the resort."

Tessa held out her hand. "Twenty dollars says you have lipstick and comb, Zoe. Hand them over."

"Twenty dollars says you do it with him before Thanksgiving."

Tessa laughed. Maybe she would. Until then, all bets were off.

Chapter Five

What the hell was he thinking? That flirting with her would get him the job? From the look he got, winking was only going to get him kicked out on his ass, jobless.

Time for a new strategy. What he had to do was cook his balls off and get the job the old-fashioned way. If he didn't find work quickly, he'd have to move on. Those were the rules he'd agreed to when Henry let him go to North America. He had to get a job, find a place to live, keep his nose clean, and watch the damn clock tick his life and hope away.

Oh, and not let anyone in the world know where or what or who he was, except John Brown, an American-born, self-taught cook.

When he walked back into the kitchen, the young kid who'd been working the line and giving him an evil eye the whole time Ian had cooked was cleaning away any trace of Ian's work.

"What are you doing?" Ian asked as the boy—he

couldn't be a day over twenty—swiped a cloth over the stainless prep top.

"Oh, I thought you were gone."

"You threw away the eggs Benedict?" Ian choked. "Nobody tasted them."

"I did. Good stuff, but I got this covered, man, so thanks for coming in."

How many damn obstacles did he have to face in one interview? Ire shot through Ian as he stared down this new enemy, all too aware that Tessa would come barreling through the door any second to end the interview.

In the meantime, Ian considered this second problem, who wasn't nearly as unsettling as Tessa, simply annoying.

"What's your problem, kid?" he asked.

"Kid?" He huffed out an arrogant breath. "The name's Marcus Lowell and, at the moment, I'm the chef de cuisine in this kitchen."

Ian huffed. "Chef de kindergarten, maybe."

Marcus narrowed his nearly black eyes, set his jaw, and squared narrow shoulders. "Fuck you, man."

A punch of déjà vu, harder than anything this boy could throw with his fist, slammed at Ian's gut.

Aaron. This kid was Aaron Shaw all over again. Something frighteningly close to hate fired through every nerve ending in his body at the thought of his young, stupid, punk of a brother-in-law. If it weren't for Aaron Shaw, Ian wouldn't be standing here, pretending to be someone else, desperate for a job he really didn't even want.

Fact was, he still hated Aaron Shaw, even though the kid had died by the same hand that killed Kate. He blamed Aaron for Kate's death. Aaron had run to his sister's house for protection after getting mixed up with the worst of a Brixton gang. Dumb as a rock, the kid didn't know the gang leader, Luther Vane, was one tube stop behind him, wielding a knife.

A familiar black anger spilled through Ian's veins as he leaned closer to Marcus. Anger that had gotten his ass thrown out of Singapore. Right now, he didn't care. "Get the hell out of my face, you little prick."

"Get the fuck out of my kitchen, asshole."

Tessa walked in right then, stopping short as she heard the exchange.

They backed away from each other, Marcus looking guilty, Ian fuming as he waited for the "thanks but no thanks" announcement.

"Marcus, why don't you check the dining room and bus whatever hasn't been done yet?"

"Bus?" His lip curled at her.

"Chef Brown needs to work alone." She gestured toward the kitchen, giving Ian a chance to notice that she'd cleaned up a little. Fixed her hair, added some gloss to her lips.

Well, that was good news. Maybe Lacey had exerted her influence or played the "owner" card, because she'd been mightily impressed by his kitchen skills. He had to do that one more time with Tessa.

"So, what would you like me to make?"

She hesitated for a moment, looking around as a way to avoid eye contact. Finally, she met his gaze, an embarrassed smile in hers. "Well, for starters, not a baby."

He choked a laugh, grabbing the humor with even more optimism. "Not on the menu, huh?"

She crossed her arms protectively but didn't look away. "I want to apologize for the other night."

He shook his head, a sudden rush of affection and appreciation warming him. That couldn't have been easy. "No, not at all. You were honest, I presume. I'm the one who should apologize for taking off like a spooked raccoon."

The expression made her laugh, lighting her amber eyes and revealing the gorgeous wide smile that had first attracted him. Within a heartbeat, the tension was gone.

"Never thought I'd see you again," she admitted.

"Never say never," he quipped, picking up an avocado. "How about I wow you with some *soupe de l'avocat avec une caviar quenelle*?"

"If I had any idea how to speak French, sure."

He flipped the avocado like a baseball. "Don't worry, neither do I. I made that up to impress you with my avocado soup with a dollop of caviar. But won't it look good on the menu?"

Laughing, she nodded, her whole demeanor relaxing with each passing minute. Success. He might get this job yet.

He tightened his grip on the fruit, grateful it was perfectly ripe. "Did you grow this?"

"I sure did."

"It's a beauty." Turning the avocado in front of his face, he examined the color—this was a Florida-style version of the fruit, with a smooth rind and a bigger body. Not great for guacamole-style dips, but perfect for blending into something silky smooth. "From *le jardin du* Tessa."

"More fake French?"

"I know just enough to be dangerous." He stepped over to the basket and picked up an onion and a lemon, his mind whirring with the recipe and the genuine desire to make the best soup she'd ever had. "Can I have a bit of caviar, or will it break the bank?"

"I'll get it."

He watched her walk away, drawn to the sway of her hips and the bounce in her dark hair. And really drawn to the change in her. What had Lacey said to her? Whatever, he didn't want to question his good fortune. All he had to do was cook another dish or two, send her off to call the fake references that Henry's team would handle, and the job was his.

Unless she wanted to take their flirtation to the next level, asking questions and trying to develop a friendship. Then he'd haul ass and fast. He couldn't afford to get too close to anyone, ever.

He was still thinking about how to navigate those waters when she came back with a small container of caviar, leaning her hip against the stainless steel to watch him work.

"Why didn't you mention you were a chef the other night?"

"You didn't ask."

"Who could ask when I was so busy getting tongue-tattooed?"

He smiled at the memory. "Sorry." But he wasn't. Not one bit.

"'Sokay. I'm still…" She casually touched her breast-bone but didn't finish her thought.

"Recovering?" he suggested.

"Grateful I didn't let you—uh, sweep me away and do, you know."

He knew. He chopped some onion with a deft, quick swipe of the knife. "Why would you be grateful?"

"Because now we're going to work together."

"Yes," he agreed, liking that line of thought, and not only because it meant he was getting the job. "Better to not *you know* when we're on the payroll." He finally looked up from the chopping block, in time to see disappointment dim her eyes.

"Of course," she agreed, although her reply lacked true enthusiasm.

He couldn't forget that the woman wanted way more than a chef. Was that why she was giving him a second chance? *Be careful what you say and do, Ian Browning. Your life—any and all of it—is not yours to give anymore.*

He glanced around the pantry shelves. "Don't suppose you have any sambal?"

"For avocado soup?"

Yes, for avocado soup he'd learned to make in Singapore. Which would beg some serious questions, like, Where'd you learn to cook like this? "Never mind, don't need it."

He'd never admit to three years in Singapore, especially since his time there ended so badly; according to all records outside of the UK Protected Persons Service, he had "died" in a car accident on his way out of town, after being recognized as Ian Browning. Thanks to the brilliant minds in UK witness protection, his death made the papers, and he hoped that was enough to keep the bounty off his head and killers off his trail. As long as they believed Sean Bern/Ian Browning was dead, he could stay alive and wait for his chance to get his children back.

If it ever got out that he was still alive and living under yet another name in yet another country...

He didn't want to think about the consequences. He'd bought one more life, and he knew what to do with it. Lie low, remain distant, stay uninvolved, and, for God's sake, don't mess around with someone who wanted to run a bloody DNA test on him.

He popped the top of a food processor and started dropping in diced avocado. "Got any dry vermouth, by any chance?"

"And here I was hoping for something made of all-garden-grown ingredients. Caviar and booze isn't exactly farm-fresh."

Shrugging, he squeezed lemon. "But they are organic. Your organs need vermouth."

Smiling, she pushed away from the table and headed around the corner. "It's back here with the wine." After a second she returned, placing the bottle in front of him.

He nodded thanks. "If you hate my soup, I make a mean martini."

She relaxed again, watching him work. "Speaks French, makes martinis, kisses like a trained professional. Where does this man come from?"

And, just like that, it was time to start the lies.

He didn't answer immediately, pretending to examine the quality of the lemon leaves he'd use as a final garnish.

"I didn't get a chance to study your resume," she pressed.

Neither did I. He'd barely glanced at the thing Henry had e-mailed him when he'd printed it at a local office-supply store this morning.

"Where'd you learn to cook?"

"I've worked in a lot of kitchens in a lot of places," he said vaguely.

"Yes, I remember: You're on the run."

His head shot up with a spike of adrenaline in his veins. "Excuse me?"

"You told me in the bar you're always running. So how do we know you'll stay here?"

"You don't," he said honestly. Fact was, he was one phone call away from a disappearing act. But that phone call might take a week, a month, or…well, they didn't have that much more time, did they? Once the kids turned four, the possibility of getting Sam and Shiloh back dropped to next to nothing. "But while I'm here, I'll be the best damn chef you can find."

"We need someone who'll stick around."

He splashed the vermouth into the processor, weighing his answer and dividing his gaze between the food and the woman in front of him. "I won't walk out in the middle of a dinner rush, if that's what you're asking."

"It's not what I'm asking. Will you stay into next year? And beyond?"

Well, that depended on some stranger in Canada he'd never met and his government liaison's mood and a few hundred other things he had no control over. "I'll do my level best. How's that?" He stabbed the food processor's On button with a little more force than necessary.

"Do you have a short fuse, Mr. Brown?"

"I don't have a short anything, Ms. Galloway."

She flushed slightly. "And you can't flirt your way through the truth."

"I'm not flirting and I am telling the truth." Or as much as he was able to, which was precious little. "Can I cook in peace or do you want to interrogate me some more?"

"Interrogate?" She straightened, angling her head in

surprise. "I know this is some kind of game of evasion to you, but to me this is a job interview. Questioning is not interrogating."

A game of evasion? He was torn whether to bark in anger or ask how she'd already sniffed that out.

He couldn't do either one. All he could do was answer her questions with lies, transparencies, and clever twists of the truth. "Of course. Knock yourself out."

"How many years have you been cooking?" she asked.

"Since I was young."

"A non-answer. How old are you?"

He glanced up, surprised at the bluntness. "Is that legal to ask?"

"I don't know, but why won't you answer?"

She was right; not answering would only wave a red flag. Anyway, he'd changed his identity, not his age. "Thirty-six. How about you?"

"Sorry, you're the interviewee, Chef."

He ignored the warning, determined to turn the conversation back to playful banter and off his dark, dark past. "You can't be much over thirty, if that."

"Define much." She settled against the counter again, giving him hope that he'd succeeded in chilling things out. "I'm thirty-four."

"Ahh."

"Ahh?" She laughed uncomfortably. "Which means…"

"It means…" *Tick-tock goes the biological clock.* "You look very young for your age."

She narrowed her eyes in doubt.

"You do," he insisted.

"So do you," she countered. "Where were you born?"

The non sequitur threw him, almost more than the

question. He'd answered "Esher, in Surrey" for the first thirty-three years of his life. He squeezed the lemon too hard and lied easily. "California."

"Are your parents there still?"

They were in London…where he should be. "No, I've lost them both. What about you?"

She smiled at the smooth switch. "This is your interview, Mr. Brown."

"Please call me…" He damn near stumbled over the name, but covered by looking right into her eyes and letting her think that was what threw him. "John. And can't it be a conversation instead of a hostile examination?"

"I'm not hostile and, honestly, I promised Lacey I'd ask all the questions, sample your food, and call your references."

Would she talk to Henry or one of his lackeys?

He turned to snag a plate from the rack. "Is Lacey your boss, too, then?"

"She's my best friend," she answered. "But I guess as the owner of the resort, she's technically my boss. You'll work for her, too."

He grinned at her. "I like the sound of that."

"Because you don't want to work for me?"

"Because it sounds like I got the job."

She smiled. "I haven't tasted the soup. Did you go to college?"

He feigned interest in the avocado shell he'd be using as the bowl for his soup, but his mind reeled with the truthful answers to her questions. University of Cambridge to earn a degree in economics, followed by a rocket-ride career at Barclays Bank full of potential and promise.

All sliced into ribbons by the hands of the leader of one of London's most notorious gangs.

"No," he said, finally getting the shell to balance on a bed of lettuce. "Didn't go to college." The lie felt like grit in his mouth. "Just a few semesters at various culinary schools, never graduated." *But don't go looking for a paper trail, my friend, because the UK's version of your witness protection program might not have produced those yet.*

"What's your best recipe?"

Okay, easier question. "Whatever I'm making right this minute." He checked the consistency of the soup, then grabbed a clean spoon for a taste. Closing his eyes, he blocked her out and let the buttery texture and subtle tang hit his tongue. "And this is definitely on track to be my best."

"Can you tell me about your personal life?"

He popped his eyes open, about to tip over this balancing act. "Look, you want to do a job interview, do it. You want to drill me down because of what happened in that bar, you can stop right there. My personal life doesn't have a damn thing to do with how I cook. Wanna taste?" He held the spoon out to her, not even bothering to clean it.

She refused the offer with a tiny shake of her head. "You're awfully defensive."

She hadn't seen anything yet. "Just trying to make it on the basis of my food, not my life story."

"I didn't ask your life story. We need to know you'll be focused on work, not leaving early or taking off for weeks at a time, so these are legitimate questions. You're not married, right?"

A slow burn started in his belly as he stirred the soup

one more time. Why was she insisting on this? Every time he lied it was like Kate died all over again.

He dropped the spoon on the counter with a clatter loud enough to drown out his answer. "Nope."

"No kids?"

Damn it. He stilled his hands on the stainless steel and kept his gaze down long enough to let the silence go way past awkward. Only then did he pin her with a deadly gaze.

"Obviously you're interviewing me for some other job, which I've made achingly clear I don't want."

She drew back, as though his words had smacked her. Well that was too bad, he thought furiously, refusing to give anything remotely resembling a shit about her feelings. Because even *that* felt disloyal to his dead wife.

"I wanted to—"

"You wanted to pry," he shot at her. "Because these questions don't have anything to do with my culinary skills, my ability to manage a kitchen, or the menu I might be able to create for this resort."

She lifted her chin, hurt ravaging her expression. "John, I'm asking legitimate questions that can affect scheduling. Do you or do you not have kids?"

Of all the lies, he hated this one the most. He despised speaking the words, wiping away the existence of the two most precious people in the world to him. He was a father like any other father, as proud as he could be, despite the fact that he hadn't held Shiloh or Sam for three long years. That didn't change the power of his love. No, time and distance made him love them more.

But if he didn't lie, he could be putting his children in harm's way, and he was like any father in that regard, too. He'd die before he'd let them get hurt. He opened his mouth to say the words: *I don't have any kids.*

But for some reason, that particular lie wouldn't roll off his tongue. Instead, he looked into those earthy brown eyes and all he wanted to do was tell Tessa the truth.

If that wasn't the stupidest fucking thing, he didn't know what was. He couldn't take chances like this. Not with his life, and definitely not with his kids.

He settled on something that wasn't a lie. "I fail to see how that has anything to do with getting this job."

"We're a family here at Casa—"

"I don't want to be a family," he growled, the words harsh enough to make her flinch. "I don't want you in my business. I just want a job as a chef. Yes or no?"

She studied him for a minute, scouring his face as if she could find answers there. She'd better not. "The last person left because she had huge personal demands and couldn't work the hours we needed."

"I can work twenty-four/seven. In fact, I'd like to."

"Why?" she asked him.

Irritation skittered over him. "None of your fucking business."

"Why are you so hostile about this? What aren't you telling me?"

God*damn* it. He shoved the plate across the stainless steel to her, splashing some soup over the edge of the avocado shell. "We're done here." Before she could answer, he stepped away and went right out the door he came in.

No job and no woman was worth the risk of the truth.

Chapter Six

⌐⌐

Of course it was the best flipping soup she'd ever tasted in her life.

But the creamy, dreamy liquid caught in Tessa's bone-dry, tightly closed, very painful throat, making swallowing nearly impossible. Okay, the "interview as a way to dig for personal information" was a cheesy technique, but what was he *hiding*? And she'd been unnecessarily snippy, but that happened when someone was so abrasive.

With a little tremble in her hand, she scooped up another spoonful of soup, letting the delicious flavors of avocado and lemon linger on her tongue. If Lacey tasted this soup she wouldn't care if he was hiding the Holy Grail. She'd hire him in a heartbeat.

"Did he bolt?" Marcus asked, nearly launching himself next to her the minute John was out the door.

"He really couldn't answer the most basic questions," she said.

Marcus grabbed another spoon and practically stabbed

the soup, slurping some noisily, then grunting with pleasure. "But he killed the most basic of soups. Shit, that's good."

"He's not right for the job," she said, as much to convince herself as Marcus. "We can't count on a guy like that. In fact, I think we dodged a bullet."

Marcus took some more soup. "No kidding. What the hell kind of loser has a bug on his neck? What was that, anyway?"

"A scorpion."

Marcus lifted his eyebrows as he sucked in another mouthful. "Dude's inked up pretty good."

"I saw the thorns on his arm and that swirly black thing down to his hand and God knows what else on the rest of him." Well, God might know, but Tessa wasn't going to find out because she was too smart and mature and together to look twice at an evasive, deceitful, tattoo-covered—

"Damn." Marcus thumped his chest on the next swallow. "I don't suppose you caught the recipe before he left."

"Nothing special. Avocado, lemon, dry vermouth."

Marcus grabbed the bottle of booze. "Who would have thought of—" He caught himself. "Hell, yeah. Who can't make soup?"

"Exactly. We're really better off without him." And his secrets.

"We sure are," Marcus agreed. "You think Mrs. Walker'll give me the job?"

She could encourage that thinking and then he'd support her position that they were lucky to lose this chef, but she knew better. "You know you need more time."

He exhaled softly. "She hates me because I'm a dropout."

"She does not," Tessa assured him. "She wouldn't let you work here if she had an issue with you not finishing school." She didn't mention that the chef who'd just left was a dropout, or so he said. Who could believe anything that came out of that sexy-as-sin mouth?

"Why'd he blow out, anyway?" Marcus asked.

"I don't know," she said vaguely.

Marcus gave her a slow smile. "I know why he left, Ms. G."

"Why?"

"He couldn't take the heat in the kitchen." His grin widened. "Sparks were flying even though there wasn't a flame, if you know what I mean."

Was it that obvious? "You were in the dining room, Marcus."

"Actually, I was around the corner." He tipped his head toward the back pantry. "You were so busy jonesing for his life story that you didn't even hear me come back in."

Oh, Lord. Yes, it was really better John Brown was gone. "Then you heard him dance around anything personal. Fact is, we don't need someone working here who can't be honest about the simplest things."

Marcus looked down, concentrating on the soup. "What are you going to tell Mrs. Walker?"

"The truth," she said quickly. "I'll go find her now and tell her we ferreted out a phony."

Outside, Tessa took a minute to regroup and look around for any sign of John Brown. But there was none, giving her heart an unwanted dip. There were a few more people on the beach and a woman sitting in the chaise right where the shell had been.

Still, Tessa took a few steps closer, just to check. But there was no shell.

"Hey, where's lover boy?"

She pivoted at the sound of Zoe's voice, her disappointment at losing the shell mixing with a splash of irritation. "Don't call him that," she said, walking away from the shore to reach Zoe. "And the fact is, he's gone. Out of the running, and we should all be glad for that."

"Why? Lacey said he really knew what he was doing in the kitchen. What did he make?"

He made me crazy. "Some kind of green soup. Not that great."

Zoe flipped a stray curl over her shoulder. "You're such a craptastic liar."

"I'm not…"

Zoe gave her an elbow. "I came through the kitchen and talked to Marcus. He was inhaling what was left of chilled avocado with caviar and vermouth. Or, as some call it, green soup. But between spoonfuls, Marcus told me you two basically started a kitchen fire."

"Marcus has a colorful imagination. Fact is, I asked Mr. Brown a lot of questions that he evaded and avoided and twisted and refused to answer."

"Bet you loved that, Queen of the Secret Haters."

"Precisely. I can't work with someone who isn't honest or hides his past." Tessa brushed her hands as if she were ridding herself of the pesky, lying chef.

"Maybe he didn't want to get personal in his interview. That's understandable."

Not to her. "Either way, he bolted mid-interview. He's gone and that's good."

The low hum of the electric golf cart stole their attention, the sight of Lacey at the wheel talking animatedly to three women passengers bringing their conversation to a halt.

"Who's that?" Zoe asked.

"Must be the group booking she went to talk to." Tessa started to walk away, but Lacey slowed the golf cart and waved wildly.

"Hey, you guys, come here for a second."

Zoe eyed Tessa. "Lucky you. A governor's reprieve."

Not much of one. "I have to tell her sometime."

"Not now," Zoe said through a smile, waving back at Lacey. "She probably wants us to impress the potential guests."

Tessa glanced at the three young women chatting animatedly in the golf cart.

"You are not going to believe who's here!" Lacey's voice was unnaturally bright, a forced enthusiasm edged with high-strung nerves. "The AABC board members!"

Tessa slowed her step as one crisis melted into a new one. The American Association of Bridal Consultants represented possibly the most important group booking they'd ever had. Except they weren't due here until July, eight months from now.

Lacey scrambled out of the golf cart, turning so the three women passengers couldn't see her face but Jocelyn and Tessa could. Her eyes were wide, her jaw open, and her whole expression screamed for help.

Then she gestured for Tessa and Zoe to come closer and the women to climb out of the golf cart. "Ladies, I want you to meet two of my partners and closest friends, Tessa Galloway and Zoe Tamarin."

They were younger than Tessa had imagined, a blonde,

a brunette, and a...*pink*? The blonde in the middle led them forward, hand extended to Tessa. "Hello, I'm Willow Ambrose, president of the board of directors for the American Association of Bridal Consultants."

Tessa took her hand and accepted the powerful handshake that screamed a Type-A alert, the woman's demeanor reminding her very much of her mother when she was in all-business mode. "Hello, Willow."

"This is our VP, Gussie McBain."

Pink Hair gave a sly grin and a wink. "Place rocks. We're already in love."

"And Arielle Chandler, the AABC treasurer."

"Sorry for the unexpected arrival," she said as they shook hands.

"Do *not* apologize," Lacey exclaimed. "We're delighted to show you around."

"Absolutely," Zoe agreed. "We didn't think you were coming until this summer."

Willow brushed back some hair. "We didn't think so, either, but we've had a significant change in our schedule, one you might love..."

"Or hate," Gussie offered.

"What is it?" Lacey asked after a second of dramatic silence.

"Well, as you know, part of our role as the board members for the organization is to visit destination-wedding resorts and make recommendations to our members."

"That's why you're coming this summer, right?" Tessa asked, already sensing that the answer wasn't going to be what they expected.

"Change of plans," Gussie said, fluttering what had to

be a set of false eyelashes, which somehow looked incredibly natural on her pixie-like features. "One of the contenders in the small-resort category fell through."

"And our annual meeting is in January," Willow added. "That's when we present our top recommendations to two thousand wedding consultants from all around the world."

"And…" Lacey prompted, although they all kind of knew what was coming.

"And we need a replacement. Fast."

Another beat of silence, this one even longer than the first, making the wedding planners laugh.

"Look, we know this is short notice and that this resort is still in soft opening," Willow said. "So we'll cut you some slack in our review, but the annual recs are one of the most important things board members do. Is there any chance we can move our preview up from July to—"

"Yes," Lacey said, making them laugh.

"—two weeks from now?"

"Yikes," Zoe said.

Willow nodded with understanding. "I know that's an impossibly tight squeeze, and if you can't do it, we are headed over to a place in Naples—"

"We can do it," Lacey assured her, looking at Tessa for confirmation.

"I don't see why not," Tessa said. Except she *did* see exactly why not. They had no chef.

"You have vacancies?" Willow asked.

"In two weeks we can put you in Bay Laurel," Lacey confirmed. "It's our most spacious villa, with room for the three of you. I'll have Jocelyn, our spa manager, clear spots for every treatment and amenity."

"Don't forget your hot-air-balloon ride." Zoe pointed

to the sky. "That's the best part of a Barefoot Bay wedding."

Gussie grinned, her bright-red lipstick contrasting perfectly with pale skin. "A Barefoot Bride! What an awesome marketing concept. I can think of three clients right now who would jump all over the idea of getting married barefoot in the sand."

"That's exactly how I got married," Lacey said with a smile.

"We're volunteers on the board for this calendar year," Willow told them. "But we each have our own wedding-consulting businesses. And, honestly, we've sent quite a few brides to the places we've visited this year, for wedding packages and honeymoons. But the top three contenders in each size category get the AABC seal of approval, and those resorts are booked for years."

They knew that was no understatement. Getting picked as an AABC rec would wipe away all the damage of that nasty review and open more doors than all of Lacey's marketing efforts combined.

"You most certainly can count on coming for the official visit in two weeks. Whatever it takes, ladies." Lacey was practically drooling as she made the offer.

But all Tessa could think was *We have no chef.* Because she'd just grilled him right out the door.

"Let's finish the quick tour," Lacey said, waving the women back into the golf cart.

As they climbed back up on the electric cart, Lacey came around to whisper to Tessa, "Did you make him an offer yet?"

She didn't have the nerve to break the news to Lacey,

especially not with the AABC reps so close. "Um, not yet," she said. "I'm going to call his references."

"Seal the deal," Lacey insisted as she slid behind the wheel.

As the cart rolled down the path, their happy voices trailing, Tessa stood stone still, the sun pounding down with almost as much force as Zoe's gaze.

"What?" Tessa barked at Zoe.

"Calling his references, are you?"

"Yes, I am. And no doubt I'll find out he's a liar who will rob us blind and can't cook his way out of a paper bag because he's a serial killer."

Zoe burst out laughing. "You better hope so, hon, because otherwise your determination to ferret out everyone's truth cost us a perfectly good chef when we couldn't possibly need one more."

"Well, if not, then…I'll get him to come back." Even though she had absolutely no idea how she'd do that. "I'm sure his number is on the resume in the kitchen."

"Hope he knows how to fix a crow pot pie," Zoe said, fluffing her hair with a laugh. "'Cause you are going to be eating some when you make that call."

"I hope I have the chance," Tessa admitted glumly. "It seems all I can do with that man is make him run away."

Ian floored the bike over the causeway, not bothering with his helmet but letting the warm wind slap his face and whip his hair. He had to work, had to show some stability, had to do something with his miserable life besides *run* and *hide* and *lie* and *wait*.

It was all so completely counter to the man he used to be—the man he still was under this pumped-up, inked-out, anger-fueled body. Ian Browning didn't run from anyone, he never hid from a problem, he'd despised lying, and "wait" wasn't in his overachiever's dictionary. Now those words defined his entire world. He knew that like he knew his name.

The thought almost pulled a sharp laugh from his belly because half the time he couldn't remember his damn name. He'd wake up, sweating, hurting, sick throughout his body, with memories of Kate and the kids and the smell in the air when he'd gotten out of the tube that afternoon.

He could still see Luther Vane's eyes when they'd bumped into each other on the street, Ian still clueless about what the man had done. And then he remembered walking into the flat, dropping his suit jacket and briefcase, calling his wife's name, listening for the still unfamiliar sound of an infant's cry, and…

The thought made him swerve into the next lane, earning a loud horn blast from a pissed-off truck driver. He ignored the urge to lift his middle finger and instead glanced to his right, the navy water of some Florida river about fifty feet below, nothing but a slim guardrail between him and blissful relief. His arms tingled on the handlebars, his right arm aching with the very idea of whipping that wheel to the side to sail right over that railing, down, down, down to end it all.

He opened his mouth and let out a low, long howl, catching air and dirt in his teeth, trying to release some of the agony in his chest.

Why did this hurt so much today?

Because of that woman. That sweet, warm, pretty, innocent, anxious, tentative, sexy woman who pressed every button he had and held them down until he wanted to scream.

She didn't look a thing like his honey-haired Kate, didn't have any similar characteristics—on the surface—that should ignite this old pain. But there was *something*.

Something that made him *want* to be honest. And that could be the last moment of security he ever knew. What was *wrong* with him? Fuck that job and forget that woman. Both of them were way too dangerous for him.

He flew down the other side of the arched bridge, heading into the congested traffic of a much more populated beach town than the one he'd just left. Maybe he should have put his helmet on. Especially in a place where there could be British tourists. Sure, he looked different from when he was Ian Browning, successful investment banker at Barclays, happy, decent, and normal. He was no longer the clean-cut, lanky businessman in suits and ties, but had his canvas of tattoos and shoulder-length hair changed him enough?

What if someone with a keen eye spotted him, and remembered the press coverage of the young woman stabbed alongside her brother with the babies left in their cribs until their daddy came home? The story had been well covered by the press, and he'd been front-page news during the trial.

Then the threats got worse and the N1L gang members closed in on him, killers with no regard for their own lives or anyone else's, not when they were hell-bent on vengeance. Ian Browning had to disappear, but not with his babies. They couldn't be together while the gang was still on the streets. A man with twin babies was too easy to find, so the kids had gone to Canada and he'd gone—to hell.

If he ever wanted to see his children again, if there was any hope of a life even remotely resembling normal, Ian had to do a few very specific things: He had to lie and he had to hide and he had to wait for British law enforcement to do their job. But he also had to work.

A childhood in Surrey along with schooling at the Royal Guildford and Cambridge had prepared him to do little in the "real" world, but his first three years under government protection had landed him in and out of restaurants in Singapore. Mostly out, thanks to his refusal to play nice. But at least he'd learned to cook.

And what had he done now that he had the possibility of a decent job in a perfect off-the-beaten-path place? This time he hadn't gotten into a drag-out with a douche bag. No, he got *lost* in a woman's eyes and wanted to tell her the *truth*. What a fucking idiot he was.

She was only trying to find out if he was available.

Well, he wasn't available. Not for her.

He'd work somewhere else, that's all. The Protected Persons rules—even tighter now that he'd blown one identity in Singapore and had to be given a new one—said lie, hide, work, and stay the hell out of trouble. No fist-fights, no bar brawls, no intimate conversations with pretty gardeners who wanted a normal life.

Henry Brooker's job was to enforce those rules, and keep Ian posted on the progress toward shutting down the gang in London. Henry didn't say he had to work in a high-end resort that needed his culinary skills. Hell, Ian could work at McDonald's if he had to.

At the thought, he caught a glimpse of golden arches and took the next turn into the parking lot, pulling the bike over and shutting it down, but his body still vibrated. He still hummed and buzzed and—

No, that was his phone—the phone that only Henry could call, making Ian practically dive to answer. Maybe this time. Maybe this call. He tapped the screen and answered with his usual, "Yeah?" Sometimes he didn't say anything; after all, they were the only two people who ever communicated on this line.

"You in Morocco, mate?" Henry Brooker's thick Yorkshire accent always set Ian on edge and made him brace for the frustration of no news.

"Not even close," Ian said. "Why?"

"Someone called the line we have set up for your messages. She said she was from Casablanca."

"Different Casa Blanca, and I'm not going to work there."

"So you have another job, then?"

"Not yet." He eyed the line of cars moving slowly into the drive-through. "But I'm about to." *You want fries with that?*

"She called all the references we arranged."

After his rude exit, the fact that Tessa had gone ahead and called the professional liars who gave him glowing recommendations sent a thud of shame through him. "I'll find something else," he said. "That's not the job for me."

"Don't be picky, mate. You'd better find a job, and bloody fast." Something in Henry's voice made Ian straighten up and take notice. Something he'd rarely heard from his liaison. Optimism.

"I'm working on it," he said.

Henry cleared his throat. "Get a good job and, for fuck's sake, don't punch out a customer who doesn't like your coconut balls."

He looked skyward. "Crab balls, and he was a dick-head looking for trouble."

"You attract dickheads like that and it isn't the kind of track record government agencies like to see when they release children back into the care of an itinerant short-order cook."

He eyed the golden arches again. "I'm *not* an itinerant short-order cook." Yet.

"You *have* to have a solid job," Henry said, the emphasis strong.

A slow cascade of something like adrenaline and terror and all kinds of *possibilities* rolled through Ian's whole body, head to toe, leaving him so weak he actually closed his free hand over the rubberized handlebar of his bike for stability.

"Why?"

After a long beat, Henry said, "We're getting close."

Close. Frustration zinged him at the word. How close? Close to what? He bit back the fury, accepting that he had no control over the situation, no way to clear out the N1L gang members who wanted him dead, no way to live safely with his children. And no way to make those who did have the power move fast enough so some arbitrary, inane rule that said he couldn't have the children back after they turned four closed in and ended all hope.

"Close to what?" he asked Henry as calmly as he could.

"Just…close."

"Henry!"

"Listen, I know how you feel."

"Like hell you do," Ian growled. "I'd kill someone to get them back."

"Well, don't," Henry deadpanned. "That'll just make this more impossible. Just trust me—"

"I'm sick of trusting you!" He kicked a stone under his boot, hearing the dead silence on the other end. "Sorry, listen, I just…I hate not being able to do anything. Watching that calendar move closer and closer to the cutoff and waiting for you to call and say I'm free to get them is killing me. I am…completely powerless."

"You're not. You can do something so that when we get those guys—and we will, Ian—you are in a position to reclaim the children from their protective custody in Canada."

"Anything," he said honestly. "I'll do anything."

"Start with getting your shit together, mate. That means—"

"A job." He'd dive into that McDonald's in five minutes and have a job. "I can do that."

"More than a job; you need stability." Henry's voice was rich with implication, but Ian would be damned if he understood.

"More stable than a job? What? Management?"

Henry snorted softly. "Sta-bil-i-ty," he repeated, dragging the word out. "The kind that says your life is together. John Brown needs to be completely on track."

"What exactly does that mean, Henry?"

Henry sighed, a sound that was out of character and not exactly promising.

"What?" Ian demanded. What did he have to do to get his kids?

"You have a little time," Henry said vaguely. "Obviously, we can't make any move on the Canadians for release until we've got every single member of N1L behind bars. So you actually have some time to do this."

"To do what?" What was Henry getting at? Was he about to hand out yet another identity and new place to live? Fine, whatever. As long as Ian could live on the mere possibility of getting his children back.

"Look, I had a conversation with my counterpart in Canada yesterday to discuss how we get the wheels rolling should we clear out the streets of Brixton."

They'd better clear, and the wheels better roll. The minute that gang was off the streets and it was safe, Ian wanted his kids back.

"The review board has had a change of personnel and they're more strict than ever."

What the fuck did that mean? More asinine rules about a man and his own offspring? He bit back his anger, as if that proved he was capable of control.

"The new board is insisting that you prove your life is together, professionally and personally, before they give you back the kids."

How together could he be in these circumstances? "Henry, what the hell do I need to do?"

"Get married."

He froze, blinked into the phone, and almost laughed. "*What?*"

"You need to get married. At least on paper. They're going to want proof that you aren't a single parent."

He coughed in disbelief, turning in a circle like he

could possibly find someone to share how ludicrous this was. "I need a *wife*?"

"You need proof that you have one. She doesn't actually have to appear in the hearing, just sign a piece of paper."

"There's a *hearing*?"

"There could be. There is a process, Ian, like any government red-tape-ridden system. I can help you through the process and we can do an awful lot in the background like, say, annul a marriage that's real on paper only. But you need to produce that paper."

"You make it sound simple to get someone to sign a marriage certificate."

"With your charm?"

Yeah, he was swimming in that today.

"Can't you guys doctor one up?" The magic they'd performed with instant legit and totally fake identification when Sean Bern "died" and John Brown, American drifter and chef, was born, had amazed him. Surely they could stamp out a marriage license and a fake signature.

"Actually, we can't. Because it involves a real person—"

"I have to marry a real person?" A man passing by threw a quick, dark look and Ian almost kicked himself, turning away and lowering his voice. "How the hell do I do that?"

"Carefully," Henry said. "Because it cannot—and I mean *cannot*—involve bringing another individual into the circle."

The circle was Henry's way of referencing the few—two or three—people who knew the truth about Ian and Sean and John and whoever the hell he'd be next.

"So I have to marry someone who doesn't know who I really am?"

"Correct."

"How do I do that?"

"Use your imagination. Make an arrangement, make something up. She never has to meet the kids. Can't you scare up a woman down there?"

A slow, burning pain rolled around the pit of his stomach. "And fool her into marrying me?"

"At least into signing the papers."

"And then annulling it?"

"Of course. After you're married, you disappear to Canada, give her the impression there's someone else, and once you're down under with your family—I'm thinking New Zealand is a good, out-of-the-way place—then we'll handle the annulment paperwork because you'll be out of the picture by then."

Holy, holy shit. "Pretty skeevy, if you ask me."

"Skeevy? I don't know what that means, mate, but maybe you don't understand me."

"I do. You want me to lie to someone and—"

"Bloody hell, listen to me!" He could practically hear Henry's teeth grinding together as he hissed through them. "Ian Browning is dead. Your primary Protected Persons identity, Sean Bern, is *dead*."

"I *know* that."

"If you ever whisper to a living soul that you are still alive, mate, and it gets back to that gang, you might as well put a gun to your head and pull the trigger. Even if you get Shiloh and Sam back—"

"When," Ian corrected.

"—their real father is dead. Even *if* we wipe the N1L

off the face of the earth, you are never safe if you tell another person the truth. Ian, you live with this lie or you
die."

For a moment, the line was silent, the words bouncing
around Ian's head.

"Did you hear me?"

He didn't answer, assuming the question was rhetorical.

"Did you fucking hear me?" he insisted.

"Yes." *Lie or die.* "I heard you."

"Good." Henry's voice dropped to its normal octave.
"So, you hit on anyone lately who might make an easy
mark?"

Two women crossed the McDonald's parking lot, one
not more than twenty-two, laughing as she gave him a
glance, slowed her step, held eye contact, and flipped
dark hair over her shoulder.

That was an easy mark. But...

He closed his eyes and saw Tessa. And that burn in his
stomach rose and fell, a cocktail of guilt and desire. He
could never hoodwink her like that, could he?

"How long do I have?"

"We're not sure. I know there are two UCs who've in-
filtrated the gang, but you know that can take a long time
to work. My connection in Scotland Yard says soon. So
get a move on someone, fast. And, for God's sake, don't
fuck this up."

"I'll be fine." But would the woman be...fine? Or
would he be sacrificing her happiness for his?

"By the way," Henry said, "they started preschool."

He winced, the words like a steel fist in his gut. "Par-
don me?"

"Shiloh and Sam. They've started a nursery school program. Just a few mornings a week, to learn their letters and such."

He muttered a curse, buckled by the news. He should be teaching them to read. He should be dropping them at preschool, packing their lunches, kissing their cheeks. He should. He was their father, they were his family.

"Ian?"

He couldn't even swallow past the lump in his throat, let alone answer.

"Do what you have to do, mate," Henry said. "The end of all this could be near."

Nodding in silence at the instructions, he got off the phone and stood for a moment in the burning midday sun. He needed a job and a wife—fortunately he knew how he could kill two birds with one stone.

He only hoped there wasn't too much collateral damage in the process.

Chapter Seven

Frustration and a silent phone sent Tessa to the store-house to hitch up her tractor and start cutting the sweet potato vines. That crop was more than ready, and she couldn't harvest the potatoes until she removed the thick tangle of greens over the beds.

The noise, sweat, and concentration would keep her from checking her phone. The same phone she rarely remembered to bring into the gardens, but, today, was tucked soundly in her pocket with the ringer on max.

Giving the shift a nudge to a higher gear, she rolled the tractor between rows of veggies, headed for one of the prettiest sections of her organic farmette. She'd started out with plans for a modest garden to grow some of the produce they'd use at the resort, but in the past two years, she'd steadily added crops and fruit trees, a huge variety of herbs and spices, and, of course, plenty of beans, greens, and the citrus that gave the whole acreage a sweet, tropical scent.

She hummed with the John Deere motor, trying to con-
centrate on the bursts of new life all around her, eyeing
the first explosions of baby strawberries and the new fruit
on all six avocado trees.

Of course, the thought of avocados made her check the
phone.

Why wasn't he at least returning her call? Ignoring her
was plain rude. Kind of like walking out in the middle of
the interview.

His references had been outstanding. Evidently, Chef
Brown was talented, reliable, and dedicated. And single,
which one previous employer happened to slip in sideways.

Single and sexy and…sneaky. Bad, bad combo.

But Casa Blanca needed a chef, so she'd have to live
with that bad combo, at least for a few weeks. She could
stand anything for a few weeks, right?

If only he'd call.

She gritted her teeth and climbed down from the tractor for a final pull on the hitch, taking off her work gloves
to secure the middle-buster blades that handled the hardest portion of the work for her.

Why had John been so evasive about her questions, she
wondered as she kneeled in the soft earth. Why not tell
her all the great stuff his references had? Was she being
paranoid, the victim of age-old secrets that shouldn't hurt
anymore, but did?

Her friends knew she hated when they kept things
from her, but the true irony was that they didn't know
why. She'd always planned to tell them her one and only
secret, but dreaded the way they'd react. She'd been so
vocal about how frustrating their secrets were to her that
revealing her own would only force her to eat crow. And

every time she imagined the conversation, she couldn't bear to actually have it.

Uh, remember how I told you my parents were hippie farmers? Well, I made that up when I got to college and never got around to telling you all the truth.

Pushing up, she swiped her hands over her work shorts and, well, since she was so close to her pocket, what was the harm in checking? Just to see if she had signal strength out here.

"C'mon, Tess," she mumbled as she pulled out the frustratingly silent phone. "You can't *will* the guy to call."

She should go admit to Lacey how bad the interview really was, though Marcus or some of the other staff probably had done that for her by now. No, she'd tell her tonight. Lacey had invited a few people to her house for a small celebration and mini planning session, so Tessa could tell her then that Chef Brown hadn't called back to accept the offer.

And tomorrow, they could dig through the resumes they'd already rejected and find someone to get them through the next few weeks.

Satisfied with that, she climbed back onto the tractor seat, gave the shift a good yank, and balanced her feet on the pedals to keep it from stalling out. Right before she put on her work gloves, she stole one more peek at the phone. She might not have heard it over the tractor engine, she rationalized, and sometimes she didn't feel the vibration.

Blank screen. No calls or texts.

"Don't take it personally, Tess," she murmured as she jammed the accelerator and rumbled onto the sweet potato bed.

Like there was any other way to take it.

Sweat dribbled down her back as the slender vines snapped away, the tractor loud enough that she barely heard a man's voice calling over the noisy engine. When she did, she turned, and then sucked in a soft breath.

Oh. *Oh.*

Now, this...*this* she wanted to take personally.

For a long moment, she sat and stared. John crossed the garden with an easy, graceful gait, his golden-tipped hair blowing back to give full exposure to his chiseled face. A white collared shirt stretched across broad shoulders, and partially rolled-up sleeves exposed tanned forearms. The shirt was tucked into crisp khaki pants, making the whole look sharp and clean and handsome.

And really overdressed for the garden.

He stopped after a moment, still fifty feet away, but she could see he'd shaved—and as much as she liked his whiskery scruff, the clean look showcased the full lips and the hint of a very inviting smile.

Tessa completely forgot to breathe.

Oh, boy. If he had come to accept the job, she was in trouble. Big, big trouble. She couldn't take this intensity for two minutes, let alone two weeks.

Finally, he lifted his hand, two fingers curled in the universal gesture for *Come here, woman.*

And, God help her, she turned off the ignition, climbed down from the tractor, and might have floated over vegetable beds to reach him, one coherent thought in her head: This was so much better than a phone call.

She refused to think about the fact that she was dressed in dirt and scented with sweat and he looked like a damn prince. What difference did it make how she looked, right?

"Tessa."

He had the most imperceptible softness to his vowels, and the way he said her name was like pure sex.

She nodded in greeting. "I take it you got my message." She hadn't offered the job, but had only left a number.

He flicked his hands toward his clothes, as if that was enough of a reply. Did he feel like he had to impress her one last time? 'Cause it worked.

Bright blue eyes danced with a tease that really made it hard to think.

"What are you doing here?" she managed to ask.

"I went to the front desk and asked for you and they sent me here." Like *that* explained the inexplicable.

He glanced around quickly, then laser-locked on her again, making her feel like he couldn't stand to look anywhere else. "This is quite a little operation you have."

How could he make a simple compliment sound so sexy? Was it his low voice? His penetrating gaze? She could spend hours thinking about that. In fact, she already had.

"Thanks."

He closed the rest of the space, coming about a foot from her. Close enough to smell a new scent in her garden. *Man.*

No wonder Eve sinned.

"And it explains why you…" He brushed her cheek, the touch like a spark. "Often have a little dirt on your face."

There was something different about him; his edge was gone. The undercurrent of attitude had been replaced by something not exactly softer, but slightly less gruff and *bad*.

"Careful." She backed away. "You might wreck your fancy clothes."

"I'll take that chance." He almost smiled, enough to make her want to see more of the dimples revealed on his clean-shaven face.

"So, why the in-person returned call?" she asked.

He angled his head in the vaguest tip of apology. "I shouldn't have walked out on you. Twice."

No, you shouldn't have. But the return appearance might be worth what he'd put her through. She slid her hands into her pockets, finally catching her breath and stability, determined not to reach out, grab a handful of hair and...*hire* him. She'd at least have to make him work for the offer.

"I seem to elicit that response in you," she finally said.

He let his gaze drop over her, slowly, warming every inch. "That's not the only one."

She tried for a casual laugh, which came out more like a bark. "Really."

"Really." He laughed, too, and she could have sworn he was nervous. "I know you're surprised by this, but I've been thinking about the best way to handle you, er, us, er, this...situation." He shook his head, flustered. Flustered? What was wrong with this picture, besides everything?

Her truth-telling radar beeped and she mentally unplugged the whole system. This minute was too delicious to ruin with doubts.

"What situation?" The one where she dissolves into a pool of helpless female hormones and he takes advantage of that and breaks her heart?

"Tessa," he said softly, looking from side to side for a second. "I have to tell you something about me. Something you didn't ask in your interview."

Interesting, since he didn't even answer the questions she did ask. Still, she waited, dying to see where he'd go with this.

"I don't shy away from anything," he finally said. "When I see something I want, I get it." He gave her a hard, straight look.

Did he mean the job as chef or...*her*?

"So, what are you here to get?"

"My plan is that we start all over again." Reaching down, he lifted her hand and very slowly drew off the gardening glove, sliding one finger out at a time out of the rough canvas. She couldn't do anything but stare at his large, tanned, masculine hand undressing her much smaller one, her throat parched and every nerve ending dancing at the touch.

"We could shake on it," he said, dropping the glove to the ground but still holding her hand. His skin was warm. A little rough, a little dry, but very warm. "But I'd rather do this."

He lifted her fingers to his lips, barely brushing the knuckles, the sensation shooting fireworks down her arms. "To new beginnings, pretty Tessa. A new job, and a new..." He looked up from her hand and met her gaze, his own so serious she forgot to breathe again. "Friendship."

For a moment, she stared at him, a thousand emotions erupting like a volcano in her chest. Disbelief and excitement and desire and disbelief and longing and—yeah, mostly disbelief.

"What is it?" he asked.

"Well, I'm not really trusting by nature, so I'm fighting the sensation that you might be full of shit."

He laughed. "I deserve a chance."

Did he? "And you'll probably get one, but what happened?"

He lifted both brows. "I want the job."

"So you're suddenly Prince Charming? After being guarded, evasive, and walking out in the middle of an interview?"

He curled his fingers around her hand and sighed with resignation. "I guess I'm going to have to do some seriously high-quality groveling."

"Major high," she agreed.

"Let's start with dinner tonight. We can finish the interview."

Obviously, he didn't know she'd called all his references and they glowed like polished gold, and he certainly didn't know about the wedding planners and the urgent need for a chef. Instead, he'd come to grovel and take her to dinner.

"I'll give you time to clean up and change for our date," he said, as if she might be looking for an excuse to say no.

As if a groveling man offering dinner and looking like a sex god fell into her lap on a daily basis.

"I thought it was an interview," she said.

He shrugged. "You call it an interview, I call it a date."

"I call it a pretty remarkable turnaround for the guy who suggested a one-night stand of tongue-tattooing the last time we talked about going out."

His smile was sinfully slow and so damn confident.

"Haven't you ever changed your mind about something, Tessa? Ever looked at a situation in the light of day and realized you'd need a new approach to get what you want?"

She tried to ignore the little thrill of his words and be smart about this. "What about trust?"

He lifted his brows. "What about it?"

"Did you change your mind about the advice you gave me in the bar? Or don't you remember when your one word about trusting you was 'Don't'?"

She could have sworn a little bit of color left his face. "How else are you going to know if you should or not unless you have dinner with me?"

She couldn't argue with that logic. Or maybe she just didn't want to.

Chapter Eight

I think he's kind of crazy, Lacey." Tessa whispered into her cell phone, hoping the running water drowned out any chance of him hearing her. The bungalow where she lived on the edge of Casa Blanca's property wasn't big, and right now John Brown was prowling about her living room, waiting for her to shower and dress for a dinner date.

"But he *did* accept the job." Lacey was completely stuck on the wrong point.

"Not technically yet, but this has nothing to do with work." Tessa shook wet hair back to look in the mirror.

"Are you sure?"

"Should I wear makeup?" The question was more to herself than Lacey, but her friend gasped softly.

"Makeup? I'm sorry, I thought I was talking to Tessa Galloway."

"Very funny." She took a breath. "He's all dressed up in khakis and a button-down shirt."

"Bet he looks hot."

"There are no words. And he came out to the vegetables and…" *Kissed my hand.* "Started courting me."

"Courting?" Lacey laughed. "Who does that anymore?"

"I know, right? He's up to something, I'm sure of it." Tucking the phone in her ear, she pulled open the bathroom drawer to root for anything she could put on her face. Way in the back, she spied the mascara and blush Zoe had made her buy for Lacey's wedding.

"You thought that this morning when he wouldn't tell you anything, now he wants to take you to dinner, presumably to tell you all the stuff he didn't tell you this morning, and you don't trust him again. Listen to yourself, Tess."

"Well, look at him." And she had. Stared like he was a two-headed alien, as a matter of fact. "How can you trust a guy who looks like that?"

"'Cause he has some tattoos and hair that touches his shoulders?" Lacey tsked. "I told you, you are asking the wrong woman."

So true. She let out a sigh and unscrewed the mascara wand, turning the foreign object in her hand. "I'm so not ready for this."

"For what? For sex? For fun? For a hot guy on a cool night? For another chance at love?"

She rolled her eyes. "For mascara. And, please, *love*, Lacey? The man wants sex. He must have decided that since we're going to work together, he has to pay for dinner first. But it's still sex." She opened her mouth in the "O-face" she'd seen Zoe make for mascara ever since they were roommates in college.

"And that's a problem, how?"

"Seems like I called the wrong number, too."

"What?"

"I thought I called Lacey but apparently I got *Zoe*." She swiped the brush, darkening her lashes.

"Zoe isn't the only one of your friends who wants you to know the pleasure of four orgasms. In an hour."

She laughed, smudging the lid. "Shit. Who would do this every day?"

"Maybe five orgasms."

"Excuse me, Lacey, you're the mature one of this group. Aren't you supposed to be wishing me happiness and not orgasms?"

"They usually go hand in hand."

Tessa didn't answer because she was too busy licking her finger to get it wet enough to wipe the mascara off. Which was stinkin' waterproof. "Damn it," she murmured, looking around for lotion. "I'm so ill equipped to do this."

"Take a deep breath and relax. He'll wait for you."

She did as she was told, or tried, puffing out a lungful of air in a long, slow sigh.

"Now what's *really* the matter, Tessa?"

Now she sounded more like the former RA nurturer Tessa had loved since the day they'd met in the dorm. "What's the matter is…" She closed her eyes, and dug deep. "He's all wrong."

"But he's all right."

"This is not a country song, Lace. He's not what I want in a man."

"Too sexy? Too big? Too interested? Too funny? Too talented? Yeah, I see the problem."

"I mean it," she insisted, frustration growing. "He's a drifter who drives a motorcycle."

"The Ducati that was parked in front of the resort this afternoon?" Lacey asked, blowing out a whistle. "Speaking of orgasms, I think Clay had one just looking at that bike. He drives that? He's taking you out on it?" Her voice rose in utter incredulity.

"He drove it over here but I'm going to take us in my truck," she said. "And what I'm saying is he's a man who wants nothing like I want. Roots, kids, stability."

"He told you all this in an interview when he wouldn't answer personal questions? Interesting."

Tessa ignored the sarcasm. "I can tell from looking at him." She finally cleaned her eyelid, and did one more cursory swipe of mascara brush, and then tackled the blush compact. She didn't need it; nature colored her cheeks enough around this guy.

"Looks can be deceiving," Lacey said. "I have two words for you."

"I know what two words they are, Lace. Clay Walker."

"Precisely. Could I have been more wrong about him when I met him? Remember how hung up I was on his age and looks and his relentless determination to get me naked? Well, I wasn't wrong about that."

"And you have the brand-new baby to prove it."

"Need I say more?"

Tessa dropped the makeup brush. "How about something that sounds like 'Be careful' or 'Have a good time' or 'Don't fall for the wrong man.'"

"You don't know he's wrong. You don't know what kind of man is under all those muscles and hair and ink."

Tessa laughed. "Well, when you put it like that…"

"Exactly. You need to find out more about him."

She was right, but still. "I can tell he's a drifter without even asking. I talked to three former employers in *three different states*."

"But they said he was a great chef and a…"

"An upstanding citizen," Tessa supplied. "Two of them used exactly the same phrase."

"Well, there you go. It's nearly unanimous."

"But doesn't that strike you as odd?" Tessa asked, giving voice to one of the questions that had been bugging her ever since she'd made the calls to his references. "An upstanding citizen? Who says that unless they're running for office?"

"He didn't say it, they did. And it's probably because he looks exactly the opposite and they want to assure you that he isn't going to steal the booze or dip into the cash drawer."

Oh, she was making entirely too much sense. "Lacey, do you or do you not want me, and all of your employees, which now includes a new head chef, to be focused on the most important weekend guests since we opened the resort?"

"Of course I do," Lacey answered. "But you're not going to stop growing great food because you're falling in—"

"I am not in love!"

"—bed with the new chef."

She burned during a second of silence. "That's at the root of this, isn't it?" Tessa admitted into the phone. "For him, it's probably about sex and for me, it could never be just sex."

"Hey, you're the one on the sperm hunt."

"He already said he wouldn't be the supplier."

"In a bar, after some scotch, when he had no idea he'd ever see you again."

Tessa grabbed a comb and started untangling her wet hair. "So, it's even more impossible now when he knows he will see me every day at work. He's officially off the sperm-donor list."

"All the better."

The comb stuck in a knot. "What do you mean? You know how much I want—"

"Tessa, you have to stop…" Her voice drifted off, and, in the distance, Tessa could hear the not-so-soft cry of a hungry infant and the low tones of Lacey's husband talking to her.

She closed her eyes and listened to the music of—a family. A life with a partner and a baby and a future. A life she might nev—

"Sorry, Elijah's starving. I gotta go."

"It's okay. I got the general gist of your advice. Go have four orgasms for no other reason except it feels good." Even though that wasn't exactly what Tessa wanted.

"No."

"No? Then what are you advising?"

"Same thing I advised earlier today. Give the guy a chance, Tess. Have dinner, find out what he's made of, get beneath the sexy exterior and let go and enjoy yourself."

Tessa looked hard at her reflection, meeting the challenge Lacey offered. "In other words, forget about a baby."

"Just have fun tonight," Lacey said. "The other stuff will work itself out. And don't forget everyone's coming over later for a nightcap, so you better join us."

By everyone, she meant Jocelyn and Will, and Zoe and Oliver. And...Tessa. "Seventh wheel."

"Oh my God, I'm going to pretend I didn't hear that. Bring John."

She tried to imagine how that would unfold: Tessa showing up for a late-evening gathering with her three best friends and their significant others. Awkward or awesome?

"Unless you're otherwise occupied." Lacey's meaning was all too clear.

"We'll see." And they would. "But I'll give him a chance, Lace. I will."

"Good girl. See you later, I hope."

She didn't commit to that, though. One step at a time. Taking a deep breath, she turned from the mirror and took the first one.

Ian paced the living area of Tessa's undersized house after she'd closed the hallway door and left him to wait for her. No bigger than a roomy one-bedroom apartment, the bungalow was part of an enclave of similar structures built for high-level employees of the resort.

Convenient, because if he lived in one, he'd be right next door to Tessa, and the more contact they had, the faster he could get his impulsive marriage plan into action. Things were already going swimmingly.

He paused at a bookshelf next to the TV, perusing the titles. A smattering of fiction, but mostly books on gardening, greenhouses, horticulture, hydroponics, permaculture, harvesting, and—*huh*?

He crouched down to make sure he'd read the title on the pink spine correctly. Yes, he had. *Every Drunken Cheerleader...Why Not Me?* He pulled out the book to look at the image of a pregnancy test reading "Not Pregnant" on the front cover.

Behind it, he found another row of books, all blocked by gardening titles. He eased out a few and found a treasure trove of books all on the same subject, with titles that sang the same song. *Empty Womb. Having Hope. Boosting Your Fertility. Inconceivable. What to Expect When You're Not Expecting.*

"Looking for a particular title?" He whipped around to see Tessa standing in the doorway in a simple black dress, sleek heels, her hair falling around her shoulders. Damn. At least he wouldn't have to pretend to be attracted to her.

He straightened slowly, still holding a book. "*Five Hundred Ways to Get Pregnant.* Who knew there was more than one?"

She fought a smile, but her color was high. "You'd be surprised."

"Nothing surprises me." He set the book down on the table and gave her a thorough once-over. Twice. "Not even how gorgeous you clean up."

She gave a self-conscious half-laugh. "You got the job, John. Flattery isn't necessary."

Actually, it was. He didn't have a minute to waste. "Not flattery, honesty." And he meant that. Coming closer, he reached out for her hand. "Thanks for saying yes to dinner with me."

She reluctantly gave her hand, her dark eyes lit with distrust and a little confusion. Smart girl.

"Consider it part of your job training," she said. "I'm happy to tell you everything you'll need to know about working at Casa Blanca." She managed to tug out of his fingers.

"You think that's why I want to have dinner with you?" He shook his head, laughing softly. "You don't give yourself enough credit."

She held his gaze for a beat, a thousand questions passing through her eyes. *Don't ask them, Tessa, 'cause I won't answer.*

"I don't date much," she finally admitted.

"Then I'm doubly honored." He stepped closer and put his hand on her back. "You sure you won't change your mind and let me take you on the bike?"

"In a dress?"

"Maybe too adventurous," he agreed. "But we can take a ride tomorrow. After breakfast."

She turned to the door, but he heard her laugh.

"What? You don't eat breakfast?"

"You're good, you know that? Really, really good." She led him to a mud-splattered Toyota pickup, the back bed loaded with bags of soil and some gardening tools. "I'm afraid my truck isn't much more elegant than your bike."

"It works for me. Do you want me to drive?"

"No, I'll drive."

"Then at least"—he scooted ahead of her—"let me be a gentleman who gets the door."

She let him open it. "The same gentleman who suggests breakfast before dinner?"

Trapping her with the door and his arm, he leaned into her from behind, inhaling deeply to get a whiff of something as sweet and floral as the explosion of purple flowers lining the driveway. "I'm optimistic."

He felt her draw in a steadying breath before sliding behind the wheel.

He rounded the truck, hoping he still had his touch in the dating department. He'd done little more than pick up stray women for easy sex in the past few years. Now he was a man on a mission.

A mission, he conceded, that was made much easier by how good she looked and sweet she smelled. He could fake a lot of things, but he sure didn't have to fake the chemistry they both felt.

Was that a good thing, or was it only going to make his full-scale seduction worse?

"There a problem, John?" Tessa asked as he got into the passenger seat.

Yes, damn it. There were so many problems he didn't know where to start. Every time he had a second, third, or fourth thought, he'd simply remember why he was doing this: Shiloh and Sam. He wanted them back in his arms and in his life. If some nameless face on a Protected Persons review board said he needed a marriage certificate to reach that goal, so be it.

"Nothing we can't solve over dinner." He added his very best smile. "And breakfast."

Chapter Nine

John approached the hostess stand oozing confidence and control. "Brown," he said quietly. "Sorry we're a few minutes late."

Tessa lifted both eyebrows in surprise, glancing around the quaint Italian restaurant tucked into an obscure Naples neighborhood. "You made reservations?"

"I told you I'm optimistic." He put a possessive hand on her back to guide her.

"You called while I was changing?"

"No, after I left you this morning."

And there went those warning bells again. The same ones she'd heard the second time a stranger called him an upstanding citizen and the same ones that had deafened her when he studied her profile so intently in the car.

"First of all," she said as she tucked into the back booth. "I wouldn't call what you did 'leaving.'"

He slid in next to her. "What would you call it?"

She glanced sideways. "Unexpected. But I overstepped my bounds with personal questions."

"Not at all." He was close enough that she could feel the heat and strength of him, the power of his thigh next to hers, the pressure of his shoulder. Instead of feeling trapped, though, she felt very—secure.

Which was flat-out nuts. "Are you really going to sit on this side of the table?"

He chuckled softly. "Am I making you uncomfortable?"

"No, but I can't see you."

He instantly transferred to the seat across from her with remarkable agility and speed for a man who had to be six-one and a good—no, a *great*—one-ninety. "You're right. Better to look than touch." But he reached across the table for her hand. "Although who says I can't do both?"

She let him close his fingers around hers, shaking her head.

"What?" he asked, all innocence and sex appeal.

"Stop pretending."

John's expression changed instantly. All the light and laughter went out of his sky-blue eyes, and his mouth grew serious. He looked almost guilty. "I'm not pretending."

Way in the back of Tessa's head, she heard that warning bell again. "I meant stop pretending that this is perfectly normal."

"Dinner dates aren't normal?"

"This," she said, freeing her hand from his grip to gesture from her to him and back again. "Like I said, we had a rocky start and you flounced out and—"

He gave a belly laugh. "I can honestly say I've never been accused of *flouncing*."

"I mean as much as a man your size can flounce."

He leaned forward, managing to snag her hand again—not that she actually made it that difficult—to weave his fingers through hers.

"Hey," he whispered, the single syllable as crazy-sexy as any kiss. "Pay attention, now. Here comes the grovel."

"Better make it good."

He cleared his throat and tightened his grip. "I am abjectly apologetic for any unexpected, abrupt, or rude flouncing"—the word made him have to fight a smile—"that I may have done this morning."

"And…"

"And? You want more groveling?"

"I want an explanation. Why did you leave so suddenly?"

For a moment he didn't speak, but she could tell his mind was whirring and he had trouble swallowing. So whatever he said next would be a lie. She knew it.

"I was hiding something."

"I knew it." She leaned back, a smug satisfaction taking hold.

"You did?"

"I knew you were not being straight with me."

A slow, evil smile curled his lips. "That's sort of the problem, Tess. I was being, uh, straight."

She frowned, not following at all. "No you weren't. You were being evasive and secretive. Two of my least favorite things, I might add."

He winced. "Well, I had good reason."

"What was it?"

"You couldn't tell?" He looked a little relieved. "Well, you'd have figured it out soon enough."

She still couldn't make sense of that. "Figured what out?"

"What I was hiding."

"What were you hiding?"

He lifted both brows like he couldn't believe she didn't know. When she shook her head slowly, unable to figure it out, he slowly glanced down at his lap, then back to her, the smile broadening.

"I was sure you'd see how much you—you know, *affected* me."

She stared for a moment, part of her wanting to hoot a laugh and call Zoe, the only person who would truly appreciate that excuse. And part of her wanted to squirm at the thought of him *affected*.

He had danced around her questions, given evasive answers, and walked out because he was aroused? No. Not possible. "Yeah, mud boots and gardening clothes do that every time to a man."

"I could see past the boots and dirt. And, what can I say? I liked it." He leaned forward, a glint sparking like gas flames in his eyes. "Didn't you feel it, too?"

Yes. "No."

He laughed. "Now who's lying?"

She was.

"So, am I forgiven?" he asked.

"You're trying to tell me that you went to all the trouble to try and get that job and made world-class, five-star, mouthwatering avocado soup and bolted out the door because you were…" She let her eyes fall to the table that hid his crotch. "Uncomfortable."

"Worse than uncomfortable." Leaning closer, he whispered, "Like a two-by-four, woman."

Oh, God. She wanted to laugh, but more than that she wanted to crawl over the table and kiss the living hell out of him. And feel that two-by-four.

"So you left."

"Abruptly," he acknowledged. "A bit overwhelmed, too."

"And then you decided to take the job after all." She played through the logic, and, like everything else about him, it left her mystified. "Why? I mean, if you think these…issues will affect you when we work together."

"Oh, they will." He came closer, seeking her hand again. "They definitely will."

Her pulse kicked as he tugged her fingers, pulling her closer like he had her on a string. "Why isn't that a problem?"

"Because." He lifted her hand and brought it to his lips. "I've decided not to let it be a problem." He touched her knuckles with his lips. "It would be crazy not to give in to this chemistry, don't you think?"

She stared at him, not really sure what "crazy" was anymore.

"Don't you feel it, too?" he asked.

What, the dry mouth, a racing pulse, weak knees, and the female version of *affected*? Yeah, she felt it all over. "A little," she admitted.

"A little?"

A lot. "I definitely thought—think—you're attractive. And terrifying," she added impulsively.

"Tessa." He pulled her hand closer to him, both hands around one of hers now. "This attraction is real. And powerful. And, please God, tell me it's mutual."

She couldn't tell him anything. Because the warning

bells in her head were ringing like it was Christmas and she shouldn't have received this particular gift.

But why not? Didn't she deserve that same kind of knee-weakening magnetism her friends felt when they'd met their one true loves?

One true love? What the hell was wrong with her?

"It's not mutual?" he asked, the tiniest note of desperation in his voice.

"You move fast," she finally said. "Way, way, way too fast."

"That's why I left. Because I know myself. I know when I feel something this powerful it isn't something I can fool around with. I was—okay, I'm going to admit it, now. I was scared."

Not a chance. "You don't look like a guy who scares easily."

"I don't." He lifted her fingers to his mouth and leaned closer for another knuckle-kiss. "But you scared me."

"Why?"

"Because when I look into your eyes, I see…"

She silenced every warning bell, demanding them to stop and let her hear what it was this gorgeous, complicated, surprising, astonishing man saw when he looked into her eyes.

"A future." He punctuated that with a kiss on her fingertips and, for a moment, Tessa died.

And then the bells rang so loud she didn't even hear the waitress come to the table. What the hell? They hadn't even ordered yet and he was talking about a *future*. The same man who'd evaporated when she used the words *sperm donor* the other night? Something was very, very wrong with this picture.

* * *

Maybe he'd gone too far. Up until "a future," Ian really hadn't lied, not technically. He really *had* left the kitchen because he couldn't wrap his head around what was happening and she *had* affected him and he most certainly *had* been scared of her—at least of her questions. Even the two-by-four wasn't a lie, although it hadn't been in his pants. It was a metaphorical plank that slammed sense into his head.

That was why he'd run off.

So everything was true, more or less. Until that last declaration. The only future he saw when he looked into her eyes was his, with Sam and Shiloh. He saw a means to an end and, damn, that made him a heartless bastard.

"A future?" From the cynicism in her voice, she wasn't buying. "This is the same guy who said, and I quote, 'I'm not marriage material and I don't do complicated.'"

Yep, he'd said that. "At that point, I really was thinking with my…" He glanced down. "You know what."

"And you're not anymore?"

"Not entirely." Of course, he'd do his level best not to be a complete asshole about the whole thing, but he had to work in certain parameters: He couldn't hint at the truth and he had to work fast.

He lifted his glass. "Let's toast, Tessa."

"I will not drink to a future," she said dryly. "But I will drink to a man who knows his way around a good line."

"It's not a line," he said softly. "But if it will make you give me a chance, I'll drink to something less intimidating than the future. How about we drink to a fresh start?"

"Your new job?"

"And our new"—he dinged the glass and went with it—"romance."

She smiled as she brought the glass to her mouth, sipping a little, but laughing more.

"What? We can't have a romance?"

"It's old-fashioned," she said. "And sounds incredibly out of place on a man who has horror-movie tattoos and is built like a human lethal weapon."

"Hey, I flounced, remember?"

She laughed again, already a wee bit more relaxed, and it was too soon to be the wine. All very encouraging, plus she was even prettier when her shoulders weren't so taut and her smile didn't waver.

"Give me a shot, Tessa. That's all I'm asking for."

"A shot at what? To do something about how *affected* you are?"

"Absolutely not." Okay, that sounded ridiculous. "Well, of course I'm physically invested, but—"

She lifted a brow. "Who says things like 'physically invested'?"

A guy who went to Cambridge and studied economics. He'd better watch the wine and be damned careful. Nothing got by this woman. "I'm trying to impress you."

"It's working."

"Really?" He grinned. "Good."

"Finish your thought," she said. "There was a 'but' at the end of that sentence."

Indeed there was. "I'm attracted to you, but"—he squeezed her hand—"I don't want this to be a wham-bam-thank-you-ma'am kind of deal."

The smile morphed into a dubious frown. "You sure wanted to wham and bam when I met you in the bar."

"Consider the setting," he said quickly. "We're colleagues now. Are you that jaded that you can't believe a man could be interested in something more than sex?"

"I'm not jaded, I'm…" She laughed and sipped the wine. "Hell, yeah, I'm jaded."

"Never been in a serious relationship?"

She almost choked on the drink. "I was married ten years."

"Really?" It was his turn to be taken aback. She'd been married? She'd been down the aisle and on a honeymoon and shared a name—like he had? For some reason that tipped him a little bit off balance.

"Why are you so shocked?"

He shook his head. "I had the impression you were more or less committed to being single."

She eased her hand out of his when bruschetta and tapenade were served, both of them taking a second to inhale the aroma of roasted garlic and chopped olives. Ian could make this dish in his sleep, and he almost told her, but didn't want to get the conversation offtrack. He was much more interested in her ten-year marriage.

For some reason, that changed everything. He wasn't sure how or why.

He waited for her to take some bread and add the topping before asking, "What happened, if you don't mind me prying."

"I don't mind." She toyed with the bruschetta, thinking. "I guess the answer to that depends on who you ask."

"I'm asking you."

She cast her eyes down. "He had an affair and she got pregnant."

"Ouch."

"After ten years of our trying and failing to have a baby."

Oh, bollocks. "That had to hurt."

"It sucked, I'm not going to lie. We had spent a decade desperately trying to get pregnant, traveling the world to start organic farms, growing everything but"—she gave a wry smile—"the one thing I wanted to grow the most."

As she talked, guilt twisted his gut. He was no better than the dickhead who'd dumped her for a baby maker. He was just a dickhead who would dump her after he used her to get his own children back.

He longed for a deep drink of wine but toyed with the stemmed glass instead, listening. She told her story slowly, as if she were in her garden and could pick only the best words. Didn't matter what words she used; it wasn't a nice story. A hopeful wife, a cheating husband, a broken heart, a single woman.

And what a lovely chapter he planned to add to her life. A lying bastard.

Self-contempt rolled through him like the aftereffects of the wine he'd yet to drink.

"However, as you know…" She finally took the time to look him right in the eyes. "I don't intend to let that stop me from having a child."

And there was that little complication. "You, uh, mentioned that the other night."

"And that sent you running as fast as whatever it was in the kitchen this morning." She eyed him suspiciously. "Giving me the impression that you, John Brown, are a runner. Or at least a drifter. Definitely not a man interested in"—she launched one eyebrow north—"settling down."

Such a smart, smart woman. "People change," he said.

She let out a heartfelt laugh, tipping her head back enough to tease him with the hollow of her throat. "Nobody changes that fast."

"You don't know that," he said, knowing how flimsy that defense sounded. He *had* made a blatant play for sex the other night, and he *had* bolted the minute she'd asked him anything more than his name in a job interview.

And really, from that moment on, he'd been lying to her in one way or another. So why was he having such a hard time now? Because this woman was tender and vulnerable and so unsuspecting. She had needs and wants, but—

A thought played in his head. Tessa wanted a baby. Why didn't he just cut a deal? *Marry me for reasons you never need to know and I'll give you sperm for a baby I never need to know.*

Except she'd need to know the reasons.

And he'd need to know the baby.

"You're awfully quiet," she said, resting her chin on her knuckles. "Still thinking about a future now that you know a little more about me?"

It would be so easy to promise her that baby—or that baby-making juice she'd mentioned the other night. And all she had to do was marry him. "Yes, I am," he admitted. "I'm thinking about it more than ever."

Her shoulders dropped as she exhaled long and slow, as if she'd been holding her breath the entire dinner. "Well, then…" She lifted her glass as if to make a toast. "Why don't you tell me everything about you? That is, assuming you can do it and not run out of this restaurant and leave me for the third time."

But this time, he couldn't run. He wouldn't. He had to go forth with this plan.

"Everything?" He lifted his glass and let it ding the rim of hers. "All right, here goes."

Let the lies begin in earnest.

Chapter Ten

Tessa made her decision sometime after John told her why he'd left California. Maybe before that, when he explained how he'd been kicked out of college his first year and went to culinary school in Nevada. And got kicked out of there, too.

The boy was trouble, no doubt about it. And he was funny and flirtatious and he might be trying to seal the job, but she suspected it was still a full-court press to get her into bed. He'd changed his tactics from the bar, so she had to give him bonus points for creativity. The sweet seduction and old-school wooing was probably going to work and work big.

But first she was going to put him through one more test.

He slid the bill to the end of the table, a wad of cash inside, and gave her an expectant look after she thanked him for dinner.

"So, now what?" he asked. "A walk on the beach? A

ride on my bike? What would you like to do now that you know everything about me?"

"I don't know everything," she said.

"More than most." And he sounded a bit wistful about that. But Tessa was too content to question that. She'd asked enough questions, and he'd answered every one.

"I don't know how you are socially," she said.

He gave her a confused look as they exited the booth, reaching for her hand. "This didn't count as social?"

"I mean in a group. My friends are getting together tonight. You've met them. Now you can meet the men in their lives, too."

He looked interested. "Is this the equivalent to meeting your family?"

"As a matter of fact, this is the only family that counts." They walked to the car, hand in hand, then he curled his arm around her back so he could pull her all the way into his side in a move that only a boyfriend made. It shouldn't have felt quite as good and natural as it did.

"Tell me about them," he said.

"Well, these women have been my closest friends since we all met in the dorm in college. Zoe and Joss and I were in a triple room, and Lacey was our resident adviser. We got close and stayed that way through the years."

He nodded, absorbing that. "What about your real family? Parents and siblings?"

"Not much to tell." Not that she wanted to share, anyway. Not yet. "I'm an only child, and my mother is…" Oh, no. Not the time for this. "Not really in my life," she said quickly. "My 'friend' family is the one that matters. And who's who will be self-explanatory, and you'll get to know them all when you work at Casa Blanca."

"Can you give me a refresher before we get there?"

"Sure. Lacey and Clay Walker own the resort and have a new baby, Elijah, plus Lacey's teenage daughter, Ashley. Zoe has a hot-air-balloon excursion business, which she has someone else piloting right now because she's pregnant. She's engaged to Dr. Oliver Bradbury, an oncologist, and they're planning to get married after the house they're building is finished and the baby's born."

"After?"

"She wants the baby at the wedding. She lives to be unconventional."

"So there are a lot of babies in the air," he noted, keeping his arm tightly around her.

"A few. None for Jocelyn, yet. She recently married Will Palmer, a local carpenter. She runs the spa at Casa Blanca."

"How did you all end up at the resort?"

"Lacey launched the project and, one by one, we came to join her." At the truck, she unclipped her key ring from her bag, handing it to him. "Don't think it escaped my notice that you barely drank one glass of wine and let me dip into a second. You drive."

He took the keys, maneuvering himself so her back was against the passenger door. "Be happy to."

She sighed as he got closer, tilting her head up to look at the full moon, but her gaze caught his instead, and stayed there, letting the power of those blue eyes nearly flatten her. For a long moment, he said nothing, just looked into her eyes.

Since he'd taken over the conversation at dinner, the warning bells had stopped ringing. He'd made her comfortable and content. He had convinced her they'd had two rocky starts—the bar and the interview—but this was all new. He had made her stop doubting, at least for now.

"What are you thinking?" she asked him.

"You don't want to know."

The answer surprised her. "Then I wouldn't have asked."

"I'm thinking about a lot of things."

"Name one."

"How perfect you are," he whispered.

"Oh, with the lines."

"That's not a line," he insisted. "You are perfect." He backed her against the passenger door with one step, stroking her cheek with a shockingly light knuckle, the feathery touch making her close her eyes. "I'm not sure how I feel about that, but you're perfect." The hint of sadness in his voice made one of those dormant warning bells ring again. Something wasn't right with that answer, or the regretful tone in his voice.

"Perfect for what?"

He frowned and shook his head, not answering.

She put both hands on his chest, not to push him away but to get a good feel of the muscles under his shirt. "What exactly are you looking for in a woman, John?"

"I don't know," he said gruffly, added some pressure so they were chest to chest, legs to legs. "But I think I found it."

Oh, God. Was it possible he was for real? Was she about to kiss a guy who could possibly…

No. Not this soon. Not this man. It wasn't—

He lowered his head, angling it one way, then the

other, as if he couldn't decide the perfect way to go in for the kill. "Damn it, you're beautiful."

His mouth covered hers, warm and wet, soft and sweet, his lips lingering like she was as delicious as the tiramisu they'd just shared.

Lifting her hands, she wrapped her arms around his neck, pulling him into her and standing a little higher on her toes to get every bit of this moment. Her head buzzed and her heart hammered and every nerve in her body quickened to life. She couldn't separate the taste of mocha and mint and man, and didn't try. She merely reveled in them all.

He opened his mouth, swirling his tongue around hers. An invitation, not an invasion, and Tessa licked him in even deeper. A soft, low groan escaped from his chest, the sound of sex and desire, a sound that made her dig her fingers into his silky long hair and press harder against his granite-like torso.

"Now I'm sorry," she whispered into the kiss.

"Sorry?" He broke the contact, frowning at her. "For kissing me?"

"For inviting you to meet my friends."

He almost smiled. "Because you want to go straight home and fall into bed?"

She kind of nodded, fighting a laugh.

"I know how you feel, but..." He kissed her again, taking her face in his hands this time, tilting her so their mouths fit perfectly, breathing life and hope and a dizzying, stunning jolt of desire all the way through her. "I really want to meet your friends, too."

Seriously? "I can't believe this," she murmured into the kiss.

"Believe it." He inched back, his eyes squeezed closed. In the moonlight, it almost looked like his lashes were damp and he worked hard to swallow.

Was he *crying*?

He squeezed her into him, fending off the question with a hard kiss, unforgiving, and completely different from the ones before. This was far more fury and desperation than seduction and sex. And *tears* rang the warning bell again. Tessa pushed back, aware of the hammering of his heart under her palms.

He kept his eyes closed and took a ragged breath. "I told you," he murmured. "You affect me."

Tessa stood perfectly still, looking up at a god in the moonlight, no question that the sides of this tough guy's eyes were moist.

She touched the tear-dampened line and brushed his long lashes. "In more ways than one, I'd say."

"Yes, in many more ways."

Believe it, he'd said. Everything in her wanted to believe him. Everything. But something wasn't *right*.

Corralling his composure, he put his hands on her shoulders as if to steady her, despite the fact that he was clearly the one in need of steadying.

Once Ian Browning committed to a course of action, he rarely veered in any other direction. That was why he had excelled in university. That was why he'd sailed up the ranks at Barclays. That was why once he decided he'd get Tessa Galloway to marry him, he pulled out all the stops and turned up the heat.

At least that was what he kept telling himself, even after he made the monumental mistake of letting himself feel something for her—enough that his emotions were all over his face.

He was no stranger to tears; he'd shed a thousand since Kate died. But these? These stunned him. Surely they weren't because he felt something for Tessa Galloway already.

"Let's go," he said, not wanting to get into the conversation here and now. "I want to meet your friends."

She gave him a wary smile. "Really?"

"No, that's a lie," he admitted. "I'd rather have a root canal and hug a cactus tree than go to a party, but"—he opened the passenger door and gestured for her to get in—"let's go."

She hesitated. "Why, if you hate parties?"

"Because you want to go."

Her eyes flickered in surprise, and affection. "That's not necessary."

"You do want to go, right?"

"Actually, yes."

"Then get in the truck, sweetheart."

She started to, then stopped. "Why?" she asked again.

"Because I want to make you happy." *And* having her friends like him was another key component to the marriage plan. Without waiting for another question, he closed the door and rounded the back, shoving down the misgivings that threatened to rise up and choke him.

There was no other choice.

Sliding behind the wheel, he felt her gaze on him, steady and definitely unsure.

"Why do you want to make me happy?"

He let out a soft laugh and twisted the ignition key. "Boy, you *have* been hurt. Tell me about it."

"I did already," she said, warming him with her directness.

"You had a shitty ex-husband," he acknowledged, happy to have the conversation off his motivations and onto her life, where it should stay until they got to the party. "Was that enough to destroy your trust in all mankind?"

She laughed softly. "If all mankind were like you, womankind would be in big trouble."

He shot her a grin. "You like me."

"Jury's out."

"You like me." He took her hand, the feeling of her fingers warm and familiar now. "You know you do."

Her head on the backrest, she turned to him, smiling. "I could," she admitted. "But we have to work together."

"So?"

"Could be awkward."

"What's awkward?" he countered. "Longing looks across the kitchen? Kissing in the cooler? Daily trips up to the garden to roll around in the dirt with my favorite farm girl? What's not to like about this arrangement?" Damn, it sounded a little too good.

But she laughed, clearly enjoying the exchange. "You make it sound fun."

He squeezed her hand. "It will be fun." Until it wasn't. "It already is." And that was no lie.

It had been a long time since he'd laughed easily with a woman, or made out in the moonlight. It had been a very long time since he'd delayed sex to linger over a romantic dinner or meet friends and family. It had been a long time since he'd…

Had a normal relationship.

Except, this wasn't normal because this wasn't real. He glanced at her and she met his gaze, giving him a warm smile.

But sometimes it felt real.

While they drove back to Mimosa Key, he let her tell him more fine points about her friends, the conversation lasting all the way along the beach road, up to Barefoot Bay to Lacey and Clay's house. As they walked across the circular drive, he took a deep breath of salt air, eyeing the darkness of the Gulf of Mexico to their left.

"Nervous?" she asked.

Not a bit. "Spitless."

She slipped her arm around his waist and reached up to kiss his cheek. "You'll be great, John Brown."

John Brown. John Brown. He clung to the new name he'd been given when Sean Bern had "died" in Singapore, which meant—for the N1L gang who wanted him dead, anyway—that Ian Browning was dead, too.

He had to be careful not to let this comfortable, easy, genuine woman make him slip and forget he was now John Brown. A man who'd bounced around from job to job but had recently been consumed with the burning need to settle down and had already fallen for this little island and one particularly appealing resident.

The front door opened and a man stepped out to greet them. "Hey, Tessa." Reaching his hand out, he greeted Ian. "I'm Clay Walker. I understand you're our newest employee."

"John Brown." The name rolled off his lips, so he added a confident nod to the other man, whose shoulder-length hair almost covered a small gold earring. The man was definitely a few years younger than his wife, but his handshake was strong and sincere.

A small group of adults gathered on an outdoor patio around the pool, but on the way out there, they walked through a family room where two teenage girls languished on the sofa, a bowl of popcorn between them.

"Oh, hi, Aunt Tess." One of the girls rolled off the sofa and popped onto her feet, her reddish-blonde hair and freckled face telling Ian immediately this was Lacey's daughter.

"This is my stepdaughter, Ashley," Clay said. "This is Chef Brown."

She gave a quick smile and then her eyes widened at him. "You're the new chef?"

He nodded. "Looks that way."

"Yeah, Marcus told me about your soup."

"Are you friends with him?" he asked, digging for his finest small-talk abilities despite the fact that they were negligible at best, especially where teenage girls were concerned.

She shifted her gaze quickly to Clay, and shrugged. "I know him from, you know, around."

"Come on out, guys," Lacey called from the patio.

Ashley looked relieved, and Clay gestured for them to head outside. As Ian stepped across the threshold, he heard a whistle from the family room.

"Hey, Aunt Tessa. Nice!"

He didn't turn to see Tessa's reaction, but he mentally counted teenage Ashley among his supporters. One down, six to go. Oh, there were seven out here.

He froze midstep when he saw the infant in Lacey's arms.

"I'd get up, but I don't want to wake him," Lacey said

from a chaise near the pool. "Hello, John. It's great to see you again."

Even from fifteen feet away he could make out the familiar shape of a baby's head, the slope of a button nose, the bundle of blanket tucked around a tiny, tiny body. Nothing prepared him for the soul-shattering impact.

"We're all celebrating the news that you've accepted the job," she said, beaming at him.

He had to hold it together. He had to act like any other guy who had absolutely zero reaction to a baby. Ambling over, he forced his attention on mother and off child.

"Thanks for the vote of confidence, Ms. Walker."

She smiled up at him. "Please call me Lacey and thank you for accepting the offer. I hope you're ready to work ASAP."

"I'm ready," he assured her, unable to fight the urge to look at the baby.

He supposed they really did all look alike, which only made this worse. Same peach fuzz of hair, same heart-shaped lips, same peaceful look while sleeping.

"This is Elijah," she said proudly, lifting him gently. "You can hold him if you swear not to wake him up."

"Sure." He had to. Vaguely aware of Lacey glancing to one of the other women, he took her bundle, familiarity mixing with pain and a sense of déjà vu so strong it nearly took his breath away. This baby was a carbon copy of Shiloh and Sam.

"About six months?" he asked, adjusting the baby a little closer to his heart. Shi had loved it there; she fell sound asleep when he held her that way.

Lacey pushed out of the chaise, smiling up at him. "Just about. You're a natural, John."

"Yeah, well, I..." Elijah shuddered with a soft sigh, the whimper as powerful as a kick in the face. "I have nieces and nephews." Two, and he'd been away at school when they were this age.

He turned, coming face-to-face with another couple watching him with interest. Lacey introduced Will Palmer and his wife, Jocelyn.

"We met at the Toasted Pelican," he said to Jocelyn, forcing himself to be social when all he really wanted to do was wallow in memories and misery at how purely hollow holding this baby made him feel.

"We didn't exactly meet," Jocelyn corrected him, an amused look divided between him and the baby. "But it's nice to see you again."

"I better give this guy back to his rightful owner," he said, looking around for Lacey but landing on Tessa, who stood a few feet away with the third couple, a look of sheer disbelief and wonder on her face.

Their eyes met for several heartbeats, and the whole patio stayed eerily silent for that same amount of time.

"Here." Lacey ended the awkward moment by swooping in and taking Elijah back. "He needs to be put down and you need to..." She hesitated for a moment as if she had so many different options for finishing that sentence, she didn't know where to begin.

"I need to meet the rest of your guests," he said smoothly, walking over to Tessa, who still stared at him. He felt the heat and hope in her look, burning him with shame.

If his plan succeeded, he'd have what he wanted and she'd—

"This is Zoe Tamarin and Dr. Oliver Bradbury," she said quickly, blessedly ending his thought.

While shaking the doctor's hand, he nodded to Zoe's stomach. "I see congratulations are in order."

Zoe beamed back. "You know what we say about Barefoot Bay? Kick off your shoes and fall in love."

Tessa choked softly. "Zoe, please."

"What? It's our new marketing slogan. Haven't you told him about that, yet?"

Ian shook his head and Tessa held up a hand. "I haven't really…"

"Did you tell him about the wedding business?" Zoe asked.

Ian blinked at her, a flash of panic. "What wedding business?"

"No need to look terrified," Tessa said with an uncomfortable laugh. "It's some really important guests you'll have to dazzle with your culinary skills."

That he could do. "Who am I dazzling?"

"You didn't tell him about the wedding-planner board?" Jocelyn asked.

"We haven't talked about weddings," she said quickly.

"Yet," Ian added. All six of them looked right at him, an incredibly brutal silence descending. "So why don't you all tell me?" He put a casual arm around Tessa. "And give poor Tess a break. I've been grilling her all night learning everything I can about her. She didn't have a chance to talk business."

Clay poured some drinks and they gathered around a long table, small talk flying while Lacey headed out to put the baby down. Ian suppressed the desire to take one last look at the wee lad, instead smiling at Tessa as she responded to Lacey's tug.

"Come help me, please?" Lacey whispered to Tessa.

When Tessa stepped away, Zoe dropped right into the empty seat next to him. "So." She grinned, a smile full of meaning and interest.

He gave one right back. "Let me see if I have this right," he said, pointing at her. "You're the instigator, correct?"

She shrugged with a smug smile. "Guilty as charged. I was also the party girl, but my wild child days are over now." She rubbed her belly again and notched her chin toward the doctor. "All settled, content, and in love."

"Sounds good."

"Does it?"

He laughed, her meaning obvious. "I like that you all look out for your friend."

Her expression grew suddenly serious. "We more than look out for her," she said. "We love her and want to see her happy."

Then shouldn't he leave her alone? Because he could never be real, could never be anything but heartache for her.

"Tessa deserves to be happy," he said.

Jocelyn moved a chair closer, jumping into the conversation. "Yes, she does," she agreed. "She's been through a lot."

He nodded. "She told me."

"Do you like her?" Zoe asked.

He looked right into the bright-green eyes that pinned him with a look full of warning and curiosity.

"Very much." Not a lie, not even close. "In fact," he said, thinking about each word before he said it, "I like her...a lot."

"Then you should know her soft spot," Zoe said.

"Zoe!" Jocelyn chastised, leaning into the conversation.

"Not that soft spot." She grinned. "The one that could implode this budding relationship."

Jocelyn rolled her eyes, but Ian was intrigued. He might need to implode the relationship. "What is it?"

"That girl will run, and I mean she will haul ass fast and furious, if you keep a secret from her."

He blinked at her, losing the fight not to let anything show on his face. Including dismay. "Excuse me?"

"Zoe's right," Jocelyn said. "Secret-keeping is her number-one, do-not-violate code. Although"—she winked at Zoe—"a couple of us have broken the rule and paid the price."

"What's the price?" he asked.

"Oh, she'll cut you off," Zoe said. "I mean, with us, we had to make her understand why we kept our secrets, but with a guy? She'll be gone before you get up to brush your teeth if she finds out you kept something from her."

Oh, bloody hell. "Then I won't."

"Keep something from her?" Jocelyn asked.

He smiled. "I won't ever leave her alone in bed."

Zoe let out a hoot. "Dude, are you legit?"

Only three years of fighting natural physical responses gave him the ability to keep from giving away the truth in his expression. "I'm as legit as they get." The lie tasted like pure shit, but he said it anyway. What the hell else could he do?

This was for his *kids*.

Chapter Eleven

⌒

With Lacey's excited cooing and Zoe's unsubtle hinting and Jocelyn's quiet nodding of approval, Ian was fairly certain he'd passed the Friend Approval test. Of course, the *real* test would be in five, four, three, two…

"You want to come in?"

Score. But was it the right move? He eased the truck into Park and took a slow breath. "I guess."

Tessa's smile wavered. "Well, that's damning with faint enthusiasm."

He turned, instantly sorry he'd replied that way. "It's not that I don't want to, Tess."

She waited for him to continue, but he reached across the small space that separated them and twirled one strand of her hair around his finger.

"It's that I really do," he said softly.

"Worried about work complications?"

He was worried about every complication as he barreled forth with his plan to pretend to be completely into

Tessa. The problem was, a few hours ago, kissing her on the sidewalk so overwhelmed him with guilt that he'd sprung *tears*. What unpardonable sin might he commit to if he actually got in bed with her and…let go of control? He couldn't take that chance.

Caring about her was not in the cards. That pinprick of guilt stabbed again, somewhere between his cold heart and burning gut. It was easy enough to soften that stab, and he did, pulling her closer and letting their lips touch lightly.

He felt her sigh into his mouth, a little bit of surrender and uncertainty and desire.

"This might be harder than I thought," he murmured, the thought slipping out as easily as the next kiss.

"What might be?" she asked.

Lying. "Waiting." It was the first thing that popped into his head.

"I don't get it. You didn't want to wait the night I met you. You wanted to take off my clothes and, let's see, do something unspeakable to my *rack*."

Just the words on her lips shot a gallon or two of blood due south. "I still do." He ventured his hand a little lower on her breastbone, nearly touching her breast. "More, in fact."

Her only response was two raised eyebrows in question. But he heard the question, read the confusion in her eyes. *What happened between now and then?*

He'd found out he needed a wife. "That night, I wanted to…" *Fuck. Shag. Screw the pain away.* "Do what I generally do with women who don't matter."

She inched back with a small grunt of revulsion.

"Don't take that the wrong way."

"There's a right way to take it?"

"Take it this way," he said, cupping the back of her head with his hand and threading some hair through his fingers. "The bar pickup was meaningless, fast, easy, and fun. But now I know you. Now I...*need* you." Again, not a lie. In fact, it might have been the most honest thing he'd said all night.

"You need me?"

He closed his eyes, fighting the urge to explain any more. "I want you. I like you. I dig you. I'm into you. I—"

She put a hand on his mouth. "I get the idea. Just so I understand...you're holding back because you think that...this might be..." She dragged out the last few words, clearly unwilling or unable to put any in his mouth.

"I think this might be real," he whispered. The guilt pinprick turned into a nine-inch chef's knife and stabbed right into his chest. Instantly, he leaned closer and tried to stop the pain with a long, sweet, wet kiss.

When it ended, she didn't even open her eyes, her breath already tight. "John Brown, you are the master of mixed messages. Give me one straight answer. Do you want to come inside or not?"

"Yes, but I'm not going to," he said. "Because I won't leave."

After a second, she nodded once, quickly. "I get it. Good-bye." She attempted another exit, but he grabbed her again.

"You're mad at me," he said.

She bit a soft laugh. "Not really. Confused."

"Understandable. Let's not rush things."

She searched his face, long and hard, the confusion darkening her eyes. "Why is it that every instinctive female alarm system that's hardwired into my body is screaming a red alert right now?"

Because that female alarm system was in excellent working condition. "Not sleeping with you doesn't mean I don't want to. It means I do. More than once."

"Okay," she whispered. "I like that."

He slowly took the keys out of the ignition and gave them to her. "Let me walk you to the door."

"No, that's okay." She gave a tentative smile. "I might never let you go."

For some reason, the words got to him.

"Thanks for dinner and coming to the party." She opened the door and stepped out, walking to the front of the bungalow. He watched for a moment, then he climbed out, closed the driver's door, and took a few steps to his motorcycle.

As he was about to get on, he looked up and saw her slip into the front door, imagining her leaning against it inside, sighing, maybe a little let down, maybe a little excited, definitely a lot baffled.

What the hell was he doing? He couldn't *use* this woman like this. He was a bastard, hurt and angry and desperate, sure, but she didn't do anything to deserve this.

Fuck this *lying*.

He pivoted, his mind dead blank for a moment, then he sprinted toward the small porch, his feet pounding on the two steps as he bounded to the door, which opened exactly the second he reached it. "What are you—"

"I have to tell you something," he said, surprised at how strangled the words were.

"What?"

"I have to tell you…" He put his hands on her shoulders, the confession jammed in his throat now. "I have to tell you…"

Suddenly, his head thrummed with blood and fear and the echo of Henry Brooker's statement of raw fact.

Ian, you live with this lie or you die.

"Tell me what?"

"That I…" *Lie or die.* He closed his eyes and pulled her hard against him, finding her mouth and slamming his over it, squeezing her whole body as if he could kiss her from head to toe.

She stiffened, bunching his shirt under her fists, a soft whimper in her throat.

Lie or die.

The three words ricocheted in his brain, so he kissed harder, opening his mouth and entering hers, tasting heat and wine and the sweet flavor of her giving in. Her fingers loosened, flattened, and traveled over his chest with appreciation. Her tongue matched his, licking and flicking in a mating dance, and her hips rocked gently at the place where they met so naturally.

Lie or…

Kiss. It was all he wanted to do. Kiss. Touch. Taste. Smell. Press his hard-on into her pelvic bone and *ride*. The reverberations of Henry's words faded into her tender moans and disappeared into nothing as he let his hands travel over her back, her hips, and cup her backside. Henry's warnings went silent with the thrum of blood and the steady, heavy insistence of his body.

He broke the kiss only to trail more down her neck, walking her backwards into the entryway, unable to stop his hands from roaming up her waist to the sides of her breasts. To her nipples, so hard his mouth watered to suck on them.

"John."

He barely heard the name, it hardly registered. He didn't have a fucking name anymore; he just had need. Kissing her mouth again, he turned her to the wall, using it for leverage to roll against her.

Breathless already, she let him, lifting her chin to offer him her throat and breasts, bracing herself as he clutched her breast with one hand and gathered up her dress with the other. He wanted under. In. All the way—

"John." She added pressure, pushing him back an inch, needing air. "Is this what you wanted to tell me?"

Was it? Wasn't he going to tell her *the truth*? Or was he going to fuck her in every possible way?

God, he *liked* this woman. This hard-on was real and way too connected to his brain, and that alone was a lovely and unwanted change.

"Actually, no," he whispered, opening his fingers to let her dress fall back around her legs. "I was going to tell you…"

A secret she had no reason or desire to keep.

He put some more space between them, taking his hand off the sexy curve of her breast and placing both hands on the wall, holding himself up and not giving her a way to escape.

She still fought shallow breaths, her eyes dark with arousal, her cheeks flushed, her lips a little swollen from his brutal kisses. She looked pretty. Hot. Ready. Willing to take him and trust him and he…

He was a total and complete fake who needed this

woman to fall for him and marry him and give him the
only thing he really wanted. Without ever knowing the
truth.

Self-loathing rose up, replacing his fiery blood with
ice. "I was going to tell you…that…I…" He closed his
eyes, unwilling to look at her when he lied. "I want more
than a one-night stand."

"You told me that."

"I wanted to emphasize it."

When she didn't answer, he opened his eyes and she
was staring hard, clearly trying to weigh that statement
with the man who'd pushed her up against the wall with
his demanding dick and hungry hands.

"Me, too," she whispered.

"That's…good." No, it was bad. Bad, bad, bad.

She smiled, reaching up to stroke his cheek. "Look,
John, I can do casual sex, honestly, I can. I think I've
proven that in the last four minutes. I can even handle a
little sideline fun with a colleague. But if you want something that lasts more than a few days or weeks, then I need
to be sure you remember that…" She struggled for a word,
biting her lip. "You remember what's important to me."

She wanted a baby. She didn't have to remind him; he
remembered.

He backed away, and she winced ever so slightly.
Enough that he saw the vulnerability that he could crush
like a roach under his boot. That he *would* crush, when he
had what he wanted…and she didn't.

There was no way. No way he would ever dream of
creating another child that grew up disconnected to him.
And no way he'd—*No*. He couldn't. He couldn't tell her
the truth, ever.

"That's fine," she said quickly, adding some pressure to push him back another inch, his answer obvious by his silence. "Just so we're clear."

He dropped one arm and she instantly stepped to the side and let out a soft, wry laugh.

"Is something funny?" he asked.

"No, just that, wow, we made progress tonight, huh? Met the friends, made out, almost had had the baby talk. What's left?"

He reached for her face, holding her chin and stroking her bottom lip. He shouldn't have picked her. She was too tender. Too precious. Too real.

All the things he wasn't.

"There's plenty left." Assuming he had the balls to go through with it. Did he?

Time would tell. He hesitated for a minute, then lifted one hand in a halfhearted wave, walking out to the porch. When he reached the driveway, he turned to see her silhouette still in the doorway.

His heart hitched and he looked away, hating that the image was burned into his brain, where he had a feeling it would stay all night long.

Chapter Twelve

ᥬ

Two days later, Tessa lounged on her back porch, angling her laptop screen so the afternoon sun didn't cause a glare. That way, she had a perfect view of the gorgeous lines of the dreamy, feminine, lace-layered wedding dress on the home page of All Gussied Up, the Web site run by the wedding consultant with pink hair.

She'd meant to spend this quiet Sunday boning up on each of the VIP guests, but for some reason she'd yet to click to Gussie McBain's bio, staring at the dress instead.

"You'd look amazing in that."

She jumped a foot and stabbed the Escape key, spinning around at the man's voice. And not just any man—the man she'd spent the last two days allowing far more of a hold on her thoughts than he should have.

But look at him. And look she did, devouring the white T-shirt molded to substantial muscle, the faded jeans clinging to powerful thighs, his honey hair tangled from the wind and face shadowed with unshaved stubble, his hand clutching—a duffel bag?

"Hey, what's up?" she asked, going for casual and friendly but getting a nervous hitch in her throat that she cleared away.

"I'm moving in."

Her eyes widened and he laughed, the sound rolling right through to her toes.

"Next door," he said, half lifting the bag in the direction of the bungalow that used to be Zoe and Pasha's. After Pasha died, Zoe and Oliver had moved off the property and the bungalow had been empty. So of course Lacey would offer him the house built for sole purpose of housing Casa Blanca's top staff.

But why hadn't Lacey told Tessa?

"Well there goes the neighborhood," she quipped, repositioning the laptop and sitting up so she wasn't flat on her back in front of him.

He grinned, climbing up the single stair to her deck as though she'd invited him. There was one other chair, but he dropped the bag and sat down on the chaise next to her, taking his time to check her out from head to toe.

"Nice." One syllable, one smile, one long look. "To see you," he finally added.

"You, too."

"It's been thirty-eight hours. Did you miss me?"

Her jaw loosened, then she laughed. "You're counting hours?"

"Mmm." He leaned forward like he might kiss her but took the laptop instead, turning it to face him, opening and clicking. "Wedding dresses?"

"Research on our important guests," she shot back.

He studied the Web site but she studied him, counting golden lashes and remembering how his lips felt.

After a second, he closed the computer and carefully put it on the cocktail table next to her. Then he leveled her with his direct attention, placing his hands on either side of her to pin her on the chaise.

"How many times did you think about me?" he asked.

She laughed again, shaking her head. "I lost count after two." *Hundred.* "You've got a big ego."

"I've got a big…" He leaned lower and she braced for something sweet and dirty. "Crush."

She closed her eyes. "That's not what I thought you were going to say."

He brushed her cheek with his, chuckling low so she could feel his chest rumble. "Come to the kitchen with me," he said into her ear.

"I thought you were moving in."

"I am." He leaned up, jutting his chin to the duffel bag. "There's my stuff."

"That's it?"

"I travel light."

Because he had no roots. "Isn't the kitchen closed after brunch now?"

"Yep, but I have my own research to do. I want to get the lay of the land, try a new recipe, and"—he ran a finger over her arm—"hang out with you."

There was no way to say no. After she showed him around the bungalow next door, they walked through the gardens toward the resort.

"One thing about living in the employee bungalows," Tessa said as they rounded the property of the northernmost villa to see the full vista of Barefoot Bay, "the commute doesn't suck."

John blew out a low, slow whistle, taking in the glorious horizon, awash with the first tinge of pink and plum, promising a breathtaking sunset later.

"I haven't been up this far north at this time of day yet. That's quite a view." He slowed his step and looked along the gentle curve of the Gulf inlet. "This is a beautiful property. This was in Lacey's family, I understand?"

"Some of it. Her grandparents were part of the original founders of Mimosa Key, and they claimed much of this inlet when they helped build the island. After they died, she and Ashley lived in an old house her grandparents had built, but it was destroyed by a hurricane a little over two years ago. She bought the adjacent lots for next to nothing from landowners who wanted out after the storm. From there, she built this."

He nodded, mouth turned up in approval. "She's a driven woman."

"Two years ago, Lacey would have guffawed in laughter over that statement. She was the original self-doubter. But then…" She smiled, thinking of her closest friend's remarkable transformation. "Clay Walker showed up on this beach and she's been a firecracker ever since."

"Ah, the love of a good man and all that."

The comment slipped under her skin, and it shouldn't have, so she nodded, pretending to enjoy the view.

"How long have you been here?" he asked.

"Pretty much from the beginning. My divorce was final around the same time as the hurricane and we—Zoe and Joss and me—all gathered here to help Lacey. I liked the area and decided to settle here and start the gardens and oversee a lot of the landscaping. Now Joss and Zoe are here, so…"

He gave her a sideways smile. "So there are a lot of roots taking hold around you, aren't there?"

Asked the man who moved in with a weekend's worth of clothes as all his belongings. She attempted a shrug in response. "It's great to live near my friends. Like I told you, they're family to me."

He didn't respond to that but put a warm, strong hand on her back to guide her to the stone trail that cut through the property.

"As far as your commute," she said, "you have two choices to get to work. This path, which will take you through the entire resort to the main building." She gestured toward the canopy of live oak trees mixed with several different kinds of palms that lined the wide walkway, meandering more or less parallel to the beach. "Or cross the bridge and walk the beach."

"Which do you prefer?" He took her hand, the most natural move that sent the most unnatural thrill through her.

"Depends on my mood," she said.

"What kind of mood are you in now?"

She made no attempt to unthread their fingers. "Let's see. Unsure? Surprised? Maybe a little tense?" And happy, excited, and wary.

He brought those joined hands a little higher, closer to his mouth. Was he going to kiss her hand again? "Tense? You're taking a walk. It's perfectly harmless."

"Harmless?" She gave a soft snort. "No one could look at you and call you harmless."

"I wouldn't hurt a fly."

"But you could destroy a woman's heart."

The slightest shadow of a reaction darkened his eyes. It was gone before she could grab hold of it, but she knew what she'd seen. Guilt. He'd probably thought all about the baby issue, and decided to…

Come and hang out with her.

She waited a beat, so he could contradict her accusation, but he didn't.

"Points for not denying the truth," she said softly.

"I wouldn't destroy a woman's heart on…" His voice faded.

She laughed softly. He couldn't—or wouldn't—even say "on purpose." "I'll give you this, John Brown. You're not a liar. I can't tell you how much I appreciate your honesty."

He bit his lip, letting out an exhale, that darkened expression clearing again. "What I am," he finally said, dragging his gaze to her face, "is interested in everything you have to say and do." He lifted their hands again, and this time he did put his lips on her knuckles, holding her gaze as he kissed.

Just relax and enjoy, Tess. She smiled at him, listening to her mental instructions and those of her friends for the past, well, thirty-eight hours. The girls had pronounced him perfect, utterly focused on how nurturing he was with Elijah.

Maybe they were right and she'd rushed him with the baby talk. Spooked him again. He was looking for sexy time and there she'd gone proclaiming her baby dreams one more time.

Vowing to keep those dreams in the background, she gave him a purposely coy smile. "You want to see my pride and joy?"

"Yes." The answer, without a second's hesitation, earned him more points.

"Then we'll take the path and start right here." She pointed to the shrub bursting with fuchsia-and-white blooms. "Because it shows some of my best work."

"Is this a hibiscus?" He fingered one of the flowers, the petals appearing delicate in his large, masculine hands.

"Actually, no, but that's an understandable mistake. And to be honest, anyone could grow hibiscus in Florida; it's just this side of a weed. But this isn't." She touched a flower. "This is rockrose, which is the name of that villa." She indicated the cozy one-bedroom villa about twenty feet away. "All of the villas at Casa Blanca are named for flowers, herbs, and spices that are indigenous to Morocco and North Africa."

"The inspiration for the architecture and the name?" he asked.

"Exactly. And I took it as my personal challenge to grow each one of the plants outside of the villa that bears its name. And, let me tell you, it was a challenge growing some African plants in Florida. But every single one is thriving." She tugged his hand, pulling him down the path to the next villa. "Come see the best one."

They wound around the curve of the path to the gates of the next villa and she pointed to the twenty-foot-long bed where she'd spent an inordinate amount of time trying to coax the purple crocuses to life. About a dozen blooms remained, but two months ago there'd been almost a hundred. "They're not as robust as they were in September, but still…" She kneeled in front of the flowers. "I'm proud of those blooms."

He crouched next to her, touching the withered petal gently, then sniffing. "Saffron?"

"Exactly, and that's the name of this villa." She beamed at him. "Of course a chef would recognize that."

"One of my favorite ingredients, living in Singa—" He shut his mouth quickly, flinching almost imperceptibly. "Saffron is one of my favorite spices."

She frowned, certain he was going to say "Singapore," but there'd been no mention of that city when he'd given her his life's history at dinner or on his resume. "Did you live there?" she asked. After a beat of silence, she added, "In Singapore?"

"Very briefly." He studied each petal of the crocus intently, as though he'd never seen one so close before. "Between California and Nevada."

"That's quite a detour between those states." Living in the Far East was a fairly major piece of a person's background. Why not mention it? "How long were you there?" she prodded.

"Not very. It was more like an extended vacation. Too short to count as actually living there."

Except he'd just *said* he'd lived there.

"Do you use this in the kitchen?" he asked quickly, brushing the orange stigma with a feathertip touch. "Or are these for show?"

"I can't grow enough to dry the stamen for cooking, but I have a good supplier if you really want saffron in your recipes." She stood slowly, the oversight on his past still pressing a familiar hot button: secrets. Not to mention men who lie about where they'd spent time. "Why didn't you mention living in Singapore when you told me your life story?"

He didn't look up. In fact, she could have sworn his fingers stilled. "It didn't seem that important." He flicked the flower. "Were these hard to grow?"

Did he really care about the flowers, or was this a way to keep her from asking more questions?

"Hard enough. How long were you there?"

"I've heard they travel deep in the soil and lots of people think they're dead when they're just deep."

She frowned at him, processing the comment on one level, but stuck in Singapore on another. "That's exactly what happened," she said. "I thought I'd failed completely when I couldn't find one bulb with life. But when I went to dig them out and start over, I realized the bulbs must have grown legs because the roots were deep in the soil."

He still didn't look up, working his way to the next blossom. Something about this conversation was way, way off.

"It wasn't that long." He looked up at her. "That I lived there, I mean."

Her heart rose with relief. At least he'd acknowledged the question. "I was wondering," she said.

"Your friends told me you hate secrets."

"Generous of them," she said dryly.

"No, I asked."

"If I hate secrets?"

He stood slowly. "Zoe wanted me to know your soft spot."

"She would. And get graphic, too."

He laughed, taking her hand and pulling her closer. "I can find *that* spot on my own." Easing her all the way into him, he lowered his head nearer to her face. "If you'll give me another chance."

Relief made room for hope. The girls were right. She'd pushed him too hard, too fast. "I'm giving you a chance right now."

This close, she could barely focus. Hell, she could barely stand, let alone wait much longer. He smelled like sunshine and sea breeze and a hint of sweet and spicy saffron clinging to his fingertips. He smelled sexy.

"Do you hate surprises as much as secrets?" he asked.

She considered that and lifted a shoulder. "Don't keep any and we'll be fine."

He closed his eyes and brushed her lips.

"John?" she murmured. "Can you make that promise?"

He barely kissed her, but it was enough to send some hot sparks through her and make her want to lean in and kiss more. She could kiss this guy for hours. "Can you?" she breathed into the kiss.

He flicked her lower lip with his tongue, then added some pressure to her lips. "I like kissing you," he murmured.

"Mutual," she kissed back, the breath trapped in her lungs.

When he ended the kiss, he placed his lips against her ear. "Tessa?"

"Yeah?"

"I've missed you." And when he kissed her again, he stroked her back and she felt every muscle in his body harden against her. Everything felt so good. So right. So absolutely perfectly delicious.

She opened her mouth and kissed him back, long enough that she almost forgot that he didn't actually make the promise she'd asked for.

Chapter Thirteen

࿉

It was the best time in the kitchen. After the resort brunch was served and cleaned up, the restaurant closed for the rest of the weekend, so on Sunday afternoons, the kitchen was dark, deserted, and very, very cozy.

Especially in the cold and dark dry-storage pantry, where two people could find a corner to kiss and whisper—and share secrets.

Except Marcus wasn't sharing anything right now but tonsil hockey. Of course, they hadn't been together in two days, so how could they keep their hands off each other?

"Come on." Marcus tugged at the sleeve of Ashley's hoodie. "Take your top off, babe."

"It's cold, Marc."

He pulled her higher on his lap, right onto an epic-sized boner. "I'll keep you warm," he teased. "I won't hurt you."

Ashley laughed softly, repositioning herself into a straddle, enjoying the little fireworks that exploded between her legs as she moved over the firm ridge between his.

"Let's just do this," she said, wrapping her arms around his neck and humping like they did last time. "It's fun."

"Fun for you." He slid a hand under her hoodie, finding his way beneath her T-shirt and heading north to her boob. They'd gone this far already, so it wasn't like she could say no. They were headed…there. Fast. But she wasn't sure she wanted her first time to be in the dry-storage pantry.

A different kind of heat slithered through her, making her stomach tighten but not in the way it did when she thought about how much she liked this boy. This was a different tightness. This was an ache. He was definitely the one. It was only a matter of time until she lost her virginity to him.

He got his thumb right over her nipple and pleasure and pain welled up so intensely she wanted to scream. All she wanted was more. And so did he.

After all, he wasn't some stinking high school junior who'd be happy making out and getting the occasional feel. This was Marcus and he was a *man*, especially since he'd be twenty in two months.

He started pumping between her legs, his eyes closing, his hands wandering to her other boob. "You're hot, Ashley."

She tried to let the compliment warm her, kissing his face. "So are you."

"Take this stupid thing off," he murmured, fumbling with her bra, underlining the plea with a hard press of his crotch right into hers. Oh, man, that felt good. "I want to see you, Ashley. I want to see your sexy titties."

She closed her eyes and tried to decide. She was seventeen, for crying out loud. It wasn't like it was a huge deal.

"Don't you like me?" he asked, coming around the back to her bra snap.

She wiggled to stop him. "You know I do. But we can just do this today, okay? Like last time?"

"You came in your jeans last time," he said, pulling back.

Oh, she had. And it had felt so freaking good she almost cried.

"So we are not even, girl."

True, she hadn't returned the favor. Yet. "You can come in your jeans," she offered, kind of hoping he didn't want to take her up on that. But what was the alternative? She *knew* the alternative. Maybe she could just kiss him and not put the whole thing in her mouth.

He took her hand and dragged it down there, making her rub his hard-on over his jeans.

"C'mon, Ash. Touch me. Put your—" He jerked away, pushing her back. "Did you hear that?"

She hadn't heard anything but the blood pounding in her head and way too many questions that didn't seem to plague any of her friends who did all kinds of smexy stuff with their boyfriends.

"Listen, Marc, we—"

"Shh!" He held a hand up to her mouth. "Someone's in the kitchen."

Her mother! "Shit." She scrambled off his lap, ice-cold fear replacing red-hot sexy in a blink.

"Quiet!" he demanded. "They might not come in here."

"They?" she whispered? Her mom and Clay? Shit monkeys! Life was over. She listened for the telltale sound of a baby's cry, because they wouldn't go anywhere without Elijah. Not anywhere, including the volleyball parents' meeting they'd missed and the parent-teachers' conference they blew off last week. Not that they needed to know she was majorly effing up calculus, but—

"It's John," Marcus said. "The new chef."

She scowled. "He's moving into his bungalow today. What would he be doing here?"

"Be quiet, Ash. Maybe he'll leave."

Ashley stayed right where she was on the pantry floor, staring at the door handle, taking silent breaths of flour and fear. Would the chef come in here? Would she be in trouble? Would he tell her mother what she was doing and who she was with?

Because this new boyfriend was probably not going to go over big.

Ashley brushed her hands over her top and jacket. At least she hadn't gone any farther.

The door handle moved, then stopped. She heard a voice, but couldn't make out what he'd said. Who was he with? Aunt Tessa? She'd die if Tessa saw her here. And of course her mom would find out and blow a gasket.

"Go." She pushed Marcus. "Go tell him you're working or something and don't let him see me."

"Why not?"

"'Cause he'll think I'm, like, a slut or something."

Marcus looked at her. "Who cares? He'll fire my ass if he catches me in the kitchen now."

Who cares? She did. But she didn't want Marcus to get

fired, either. "Then tell him you're doing inventory. You'll get promoted, not fired."

He looked at her, a mix of fear and hope in his dark, dark eyes. God, he was cute. "Please, Marc."

The handle moved again and, to his credit, Marcus shot up, taking two long strides and opening it himself, using his body to block any view of the pantry. Ashley pushed to her feet and slipped out of view behind shelves.

"What are you doing here?" Marcus asked, sounding like the guiltiest person on earth.

"What are *you* doing here?"

"Um, just…" *Inventory, you moron!* "Working."

Ashley closed her eyes and let out a silent grunt.

John pushed the door farther open. "Working on what?" he demanded, accusation in the question.

"You know, like, stuff that needs to be done."

"In the pantry?" John asked. "What exactly are you doing in there?"

"Nothing, man. You don't have to be a dick—"

"Marcus?"

Oh, *gawd*. Aunt Tessa was here.

"What's going on?"

Marcus didn't answer, but glanced to his side, where Ashley stood. *Why not scream my name, pal?* She gave him a pleading look and put her finger to her lips.

"I'm counting inventory," he finally said.

"Counting inventory?" John definitely wasn't buying it. "Or stealing inventory?"

"I'm not stealing anything!"

"Then let me in to see what you're doing."

Marcus stood frozen. "Tell him it's cool, Tessa. I come in and do inventory a lot on Sundays for overtime."

"Are you alone in there?" she asked.

Ashley almost slid back to the floor. Shit, shit, *shit*.

"Yeah," he said, about as convincingly as a two-year-old with chocolate on his face. He started to step out of the pantry, carefully keeping them from coming in. "I'm done anyway."

"You want to show me your jacket pockets?" John demanded.

Ashley's jaw dropped. He really thought Marcus was a thief? Would Marcus subject himself to a search or sell her out? That would really tell her what he was made of, wouldn't it?

"Eff you, John."

"That's Chef John to you. Empty your jacket pockets."

From her hiding place behind the door, she couldn't see Marcus's face but could imagine the hot look of hatred he was giving John right now.

"Empty them or don't come to work tomorrow."

She heard a brushing of sound, probably his hoodie. "I don't have anything, see?"

"What's that?" Tessa asked.

Silence, then Marcus kind of laughed. "Like a Boy Scout, you know?"

"You take condoms into the pantry?"

Ashley closed her eyes and dropped her head back.

"Who's in there?" John demanded.

Ashley put her face in her hands and bit back tears. She was so totally screwed.

"Nobody," Marcus said.

She pulled her hands away, the first bit of hope curling through her. Of course he'd cover for her. He liked her. A lot. It wasn't just sex.

"You're in there alone?"

"Of course I am," he said, his foot scuffing as he started to walk away. "Now I'm gonna book. See you guys tomorrow."

"I'll walk you out," John said.

"I'm cool, man."

Ashley stood stone still, waiting for the door to close, for the nightmare to be over. Instead, it opened a little wider and a familiar dark-haired head peeked in. Ashley stayed stone still, holding her breath, praying Aunt Tessa wouldn't see her hiding in the corner.

"Ashley?" No such luck. She walked in, frowning. "What are you…"

"He's gone," John said, walking right in behind her, then halting at the sight of Ashley. "Don't tell me, you were working on the inventory with him."

"She won't tell you that," Tessa said quietly. "Because Ashley doesn't lie."

Ashley gave her aunt-by-friendship a pleading look. "Please don't tell my mom, Aunt Tessa."

Tessa blew out a slow breath. "I'm going to walk Ashley home, John."

And that might give Ashley time to make her case. She hoped.

Ashley was silent all the way out of the restaurant and onto the sands of Barefoot Bay, and Tessa racked her brain for the right way to handle this. Carefully, of course. Tenderly. With mature understanding and patience. Like a loving aunt, not a worried mother.

Ashley shot her an expectant look.

"What the hell were you thinking?" Tessa demanded. So much for tender and patient.

"Right now, I'm thinking that only I would have the luck to get busted by the aunt who would die before she kept a secret. Why couldn't Aunt Zoe have come in there?"

"Zoe would kill you. I'm only going to yell. Ashley, what are you doing with him? He's twenty years old!"

"Nineteen, so we're only two years apart."

By whose math? "He's *almost* twenty and you just turned seventeen about five minutes ago."

"Three weeks ago, Aunt Tess."

"I don't care." She guided Ashley around some shellers, lowering her voice so they didn't hear. "That's too much of an age difference."

"Age difference?" Ashley shot back. "My mom robbed the cradle."

She suddenly sounded much, much younger than seventeen. And a lot more like the tempestuous and sometimes sullen young teen she'd been after the hurricane. Since then, Ashley had matured in so many ways.

Obviously, she'd matured as far as boys were concerned. "Ashley, Clay is only six years younger than your mother. And they're *both* adults."

She huffed out a breath. "I knew this was going to happen."

"Look, I'm saying this as someone who loves you dearly and deeply. A boy his age—no, a *man* his age—is not appropriate for a girl who just turned seventeen."

"Appropriate? Who even says that anymore?"

"You want me to spell it out? An almost-twenty-year-old young man is thinking about sex every minute of every day. I'll bet a month's salary you weren't in there doing inventory."

"I was saying no," she said quickly but with not nearly enough conviction.

"He had a condom in his pocket."

"At least he's smart and careful."

Tessa stopped suddenly, kicking up some sand. "Are you still a virgin?" The question slipped out with a little pain in her voice. Not that she had any right to ask or even that seventeen was *that* young, but she loved Ashley like she was her own daughter and she—

"Yes, Aunt Tessa," she said, grabbing her arm and pulling her forward. "I am. I swear on my life, my name, and the Bible, I am a virgin."

But Tessa hadn't picked up speed yet. "You're thinking about it, though, aren't you?"

Ashley didn't answer. Oh, boy. Oh, *man*.

"Ashley." She slowed again to make her point. "Please be smart, and I don't mean use protection. I mean say no."

Ashley rolled her eyes. "I have."

Tessa sighed a hearty breath of relief.

"So far."

Damn. "You don't want your first time to be with just anyone," she said, choosing each word carefully. "And you sure don't want it to be in the kitchen of your mom's resort."

Ashley closed her eyes. "Please don't tell her."

Tessa didn't answer, unwilling to make promises she couldn't keep. She zipped through a mental file, trying to remember what she knew about Marcus Lowell, other than that he'd been in trouble with the law once, dropped out of Mimosa High—or was kicked out—and came from one of the most broken homes on the island. Lacey had hired him as a personal favor to the sheriff, who was trying to give the kid another chance.

Okay, so not the Most Likely to Succeed from Mimosa High, but why would Ashley hide him from her mother and stepfather? "Why can't I tell her?"

"Because"—she finally faced Tessa—"she'll fire him."

"Why would she do that?"

"For the same reason you're marching me home like I'm nine years old and I stole a candy bar from the Super Min."

"I still don't understand why you can't tell your mother you're…" She glanced sideways. "What exactly is going on with this guy? He's your boyfriend?"

"I guess."

"You guess? You were condom-close in the pantry." She tried not to think about how hypocritical that statement was, considering what she and John had done against the wall last night. Ten more minutes and she'd have been naked.

Then she had to blabber about a baby.

"Well, I like him and he likes me."

"Of course he likes you." Tessa toed a shell, barely seeing what it was since something far more delicate was in her hands. "What's not to like? You're pretty, smart, fun to be with, and…" She probably shouldn't add the obvious, but she did anyway. "You're the boss's daughter."

"Aunt Tessa! That's not why we're dating!"

"So you *are* dating him?" Which made sex only a little less horrifying. She *was* seventeen, even if they'd celebrated her birthday less than a month ago. Not a child anymore, but definitely not a grown woman.

"We've been talking for a while now, but it's official," Ashley said.

"Talking about what?"

She rolled her eyes, tsking as if Tessa was a dinosaur. "Talking is, like, pre-dating. First you check each other out, then you friend each other on Facebook, then you talk."

"On the phone?"

"Text, mostly."

Except they weren't texting in the pantry. With a condom.

"Then he asks you to go out," Ashley said.

Which was okay, wasn't it? Of course Ashley was old enough to date. "So you've been out with him?"

"Not out-out. But out."

"I don't speak teenager, Ashley. What does that mean? Has he taken you to dinner and a movie? Miniature golfing? The mall? Out for ice cream?"

Ashley laughed. "You sound like you're hyperventilating, Aunt Tess. We hang out."

Which, Tessa remembered, was what she was supposed to be doing with John right now.

Too bad. Ashley was more important. "So do you usually hang out in the pantry?"

"He was working and…" She let the sentence fade to nothing. "He lives at home and so do I, so sometimes we—"

"Of course you 'live at home,' Ashley—you are a teenager. Barely seventeen, still in high school, and he's old enough to…vote." Among other things.

Her smile faded. "You're going to tell my mom, aren't you?"

They were almost at the end of the resort property, where the beach curved and Lacey and Clay's house sat. "Listen, Ash, if you're dating a guy—any guy—you have to tell your mom."

Ashley stopped walking, looking down at the sand, silent.

"When are you going to tell her, Ash?"

She shook her head. "If I tell her, it's over."

"What does that mean?"

Struggling for a second, she looked out to the Gulf, emotion and the reflection of the water turning her eyes to a deep green. "Either she'll fire him or he'll leave me."

"Ashley, you have to tell her." Tessa reached for her hand to underscore her point. "First of all, you don't keep secrets like that from your mother. Secondly, you haven't given her a chance to fire him or not." Although, knowing Lacey, she wouldn't be happy. "And, third, I don't know how you 'leave' someone you're just hanging out with, but on principle, what kind of guy is he if he bolts at the first sign of trouble?"

Like he'd done about ten minutes ago.

"No, no, it's not like that," she said.

"Then what's it like?" Tessa knew she should back off, but couldn't. Every red flag ever made was flying in front of her face and this was *Ashley*.

"It's like this," Ashley said, lifting her chin and squaring her shoulders as if preparing for a fight. "He needs this job so bad, Aunt Tessa. His mom's…he doesn't know where his mom is."

And that was heartbreaking, but not what concerned Tessa most about this boy-man.

"And his dad is…"

What was commonly known as the town drunk. Only, word on the street was he was more like the town stoner.

"His dad lost his job at the hardware store. Marcus needs the money from this job so much."

"He's supporting his dad?"

Ashley shook her head. "He has a dream, Aunt Tess. He got his GED and now he really wants to go to a culinary school. He's a good guy, honestly."

Tessa exhaled. "Dreams are…important," she said, striving for encouragement but not wanting to offer too much of it. "And, after he goes to culinary school and you go to college, and maybe graduate school, then you both work for a few years and figure out who you are, then…" She'll never remember Marcus Lowell. "Then you can date him."

Ashley laughed softly at how much Tessa stretched the timeline. "What if I want to date him now?"

Then they were back where they'd started. Tessa didn't answer.

"Because of the color of his skin?" Ashley challenged.

"The color of his skin has never even occurred to me," she said honestly. "And you know damn well that would never, ever matter to your mother or Clay or even your father."

"Oh, Dad really likes him."

Tessa blinked. "How does David know him?" David Fox hadn't been on Mimosa Key for two years and the last time he was, he'd done his damnedest to ruin Lacey and Clay's budding romance. Since then, Ashley had gone to see her father, rekindling a long-dormant relationship, but he certainly hadn't been here.

"They're Facebook friends. Dad's excited for me."

Tessa tried not to respond to that. David Fox, of all men, should know the dangers of young and impetuous love. Ashley was the result of Lacey's college romance with the world-traveler trust-fund baby who called himself "Fox."

Another thing that would make Lacey uber-skittish when it came to Ashley dating.

"Please don't tell my mom." Ashley's voice cracked with a mix of plea and fear.

"Ashley, you and your mom have never had secrets."

She finally looked up, her eyes brimming with moisture. "But that was before." Her voice cracked, and so did Tessa's heart.

"Before what, honey?" She took Ashley's hand between hers, dying to pull the girl into her arms but knowing that might stall whatever she was about to admit.

"Before…"

Before Clay? Ashley and her stepfather had a great relationship. Before the resort? Her life was a thousand times improved now. Nothing had changed, except…

Oh, of course. "Before the baby," Tessa said.

Ashley's face confirmed the guess. "It's like their whole lives are consumed by twenty pounds of screaming, shitting, wide-awake-in-the-middle-of-the-night monster!"

Tessa almost laughed at the description. "He'll get better, Ash, and you love Elijah."

"Of course I love him." She swiped at a tear. "I feel awful even saying anything, but my mom's barely looked at me since he was born."

A total Ashley Exaggeration. "You know that's not true."

"Everything is Elijah. He needs to be fed. He needs to be changed. He needs to be picked up. And, then, there's the resort. And Clay. She's out of time and I think she…" The tears were streaming now as they got to the heart of the issue. "She forgot about me, and we used to be so close."

Tessa's whole chest swelled with sympathy. No, not sympathy. Empathy. There was nothing worse—no emptier, achier feeling—than being ignored by the one person you count on to pay attention to you. God, she knew that.

"Please, Aunt Tess." Ashley's mouth quivered. "Just for a little while, let me figure this out."

She didn't know what to do, but her heart folded enough to give Ashley that much. "Okay. But don't do anything stupid, and let me think about how to handle this."

"You don't have to handle it. Don't do anything."

At least she could ask John to keep an eye on that boy.

"If I don't tell your mom, I'll be…" Doing the thing she abhorred: keeping secrets.

"You'll be an awesome aunt who loves me so much." Ashley smiled. "And pays attention to me."

Of course, that got to her. "For now, Ash. Just for now. And, please, whatever you do, be careful."

Chapter Fourteen

Tessa had no idea how long she sat on the beach, halfway between Lacey's house and the resort, halfway between certain she knew what to do and total indecision. Long enough for a few sanderlings and terns to pitter around her, their bird feet etching prints in the sand as they pecked for food she didn't have.

Rubbing the silky smooth inside of a duck-clam shell, she stared at the undulating navy water of the Gulf, watching the blue morph to fiery orange as the sun slid closer to the horizon. The colors faded in her mind, though, replaced by images of mothers and daughters, and a poignant awareness of how much damage and love and emotion could be folded into one complex relationship.

Did she think her relationship with a child would be any different? Of course, it could—

"Hey."

She startled, pulled back from her deep thoughts and

drawing in a quick breath at the sight of John walking toward her, his silhouette and long shadow spotlighted in the burnished-gold rays like some kind of sun god casting a long, strong, daunting shadow.

"Hey." Really, it was all she could manage. The T-shirt clung to broad, strong, endless muscles and the sun highlighted the smattering of artwork on corded forearms.

"I thought you forgot about me." He approached slowly, giving her a chance to appreciate every inch, from the soft waves of milk-chocolate-and-hot-caramel hair all the way down to the bare feet that left a wake of sandbursts as he walked.

"I kind of did," she admitted.

He thumped his chest as though her words had stabbed him. Slowing down, he searched her face, glancing around for clues, or maybe a sign of Ashley, and then he crouched next to her. A hint of kitchen aroma clung to him, floating toward her on salt air along with that raw scent of masculinity he seemed to exude.

"You okay?" he asked.

And then there was that *tenderness*. Affection and interest and kindness seemed so utterly out of place on a man who looked anything but tender or kind.

"Yeah, I'm fine."

"Need some help? Advice?" He reached into a breast pocket on his T-shirt and whipped out one of the after-dinner candies Lacey had ordered with the Casa Blanca logo on the wrapper. "Never met a woman who didn't think chocolate could cure all ails."

She laughed softly, taking the candy. "Do you have to be so utterly perfect?"

He eased onto his backside, right next to her. "Your

bar is low, my dear. What's going on? I missed my sous-chef."

He missed her. Why did that make her stomach do incredibly stupid things? What was it about this man that made her as gooey as this chocolate would be if she held it much longer in her hand? "What'd you cook?"

"Delicious in a dish. Come back with me. We can have my very first chef's kitchen dinner. It's private and, evidently"—he lifted a brow—"quite the romantic setting."

"So it seems." She attempted a laugh. "Sorry I disappeared. I had a little disciplining to do."

"What's the problem? You don't approve of her choice of friends?"

"It appears to be far more than friendship," she replied, unwrapping the candy. "He's a little old for her and she's…"

"Naive and innocent?" he suggested.

"Yes, but that's not why I'm troubled."

He inched closer, managing to let their shoulders and thighs touch, somehow inviting without being invasive. "Tell me."

And, just like that, she wanted to tell him everything. Dark, light, happy, sad, personal or public. He somehow drew her out that way. She took a bite of the chocolate, the creamy, minty flavor sweet on her tongue. As it melted in her mouth, she held the rest up to him. "I can share."

He closed his eyes and opened his mouth enough for her to slip in the candy. She stole the opportunity to look at his lips, his teeth, the sexy growth of beard…and remembered how all that felt against her throat and cheeks.

"Waiting," he murmured, eyes still closed.

"Watching," she replied.

He opened his eyes and held her gaze. "Watching what?"

"You." She leaned a little closer, so attracted to his mouth she couldn't even pretend to not want to kiss him. But she slipped the chocolate onto his tongue instead, and before he tasted it, he closed the space and kissed her lightly.

Bathed in sunset, warmed by chocolate, close to a man who made every cell want to dance, Tessa grabbed the two seconds of pure bliss and tucked them into her heart, to be relived soon and often.

After a moment, he nudged her. "So? What's the problem?"

"Ashley asked me not to tell her mother about him."

"Difficult for you, I'd imagine."

"Mmm." She nodded, combing the sand next to her and closing over the duck-clam shell she'd dropped when she saw him. "Very difficult."

She ran her nail along the shell's ridges, mentally counting in tens, then multiplying that by a hundred. "What's five thousand divided by three hundred and sixty-five?"

He looked surprised. "Why do you need to know?"

"Didn't you say you do math like that in your head?"

"I did, and the answer is about thirteen and a half."

She nodded, impressed. "You *are* a math whiz. Who'd guess that from a man with long hair, big muscles, multiple tattoos, and drives a motorcycle built to race off into the sunset?"

"Those may be things that terrify you, Tess, but none of those things says I can't do simple division."

"You're right."

"About the things that terrify you or simple division?"

"Both." She held up the shell. "But, for your information, you figured out that for thirteen years, a sweet little
mollusk called this home and lived in it, protected from
all the dangers of the sea, until he was forced out to be
food for some big shark."

He looked equally impressed. "And you are a shell
whiz." He reached for the seashell but took her hand
instead, clasping both in a strong, straightforward grip.
"Who'd guess that from a woman with soulful eyes, sinful lips, no visible tattoos, and drives a truck big enough
to haul a half ton of dirt."

She laughed at the echo of her words. "Guess we're
both full of surprises."

"That's the fun part." He got closer. "So, are you going
to tell Lacey her daughter was making out with the line
cook?"

Taking a deep breath, she managed to pull her gaze
from the crystal blue of his eyes and look at the sunset,
which was only slightly less breathtaking. "I don't know.
Let's keep flirting instead."

"Done and done." He fingered some of her hair,
twirling it slowly, a habit she was starting to like a lot.
"You're even prettier when you're pensive."

She closed her eyes, tilting her head back, giving him
more hair to play with. "God, you're good. Like world-
class, you know? Where did you learn how to work a
woman like that? California? Nevada?" She turned to
look at him. "*Singapore?*"

She could have sworn he paled, but that might have
been the changing light. "I was born with this curse. Just

like you"—he tipped her face toward him—"were born with a very big heart."

"How do you know that?"

"You love living things," he said with absolutely no hesitation. "You love fruits, vegetables, flowers, and shellfish."

And babies. "And I love that girl." She tipped her head toward Lacey's house. "So I don't want her to do something monumentally stupid or dangerous."

"You think Marcus is trouble?"

"I think he's a condom-carrying twenty-year-old boy who is taking advantage of a girl who…" Maybe he didn't need to know all the details of that little family problem Ashley had described. He didn't need to know his new boss was slightly overwhelmed by life's responsibilities.

"Who what?"

"Who's still young and probably feeling a little squeezed for affection right now."

He nodded. "Yeah, the new baby. Kids'll do that."

Wow, perceptive. In fact, something in the way he made that statement was so laden with familiarity it took her by surprise. "That sounded like the voice of experience."

"God, no." He gave her hand a squeeze. "Marcus doesn't seem like a bad guy," he added quickly. "Maybe has a bit of a chip on his shoulder. Wanted to be the chef and resents my appearance, but he's smart enough to know he can learn from me. Not easy to be the low man in the kitchen."

More experience speaking, but this time it made sense. "Will you talk to him?"

"Not sure he'll listen."

"She didn't listen either. Still, I really want to respect Ashley's request. In a weird way, I understand what she's going through and maybe she has to work it out for herself. Or maybe Lacey…" The thought formed and wrapped around her heart. "Needs to see what she's doing to her daughter."

He frowned. "Because she's preoccupied with a baby and a brand-new business? Can hardly blame her, and Ashley isn't exactly a child."

So, so perceptive. "You can't ignore a kid because of another kid. Or because of your job."

"Speaking of sounding like the voice of experience."

She turned to the sand, finding a tiny white cockle-shell, the kind that were on Barefoot Bay in the millions.

How had he gotten *there* already? How had he spent a few hours with her and managed to dig right to a place that she never, ever shared with anyone—not even her closest friends?

"I have to figure out what's the best thing to do about Ashley."

"I think you should keep her secret."

"Why?"

"Because if you tell her mom, shit will hit the fan and she'll keep seeing him anyway, but on the sly and then they really might get into some trouble. If you keep her secret, Ashley's got an adult she trusts and then you have a chance to talk to her, to advise her, and give her the kind of attention you think she's not getting. She'll confide in you, and you can be more help to her that way."

She considered that, the wisdom of his words pressing on her chest. "You're right," she admitted. Absolutely, dead-on right.

"And in the meantime, I'll get to know Marcus for you and find out what his intentions are. Although his pocket change tells me exactly what they are."

"And maybe you can keep him from doing anything stupid."

He laughed. "A twenty-year-old with raging hormones? Unlikely, but I'll give it my best shot if it'll make you feel better."

She leaned back to get a good look at him. The sun, almost below the horizon now, cast indigo blue in his eyes. "You really are amazing," she whispered, unable to keep the hint of awe out of her voice.

"'Bout time you noticed." He closed the rest of the space between them. "So are you, by the way. Are you so fond of sea creatures that you won't eat them?"

That made her laugh. "I'll eat them."

"Good, because I have made you the best shrimp scampi you've ever had and I found a great bottle of sauvignon blanc that I'm happy to have taken out of my first check. It was in the wine vault, where not a soul was liplocked, but"—he stood, tugging her up, but she stayed on the sand—"we can change that."

She didn't rise when he added some pressure.

"No?"

"Yes, I mean…" She laughed, dropping her head back in surrender. "I'm trying not to be so easy."

"You're not easy, trust me."

"I'm an open book."

"Not completely." He gave another gentle yank on her

hand. "There's lots you haven't told me. Like how you know so much about seashells."

"Shelling has become one of my favorite pastimes."

As she rose up, he pulled her right into his chest, melting her into the sweetest embrace. He nuzzled her neck with a few kisses and then slipped up to her ear. "I want to be your favorite pastime," he whispered.

A million chills exploded all over her, her legs almost buckling at the sexy sound of such a harmless request. "There you go again."

"You told me to flirt."

"I didn't tell you to turn me into a helpless mess of brain-numbing female hormones."

"Is that what I do?" he asked innocently. "I'll stop immediately." He took a step back, but she reached for his hand, bringing him to her side.

"'Sokay. I can handle it."

"Good girl." He slipped his arm around her back and guided her down the beach. "Now, teach me about your seashells. Which is your favorite?"

"The junonia." The word popped out without a moment's hesitation.

"A junonia." He dragged the word out, rolling it around his mouth like a piece of sticky candy. "Never heard of that."

"Well, if you hang around here long enough, you will. She's the pride of the Gulf Coast barrier islands. Find a junonia and you get your picture in the paper and become the envy of all the shelling professionals."

He laughed. "There are professionals?"

"Of course. And lucky beginners."

"I bet I could find one."

"Oh, the cockiness of a newbie. And if you do, I'll kill you."

"What's it look like?"

"About this big." She indicated about four inches with her thumb and index finger. "A spindle shape that's technically known as a fusiform. Like that." They stopped and she picked up a Florida cone, the most common spiral on the beach. "But the junonia has the most distinctive spots, like little brown squares, and it reminds me of a giraffe."

"Really?" He hesitated and frowned. "That's rare?"

"Oh, I know you think you've seen them, but a real junonia is nearly impossible to find, and goes for up to fifty bucks in a shell store. Also, because of its unusual shape and the fact that it doesn't have this little ridge like other pillar shells"—she took his finger and ran it along the inside of the shell—"that's called an operculum or a trap door. Anyway, it's an amazing texture, and there's a lot of folklore about it."

"What kind of folklore?" He tucked her deeper into his side, a protective, interested, precious gesture that made Tessa almost tilt her head back and reach up for a natural, delicious kiss.

"Well…" Should she tell him? Would it scare him off? Would he think she was crazy? He already knew what she really wanted in this life and the very conversation had brought things to a fairly sudden halt twice now. But why lie? The last thing she wanted was a friendship or romance built on lies.

"It gets its name from Juno, the Roman goddess…" *Of marriage and childbirth.* "Who is generally considered a protector of women."

"Ah, I see."

But, he didn't, of course. Not really. "So, I'd like to find one, because if I do…" She slowed her step and took a breath, finally looking up, her face at the perfect angle for that kiss.

"Yes?" he waited.

Then I will have a baby. "Then my…" She couldn't say it. He'd slip through her fingers again, running scared and far, and right now, she couldn't stand that.

"Then your what?" he prompted.

"Then my every dream will come true."

He tucked her deeper into his side. "Sounds like a fairy tale."

Maybe it was. "Like I said, finding one is really rare and almost never happens."

"But not impossible."

The way he said it made her light-headed with possibilities. She gave in to the sensation because, right that minute, nothing seemed impossible. Not hope. Not love. Not even finding a junonia.

Chapter Fifteen

The Batphone buzzed. Right in the middle of a sodding lunch rush.

Ian slipped the device from his pocket, knowing who'd sent the text before he looked; only Henry Brooker could reach him on this line and the only outgoing call the phone could make was to Ian's government liaison. That made every contact urgent.

The text was simple, and short: *Call me now*.

Ian looked around the kitchen for help that wasn't there, but then he'd only been running this kitchen for a few days. Still on abbreviated hours for food service, he was far too shorthanded to walk out. With one prep cook/dishwasher peeling and dicing and Marcus on the line, Ian was far more than an expediting head chef in this operation. He was up to his ass in crabcakes and steaks and no time to breathe, think, or take a piss, let alone find a quiet corner and make a critical call.

Orders from the floor were coming in at a steady clip,

the small kitchen finally thrumming with something close to a solid heartbeat. Well, too bad. Nothing, no customers, orders, or rush, could keep him from calling the man who held the key to Ian's future with his children.

Marcus cruised by, carrying a pan of veal chops from the oven. Anthony, a silent, hardworking prep cook who'd clearly been in a lot of restaurants but had near zero ambition, was head down, dicing ingredients for more pineapple salsa, an unexpected hit on the rum-soaked chops.

"Hey, Marc, can you cover this grill?" Ian asked. "I have to run out."

The young man whirled around, disbelief in his midnight eyes. "Out?"

"Emergency. Can you flip these steaks to order and finish the crabcakes?"

Marcus raised the dish of veal, along with his eyebrows. "Got four orders for these and those customers are getting antsy as shit."

They *had* been waiting, Ian agreed silently, scanning the room again to weigh his options. He could ignore Henry and get the orders up. He could threaten, cajole, or otherwise strong-arm Marcus and risk the chop customer's order. Or he could walk and get fired.

In his pocket, the phone vibrated again. He knew what it said but looked anyway. One word, clear message: *Now*.

A cold sweat marched up Ian's back and iced the nape of his neck. Left hand on the crabcake pan, right-hand thumb out, ready to check the temperature of the steaks, he bit down hard on his jaw.

"Got the fresh parsley and extra pineapples!" Tessa's

voice rang through the noisy kitchen as she sailed in the back door, carrying a bushel-sized basket of greens and vegetables.

Instantly, Ian felt better. He didn't know why, because she certainly wasn't the answer to his immediate problems, but that was what she did. She made him feel better. Until he got into bed at night and felt like shit on a stick for lying and pretending and totally fucking with her heart and head.

He squeezed his eyes shut. One problem at a time.

He glanced to the side to catch her distributing her garden goods. The instant they made eye contact, he felt the zing down to his toes and, from the look in her eyes, so did she.

At least he didn't have to pretend that part. Didn't pretend to like kissing her or holding her hand or making her laugh or listening to diatribes about seashells and saffron. He had to pretend to be someone he wasn't and convince her she wanted to—

The phone vibrated again.

He checked the steaks and gauged the rest of the orders. If he could get these out and then—

"You look shell-shocked." Tessa came up next to him, her cheeks flushed, her hair mussed, her smile as fresh as the food she carried. He didn't return the happy grin, too torn by the vibrating phone, the half-cooked food, and the need for a savior right now.

"In the weeds."

"I'd offer to help, but—"

"I'd take that offer." He tapped the crabcake pan. "Can you flip them for me?"

"Now?"

"In a minute." He angled the fork to the steaks. "Do you know how to test for doneness? Use your thumb. I have two medium rare, one rare, and one a hint under well with a bit of color left in it." He waited a beat as the words hit her, clouding her eyes with confusion. "Tessa, can you cover for me?"

"Me?"

He grabbed a spatula and pressed it into her hand. "Just flip the cakes. Look for a deep gold, but no hint of brown, and turn them until you have the same thing on the other side. And the steaks you press until they feel…" How could he describe it to her? "You can do steaks, right?"

She lifted her brows. "He asked the vegetarian."

"You don't have to eat it, just cook it." His voice grew gruff with frustration. "I have an emergency."

She hesitated one second, then shooed him away. "I can handle it. Go do what you need to do."

An unexpected wave of affection rolled over him at her attitude. "Thank you," he said, taking one second to brush her cheek to let her know how much the assist meant to him.

"No problem." She waved the spatula. "Off with you."

No questions, no argument, no complaints. Another tsunami of affection threatened, inexplicable but real. "I'll thank you later," he promised, taking a step backward but still holding her gaze.

"You better hold that gratitude in case I totally wreck your work."

"You can't. Turn the cakes in thirty seconds, dress them with that remoulade and a few sprigs of your unparalleled parsley. The rare steak's done now. Be back."

She winked at him. "Hurry."

God, she was sweet. Just…perfect. He was so, so wrong to think he could bamboozle her into some meaningless marriage to help him out of a jam.

One more vibration had him darting through the kitchen to the dry-goods pantry. The door didn't lock from the inside, but he put his whole body against it, and that was as good as any lock. With remarkably steady hands, he tapped the phone and Henry answered on the first ring.

"What took so long?" the gruff Brit asked.

"Work. What's up?"

Henry didn't answer right away, but blew out a maddeningly noisy breath. "There were some arrests in Brixton last night."

An imaginary band squeezed Ian's chest, stealing his breath or ability to reply. Brixton, the gang-ridden south London neighborhood where the last of the N1L members purportedly lived and worked. A group of murderers, thieves, drug dealers, addicts, and the scummiest of the world's scum who proudly called themselves "No One Lives" and made sure that was true for anyone who got too close to the operation.

No one lived. Including innocent young mothers who were simply doing a favor to help a scared little brother.

"How many arrests?" Because if they weren't all behind bars, Ian's life remained on hold.

"All but two, but they're on the radar."

"Okay." He heard a new order for crabcakes get called in from a frantic server and could have sworn he heard Tessa respond. God love that girl. "Okay, that's good, Henry. But why the barrage of texts to call you?" Henry never made a big deal out of good news, only trouble.

That ice up his back chilled to a fine, freezing sheen at the thought.

"I contacted Canada."

Oh, here we go. "Canada" was Henry's shorthand for the Canadian arm of the UK Protected Persons Service, who had placed and monitored two innocent babies three years ago. Ian had been allowed no contact, not even a picture, for thirty-eight months. And six days.

He didn't speak, waiting for the verdict.

Behind him, a sharp knock. "John?"

"I told you the kids started pre-kindergarten."

"You said nursery school," he corrected. "Like day care, I assumed."

"It's a little more formal than that."

"So?"

"So, they feel if the children are in the program too long, then removing them will cause anxiety issues, separation issues, you know, the kinds of things social services people hate."

No, he didn't know. And he didn't know what the hell it had to do with him getting his kids back. "So what's the problem?"

"It's a timing thing, Ian. If the kids are in the program more than three weeks, that passes some arbitrary twenty-one-day limit and—"

"What the hell are you saying?"

On the other side of the door, Tessa's voice rose, but the blood in Ian's head drowned out her voice as he worked to make sense of Henry's words.

"I'm saying that assuming all goes well in Brixton, and I believe we are that close, that you'll need to be in Canada in less than three weeks."

Less than three weeks! He dropped his head back and closed his eyes. Shiloh and Sam would be in his arms in less than three weeks.

"So you can see the problem."

No, he didn't see any problem at all.

"I don't suppose you're going to get all the proper paperwork in less than three weeks and—"

"Of course I am."

"You'll have a marriage certificate?"

"John, please." Tessa's voice rose. "Can you answer a quick question?"

Tessa. Sweet, unsuspecting, salt-of-the-earth Tessa.

"Do I absolutely have to marry someone?"

"Yes. This new board is quite inflexible where Emma and Eddie are concerned."

Emma and Eddie? "Who the fuck are they?"

"Your kids."

"Their names are Shiloh and Samuel."

Henry hesitated. "Not anymore."

Ian's heart scudded around and fell down to his belly. Someone else was raising his children. Someone else was loving them, naming them, *keeping* them. Way deep inside him, something angry and achy and uncontrollable erupted, bubbling up like hot lava. The power of the emotion choked him with the burning need to change everything, do anything, punch someone, to fight and claw and lie and kill his way back to the only thing that he had left in the world.

His children.

The door handle rattled. "John, if you need help—"

"You got three weeks, Ian, not months. Make it happen."

Stabbing the phone with one hand, he yanked open the door with the other. Tessa almost fell in, letting out a small shriek as she tried to gain her balance. Before she took a breath, he pulled her into the room, spun her to the side, and used her whole body to close the door again.

Her eyes went wide as he lifted her up a few inches and brought her face-to-face with him.

"I do need help." The words were little more than a groan, part of that pain and determination that took over his whole being. He needed her to say yes, to help him, to get back Shiloh and Sam.

"What can—"

"I *need* you," he growled again, pressing into her, gripping her with all the utter frustration that rocked him. "You…have to…"

He crushed her mouth with a kiss, their teeth cracking with the impact, his mouth open wide to delve into hers. He felt her fingers tighten on his shoulders, her mouth slacken with response, and her whole body respond to him.

How did he ask her to marry him? Instead he pressed harder. "More," he murmured into her mouth. "I want more. I want it all. I want you."

She answered with another kiss, clinging to him and intensifying everything by battling his tongue with hers. "I want you, too," she admitted on a soft choke.

He dragged his mouth down her jaw, to her neck, kissing and sucking with all the fury that rocked through his body. Sex and fear and a crazy sensation of being alive again made him suck her skin so hard it made noise.

"John," she laughed, tilting her head, squirming away. "You're leaving a mark."

He lifted his head, burning her with a look as he held her so close he could hear the echo of his own heart in her chest. "We have to move fast," he murmured.

Her brows drew closer, her eyes confused. "To do what?"

"Everything." He kissed her, not trusting himself to keep all this emotion and need and urgency inside.

"Oh." She melted a little, sighing, resigning, letting him know she was his. "Then I guess you won't mind that I burned the crabcakes."

He smiled into another kiss, wishing like hell he didn't like her so damn much. "I don't mind as long as you give me...everything."

She kissed her answer and left no doubt she would.

Chapter Sixteen

⌒

Somehow, Tessa made it from the kitchen into the spa. Instantly soothed by the waterfall, the new age music, and the soft lighting, she collapsed on the overstuffed lounge in the waiting room.

What just happened?

In less than five seconds, Jocelyn stepped out from the back, obviously expecting a spa client, and then frowning in concern at Tessa. "You okay?"

"Define okay."

"Breathing regularly, seeing straight, and generally aware of what day it is."

She shook her head. "Then I'm not okay. My head is spinning, my heart is hammering, and is it day?"

Jocelyn snapped her fingers into the doorway behind her. "Zoe, get out here. Tessa's in love."

Tessa managed to close her eyes and open her mouth, but nothing that sounded anything like a denial came out. "Zoe, come here," Joss repeated.

"Chill for a sec. I'm calling Lacey," she called out. "Bring Tessa into the massage room."

Jocelyn gave a wary look as she rounded the reception desk and reached out her hand. "Come on."

"Intervention?"

"Emergency Fearsome Foursome meeting. In the back, Jack."

Tessa did as she was told, knowing she'd come over here for exactly this kind of support. She let Joss lead her down the hall to the vestibule outside of the massage room, where Zoe joined them, inspecting Tessa's face like it held clues to the deep secret of life. Then Zoe pointed and gasped, obviously finding that secret.

"Holy Hickey, Batman!" Zoe cried. "He really did tattoo you."

Tessa slammed her hand over the still-warm spot on her neck, a heated memory of John's demanding, relentless mouth rushing over her. "Now I have to wear turtlenecks for a week."

"Are you kidding?" Zoe gave Tessa a playful tap on the shoulder, nudging her into the massage room. "That sucker—and I do mean sucker—is a red badge of courage. Got it on the job, too."

"Got what on the job?" Lacey burst in, a little out of breath.

"That." Jocelyn pointed to Tessa's neck.

Lacey shot a brow up. "I heard there was some kind of dustup in the kitchen."

Zoe snorted. "Apparently Tessa has given new meaning to the term 'lunch rush.'"

"Do you mind?" Tessa glared at her.

Zoe had the good grace to back off, but Lacey stepped

forward, closing the circle around Tessa. "What's going on?"

Tessa held Lacey's gaze for a long moment, trying to gather her thoughts into something cohesive. "John."

It was the best she could do, and Zoe cracked up. "She's gonzo, girls."

"What about him?" Lacey asked softly.

"I'm…" Tessa exhaled again.

"Scared?" Lacey offered.

"Nervous?" Joss added.

"Like melted butter from the waist down?" Zoe finished.

"All of the above." Tessa laughed, shaking her head and covering her face with her hands. "I can't believe this is happening. So fast, so right, so…so…so…"

"Real?" Jocelyn asked.

"Is it?" Tessa countered. "Because it's too fast. I still can't help feeling that he's not telling me everything. And let's not forget the idea of a baby sent him screaming into the night."

"But holding Elijah turned him into something that resembled this morning's jar of baby food," Lacey interjected.

"So why does he do a caveman drag into the pantry and kiss the living hell out of me?"

Zoe puffed out a frustrated breath. "*Why* do you have to question good fortune?"

"I just gave you a list of compelling reasons."

"And we're ignoring them," Lacey said as they closed in around her, grabbing at her hands and squeezing her into a hug.

"It's so wonderful to see you this happy," Jocelyn said.

Tessa inched back for some air, touching her face as if

she could feel how happy she looked. "Is this happy? Because I don't feel happy. Well, I do, but I…" She laughed again, then let out a little scream. "He's freaking perfect and that's what's wrong."

They all looked at each other like she'd lost her mind.

"Seriously," she insisted. "Don't you guys think this is kind of fast and a little confusing? He even said 'We have to move fast' but didn't give me any reason why."

"So ask him."

"I did."

"What did he say?"

She tapped the love bite on her neck. "He's a man of few words." She shook her head, replaying the short, intense conversation. "Too few."

They shared a look, smug enough to piss her off.

"Look, just because you three got lucky and met great guys doesn't mean I automatically have the same thing happen the first time an eligible man cruises by. There are issues. And there's a right way and a wrong way to go about handling them. Things take time, we have to get to know each other, meet families, spend months and even years learning about each other. And I don't have that kind of time."

One more group look made her close her eyes. "Go ahead, pass judgment on me because I don't believe things just happen, they have to grow. You plow, you plant, you water, you wait. Then you harvest. You don't…dig a hole and get a tomato."

Zoe leaned back. "Who is talking about tomatoes, Tessa?"

"It can happen fast," Lacey said. "I met Clay and wham, it wasn't three weeks and I was completely in love. Next thing I knew I was"—she laughed and gestured around—"in this room, having his baby."

The last word fell on the floor with a thud, and everyone got quiet.

Tessa couldn't resist a dry snort. "And there, my friend, is the heart of the problem."

After a long beat, Lacey said, "I still think you need to soft-pedal that a little and he'll come around."

Irritation blasted through her. "Soft-pedal, Lace? Did you soft-pedal your desire to build a resort when you met Clay?" She turned to Jocelyn. "And did you soft-pedal the fact that Will was taking care of the man who broke you two up in the first place?" And Zoe—

"No," Zoe said, holding up her hand. "I didn't soft-pedal with Aunt Pasha's cancer, either."

At their moment of silent consent, Tessa allowed herself her own smug look. "Then I'm not going to soft-pedal the one thing I want most in the whole world. A baby. Either he's all in or he's out to get laid. I don't care which it is, but I need to know. The next time I see him, I'm going to demand he tell me exactly what he wants, when he wants it, and how he expects to get it."

"And what if that doesn't include a baby?" Lacey asked. "Is he automatically out of the running?"

"I guess so, because I am still planning to have one with a surrogate and a—"

Tessa's phone chirped. They all looked expectantly at her.

"That's probably him," Zoe said. "He's in the walk-in cooler waiting for more."

Tessa gave her a stink eye. "He better not be. Cold lowers sperm count."

They all laughed as she slipped the phone out of her pocket and checked the ID.

Maryann Bartlett, North Naples Reproductive Center.

"Speaking of sperm count, it's the clinic." Her insides tightened a little. "I bet they had the site visit with the surrogate. That means I can meet her next. I have to take this, guys." She turned, walking to the door as she answered the phone. "Hey, Maryann."

"Tessa, I'm so glad I got you."

Outside, Tessa closed the door and sat on a cushioned seat in the vestibule. "What's up?"

"I'm afraid I have some bad news."

She closed her eyes and tensed. "A problem with the site visit?"

"She's found another couple, Tessa, and they've visited, met her, and she's passed every test with flying colors."

Disappointment rose like bile. "Another couple?" she asked in a strangled voice. "How can that happen? I put a deposit on her."

Of course she wasn't a house you can hold off the market.

"It happened because this couple is ready to pull the trigger tomorrow." Maryann's tone was gentle, but that did little to quell the hot cocktail of regret and frustration. "Tessa, you've delayed this several times. I understand you haven't found the right donor, but other couples are as anxious as you are. And we have plenty more candidates."

"What if I found a donor? Today?" Her voice rose with desperation.

"It's too late, Tessa. But I have several files for you to review. All very high quality, and I'm certain…"

The rest of her words faded away as hope crumbled into a million pieces, a feeling so familiar Tessa was almost comforted by it. The cracking of her heart, the sinking of her joy, the final pool of bitter disillusionment. She'd felt the same thing every time her body confirmed it wasn't pregnant, month after month, year after year after year.

"Do you want to set up an appointment, Tessa? I have candidates' files ready for you to look at."

She shook her head, the tight fist in her throat making it impossible to speak. "No, thanks," she rasped.

"Still no luck with a donor?" she asked.

"I need a little more time." Even though the man she had in mind wanted to rush "everything," he didn't seem to want to rush that. "I'm working on it."

"Well, Tessa, you know we have a great selection of anonymous donors and I promise you I stand behind the quality of that sperm."

The quality of that sperm. Could it sound any less romantic? Any more brutally clinical? Any riskier?

"Good to know, Maryann. Thanks."

She hung up and stood to go back into the room, knowing she'd get all the comfort she needed when she told her friends, which she would do right now. But nothing was going to fill the void.

As she reached for the handle, her phone chirped with a text and she almost didn't look at it because, right that minute, nothing mattered.

But she looked anyway.

John Brown: *See you at the meeting this afternoon. I can't wait.*

She couldn't wait either. Problem was, they were both impatient for different things.

Chapter Seventeen

⌒

Tessa cleaned up after a few hours in the greenhouse and headed to the all-staff meeting in the restaurant, still nursing the disappointment of Maryann's news. Even an hour of composting hadn't made her feel better, but knowing she'd see John did lift her spirits.

Once again she toyed with his "excuse" for running off and disappearing behind the pantry door. He'd said he had an emergency call from one of the restaurant suppliers but had never really explained the nature of the crisis.

Wasn't that just like him? A little too evasive to trust. The minute she started to get comfortable with him, a little buzzer went off in her head that said—what was his advice in the bar about trusting him?

Don't.

So what changed?

She breezed through the business offices, stopping at Lacey's closed door. Shouldn't she be in the restaurant setting up for the all-hands meeting? Tapping lightly, she poked her head in to see Lacey with the phone tucked between ear and shoulder, furiously scribbling notes. She barely looked up, waving Tessa off with her pen.

As Tessa backed up, closing the door, she stepped right into Ashley, who was barreling toward the office.

"Don't bother her now," Tessa said. "She's on a call."

"Of course." Ashley gave a put-upon sigh. "I really need to ask her a question. Doesn't she have a meeting starting?"

"Yes, so she won't be long. Get her when she's on her way."

Ashley leaned against the wall and smiled. "Guess I'll camp."

"So," Tessa said. "How are things with Marcus?"

"Actually, things are…" Her gaze slipped down to Tessa's neck. "Whoa, is that what I think it is?"

Immediately, Tessa whipped her hair over the offending mark.

"WTG, Aunt Tess." She held up her knuckles for a tap, but Tessa didn't reciprocate. "So the rumors that you two were making out in the kitchen are true."

"We were not…" She rolled her eyes instead of lying. "Don't delay your mom too long, Ash. I'm going to head into the restaurant."

Ashley made a tiny clap of happy-fun over her grin. "Yay for you."

This would be all over the resort in no time, Tessa thought as she made her way toward the restaurant. She'd be employee-gossip fodder for a week. But did that stop Tessa from scanning the whole room, looking for one pair of steel-blue eyes and that sexy smile? No.

Except he wasn't there.

Jocelyn sidled up next to her. "Lacey's on the phone with Willow Ambrose from the AABC," she said. "Something big. She told me to start the meeting."

"Holler if you need backup," Tessa said, sliding into a corner table in the back of the room, where she could see the main entrance and the kitchen door. Not that she was waiting breathlessly for John or anything.

That breath came out in a whoosh when he walked in, stood perfectly still, and searched every table, finally landing on Tessa. For what seemed like thirty seconds but was probably a nanosecond, they held eye contact. Then he smiled, all slow and sexy and crazy, crazy hot, and headed toward her, so focused on his target she actually felt herself back up at the power of his stare.

When he reached her table, he stopped right there and leaned in close enough that she could smell a hint of shampoo and see that he'd recently gotten out of the shower, as she had.

Shower. Wet. Naked.

Oh, this was going to be a long meeting.

"Can't we blow off this business and go for a bike ride?" he whispered. "It's gorgeous out."

It was gorgeous *in*, too.

"We're already in trouble with the boss and the talk of the break room, so no." She gestured to the other seat at the two-top. "You can sit here if you don't distract me." Like that was remotely possible.

He dragged the other chair close to her, sitting so his leg brushed hers under the linen tablecloth. Reaching over to her face, he pushed back the lock of hair she'd wound over her neck. His fingers tickled her skin, the move pure possession and sex.

"Whoops." He sounded more proud than apologetic. "Did I do that?"

She slid him a sideways look. "I owe you one."

"More than one, I hope."

She laughed softly, shaking her head. "What am I going to do with you?"

"I can't believe you have to ask that question." He pressed his thigh against hers under the table. "But since you won't leave this meeting, how about a late dinner tonight? Walk on the beach in the moonlight? We could find your junonia."

"We'll see."

"I want to ask you something."

"What do you want to ask me?"

"Not here. Somewhere romantic."

Her pulse skyrocketed, along with her curiosity. "Ask me now."

He settled his large hand on her thigh and gave a squeeze. "Patience."

"Like you had in the pantry?"

He gave a sly smile, but Jocelyn called for everyone's attention with a clap.

"Lacey wants me to get things started, team." Jocelyn stood with the windows behind her, the cobalt water and baby-blue sky as her backdrop, her dark hair pulled into its usual ponytail of perfection, not a stray hair out of place. Still, Jocelyn wasn't the uptight life coach she used to be, thanks to Will and a nice life running the spa at Casa Blanca.

"So since Lacey's not here, let me take a minute to tell you all how amazing this opportunity is. We have a chance to really kick this resort to the next level and it's going to take some work. I'll start with…"

Ian leaned closer and stroked the inside of Tessa's thigh. "So, tonight?" Goose bumps rose on her bare arms and he nodded to them. "Is that a yes?"

"Depends on what you want to ask me, but we better pay attention. This is an important meeting."

"So is the one I'm *proposing*…" He drew out the last word, the emphasis so obvious and powerful enough to fire one seriously unholy heat through her.

Why did he say things like that? He didn't want what she wanted. He wanted sex in the kitchen; she wanted a baby in the belly. Or did he? Sometimes she'd swear he wanted more. Was that possible?

She didn't take her eyes off Jocelyn to look at him. She was almost scared she'd find out that thought was wrong. Or maybe she was scared it was right.

Either way, she was scared.

Jocelyn walked across the front section of the restaurant, handing out some papers to be passed around. "In case you haven't had a chance to do your homework on the American Association of Bridal Consultants, this will tell you what we're dealing with and how important this weekend will be for our budding destination-wedding business. If we are selected as one of their AABC-approved resorts, that means many of the country's wedding planners will be bringing brides for site visits and, of course, we can plan on a steady stream of destination weddings."

A buzz of response hummed through the room as she continued. "Those weddings will fill our rooms and villas, keep our kitchen running full speed, pack the spa to capacity, lift the hot-air-balloon business to an all-time high, and kick up our entire event and catering business."

She paused to take a breath and let it all sink in. "In other words, this is the most important weekend we've ever had that could make or break this resort."

The staff reacted with the appropriate cheers and claps and a barrage of questions, all so fast and furious that Jocelyn held up her hands "Hang on, troops. Lacey will answer everything when she's off the phone."

John leaned closer, his face so, so close to hers. "You thinking about it?"

She was certainly thinking about *something*. "The weekend with the wedding consultants?" she asked, trying—and failing—to keep the smile off her face. "I am, and so should you, since it's the only reason we hired you."

"The only reason?" He feigned a hurt look. "I thought it was my boyish charm and irresistible kisses."

"*And* because we need you to cook when they're here. Shh." She jutted her chin toward Jocelyn. "She's going to talk about the menu any minute."

He moved closer, kicking up the assault of a soapy scent and a warm, comfortable hand, reminding her of how it felt on her breast, on her backside.

"Now you're thinking about sex."

She straightened guiltily. "Speak for yourself."

"I am." He drummed his fingers on her thigh, way too high, way too close to a spot that grew warmer and damper by the moment.

"Is that what you want to ask me tonight? To have sex with you?"

"Not exactly."

Not exactly? "What does that mean?"

"It means come out with me tonight and I'll tell you."

He slid his hand one more inch up her thigh, heat pressing through her jeans. "Please?"

"Maybe." Who was she kidding—*maybe*? She was already thinking about what she'd wear: black or red undies?

As if he'd read her mind, he flicked his thumb right between her legs, making her gasp the very second things quieted down. At the next table, a nail tech in the spa shot them a curious look. Tessa tried to smile and cross her legs. Impossible.

"Of course, we were thrown a huge monkey wrench," Jocelyn continued. "When we found out they wanted to move up their visit from next summer to later this month."

"That's not the only monkey wrench that hit us." Lacey bounded into the restaurant, her eyes bright, the cell phone still clutched in her hand. "I just got walloped with one more."

Tessa sat up, and the chatter in the room quieted down.

Lacey took a moment to cross the room, set the phone dramatically on one of the tables, and put both hands on her hips to make her announcement. "It seems that the whole site visit is now contingent on one thing."

The entire room hushed to silence.

"We need to have a wedding that weekend."

Instantly, John pulled his hand away and sat forward. "What?" he asked.

"I know," Lacey replied, nodding his way. "It'll be a challenge for the kitchen, but I promise you we'll bring in help, Chef Brown. We'll get a pastry professional and more hands for you in the kitchen."

"Just what you need," Tessa mumbled under her breath. "More hands."

But he didn't laugh, his attention still on Lacey. "Do we have a wedding scheduled that weekend?"

Lacey threw her hands up. "That's the problem. We do not, nor do I have any couples that could possibly be coerced into changing their date. Unfortunately, our competition in Naples does have a wedding scheduled and the planners are considering moving their weekend visit there."

Jocelyn stepped forward, frowning. "Why didn't they mention this to us when they were here?"

"It came up when they met with the regional directors," Lacey replied. "Because we are so new and untested, the directors feel that the only way they can make a real recommendation is if they witness a ceremony, sample a wedding dinner, and assess how we handle logistics, decor, staffing, everything."

"That's crazy," Tessa said. "We can't pull off a wedding in two weeks."

A few disappointed moans of agreement traveled through the room, then the nail tech at the next table called out, "Zoe! It's your time."

"Yeah, Zoe!" A few others agreed. "You're engaged."

"Move your date up with Oliver!"

"Can it," Zoe said, standing up from her seat in the front to turn and face her colleagues. Rubbing her small but distinctive baby bump, she shook her head. "I'm not walking down the aisle until my baby of honor can be there." When Jocelyn and Lacey gave her pleading looks, Zoe shook her head. "Oliver and I agreed, and there's no way I'm throwing my one and only wedding together in two weeks, sorry."

"So what do we do?" someone asked, giving voice to the question on everyone's mind.

Next to her, John's body language had changed as he leaned forward, his torso tight, his jaw set. He must realize how important this weekend is, Tessa thought with a rush of affection.

Lacey sighed audibly. "She did tell me we could back out and maybe get rescheduled for next year, but this is the end of her tenure as president, so there's no telling where the next board will want to go. So I guess we have to—"

"Have a wedding." John pushed back and stood so fast his chair toppled.

Everyone in the room turned to him, and Tessa drew back an inch, that affection soaring now. He really, really cared about the resort.

"Suggestions are welcome," Lacey said. "You have any ideas?"

"Yes." A slow, broad smile broke over his face, turning it from merely handsome to unspeakably hot. And then he looked down at Tessa, expectantly. "I have a capital idea."

A capital idea? The foreign-sounding phrase was the least of the things that sent a blast of heat through her. The warmth in his eyes, the certainty, the overwhelming sense that he meant...

No, no, *no*. That was her overactive imagination at work.

"A perfect solution," he continued, kind of shaking his head like whatever idea had just occurred to him was too good to even be contained there. "It's the answer to *everything*."

The entire room stared at him, including Tessa.

Very, very slowly, he lowered himself, bypassing the toppled chair and landing right on—one knee.

The whole room drew in one loud, collective gasp, but not Tessa. Gasping would require breathing, which, right then, was physically impossible.

"You'll marry me," he said.

Not a question, not a joke, and not a fantasy.

"Are you out of your mind?" she whispered.

Someone squeaked—Zoe, no doubt—and a few people hooted and somebody else shouted "Say yes!" but mostly the room tilted so far off center Tessa thought her own chair might topple with her in it.

"You'll marry me," he repeated, still on one knee, as if those three words made *any sense at all*.

He took her hand and looked right into her eyes, his voice barely audible over the room noise and the thunder of blood in her ears. "You know it's going to happen. It's inevitable."

Inevitable? "It is?" Her voice cracked again.

"What do you think I was going to ask you tonight?"

Her jaw dropped, but he pulled her right into him and kissed her, and the whole room, along with Tessa's head, exploded.

Chapter Eighteen

Ian could taste the shock in her mouth. Shock and mint and raw confusion sparking in her open lips that didn't exactly respond to his. Unless her *response* was to tense every muscle and use all her power to whip away. But he held her firmly and kissed her solidly until the noise in the room and the buzzing in his head abated.

The answer had been handed to him and he wanted a celebratory kiss.

Finally, he let her win and pop backwards, her mouth still hanging open in disbelief. "What the—"

"It's for the resort," he insisted in a whisper.

"No, I wo—"

He put his fingers on her lips, still warm and so soft. "Don't say no."

She blinked at him. "No."

"No, you won't consider it, or no, you give the idea a chance?"

"Are you nuts?"

He grinned. "Do I have to state the obvious? I'm nuts about you."

Behind him, he was aware that Lacey had walked over to the table and he had no doubt the other two in Tessa's entourage would be here in a moment. The question was, Would her friends be on his side, or the sane side?

He had to move fast. "Tessa, give me a chance."

"A chance? You're asking for…"

"You don't mean a real wedding?" Lacey asked from behind him.

Tessa looked up at her, relief and gratitude on her face. "I'm sure he doesn't."

"Of course I…" He finally got up from his knee, taking the chair someone had righted for him, scrambling for the best strategy. "Don't," he finished.

For the first time in a minute, Tessa breathed.

Okay, let her think it was pretend. Until the very last possible second, then, somehow, as part of the act, he'd get her to sign the papers. Henry could pay off a justice of the peace and she wouldn't even know she'd signed a real marriage certificate. Or…or…

Or nothing. He didn't have another idea, but he'd think of one. All that mattered was that this cut so much precious time out of the process and he could be married in two weeks, meeting the Canadian board's ridiculous time line.

"You mean like a re-enactment?" Zoe came in the other side.

"That's not a bad idea." Jocelyn flanked the left.

"What do you think?" Lacey asked Tessa.

"I don't know." She dragged the words out, searching his face. "I mean, it seems kind of…impulsive."

"It's a great solution," he said quickly.

"A fake wedding." Tessa's words weren't a question, and they were thick with disgust.

No, not fake.

Lacey dropped into a chair across the table. "I guess we don't have to tell the AABC board that it's fake. They want to see a wedding and we can re-create what we did for Gloria and Slade's wedding last month. We still have a lot of the decorations, so everything will be real except—"

"Except it won't be," Tessa said flatly.

"Unless you want it to be," Ian replied, his voice low, but the other women heard him.

"Awww," Zoe said, balling her hands up under her chin. "So sweet."

Tessa mowed her down with a look. "He's kidding."

Not exactly.

"We could do it," Lacey said, getting a lot of nods and "Yeah"s from the staff. "Honestly, it wouldn't be that hard."

"But you have to run the kitchen," Tessa said to John. "You can't be the groom and the head chef. If we're going to do a faux wedding, we should have someone who's not so critical to the resort and restaurant."

"Sure I can." He shoved confidence into every word. "Marcus will back me up and I'll organize and plan everything ahead of time. Lacey said we'll add temporary staff and all I have to do is quick supervision. We can do it easily."

"We need guests," Tessa said, grabbing metaphorical bricks to build this wall and stop the train.

"Invite the whole town."

"And cake."

"New pastry chef, right, Lacey?"

"And…" She was running out of ideas. "A dress."

"I thought you'd picked one out," he replied.

That silenced all the questions and sent every eye directly to Tessa, who was still staring at him, her face bloodless and blank. "I was just…looking."

He rescued her by taking her hand and laughing. "Don't worry, Tess. It'll be fun, and think of how important this is to the business."

"He's right," Lacey agreed, beaming at him. "If we don't come up with a solution to this problem, we may never have this opportunity to impress the AABC again."

Tessa nodded. "I mean…can't it be…someone else?"

"I'll do it." Everyone turned at the sound of Ashley's voice. At the attention, her face reddened. "I mean, if you want another stand-in bride, I'll do it." A few feet behind her, Marcus straightened from the wall he leaned against, his eyes wide.

"Why would you do it?" Lacey asked.

"Because." She shrugged and took a quick glance over her shoulder. "It might be fun to, you know, be a bride."

"No," Tessa said, sitting up straight and adding some power to her voice for the first time since Ian had been on his knee. "No you won't. I'll do it. John and I will… do it."

Ian understood her turnaround—she probably thought the girl and Marcus would make the ceremony real. Never mind that was exactly what he planned to do.

"You will?" Lacey asked, looking relieved.

"Mom, I want to do it."

"They'd never buy a sixteen-year-old bride, honey."

"Seventeen," she corrected.

"And who'd be the groom?"

"I'll find one."

Ian looked over the girl's shoulder again, but Marcus had disappeared back into the kitchen.

"It's better if I do it," Tessa said, her change of heart obvious even if only he knew the reason. "If you really think that's better than having you handle the wedding feast."

"We'll make the logistics work," he assured them all. And the logistics would somehow include a legitimate certificate.

But Tessa still looked entirely doubtful.

"Listen, Tess," Lacey said. "We can iron out the details of this at a smaller meeting. Since we have all hands here, let me finish the rundown of the whole weekend and you two can talk about this."

"Over dinner." Without a word, he reached under the table and found her hand. Closing his fingers around hers, he gave her a soft squeeze, something dark and achy pulling inside him.

Why wasn't he simply overjoyed at this perfect solution?

He glanced at her again, and a longing so physical and potent he could actually taste it welled up and seized him by the throat. Because he wanted to tell her the truth and he could not do that. Even though this gentle-hearted, child-loving woman would probably help him, with no questions asked.

But he couldn't take that risk. So he'd fuck up her life instead of his.

* * *

"What did I just agree to?" Tessa dropped into the chair in Lacey's office, the rhetorical question answered by an avalanche of female voices the minute all four of them were behind closed doors.

Lacey, the organizer, pushed her sweater sleeves back like a woman ready to dive into a new project. "We can totally make this work."

Jocelyn, the analyzer, angled her head thoughtfully. "I think it says a lot about him that he came up with this idea."

And the queen of a good time clapped like a kid who'd just won a trip to Disney World. "Dress shopping!" Zoe exclaimed.

Finally silent, they all stared at Tessa as she nearly choked on frustration. "Guys, do you really think it's a good idea for me to stand out on that beach in a white gown and exchange wedding vows with a virtual stranger for the *good of the business*?"

They glanced at each other, then at her, still silent but communicating volumes. And Tessa didn't like one unspoken word. She fell into the guest chair with a sigh of exasperation.

"It's not like it's real, Tess," Lacey said.

What do you think I wanted to ask you? His words echoed. Was it…no. It wasn't even remotely possible that was what he wanted to ask her. But now she'd never know.

"It's crazy." Tessa closed her eyes, shaking her head, looking for some sanity and seeing nothing but John Brown's sexy eyes boring a hole right through her heart. "I said yes because Ashley was so determined and—"

"So was he," Jocelyn said.

Yes, he was. Freakishly determined. "Okay, I'm going to pretend to get married, but you guys don't have to blow it into something it's not so I look like some kind of fool out there."

"Tessa." Jocelyn curled up on the couch. "There's nothing foolish about love."

"Love?" The word catapulted her back to her feet. "You guys are blind, I tell you. Just because you all won some kind of lottery or cracked the code or found the key to ultimate happiness, you think I should melt into a pool of helpless lust because some complete stranger drops onto the property and has a boner for me. That's not how it's done."

Once more they exchanged knowing looks. Superior, self-righteous knowing looks, too, which fired Tessa up even more.

"Oh!" She balled her fists and double-punched the sky. "Don't you see that I'm…I'm…I'm…"

"Terrified," Zoe suggested.

"Looking for excuses?" Lacey added.

"So hung up on your own expectations you don't see the possibilities right in front of you?" Jocelyn finished.

Oh, God. How could she fight this tsunami of friendship?. "I give up." She fell back into the chair and let her arms drape open.

"Thank God," Zoe said.

Lacey kneeled next to her. "Listen, Tess, forget the fake wedding for a moment. And we all know it's fake, even if we secretly hope that someday it won't be. But, seriously, what exactly is *wrong* with this guy?"

"Nothing. And I told you, that's the problem." At their

group look of dismay, she held up her hand. "Hear me out, okay? He's...*perfect*. Everything he says, everything he does, every touch, every kiss, everything. And then he talks about 'us' like...like we actually might be an us."

They let out a collective and sickening sigh.

"But we just met," she insisted.

"So? What's wrong with that?" Lacey asked.

"What's right with that?" she shot back.

Jocelyn came closer. "Better question, Tess: What's right with *him*? Obviously, there are things you like a lot."

"Of course. He listens to me, he makes me laugh, he's sexy, he's smart, he's kind, he's..." Freaking perfect.

Three sets of wide eyes stared at her, stone silent.

"Well, don't you see? It's too fast, it's too much, it's too right to be real."

"You're too stupid to be real," Zoe said.

"She's not stupid." Of course Lacey jumped to her defense. "She's cautious and I understand that. And, for God's sake, we don't expect you to really marry him."

"Thank you." Tessa puffed out the words with true gratitude. "And I'm not so stupid that I'm not interested, Zoe," she fired at the other woman. "I'm interested. But when I bring up my desire to have a—" A sudden punch of pain hit her chest.

The phone call. The surrogate. The disappointment. "Shit," she murmured. "I forgot about that call from the clinic."

"See?" Zoe said, her voice softening. "He's good for you like that."

She shook her head. "I don't know. I have to get used to this wedding idea. It feels like a farce."

"It is a farce," they all said in unison.

And that was what hurt, but she couldn't possibly make them understand that.

"I know you're all hung up on things happening just so," Jocelyn said, moving from the sofa to get closer to Tessa. "And since you think you can't get pregnant the standard way—"

"I can't."

"—you have to do it this scientific, surrogate way or not at all."

True enough.

"And now," Zoe said, coming around to get down next to Jocelyn so they could all three be in her face. "You meet this guy and he's 'perfect' and that upsets your apple cart."

She looked from one to another, a little jolt of love swelling in spite of how much they could frustrate her. "I like apples," she said with a laugh. "And I like my cart to be organized."

"Yes, you do." Lacey squeezed Tessa's knee. "But sometimes that cart has to be turned over, spilled out, and stripped bare."

"Oooh." Zoe moaned. "And he's just the man for that job."

"Listen," Lacey said. "All kidding aside, we really do have to have a wedding on this property that weekend or we won't be considered. If it really makes you uncomfortable, Tess, or you feel we've snowed you, I'll call more potential couples—from a list of people who've made inquiries, or maybe in town—and see if I could offer someone a free wedding if they'd hold it that weekend." She didn't sound too promising, but Tessa appreciated the offer.

"Then what?"

"Well, if that works, you're off the hook. If it doesn't, you gotta take one for the team."

Tessa's heart slowed as she realized how much of this important weekend fell on her shoulders. And what it would feel like to walk across the beach at Barefoot Bay and stand in front of an official next to John Brown and—

And *lie*.

"You know, I already got married once, and you were all there. You"—she pointed to Jocelyn—"made a toast that brought me to tears. And you"—her finger moved to Lacey—"caught my bouquet. And you—"

"Made out with that really cute guy from Boston." Zoe grinned. "*And* went the lowest under the limbo stick."

They all laughed, except Tessa, who could barely swallow the lump in her throat.

"Tessa." Lacey, of course, noticed. "What's wrong?"

"I wanted the next time to be forever." Hot, hated tears stung her lids. "Not an…act."

For a long moment, no one said a word. Then Lacey leaned closer, squeezing Tessa's arm. "You still have two weeks. By then maybe it won't feel like pretend. Maybe it'll feel like practice."

"Stranger things have happened," Jocelyn said.

"Right here in Barefoot Bay, as a matter of fact." Lacey laughed. "I didn't even know I was at my own wedding, remember?"

"I'm not going to be thinking about marriage in two weeks." Tessa closed her eyes, her head and heart going back to John. "I still think he's hiding something."

"Oh my God." Zoe shot up, disgusted.

"You might be looking for trouble where there isn't any," Lacey agreed.

"Maybe he really does know something you don't," Jocelyn said. "Like the fact that you two are meant to be together."

Tessa didn't answer any of them, pressing her hands to her temples as confusion ricocheted around and gave her a headache. "I'm going to find out what it is."

"In other words, you're going to doom this relationship." Zoe folded her arms and gave Tessa her darkest look.

"No, I'm not. I'm going to dig a little deeper and not let him derail me with…kisses and promises and all that certainty."

Before she got "married"—even if it was a charade—she intended to know the answers.

Chapter Nineteen

ᡩᡪ

W e done here?" Marcus already had the first two buttons of his chef's jacket open, one eye on the clock. "Everything's cleaned, dining room is ready for tomorrow, and the cooler's organized."

Ian glanced around the kitchen, satisfied that they were finished, even though it was only ten-thirty. "I suppose," he said. "But don't get used to being through with dinner service this early. Once we get this place up to speed…"

What was he thinking? He wasn't going to be around that long, was he?

The sickening feeling that had been eating away at him all evening settled low in his belly. He shook it off and settled his attention on the young man in front of him, who'd done a great job that night. He still reminded Ian a little of Kate's brother, but he couldn't hold that against the kid.

"You got a date, Marcus?"

He gave a hesitant smile and nod.

"The boss's daughter, by any chance?" Ian pressed.

Another nod. "That's cool, isn't it?"

"Depends." Ian unbuttoned his own coat, eyeing Marcus as he shook out of it. "Ever hear the expression 'You don't get your meat where you get your bread'?"

He laughed softly. "No, and neither have you, based on the news that you're going to marry Ms. Galloway."

"Not exactly," he corrected, pushing away the bad feeling that gnawed.

"Yeah, but everyone's starting to say it could be real. Waitstaff placed bets already."

He smiled. Which side would he bet, if he were a gambling man?

"They're telling the customers, too."

Oh, man. Tessa would hate that. "Probably best if we keep the whole thing quiet." That way, when it was all over, he could slip away with his kids and this would be a memory. And Tessa would still have her pride.

"Sorry, but Marcia had to do something, otherwise you'd have had unwanted company back here."

Ian frowned, not following. Marcia was the head server, but who was this company? A quick stab of a worry pinched. "Someone was asking for me?"

"Grace Hartgrave."

It took a second, but then he placed the name. "From the Fourway Motel?"

"Dude, you could totally do her."

"No, thanks."

"Well, yeah, that's what Marcia figured, so she told Grace and her buddy that you'd gotten engaged this afternoon."

He had no idea how to respond to that.

"Not that Mrs. G. ever let a man's wife stop her. Or her own husband." Marcus grinned. "Man, you got it goin' on in the sack, don't you?"

A little irritation flared at the disrespectful comment. "Not your business, Marc."

He held up his hand. "Just talkin' man to man, Chef. It's cool. When you're getting a piece, it's nice to talk about it."

The irritation did more than flare now; it sparked, and Ian took a step forward, eyes narrowing. "First of all, it's not nice to talk about it. Second of all, you better not be getting a piece of Ashley Armstrong."

"Dude." Marcus laughed. "She's hot."

Ian raised an eyebrow. "You think that's enough?"

"I dig her." He put a hand on Ian's shoulder and squeezed. "It's all good, man. We'll take care of business, if you know what I mean. Everything's cool and there's no reason not to take what the chick is offering."

Ian fisted his hand, and only the soft echo of Henry's warning kept him from taking a swing. "You want a reason? I'll give you three. You work for her mother, she's barely seventeen, and if you lay a fucking hand on her, I'll kill you."

Marcus backed up a little. "What's your deal, man? Why does it matter?"

Because it mattered to Tessa. The thought scared him almost as much as his fisted hand.

"It just does. So fly straight." Ian gave him a solid push out the back door. "I'm watching you, kid."

With a nervous and pissed-off look over his shoulder, Marcus left. Still fuming over the conversation, Ian finished one last pass at the kitchen and grabbed the to-go box of the last two orders of stone crabs he'd kept in the cooler. He dug through the bag for his regular phone since the one he kept in his pocket could only call Henry. When he had it, he tapped in Tessa's number to text a message, as he promised he would when he was on his way over for the late dinner they had planned.

Leaving the restaurant. His finger hovered over the screen, considering how to close the message. *Can't wait,* he typed.

But how would these words on her phone make her feel when he was finished with this charade? Hollow and hurt.

He deleted those last two words, stepping outside, still debating how to sign off the text, if at all. Oh, hell, how to sign off a text was the last thing he should be worried about. As the evening had worn on and his outrageous plan took hold, he'd battled hope and guilt.

Hope that he'd somehow found an answer for Henry's request that he have proof of marriage when he went to Canada to get his kids. But guilt pounded harder, because signing that piece of paper would mean something to Tessa Galloway. So how would he make that happen?

He still didn't know, but he hadn't talked to Henry yet. Maybe Henry would give him the go-ahead to be straight with her.

His finger still over the screen, he sucked in some of the cooler evening air, hoping for a clear head in the salty breeze but getting a douse of cloying perfume instead.

"I thought you'd never come out."

Blinking into the darkness, he spied a woman standing next to his bike. Oh, hell. Apparently "He's engaged" really didn't mean anything to Grace Hartgrave.

"I had dinner with a girlfriend," she said as he crossed the parking lot. "We asked the server to send our compliments to the chef."

He reached the bike, averting his gaze from hers. "I got them, thanks."

"We also asked that you visit the table."

"It was the middle of a rush." He shifted from foot to foot, keeping the bike between them. "Kinda late to be hanging out in the parking lot, Mrs...." He pretended to search for a name he knew. "Sorry, I can't remember your *husband's* last name," he added deliberately.

She gave a slow smile. "Don't worry. I can't remember his first name half the time." She rounded the bike. "Want to walk the beach?"

"No."

She peered up flirtatiously. "Want to take me for a ride?"

"No."

She smiled, undeterred. "Want to skip the preliminaries and go back to your place for a nightcap and a—?"

He put his hand over her mouth. "No, Mrs. Hartgrave, I don't want to do anything with you."

Under his palm, her smile faltered. He dropped his hand and cocked his head toward the bike. "'Scuze me..."

She stepped closer, the perfume as offensively strong as she was. "I think you're hot."

"I think you're married."

That made her grin. "Nothin' wrong with a little fun on the side."

"Yes there is," he said simply. "I need you to step out of the way so I can get on this bike."

"I need you to think about what you're missing." She arched her back to press her breasts to his chest. "'Kay?"

He shifted to the side, smelling trouble as much as the cheap fragrance. Even if he was the least bit interested—which he wasn't—he knew bad news when it batted over-made-up eyes at him. For years he'd trained himself to avoid anyone or anything like this.

"Bet your husband is worried about you," he said, attempting for diplomacy.

"Bet my husband is on his ninth beer." She splayed her fingers on his chest, hissing in a breath as she pressed against his pecs.

He closed his hand over her wrist and removed her hand.

She circled the other around his neck, pulling him down. "One kiss. I made a bet I could get one." Up on her toes, she smashed her mouth against his the very second bright lights of a golf cart bathed them in yellow.

He jerked away, blinded by the lights and unable to see the driver. Instantly, the golf cart whirled around to head back up the path, and the moonlight shown on dark hair spread over narrow and familiar shoulders.

Damn it! "Tessa!" he called, practically tossing the woman in front of him to the side. "Wait!"

But she barreled the cart back up the path without even glancing back.

"Come on." Grace put both arms around his waist. "Let's—"

He gave her a gentle but solid push back, still watching the retreating golf cart. "Get the hell off me, lady."

She stepped back, wiping the corner of her mouth, her eyes transforming from sultry to icy in an instant. But he barely noticed, his entire focus on that golf cart disappearing into the darkness of a winding path.

The second he had space, he threw one leg over the bike. He twisted the key and revved hard, not even looking at Grace as she dramatically threw herself backward.

He turned the wheel and shot out of the lot, his engine not quite loud enough to drown out Grace's parting shot. "Fuck you, asshole!"

He hoped Tessa heard that, too.

Tessa parked the cart on the path, cursing her decision to go meet John at the restaurant and take that beach stroll he'd wanted. Marching across the grass toward the gardens, she heard the motorcycle engine rev, but the sound of her name called out in shock still reverberated in her head.

She slowed down when she reached the root-vegetable section, the burn of embarrassment finally subsiding.

Grace Hartgrave! How low can you go? Not that she thought for a minute he was interested in her, but did he take what any woman offered? Was that the thing he was hiding from her?

He'd certainly acted that way the night they'd met. Since then, he hadn't shown any indication that he was a man whore, but *she really didn't know him.*

She squeezed her eyes shut, the truth of that burning.

The motorcycle engine grew louder, coming up the path on the same route she'd taken. Maybe she shouldn't have run, but she had. So now what? Hide in her own garden?

"Tessa!" His voice carried over the garden, more angry and frustrated than desperate.

Why *had* her instinct been to run?

She knew why. An image of another man in a parking lot flashed in her head, the memory of that moment when she saw Billy leaning against the yoga instructor's car, reaching down to touch her possessively, and that very first twinge of disbelief and suspicion started to simmer in Tessa's chest.

"Tessa!"

Of course, this was déjà vu. At least Billy picked someone worthy of Tessa's jealousy. Grace Hartgrave wasn't—

She spotted him rounding a live oak tree, pausing as if he'd picked up her scent, scanning the garden. Staying in the shadows of the citrus trees, she inhaled the sweet scent of orange and tried to erase both bad memories.

John wasn't Billy, not by a long shot.

"Bloody hell." The words floated over the garden, making Tessa draw back in surprise. "I could kill that fuckin' woman."

The words…spoken in a perfect *English* accent.

"What did you say?" Tessa's question popped out at the same time she jumped from the shadow.

"Tessa!" He lunged toward her. "Holy crap, that was *not* what it looked like."

But was *that* what it sounded like? "What did you say?"

He shook his head. "She threw herself at me, I swear." He reached her, his hands out, a backpack hanging off his shoulder. "I'd just texted you that I was on the way." He opened his hand and showed her his phone.

"I didn't get a text." Had she imagined that accent?

"I didn't get to send it," he said, stepping closer, his hair wavy from being pulled back in a ponytail, a shadow of whiskers darkening his cheeks, his eyes glittering shiny blue in the moonlight. "That woman freaking threw herself at me, I swear."

Bloody hell. She shook her head as if she could make the words tumble out of her memory. Who said that? No one—in this country.

"Tessa." He closed in on her, his large, masculine torso so close she could smell the scents of the kitchen. "I know what you're thinking, and it's completely wrong."

But now he sounded normal. American. Like someone from California and Nevada where they had zero accents and didn't say things like bloody hell.

He stroked her cheek. "You were coming to meet me, weren't you?"

She looked up at him, searching his face for a clue to any kind of secret. All she saw was perfection. Almost *too* perfect.

"To take a walk?" he asked.

He flipped the backpack over his shoulder and dropped it on the ground. "Let's have a picnic right here in the garden. I brought stone crabs. I was going to take a shower, but…" He took her hand and pulled her down to the ground. "Sit down and please, please tell me you know me better than to think for one second I'd be attracted to that piece of trash."

"John." She refused to let him do this, steadfast in her determination not to be sweet-talked or coerced or lied to. In any accent. "I saw you."

What she meant was I *heard* you, but she couldn't bring herself to say that yet.

"What you saw was a pathetic woman throwing herself at a disinterested man." He tugged her toward the ground. "C'mon, Tessa. Sit here. Talk to me."

She let him pull her down. "I did see you kiss her," she said softly as she let her backside hit the ground, a soft spot of orange-scented leaves.

"No, you saw her kiss me." He settled right next to her, the backpack in front of his knees. "I have had exactly three conversations with the woman and hope that was the last."

"She's a…" She couldn't quite think of anything bad enough.

"I know the word for what she is."

"In what language?" she asked.

His eyes widened in surprise. "I only speak one."

"Maybe I should say in what accent?" At his look of confusion, she took a breath and let her thoughts out in a rush. "I heard you when you were looking for me. You said 'bloody hell' and something in an English accent."

"Did I?" For one second, one lightning flash of a millisecond that was so fast she almost missed it, she read a little fear in his eyes. Or guilt. Or…*something*. Damn it, there was something.

"That's…odd." He reached for the backpack, yanking the zipper. "I have everything we need for a moonlight picnic," he said quickly. "Even a corkscrew. But no glasses. We have to drink from—" He finally looked at her, his expression changing as he took in hers. "Tessa, I swear I have no interest in that woman. She's obviously the town slut, a complete—"

"You spoke with an English accent. I heard it. I know I did. Why?"

"I don't know," he finally said, so softly she almost didn't catch it.

He pulled out a to-go white foam box, and then a bottle of wine. "I told you I lived in Singapore, and I picked up a lot of expressions from the Brits there."

She didn't answer, swallowing the temptation to remind him he said he'd lived there for such a short time it was more like a visit.

"Tess, why are you looking at me like that?"

"Because I need to trust you," she finally said.

He set the box and wine on the ground, turning to put both hands on her face. His fingers were calloused and rough and so large that his palms covered her cheeks. "Listen to me, okay? I know what happened with your husband. I know that you saw what you think was me"—he searched for a word—"cheating on you."

"Cheating? I barely know you."

"We're getting married," he shot back. "Or did you forget?"

"We're talking about a stunt on the beach to help build business," she corrected, trying to ease out of his grasp. "So there's no 'cheating' involved."

"Then why did you turn and fly away into the night?"

"I didn't want to…" *Relive old pain.* "Watch."

He stroked her chin with his thumbs, a sure, warm touch that sent a thousand sparks to every nerve ending in her body. "Like I was saying, I know that your husband ended your marriage by cheating on you. So I'm taking a wild guess that you had a little flashback and a very understandable moment when you doubted me."

"Am I that transparent?"

"No, I'm that keen."

Keen. Another word spoken more in England than the US. Had she ever noticed that before?

"And you are not transparent." He came an inch closer, erasing space and doubts and common sense. "You're beautiful and sweet and smart and good." His voice got so soft it almost sounded pained. But Tessa's eyes were closed and she couldn't read his expression. All she could do was feel his hands, his breath, his...lips.

He kissed her so tenderly she could barely feel it.

"I'm sorry," he whispered. And he sounded truly sorry. Really sorry. Like—she pulled back from the kiss to study the misery on his face.

"You're *too* sorry," she said. "If that was as innocent as you say, you wouldn't look quite that sorry." Or was he sorry for something else? God, he confused her.

"I'm apologizing in advance for all the stupid things I'll do in a clumsy effort to"—he closed his eyes—"get what I want." Another kiss, this one slower, deeper, and hotter. "And what I want, woman, is you."

She barely heard those last words, the blood rushing through her veins, pulsing in her head and a whole lot of other places. Everything felt so good, so alive, so *real*.

But was everything real? Was he? Here in the moonlight, the smell of oranges and oak, the touch of salt air and sweet lips, was anything real? His tongue traced her lips and he finally let go of her face, dragging his hands down her throat, onto her chest. She bowed her back into the kiss, dropping her head back to offer him whatever he wanted to touch.

He kissed his way down her throat, lingering there to suck gently, tangling one hand in her hair and letting the other slide lower until his palm grazed her breast.

More nerves tingled, tightening every inch of skin, twirling a ribbon of desire through her body until she had to moan with the need for him to untie every bit of her.

Who cared if he was real? She wanted this. She wanted him. She wanted everything.

As he caressed her breast, she dropped back and he came with her, both of them falling to the soft earth as they kissed. Her nipple budded under his palm, drawing a moan from her throat, or maybe it was his. Everything was connected.

He slid on top of her, a solid, huge erection pressing on her stomach and stealing her breath.

"Tessa," he whispered into the kiss.

"Mmmm."

"I'm still waiting for an answer."

What the heck was the question? She turned her head, letting him nibble at her neck and ear, squeezing his mighty biceps and finally giving in to the urge to rock her hips into his.

"Do I believe you?" she asked.

He slipped his hand under her T-shirt, up her belly, and onto the thin silk of her bra. "The other question."

She rocked again, the knot between her legs twisting tighter with need to ride his long, hard ridge. What other question? Did it matter? "Just…don't stop."

He chuckled softly, purposely holding still. She rolled against him anyway, the shock of arousal electrifying her whole body.

"I need an answer."

"Ask again."

He laughed once more, lifting his head to look into her eyes. "Are you going to marry me?"

She held his gaze for so long, it felt like the world shifted on its axis. If only this were real, she thought. If only this were love and not pretend. If only…

He ground against her, harder this time, giving her full access to his hard-on, grunting as the pleasure hit him, too. "Come on, say yes." He pounded into her, torturing her with the exquisite feeling.

"Well, not for real."

"Then for pretend."

She finally held him still, grabbing his shoulders, looking into his eyes. "I'm lost," she admitted. "I don't know what's real or right or pretend or play. I don't know what to say except…"

Harder and faster he rolled against her, pulling her right into a vortex. She couldn't think. All she could do was slide against him, sounds of sex and need whimpering in her throat.

"Don't say anything," he whispered.

She closed her eyes and gave in to the first helpless hitch of pure pleasure, an orgasm building so fast she knew it couldn't be stopped.

A delicious heat coiled through her, spinning at the most tender spot as she rubbed and rode and rocked against the sexiest body she'd ever held. "I…want… you…to…be…"

She came fast and hard, biting her lip to keep the word from slipping out. But as she fell over the edge of pure, raw, crazy pleasure, she lost control, one word tumbling helplessly from her lips. "Real."

"It can be real." His voice was rough in her ear.

What did he mean? Sex? Love? This farce of a wedding? What did he mean by that? She closed her eyes as he rocked again, relentless and rhythmic, firing arousal through her, letting that orgasm flow and then subside.

"I said I want you to be real."

She felt him sigh. "I'm real enough, Tess."

Real enough. *Real enough.* And once again, he'd deflected her questions and probing with kisses and heat. And she let him. So maybe, deep inside, deflected questions and nonanswers were what she really wanted.

Chapter Twenty

~

Was that a lie? Was he real enough?

Ian didn't know and, at that very second, didn't care. His own release was far too close at hand, forcing him to clench his jaw and hold back while Tessa melted under him like butter in a smoking saucepan.

He allowed his body one more hard press against hers, the move firing more blood to his already aching hard-on. After a second, he lifted his head to look into her eyes, glittering in the moonlight, bright with arousal.

Still clutching his arms, her breathing as strangled as his, she held his gaze. "John," she whispered.

John. What would it be like to hear her call him Ian? Could it ever be *that* real?

Not unless he was insane. Wasn't it bad enough she'd overheard him slip into his native accent when he thought he was alone?

"I can't think straight," he admitted. "No blood in my brain." Slowly, he rolled off her and sat up, leaving her lying on the leaves, looking sated and sexy while his boner strained his jeans. He was lying in every way already—he wasn't about to throw salt on the wounds he'd leave by screwing her, too. "I think we need food and wine."

She repositioned herself, pulling down her top and brushing some hair back, trying to get composed but only managing disheveled and sexy.

"You really want me to drink from the bottle?"

He took his time getting the corkscrew, letting his arousal subside. "Yeah. I think it'd be hot."

"Making out in the garden, drinking wine from a bottle." She drew in a breath, then smiled as she exhaled. "And I'm giving Ashley a hard time. We're as bad as they are."

"Not quite."

She sat up. "What does that mean?"

"It means I think there's more than what we just did going on between them."

Tessa closed her eyes. "Ugh. I don't know what to do. Should I tell Lacey or not? I can't stand lies. I can't stand secrets. Absolutely nothing drives me crazier, except...I totally get what she's going through."

He popped out the cork with one easy pull and handed her the bottle, happy for the chance to talk about something other than lies, truth, and his slip of the accented tongue.

She eyed the bottle. "I don't generally do things like this."

"See? I'm good for you." He wiggled the bottle.

"I like to do things in their proper order. You know, wine in glass and then in mouth. Kiss like crazy in the house. Or maybe fall in love then get married, not fake it for an audience."

He swallowed hard. She'd want love, of course. What woman wouldn't? And he was offering her nothing like that. Self-loathing roiled through him. "Drink up, pretty Tessa."

Frowning, she reached for the bottle. "I'm not that pretty."

"Speaking of 'Ugh.'" He looked skyward. "I hate when pretty women say that."

"No, honestly, it wasn't a ploy for compliments. I don't see myself like, you know, Zoe. Now she's pretty."

"Not my type. Have a sip."

Still, she didn't put the bottle to her lips. "What is your type, John Brown?"

He thought for a moment, expecting an image of Kate Shaw Browning to burn his brain. But for one second, he couldn't remember what his wife looked like. Oh, *hell*.

"John?"

"I'm trying to think of all the ways I could describe you," he said, hating his glibness but he had no choice. "If you want to know my type, look in the mirror."

"Mud-brown hair, too-high forehead, unimpressive cup size."

He leaned back and scrutinized what she'd said. "Your hair is about fifteen shades of hot fudge. Your forehead, cheekbones, and chin are heart-shaped, which I read once is the sign of a person with a big heart. And as for your cup size…" He let his gaze fall on the chest he'd caressed. "Those are…sweet and they do exactly what they're supposed to do to me." He leaned over and kissed right above her breast. "Make me want more."

Still holding the bottle of wine poised to her mouth, she smiled. "Where'd you learn to talk like that?"

For a second, he thought "like that" meant "like an American."

"You said you didn't go to college, and I doubt they teach you romantic poetry in culinary school."

No, but they did in the Humanities classes at Cambridge. "I read a lot."

"What do you like to read?"

He shook his head and gave the bottle another nudge. "No stone crab for you until you drink. And make a toast."

She raised the wine and dropped her head to one side, thinking. "I would like to toast to the first man who made me…ahem…in the dirt." Lifting it to her lips, she winked. "Guess yours will have to be in the kitchen, since we're doing each other on our home turfs."

He didn't answer, watching her bring the bottle to her lips and sip. After a second, she handed it to him. "Your turn."

"All right." He lifted the bottle. "To…" *My children, lost and waiting for me to deceive this woman just so I can get them back.* "Us."

He closed his eyes when he drank, deep and long, letting the dry Cabernet cover his tongue and, hopefully, take the sting out of his thoughts and the guilt out of his soul.

"Never been married, John?"

The wine clogged his throat and made him choke softly. "No." He managed to cough out yet another lie. Then he lifted the bottle and drank again, this time to wash it away.

Tessa settled back on her elbows, relaxed as she studied him. "How'd you go so long without getting snagged?"

He hadn't gone so long. He'd met Kate in college, at a pub. She'd beat him at darts and downed a pint faster than he had.

"Haven't met the right person," he mumbled, the wine good and stuck in his esophagus now. He gave her the bottle and busied himself by opening the box of stone crabs, presenting the array of pinkish claws. "Here we go, all pre-cracked and ready to eat with our hands. It's like I knew we'd have a picnic."

"Have you been looking?" she asked.

"For stone crabs?"

She gave him a playful kick with her foot. "For the right person."

He shook his head, grateful to be honest. "I've been focused on me," he admitted. "Learning how to cook, doing my thing, traveling. What about you?"

"I told you, I was married for ten years."

"I mean since then?"

"Nah, just working."

He had to keep the conversation off his past. "What about your parents?" he asked.

A reaction flickered over her face, impossible to read in the dim light. "What about them?"

"Tell me about them." He handed her a stone crab. "Just peel the shell off the outside and dip it in this." He popped the lid on the tangy mustard sauce he'd prepared.

It was her turn to pretend to be so involved with the stone crab that she didn't answer his question. She dipped the edge of the crabmeat in the sauce and slowly put the claw in her mouth, sucking the meat and closing her eyes as the taste hit. A soft moan of delight followed, a lot like the ones he'd heard a few minutes ago.

"Mmm. Perfection," she finally said, dabbing at the corner of her mouth. "I don't suppose you included a napkin in your bag of fun."

He got on his knees and leaned close to her face, giving a swift lick to her lips. "We'll be each other's napkins."

She smiled, running her tongue right over the spot where his had been. "You're determined to take me to places I don't want to go, aren't you?"

"Yep. Your parents?"

Looking down, she played with a piece of the shell, breaking it off to reveal more meat on the claw.

"You don't want to talk about your parents?" he urged.

"I don't…" She made a face, obviously struggling with something. Then she reached for the wine bottle, which he'd balanced next to his leg. "Lubrication, please."

He gave it to her and she took a solid swig. Then another.

"Whoa. Must be some story."

She eyed the bottle as if she was considering a third, but gave it back to him. "I don't talk about my parents, to anyone. And I mean *anyone*."

He lifted a brow and held his stone crab still without biting. "Even your close friends?"

"Nope."

"Says the woman who hates secrets."

She flinched, acknowledging the truth. "It's not that I want to keep secrets from them, but I don't like to talk about my mother." She gave a dry laugh. "The irony is that my mother *is* the reason I dislike secrets and she's the reason I made up a story about having parents." She draped her arm over her face, covering it completely. "I can't believe I'm going to tell you this."

He leaned closer, holding the bottle with one hand so it didn't spill, but using the other to lift her arm and see her face. "Why not?"

"Because it's letting you…in."

"I want to be in," he admitted, a little taken aback by how much truth there was in that statement. Right that moment, looking at her with moonlight on her hair and conflict in her eyes, he wanted to be right inside that whirlwind of emotions.

Where he really had no fucking right to be.

"I don't tell people this bit of my history. I say my parents were nice and normal but we're not close at all. End of story."

"Did you tell your husband?"

"Of course. He met her."

"Did he meet your father?"

She closed her eyes. "My father is dead."

"I'm sorry," he said softly, stroking her face. "Were you close to him?"

Giving her head a negative shake, she brushed off his touch. "Long story. And, honestly, I don't want to talk about it. I don't want to…" She bit her lip, reaching up to touch his cheek as he'd touched hers. "Damn it, yes I do. How did you do that? In this short time? How did you get me here?"

He turned to kiss her palm. "Same way I got you to drink with no glass and eat with no napkin and have an orgasm under the stars."

"How *did* you do that?"

Lowering his head, he kissed the answer. "Now that's my secret."

She curled a hand around his neck, nestling her fingers into his hair. "You're a professional apple-cart upsetter," she said with a smile. "You know that?"

"Mmmm." He kissed her. "That I am."

She pushed him before he could deepen the kiss. "You did it again."

"Did what?"

"That accent. 'That I am.' The way you said it was…English."

Actually, it was British, and troubling. She made him relax and forget and share far too much. "You're imagining things, pretty Tessa." He got the kiss accomplished, and kept it long and slow and a little bit dirty. But she pushed him back one more time.

Damn it, he didn't want to keep making up any more lies. "Tessa, please I—"

"I want to tell you."

He stopped the plea, looking at her. "About your parents?"

"Yes. I want to tell you," she repeated. "I don't want any secrets between us. None at all. I'm going to tell you everything and then…"

He would tell her nothing. "And then?"

"Then I'll feel better about that fake wedding business."

And he'd feel worse when he somehow made it real. But he forged on, kissing her again. "You keep letting me in and you know what's going to happen, don't you?"

She shook her head.

"It might not be a fake wedding."

Her eyes popped open and he kissed her long and hard, until he was certain they were closed again.

* * *

Had he really just said what she thought he said or had the wine hit?

By the time the kiss was over, Tessa was good and confused again, and ready to share anything. Including her past.

"It's not a huge deal," she said, confirming she was at least a little tipsy even to say that. Her issues with her mother had always been a huge enough deal that she'd buried them and thrown away the shovel.

Until now.

"I was raised by a career-crazed single mom who put her job before her daughter and basically lied to me for almost seventeen years about who my father was."

"How'd that happen?"

Good question. "Well, she was never home," she said softly. "She was always, always working. Which meant she was always, always with him."

Frowning, John shook his head. "I thought you said he was dead."

"He is now. He wasn't then. He was my mother's partner."

His expression grew more confused. "They lived together?"

"Law partner. Look, it's complicated, which is one of the reasons I don't tell people, even my friends." She gnawed her lip, thinking about the vacuum of information she'd kept from Lacey, Zoe, and Joss. "I've always planned on telling them someday," she added quickly. "At first, when I met them in college, the wounds were still so raw I couldn't be straight with strangers. After a few years, after we were so close, the whole subject embarrassed me because they knew I hated secrets. But only because my mother's secret hurt me so much."

"Tell me the whole story." He repositioned himself next to her, aligning his large, strong body along hers, sliding a leg over her, as if they were lying in bed together.

Taking a slow breath, she closed her eyes and leaned her cheek against his head, a few soft hairs tickling, the lingering scent of food on him and the garden in the air like a balm over her old wounds. Maybe telling him would erase the scars completely.

"My mother is a lawyer in Seattle. In her first year out of law school, she got involved with another lawyer in her firm. I was the result."

"Why didn't she marry him?"

"Because his wife would have hated that."

He grunted softly.

"Yeah. So, she had me and promptly returned to work, and her affair, which lasted for another sixteen years."

"Seriously?" He lifted his head as if he hadn't heard that right. "He was married the entire time?"

"Oh, yes. Married, with children."

"Did you know he was your father?"

That was probably the thing that hurt the most. "No. When I was old enough to understand, my mother told me I was an accident, the result of a one-night stand whose name she didn't know."

"Did that other lawyer know you were his?"

"Uncle Ken? Of course he did." Another aspect of her screwy life that always irked. "And I knew him quite well, only I never had any idea he was my father. When

I was about five, they started their own firm, Donnelly & Galloway, and it was hugely successful. My mother was the quintessential workaholic, putting in long days and"—she gave a dry smile—"lots of out-of-town trials that she and her partner handled together."

"Who raised you?"

"Nannies when I was little, then I pretty much learned to fend for myself." She'd been the original latch-key kid.

"How did you find out he was your dad?"

"He died and she was…" She shook her head, remembering the dark, dark days of her mother's grief. "Devastated would be an understatement. That's when she told me, in the throes of her grief." Damn it, her voice cracked.

Instantly, he was up on one elbow and his grip around her waist tightened. "That must have been rough."

"I think the hardest part was I had a father and didn't know it. No, no, the hardest part was I shared him with another family and my mother…" The lump in her throat made it hurt to swallow, even to get air. "No, it was all hard. Including the fact that my mother was willing to settle for second best and live a lie. And, of course, she kept that secret from me and from the world. To this day, his family doesn't know."

For a long time, John stayed quiet and still. She waited for a reaction, a question, some sympathy. But he didn't say a word.

"Anyway, she's fine," Tessa said, as if he'd asked. "Still runs the law firm, still works long hours."

"Only now she's alone."

So very much alone. "We talk, but not often. Mostly by e-mail. She came to see me when Billy left me, and it only made things worse." She snorted softly. "Like she was a good role model for marriage."

"And the fact that she didn't tell you about your father is why you hate secrets," he stated, as if he'd snapped the last piece of a puzzle into place.

True enough. But was that the reason she'd shared this one? So he knew that about her? Because something about this man, this night, this…*possibility*…had taken down a wall she'd always kept up.

If he was going to push this to the next step, then so was she.

"That's why…" Her voice trailed off as she struggled with the admission. "I want a child so much. I think the worst way you can end up in the world is alone. And, honestly, I'm headed right there."

"Your mother had a child and she's still alone."

"I'll do better," she said without hesitation. "I learned from her mistakes."

He nodded, considering that.

"Aren't you afraid of being alone, John?" she whispered, fighting the urge to touch his face to punctuate the question.

"No. I've been alone for a while—no."

So he hadn't *always* been alone. "You know what I think?" She lost the battle and grazed his whiskered cheek with her fingertips.

He didn't answer, but slowly closed his eyes.

"I think"—she turned onto her side, facing him—"that there is much more to you than brawn and good looks."

Still, silence.

"I saw it in your eyes the very first night we met. Something deep, something real, something…pained."

He squeezed his eyes shut as if he couldn't take the words. Or didn't want her to see that pain.

"Will you share?"

His only response was to angle his head down, as if he couldn't face her, even with his eyes closed.

She'd shared her deepest and darkest. Wouldn't he?

He finally looked into her eyes. "No."

There was more, and he didn't deny it. But he wouldn't share. And, really, that told her all she needed to know about how "real" this was.

He let out a soft sigh. "I'm sorry, I can't."

Can't or won't? Either way, it hurt.

Chapter Twenty-one

⌒

This time, nothing would stop her. Tessa waited until late afternoon the next day, when it cooled down a bit, kneeling in the soil behind her tractor, threading the three-point hitch. The vines would be cut come hell or high water. Plus, a good long ride could clear the confusion of—

"Hey, Aunt Tessa! Whatchya doin'?"

Or not. With a nearly silent grunt of frustration, she turned, smiling at Ashley as the girl loped over a row of English peas, her long stride surprisingly easy and fast considering that her jeans had been sprayed on.

Tessa wouldn't demand to know what was going on, but any opportunity to talk could only help Ashley. She hoped.

Standing straight, Tessa took a moment to watch the younger woman approach, a deep-seated love swelling inside her. Ashley hadn't been the easiest child to raise—and still wasn't—but Lacey, a single mother for every minute of the first fifteen years of her daughter's life, had done a remarkable job.

"I'm harvesting sweet potatoes," Tessa called back. "Want to help?"

Ashley made a face, then brightened. "I'll drive the tractor!"

"Not a chance." The soil was soft and, despite the fact that she used a fairly small gardening tractor, it was top-heavy and required a deft touch and experienced driver.

Ashley's expression fell again. "Can we talk before you start?" she asked as she got closer.

"Of course," Tessa answered without a second's hesitation. She stood, yanking off her oversized gardening gloves. "I always have time for you."

Ashley gave a dry smile. "Good thing, since Mom is MIA."

"Ash, come on. She's running a business."

"She's at the pediatrician."

Tessa drew back. "Is Elijah sick?"

"No, he needs some shot thing. I don't know. Clay's with her and they left me a note on the kitchen counter. Not a soul in sight." She sounded defeated, and Tessa immediately wanted to defend her friend, in spite of the age-old resentment that rose.

"Well, you're seventeen, Ash. It's not like you're coming home from kindergarten to an empty house." Though Tessa knew that feeling, too.

Ashley leaned against the tractor, looking over Tessa's shoulder. "You know, I'm a little sick of it. It's annoying to always come in second. Or third."

"Did you come all the way out here to complain about

your mom?" Tessa asked gently. "'Cause if you did, I *will* make you dig in the dirt."

"No, I just want to talk to somebody." Kicking the soil with a bright-green Converse sneaker, she kept her eyes cast down. "Did you decide what to do about, you know, telling my mom about Marc?"

"I'm still thinking about it," she said, remembering John's sage advice to keep the lines of communication open.

"What are you thinking about?" Ashley asked.

Nothing but myself and my own crush. "Well, are you still seeing him?"

"Uh, yeah." She choked softly on the word. "Was with him all last night."

"*All* last night?"

"No, but until one in the morning. We were out on the beach."

So she hadn't been the only one kissing under the stars last night. Except—had Ashley stopped things the same way Tessa had? How could she find out without prying too far into Ashley's privacy?

"You were out until one on a school night?"

Ashley let out a sharp laugh. "Aunt Tessa, I'm almost in college."

"You're a junior in high school," Tessa said quickly. "What did your mom say when you got home that late?"

She shrugged. "She was crashed. I guess Elijah had a feeding at midnight and Mom grabs every minute of sleep she can."

"Clay didn't hear you come in?"

Another shrug, then a guilty look. "I told him I was at my friend Kaylee's house."

Tessa closed her eyes. "Ashley, you can't lie and sneak around. I won't help you do that and you know it."

"I know. I…" She let out a little moan and shivered. "Oh, God."

Oh, God, *what*? "What does that mean?"

She hugged herself and gave up a rapturous look. "I really, really, *really* like him and it has me all crazy inside, you know?"

"Oh, yeah," Tessa said with a dry laugh. "I know."

"See?" Ashley nudged her. "Hard to say no to a little of the good thing."

"The good thing?"

"That's what Marcus calls it."

Which said a lot about his feelings regarding sex. Tessa leaned on the hitch, trying to decide what to say. "Look, you're not a child, and I know kids at seventeen have sex."

"A lot of them do," Ashley said. "Like, half my friends lost their virginity last year."

Tessa cringed. "But is that the right thing to do? I mean, it feels like fun in the moment, but what about when he never calls again and you've given him that part of yourself? What about disease and pregnancy and self-respect?"

She expected an argument, but Ashley just looked at her. "I know, Aunt Tess. I'm careful."

"I'm carefuling," Tessa said with a smile.

"What?"

The memory teased. "When you were little, we were at the beach with you and your mom kept saying 'Be careful, Ash' when you went in too deep, and you turned around and said, 'I'm carefuling.' You know, you're still that baby to me and your mom, Ash."

"But I'm not," she replied. "I'm grown up."

"Enough to have sex?"

"Enough to make my own decisions."

"Ashley, don't…" Tessa rooted around for the right words. "Please be smart about this boy. This man," she amended quickly. "You can get in way too deep, way too fast."

"I promise I won't do anything stupid, Aunt Tess. God knows I don't want to mess up my life like my mom did."

And Tessa's mom. "Ashley, your mother doesn't feel like she messed up her life by getting pregnant with you," she said. "I know that, because I was there. I was with her the day she took the pregnancy test. I've known you since before you were born."

"Which is why I'm asking you not to turn me in."

Tessa rolled her eyes. "Just using the words 'turn me in' makes me feel like you know you're doing something wrong, Ashley."

She shook her head. "Is it wrong if you're in love?"

"You're too young to know what love is."

She got a shaky smile in response. A smile that said Ashley thought she knew exactly what love was.

"You hardly know him, Ashley."

"I know him as well as you know John Brown. Aren't you doing it with him?"

"No." But it was only a matter of time, right? "And even if I were, I'm in my thirties. Listen to me."

She reached out for Ashley's hands, wanting so desperately to talk sense into someone who was way past sensible. "You have to promise me you won't lie or sneak around anymore."

"I can't tell my mom I'm dating Marcus, Aunt Tess.

She'd fire him, I know she would. He needs this job so bad."

"Will you promise me you'll think long and hard before you do anything you might regret later?"

"I'll try, Aunt Tess."

Should she tell Lacey? The question pressed hard, making her shake her head. "Your mom needs to know this, Ashley."

"No!" She squeezed Tessa's hands. "Please, I promise, promise, *promise* we won't go any further than we have. I won't do anything that could get me a disease, a baby, or..."

"Or a broken heart."

"Oh, he won't break my heart," she said confidently. "He loves me. He told me last night."

"He could be lying to get into your pants."

She just smiled.

Damn. He probably said it when he was already *in* her pants. "Oh, Ash—"

"Hey! You better not be planning to get on that thing."

They both turned at the sound of Zoe's voice, the sight of her plucking her way across the garden in a flowing yellow sundress ending the conversation.

"Don't tell her, either," Ashley whispered, a soft desperation in her voice.

Tessa closed her eyes. "Why are you trusting the person who hates secrets?"

Ashley didn't answer as Zoe came closer, pointing to the vehicle that apparently wasn't going to get used at all in the near future. "So, does he think your tractor's sexy?"

"Very funny, Zoe. I'm harvesting sweet potatoes and I need to get back to it."

"Not today, you're not."

"I have to," Tessa said, pointing to the tangled vines that were fast becoming her nemesis. "Under that lies hundreds of sweets, and they aren't going to unearth themselves." She frowned at Zoe. "I don't suppose you'd go change and follow the tractor with a basket, would you?"

"The only one of us who's going to change is you. Take a shower and put on some pretty undies." She curled her lip and gave Tessa's overall shorts a disgusted look. "Do you have pretty undies?"

Ashley giggled. "For sweet potato harvesting?"

Zoe reached out a hand to both of them. "Come on. The gang is waiting."

"My mom's at the pediatrician's," Ashley said.

"Not anymore she's not. She's looking all over for you."

Tessa shot an I-told-you-so look at the young girl.

"Does she need me?" Ashley asked.

"She wants to make sure you come with us, of course."

Ashley's eyes brightened. "Where are we going?"

Zoe grinned and yanked Tessa closer. "Wedding-dress shopping!"

Tessa froze. "I thought Lacey was still checking out other possible couples. This isn't a definite thing yet."

"We're dress shopping for me," Zoe said, tugging her. "I need you to be my thinner version. And if we find something you might want to wear for the faux wedding, all the better."

With one last look at the vines, Tessa let Zoe lead her away.

* * *

The minute he could escape the restaurant, Ian grabbed his safe phone and jumped on his bike, not bothering to say good-bye to anyone. Let them look if they needed him, but he would not be found. Not until he made a call to Henry.

He revved the bike engine and peeled out of the resort lot, heading through the gated exit to the winding road that connected Barefoot Bay with the rest of Mimosa Key. A cloud drifted and let some late afternoon sunlight filter through overhanging palm fronds to warm him through his T-shirt and jeans.

But deep inside, he was as ice cold as he'd been since he'd left Tessa the night before.

Glancing to his right, he studied the cobalt expanse of the Gulf of Mexico, wondering for a moment if he should get across that body of water and start over somewhere else. He'd never been to Texas. But hey, he'd never even been to Nevada, but Tessa thought he'd lived and worked there. Bloody hell, why was this lie so hard?

He'd been living a lie for three years, since the day he'd said good-bye to his kids, taken his new identification, and Ian Browning became Sean Bern. Not a word that had come out of his mouth for the better part of those three years had been honest. He lied about his name, his life, his opinions, his language, his feelings. Until he got into it with some idiot and fucked up his cover by landing in jail; he could still be in Singapore, working, drinking, hiding from anything that resembled *caring* about someone other than himself.

But too much more time with Tessa Galloway and he wasn't going to be able to keep up with the lies. He liked her. He liked her a hell of a lot. He liked everything about her, and he hated what he was doing.

There had to be a better way.

He took a curve too fast, veering so far he damn near laid the bike on the pavement, but he whipped it back, narrowly avoiding a wipeout. Which, he thought bitterly, was another option he had.

No, checking out of Barefoot Bay and the situation he'd gotten himself into wasn't his only option. He had one more, one that had kept him awake all night, brewing and stewing. There was another way to handle this; a possibility that, once planted in his brain, wouldn't get loose.

He could tell Tess everything.

No matter how he played out that conversation in his imagination, he knew it wouldn't be in any way pleasurable or easy. He lifted his face to the sky for a moment, but a cloud had covered the sun again. He had to call Henry and convince him that this woman could be trusted.

There'd be some aftermath, of course. Even in this short bit of time, she'd be hurt that he'd lied. She might refuse to help him, but he doubted that. They could start over, on honest ground.

He wanted that so much he could taste it. How had that happened? How had she wormed her way into his psyche already?

It didn't matter. She had, and he had to get out from under this anvil of lies. This time, it was different. This time, she mattered. A lot. Too much.

Far enough between the resort and town that the road was deserted, he slowed down and pulled to the side, spitting up some sand and gravel as he brought the bike to a halt. This was as good a place as any to—

An engine screamed from around the bend, and he whipped around to see a cherry-red 4x4 with the top down, music blaring almost as loud as the engine. As it got closer, he saw the passengers were all female and—*shit*.

At the wheel, Zoe laid on the horn as they approached, and from the back, Lacey's daughter waved.

Tessa sat in the passenger seat, her expression unreadable as they slowed down next to his bike.

"You okay?" Zoe called out.

He nodded, grateful he hadn't been on the phone with Henry when they came by. "Where you off to?" he asked, unable to tear his eyes from Tessa.

She responded with what appeared to be a shaky smile, lifting her shades so he got a good look at her eyes and read a mix of worry and—affection. Damn, she was feeling everything he was. Maybe more.

He had to make that call.

"Don't ask where we're going," Tessa said, a note of wry humor in her voice. "I've been kidnapped."

Zoe leaned over in front of Tessa. "He should know."

"Know what?"

From the back, Ashley leaned forward. "We're going shopping for a wedding dress!"

He blinked at that, the words hitting him harder than they should. "Really?"

"For Zoe's dress," Tessa corrected.

"But the love child makes it impossible to try on dresses," Zoe added, tapping her belly. "Tessa's my size, so she's going to model for us."

A slow smile pulled as an impression settled on his brain: Tessa in a long white gown. Pretty, pretty Tessa. "Not getting anything for our big event?" he asked.

Her color rose, but Zoe leaned in closer to answer. "I might let her borrow."

Deeper. They kept getting in deeper. Now a dress was involved. Of course, this was his idea, so he should support it. "Sounds like fun."

"What are you doing parked out here?" Tessa asked.

And here went one more lie. "Bike sounded weird, so I wanted to check it."

"Do you need a ride somewhere?" Zoe asked.

"Clay could come and pick you up," Lacey offered from the back, the offer so natural and genuine. Of course it was; they were friends now. He was part of their community.

He shook his head at the realization of how they'd all hate him once he disappeared. Even if he succeeded in persuading Henry to let him tell Tessa the truth, what would she tell them when he left?

Holy hell, he was in a bind. Henry had to help him. The safe phone practically burned a hole in his pocket.

"I'm fine," he assured them. "You have a good time shopping, ladies." He gave them a wave and stepped back, and, thankfully, Zoe threw the Jeep into Drive.

"We will!" she promised, hitting the accelerator and taking off, only Ashley turning around to wave good-bye.

The minute he was alone, he pulled out the phone and stared at it. The instructions for use of this had always been clear: Answer when Henry calls, and never call him first unless it was a life-or-death emergency.

He was pretty sure Henry would say this didn't qualify, but screw that. He closed his eyes and saw the image of Tessa's smile. He couldn't go another day lying to her. She'd told him all her secrets the night before, and all that

had done was make him care more for her. And hate himself.

Turning away to get the glare off the screen, he tapped
the only number the phone was programmed to call.
"What?" As suspected, Henry didn't sound pleased to
hear from him.

"I got a problem," he said, slipping naturally into his
native accent, which usually made his whole body relax.
But not today. Henry was sure to put up a fight about this.

"They found you?" There was enough edge in the
other man's voice to let Ian know he wasn't completely
safe, not yet, anyway.

"No. No news on that front?" He had to ask.

"I'll call you, mate. What's wrong?"

"It's this marriage thing."

Henry barely grunted. "I thought you had that covered."

"You told me to get it covered and I told you I'm working on it. But I—"

"You want your kids or not?"

Fuck it. He refused to even answer that. "What I want
is to trust someone."

A long silence.

"I really believe I can trust her, Henry. I know I can."
Did he, though? She'd shared a secret with him, but it
wasn't life-changing or, hell, life-ending. It was a little bit
of dirty laundry, not the fact that he was living incognito
to stay alive.

"You can't afford to have a conscience, Browning." Of
course, Henry nailed it. "You can't trust anyone. Believe
me, I've seen this happen before, and it never ends well."

It was Ian's turn to be silent.

"And you also can't afford to have feelings for someone," Henry added.

Why did the man have to be so flipping smart? "Might be too late," he admitted softly.

Henry sighed. "Look, mate, ultimately, it's your call. I can't force you to do anything. I can't even force you to stay in this program. It's voluntary, as you know. So you do what you have to do, but before you do it, I will counsel you to remember two things."

"What?"

"Don't you know?" Henry asked, sounding a little bewildered.

"No," Ian admitted.

"Shiloh and Sam."

His gut dropped at the thought of the two babies he needed to see and hold more than he needed his next breath.

"You leave this program or break our rules, they are off limits to you."

"But just this once, I—"

"Not to mention," Henry continued forcefully, "that it's one thing to put yourself in danger, but it's something else altogether to jeopardize your kids."

Ian stared at the horizon, then closed his eyes, the horizontal slice of the sea against the sky burning his lids like a negative picture.

"We're close, Ian, close to shutting down that gang. But we haven't succeeded completely. Listen to me." He lowered his voice as if he wanted Ian to press the phone closer to his ear and not miss a single word. "One of the two remaining members is Luther Vane's younger brother, Darius."

Luther Vane. Who had admitted he'd stabbed Kate ten times.

"So if you want to whisper one word of your history and identity, you remember that. It's not about money for Darius Vane. It's about taking out the guy who put his brother in jail, and, frankly, that's a more dangerous motivator. You understand that, don't you?"

He didn't respond, the pressure of that reality too hard.

"Then let me remind you. Once N1L is shut down, you have a chance at getting your kids. A chance. Once you get them, you are still in a government protection program, and so are they, only you'll take on another identity and live in another country as their father. There's no getting around that. If Darius gets wind that you are alive and well and have your kids, he might stop at nothing for revenge."

The truth actually hurt when it was spelled out like that. There was no room in his life for a woman. Even when he had the kids—he wouldn't let himself think "if"—he couldn't subject Tessa to a life under protection. A woman who recoiled at deceit? A woman whose whole personality was formed by her mother lying to her?

No, he couldn't do that to her.

"Are you there?" Henry barked.

He was there…but dead inside. "Yeah."

"Okay, then you heard me. For God's sake, don't let your cock or, hell, your *feelings* get in the way of that reality."

He dragged out the word *feelings* like they were nothing but repulsive.

Ian blew out a breath. "I won't." The promise sounded vacant and weak, kind of like he felt right then.

"And I'll keep you…" The rest of Henry's sentence was drowned out by a loud truck engine coming up from town, on the other side of the road. Ian automatically turned away, not wanting to make eye contact with anyone, all his protective instincts on alert with the news that rang in his ears.

Luther Vane's brother was out there—somewhere.

A door slammed and he had to turn, coming face-to-face with a bull of a man crossing the street. "Hey, dickhead!" the man called out.

"What the hell was that?" Henry asked.

Grace Hartgrave's husband. Son of a bitch! "Nothing. I gotta go."

"Remember those two things, mate. Oh—and for Christ's sake, stay out of trouble."

Ian tapped the phone and stood with his feet splayed as Hartgrave ambled over, silent, menacing, and really pissed off. Well, Grace's parting shot had been "Fuck you." And Ian had a feeling he was about to get fucked.

Hartgrave stopped about two feet from Ian, who didn't say a word. They were about the same height, but the other man had marshmallow where Ian had muscle. He could kill Grace Hartgrave's husband, but the last thing he ever wanted to do was land on the radar of local law enforcement.

"I talked to my wife."

He should do more than talk to her; maybe then she wouldn't throw herself at strangers. Ian just nodded.

"She said you made a pass at her."

"She's lying," he said simply.

"Gracie don't lie." Beads of sweat formed on his oversized forehead, his face the flushed red of a heavy drinker.

Ian pressed his lips together, meeting his opponent's narrow gaze. "She did this time."

"You see her last night?"

"I *saw* her, but I didn't *see* her."

Hartgrave's fist balled as he raised it. "See this, mother-fucker?"

Ian didn't look at the fist, instead hearing Henry's parting shot. *Stay out of trouble.* "She was in the restaurant."

"And you stalked her in the parking lot."

"That's not my version of the events."

He took another step closer, his gaze flickering to the bike behind Ian, then back to Ian's face. "You touch my wife, you'll never see that motorcycle again."

Ian nodded.

"It'll be in the bottom of that bay."

Another nod.

"With your dead body on it."

Ire shot through his veins, the image of Luther Vane flashing in his brain at the threat. He wasn't the least bit scared of this blowhard in front of him, but what if the N1L got to Hartgrave somehow? As preposterous as that seemed thousands of miles and an ocean away, what if Ian told Tessa the truth and she whispered it to a friend and that led to a stray comment? Really, how many degrees of separation was this man from Darius or Luther Vane?

Right then, he knew without a shadow of a doubt that no matter what he felt, how much guilt pained him, how hurt she'd be, he couldn't tell Tessa the truth.

In fact, he had to do the opposite.

"Did she mention to you that I got engaged to Tessa Galloway?"

The other man frowned. "What? You just got here."

Ian shrugged. "Love at first sight, my friend. She's wedding-dress shopping right now. We're hoping you and Grace make the beachfront wedding."

He scowled, slowly lowering his fist. "That don't mean you won't try and get what you can from my wife before you got your own problems."

Not bothering to argue, Ian shook his head. "I like what I have, pal."

Hartgrave snorted. "You like what I have." But the conviction was gone from his voice, and maybe a little bit of the threat. "Remember what I said."

He took a few steps back and turned around to go to his truck, throwing one last glare over his shoulder at Ian, who stayed right where he was until Hartgrave's truck had disappeared, taking any hope of telling Tessa the truth with it.

Chapter Twenty-two

⌒

Tessa's soft gasp as she looked in the mirror was drowned out by Zoe's squeal and Lacey's "Aww" and Jocelyn's slow clap of approval. Ashley watched from the floor of the dressing area, smiling up when she wasn't texting.

"That's so totally it," Zoe announced, fluttering around the dressing stage like a robin over her nest. "That neckline, that bodice, that little row of pearls. Love!"

Tessa took a minute to look down and smooth the cool silk over her hips. The handkerchief hemline rose and fell flirtatiously around her ankles and calves, making it perfect for a beach wedding. The fabric had a shell-pink cast to it, so it didn't scream virginal first-time bride. And the tiny rosebuds along the portrait neckline made her hurt with how perfect they were.

Perfect for Tessa, not Zoe.

"You'd never wear this," she said. "I should have tried on that one with the gold belt and plunging neckline."

Zoe's eyes widened. "Yeah, I loved that dress, but this one is…it's you."

"Precisely," Tessa said, glancing at the others for an assist that was clearly not coming. "I thought this was going to be *your* wedding dress."

"Well, just in case, you should buy it."

Three—no, four—heads nodded in agreement with Zoe.

"You guys! I'm not spending…" She reached down to look at the tag, but of course there wasn't one. She wasn't in a department store; they'd come to an exclusive Naples boutique that reeked of money. "Whatever it costs."

"It's so pretty, Aunt Tess. You could wear it for any fancy thing."

"But you all want me to buy it for a farce of a wedding?"

"What makes you think it's a farce?"

"Lacey!" Tessa choked on her name.

"Seriously, Tess," she continued, getting up from her comfy viewing chaise to approach the stage. "The way he looks at you, the way he talks to you. I mean, did you see the look on his face when you said you'd be trying on dresses? Maybe you can wear it twice—once for the bridal consultants and, again…later."

Why were they all helping to build up her hope?

The next "You guys are nuts" welled up, but somehow the words didn't come out. They weren't completely nuts. He *had* given her the dreamiest smile. And last night, under the stars, they'd kissed for hours and talked more—not about him, but about all kinds of things.

There was no way that guy didn't like her a lot. And vice versa.

She turned back to the mirror, the rush of seeing herself in the dress washing away common sense and reality and questions.

"Buy the dress, baby," Zoe said. "No alterations and it fits like a dream. And you have to have something to wear for the big event."

"Can't I just wear a pretty dress I already own?"

"I'm afraid the consultants won't buy it," Lacey said.

"Ash?" Tessa asked, but she was texting. Finally, Ashley tore her gaze from the screen to look up and, from the glint in her eyes, Tessa knew exactly whose name was on that phone.

"What?" Ashley asked from her residence in la-la land.

"I was hoping for the voice of reason."

"I think if he makes you feel good and you really love him, then go for it."

Tessa narrowed her eyes. "I'm not going to pretend I love him," Tessa said. "But…" She grazed the smooth fabric again. "If I have to pretend to get married…"

They all waited, hanging for the verdict, but she blew out a breath and looked around, as if he might show up at any minute.

"I'm really falling for him," she whispered, so softly Zoe had to step closer to hear her. "I mean, like, whoa and damn, girls, I am *really* falling for him."

Jocelyn joined Zoe, closing in. "And that's a problem, why?"

"Because I still sometimes think—no, I actually know—he's not telling me everything about himself. He even admitted there was more than he was telling, but refused to disclose."

"Give him time," Jocelyn said. "Some men take eons to open up."

"Still," she said. "It scares me."

"Relationships are scary," Lacey said. "You think he's not telling you everything. And I thought Clay was too young and Joss thought Will was too close to her father and Zoe thought Oliver would tie her down."

"He does, occasionally."

On the floor, Ashley giggled. "Aunt Tessa, I think they're trying to tell you that every new guy has problems but, if it's true and lasting and honest, you'll overcome them."

Lacey beamed at her. "Right you are, baby girl."

Ashley smiled back, then gave a knowing and hopeful look to Tessa. "Are you listening?"

"Yes," Tessa assured them. "But this is different. It seems like every time we get close, he shuts down."

"He's a *guy*," Jocelyn said. "They don't see the need to spill their guts. It doesn't mean he's not getting ready to. He obviously really cares about you."

Tessa nodded, then looked in the mirror again as Zoe climbed up on the bride's stage and slipped an arm around her. "He's got a lot of promise, is all we're saying."

She curled her arm around Zoe and, as she pulled her in for a hug, got a nudge from the baby belly. "There is the little matter of how much I want a child."

"Is he opposed completely to the idea?" Zoe asked. "My God, surely he'd offer up some of his liquid gold when he sees you in that dress, if not before." She shot a look at Ashley. "I guess you're old enough to get those jokes now."

"I know what liquid gold is, Aunt Zoe," Ashley said quietly and held up a hand to Lacey. "Don't, Mom."

Lacey shot her a surprised look, but then turned to Tessa. "Honey, I don't care what he says. I saw that man hold Elijah and he *wants* a baby. It was all over his face. He's probably terrified to admit it, but he couldn't hide how taken he was with that child. Give him time, Tess."

Maybe she was right. Maybe they all were. "I'm cautious," Tessa said. "And I don't trust easily. I don't really know if he's marriage material or daddy material or donor material or a good time in the garden."

"In the garden?" Zoe spat. "You did it in the garden?"

Ashley's head shot up, her text forgotten.

"We did not do it," Tessa said. "We talked, really. And kissed."

"That tells you so much about him," Lacey said.

"That he's made of titanium?" Zoe asked.

"That it's real for him," Lacey insisted. "He respects you."

Tessa fought the urge to underscore the point with Ashley, who was facedown in a text, anyway.

The boutique attendant knocked on the dressing-room door and peeked in. "Do we have a winner?"

"Not yet," Ashley said.

"Maybe," Zoe added.

"Working on her," Lacey chimed in.

They all looked at Tessa, waiting for the final answer. "Possibly" hung on her lips to finish the chorus, but then she turned and looked in the mirror and went a little crazy. "I'll take it."

* * *

The last dinner customer left the Casa Blanca restaurant at eleven, so Ian texted Tessa that he'd be at work until well after midnight, too late for a rendezvous dinner like they'd had the past few nights. It was actually well after one by the time he finished the kitchen cleanup.

So he wasn't surprised to see her bungalow shrouded in darkness when he got home. The only thing that surprised him was how disappointed he felt. All he wanted to do was be with her. Kiss her. Make her laugh. Take their constant touching and foreplay one step farther.

Not good, mate. Not good at all.

Swearing softly, he turned off his bike and sat in the circular drive shared by both little houses, staring at her darkened windows. This was probably better.

The more time they spent together—and the hours were adding up—the more he wanted to tell her the truth. Among other things. God, so many other things. He'd touched her, felt her quiver with an orgasm, kissed her breasts, and walked away with a woody the size of Big Ben.

He could feel one growing right now, thinking about her in bed.

Why the hell wasn't he in there with her?

Because of some trumped-up, fucked-up plan to fool her into signing a piece of paper. He'd talked to Henry once more, and although they weren't quite sure how it would unfold yet, he was onboard with the wedding plans. It was possible that Tessa would sign a piece of paper thinking it was part of the act, but, in reality, it would be a legitimate wedding certificate.

Then Henry could get the whole thing annulled when Ian disappeared. Tessa quite possibly wouldn't even know she'd ever been married. The only other plan was to actually convince her to marry him, then claim cold feet and disappear after the wedding.

She'd hate him and be heartbroken, but he'd have Shiloh and Sam and they could start a new life, hopefully while they were so young they wouldn't even remember the old one.

"John? What are you doing out here?" He hadn't even heard the front door open.

In the doorway, she was bathed in moonlight that shimmered over a thin tank top, so silky sheer that he could see right through it. Her long legs were exposed all the way up to the top of her thighs, barely covered in black shorts that looked like a very sexy version of men's boxers.

Holy bloody hell, he wanted her.

"Somehow I imagined you slept in a men's nightshirt."

"Nice to know you think about such things."

"Only constantly."

She leaned her head against the doorjamb, a sleepy sigh carried on the breeze and giving him chills. "I heard your bike, but not your bungalow door."

He liked that she listened so carefully. "Can I come in?"

She swallowed and lifted a narrow, toned shoulder, the skin glistening from recently applied lotion. "It's late."

He climbed off the bike and walked to her door. "I need…" *You.* "A shower."

She lifted a brow in question and pointed one finger toward his bungalow. "You have running water."

"So do you."

She crossed her arms as he reached her, the act pure self-defense. "Not sure I can take the torture."

"Torture?" He got right in front of her, the scent of that body lotion a mix of flowers and fields and female.

"Of having you naked in my shower."

He lowered his face. "You could join me."

She lifted her lips and let him brush hers, the contact electric, the need instant. He opened his mouth and she did the same, letting their tongues tangle in an easy familiarity.

She moaned softly in response, taking one step back into the bungalow. Behind her, a few candles flickered on the table next to two glasses of wine, very soft music coming from a sound system.

"You were waiting for me," he accused, a tease in his voice.

"Maybe."

He stroked from her shoulder over her breast, palming her, thumbing her, instantly getting rewarded by a puckered nipple. "I like that." He ground the words into her mouth, his dick already high and mighty and not giving a shit about why and when and what he was doing.

"I thought you might come over."

He tore his hands from her breasts, placing them on her face to push her hair off and look at how pretty she was. "I might not know too much about these things, but isn't anything after midnight officially considered a booty call?"

She grinned. "Yeah."

"So, is this…?"

She shrugged both shoulders playfully. "Could be."

Before any voice of reason, guilt, or doubt could scream "Stop!" in his head, he kissed her and everything went silent except for the hum in his veins as blood began its journey to the one and only place that didn't listen to reason, guilt, or doubt.

"Tessa," he whispered, inching her back into the house, kicking the door closed behind him. "I can't stop thinking about you."

She responded with an equally hot kiss, pulling him deeper into the bungalow, pressed completely against him.

"Then don't," she said. "I was just thinking about you, as a matter of fact. I was…" She grunted softly into the kiss. "*Thinking really hard.*"

He half laughed, half moaned at the sexy, sexy way she said that, guiding her into the living room. "What were you thinking about?"

"You."

He caressed the silky top, lingering over her sweet little breast.

"That."

Taking the nipple between his thumb and index finger, he gently tweaked, kissing her throat and jaw and ears.

"And that," she said.

"Anything else?" he asked.

"*Everything* else."

Forget the shower. The sofa was closer. "Everything else," he repeated, adding pressure to lay her down. "I better hear about this."

She kissed him as he dropped onto the cushions; all the while he touched her breasts and hips and stomach, the round, feminine curve causing a fire hose of blood and heat and pain to rush to an already stiff cock.

"Oh, I can't tell you exactly what I was thinking about. Too…personal." She wrapped her legs around his, letting him take the most natural place on top of her, their hips already rocking, pulses pounding.

"Were you touching yourself?" he asked, devouring the idea of her making herself come while thinking about him.

"Maybe a little."

Oh, the admission squeezed his balls. He slipped under the satin top to touch air-soft skin, thumbing her budded nipple to make her whole body shudder. "Like this?"

"No," she whispered. "Nothing like this. This is better."

He tweaked her nipple playfully, his erection slamming against his jeans, forcing him to press it against her pelvic bone. He dragged his hand lower, over ribs, toward her hips. "Where else did you touch?"

"Here." She reached between them, sliding her hands down to rub the ridge of his cock. "You know, in my imagination."

His hard-on damn near danced. "Like that?"

She sighed, then slipped her hand behind the button of his jeans, reaching in and closing over his hot shaft. "More like this."

Murmuring and moaning, he closed his eyes and lifted off her enough to let her get the zipper down. He burst out, making them both suck in a shocked breath.

"Oh, it's better than I imagined," she admitted, stroking him slowly from top to bottom.

And better than he'd dreamed. Her fingers squeezed, slipping over the already wet tip, then all the way down, burning from top to bottom, making him throb with the need for even more.

He kissed her hard, his hands traveling everywhere,

his head screaming conflicting orders to stop or go, touch or talk, think or feel, and, oh, man, just *fuck*. The need swallowed him whole, wiping out everything else, raw relief engulfing him because he was finally, finally going to have her.

She stroked again, the ache of pleasure and pain eliciting a low growl from his chest as he buried his face in her neck and let her take him to the damn near edge of an orgasm.

He could come in a blink of an eye. "Again," he murmured. "Do that again."

She did, slow and easy, and again and again until his body threatened to erupt.

His hands shaking, he repositioned himself, giving her more room to fondle him, and letting him slide her little shorts to the side and touch her soft, wet center.

She cried out softly, squeezing him harder and lifting her hips for more.

"Do I touch you in your fantasies, Tess?"

Eyes closed, she nodded, still pumping him, spreading her legs a little more. He twirled the tiny tuft of hair between her legs, then stroked the opening, slipping his finger in and out no more than a centimeter.

She bit her lip, her head going from side to side with pleasure, never missing a beat as she practically pulled an orgasm from him with her hands. He fought it with everything he had, holding back, watching pleasure rock her, sliding his finger deeper into her hot, hot body. Every cell in him was on fire, burning with the need for release.

Finally, she opened her eyes and slowed her touch, each breath a battle.

A mere centimeter and a flimsy piece of satin separated their bodies as he pressed her against the cushions, both of them naked enough to do what both of them desperately wanted. Wet, hot, they connected in every way but the only way they both wanted desperately, their mouths attached with a strangled kiss.

"In me," she pleaded, lifting her hips so it was almost impossible not to go inside her. "I want you."

He pulled back an inch, a sudden, aching realization floating to the front of his hormone-addled brain.

He was going to leave her, damn it. High and dry and completely alone, with no explanation except that—no. No explanation. The cruelest, most despicable act he could imagine. And he was going to do it to her.

So what? Did that mean they couldn't...

He slammed his hands against the sofa, the noise startling her. Eyes wide, she stared at him, both of them fighting for each precious breath.

"John." She barely whispered the name. "Please don't make me beg."

He closed his eyes.

She let out an uncomfortable laugh. "It's so embarrassing when a woman begs."

"You don't have to beg." He leaned down and kissed her. What the fuck kind of excuse could he make if not the truth? Anything else would crush and insult her. He needed something real, honest, or else they could...

"I don't have a condom," he murmured.

She made a little "O" with her mouth, then very slowly shook her head.

"I don't," he said. "Do you?"

She let out a mirthless laugh. "I have a library on the

subject of how to get pregnant. Do you think I stock condoms?"

"Well, for protection against…more than babies."

Taking a slow, deep breath, she pushed him up and off her, fighting to right herself. "John, I don't have casual sex with people I don't know very well."

Of course this didn't surprise him in the least.

"In fact, I don't have sex at all, because you're the first guy I've dated or liked since I got divorced, so, no, I don't have condoms."

He started to answer, but she put her hands over his mouth.

"The truth is, I'd bet you have a box of them in the back of your bike and at least three in your wallet."

That was, mostly, true. Two in his wallet. He didn't answer, and his hesitation made her close her eyes and puff out a breath.

"So you lied to me when you said you didn't have a condom."

Even he didn't have a soul black enough to deny that. He just looked at her.

"Why?" she demanded with a hitch in her voice. "Why lie?"

He still couldn't answer. Anything, any single word he spoke, could only be the truth, and he could not tell her the truth.

"You want me as much as I want you."

"Yes," he said, grabbing something he could hold with two hands. "Every bit as much. Probably more."

"But something is holding you back."

Something like a conscience. When the hell had he developed one of those?

"And I know what it is."

He was quite certain she didn't, but he still didn't answer.

"It's the baby," she said flatly.

He flinched for a second, his guilt-ridden brain thinking she'd said babies, his babies. But, of course, she hadn't.

"See?" she accused. "That's what it is. You know I want a baby."

"I know you want a baby," he repeated slowly, like a witness on the stand dancing around the truth but so determined not to lie under oath.

Even in the candlelight he could see some color fade from her face. "So you think it would be wrong to have sex with me because you think…" She dug around, obviously trying to figure out how his mind worked when, in truth, she was miles and miles and *miles* off base.

The simple truth was that right this minute, he could absolutely see himself having a baby with Tessa. He really could. At the thought, a longing deep and powerful squeezed his chest, shocking the breath right out of him.

He could. Holy hell, *he could fall in love with her*.

What did that mean? Where did that leave them? Both living in a government protection program? Gone from here, from her life and her friends, disappearing into obscurity and lies, like he had to live? No. She didn't have to live that way just because he loved her.

After a long moment of him staring at her, she pushed him all the way off her, sliding her legs out to stand up. "I'm glad you're honest about it."

Honest? He was choking on lies. "I haven't said a word."

"You don't have to." She smoothed her top and straightened the tiny shorts she wore, self-conscious of her sex-inviting outfit. Leaning over to blow out a candle, she held the V-neck to her chest modestly.

With a puff, the room was completely black.

"Good night, John."

From deep, deep inside him, something welled up. Something hot and mad and so damn frustrated. He wanted to howl, to cry, and punch a hole through the wall.

This was *not* how he wanted to live. Tears stung his eyes and every muscle quivered.

With a shaking hand, he reached up and grabbed her arm, pulling her right back down on the sofa with a gasp.

"You don't know anything," he ground out. Even in the dark he could see her eyes widen in shock. "You don't know…*anything*."

He didn't care that she could see his eyes wet with tears. Didn't care that his voice cracked and his body quaked. Let her see how torn up he was inside. Even if she could never know why.

"Then tell me," she whispered, searching his face, touching his cheek in wonder when she saw the moisture. "Tell me anything. Tell me…everything."

"I…" A sob welled up, a sorrowful, pitiful, aching hole of need. He didn't want to make love to her. He wanted her to be part of him, the part that knew every ugly thing about his life and loved him anyway. In spite of his past. *Because* of it.

"You what?" she urged.

"I…want…you." For real. For real. Why couldn't this be real?

Because Luther Vane stole more than his wife and his

life. He stole every chance that Ian had to be normal, happy, and whole again. But Tessa…*Tessa*. She could make him whole.

If she were willing to give up everything.

She held his face very still, clueless as to what he really needed. "Then take me right now and forget about whatever it is that's torturing you so much."

White-hot agony ripped through him. One kiss, that was all it would take. One touch of her lips, one single kiss, and they would melt into each other and find pleasure and release and the ultimate, perfect bliss. For an hour, or two. A night, maybe.

And two weeks from now, he'd fuck her again, in a whole different way.

The need to tell her the truth actually burned in his chest, far hotter and more demanding than anything in the lower half of him. He didn't want to "take" her. He wanted to *tell* her.

He had to. Right now. Right bloody now.

Chapter Twenty-three

The wild, raw pain in John's eyes reached right into Tessa's soul and kind of horrified her. She'd never seen anything so—dark.

"I lied to you." The words came out like burlap through his throat.

"About what?"

He closed his eyes, clearly buying time. Everything knotted—her chest, her stomach, and the blood in her ears seemed to gush like whitewater.

"I've been married."

"Okay." She merely mouthed the word. "And?"

"She died."

Oh. She might have said the word, or just formed the letter, or barely breathed.

She died. The many, many implications of that rocked her, so she grabbed the easiest one. "That must have really hurt you."

"More than you know." He inched back, enough that she got cold and hollow inside. Deep down, the first tendril of a realization started to twine through her, but she was too busy taking in the torture on his face to think too hard about her own.

She backed away, too. Not to mirror his posture, but from the sheer anguish that emanated from him. This was no ordinary tale of loss, she realized with a shudder. Not that there was anything ordinary about death, but this was dark. "What happened?"

He tried to swallow, his moist eyelashes crinkling as he squeezed his eyes shut. "I found her," he rasped. "I found her body."

She let out a low exhale. "No."

He nodded, still struggling for his voice.

"Did she..." Have a heart attack? An accident? Questions ricocheted as she waited for more.

"She was murdered."

Gasping, she put her hand to her mouth, icy chills dancing over her. "How awful."

Another nod, and he slowly moved even farther away, like his body and soul simply had to make distance from her.

And a wisp of a thought started to take shape: *He's not over her. He may never be.*

"How long ago?" she asked.

"Three years." He stabbed his hair, dragging his fingers through it as though counting. "And eight months."

Oh, no. Not over her yet. Not even close. "You still..." *Love her.* "Are healing."

He snorted softly. "There's no healing from something like that, Tess. There's merely existing."

The words kicked her in the gut. "Did they…get the murderer?"

He nodded. "He's in prison."

"Do you want to tell me about it?"

Very slowly, he shook his head, sliding back another few inches. She could practically feel the bricks go into place as he built a wall around himself.

"Why are you telling me if you don't want…help?"

"You can't help," he fired back, the shot actually hurting her.

"You don't know that."

He searched her face again, his eyes red. "I shouldn't have told you," he said quickly. "You'll want to know…" He shook his head as if he were trying to stop himself from talking. "I shouldn't put you in this position."

In what position? "You don't want to talk about it? To a friend? To cry about it and…" *Maybe move on?* "Fix yourself?"

"I'm fine," he said, standing abruptly.

She coughed a laugh, despite the weight of the topic. "I beg to differ."

"She's dead," he said. "And…I'm…"

"Also dead," Tessa whispered, standing as well. Dead to love, dead to possibilities, dead to the chance at a new life. The gardener in her ached to tend him and nurture him back, but something in his eyes told her that wasn't possible. "Until you're ready to talk about it, you'll stay that way."

"I can't talk about it, Tessa." The statement was flat and unequivocal, the complete lack of emotion cutting deeper than when he'd been ragged with feeling. "So don't ask me to."

"Then why did you tell me at all?" And, Good Lord, why had he lied all this time? The question shocked her, both because it hadn't occurred yet and and—well, why?

"Because I can't talk about it."

"So you pretend it never happened?"

He swiped at his hair again, the anguish a little different now. He'd gone from jagged pain to regret in the space of a few minutes. "It's easier that way," he finally said.

"Easier for who?" she demanded, hating the rise in her voice but unable to stop it.

"Just easier." He rounded the table and put still more space between them. "I shouldn't have talked about it. I really shouldn't have."

Definitely regret. But why? She stood speechless, the truth descending like a mid-summer storm cloud.

"You know now," he said, waving his hand like he was absolved, somehow. "You understand."

Was he kidding? She didn't understand anything. Only that he was still in love with someone else. Dead or alive, it didn't matter. He was in love with another woman, and that was the little something he'd been hiding all this time.

He was at the door in a few steps, his hand on the knob, the unspoken good-bye echoing through every dark corner of the room.

"Sorry," he mumbled, letting himself out.

Stunned, she didn't breathe until he was gone. "Yeah," she whispered to the emptiness. "So am I."

She heard the growl of his motorcycle starting up and the whine as it took off into the night.

She was sorry, all right. Sorry and vindicated. Because,

deep inside, she'd known this from the very beginning. Sure, the girls could say it was her silly fear of secrets, and she could rationalize and rationalize along with them, but she'd known deep in her gut that he was holding back something important, something truthful.

From her bedroom she heard the soft digital ding of her phone.

That didn't take long. Of course he had to finish this conversation. Resentful of the hope that bubbled up, she ignored the call, dropping her head into her hands until the sound stopped.

A few minutes later she washed up in the bathroom, and she heard the ringtone again. Turning the water on harder, she tried to drown it out. What was left to say at this hour of the night?

As she climbed into bed the phone rang again, and this time she could see the screen light up on the nightstand.

Catherine Galloway.

Her mother was calling now? At two in the morning? That couldn't be good. She picked up the phone and answered, "Mom?"

A sniff was all she got, making Tessa sit straight up in bed. "Mom, is that you? Are you all right?"

"I…I need to talk to you, Tess."

"Now?"

"I know it's late out there. Did I wake you?"

"Actually, no. What's the matter?"

"She's dead."

For a moment, Tessa thought of John's wife. But of course that wasn't who her mother meant. "Who's dead?"

"Finally, after all these years, she's dead."

Oh. The answer landed on Tessa with a thud. Uncle

Ken's wife. She couldn't even remember the woman's name since "Uncle Ken" never brought his wife with him when he visited their home. Because it was business, her mother would say.

Yeah. Monkey business.

Her mother shuddered another sob. "I wanted her dead for a long time, and now she is."

Tessa cringed, so ashamed that her mother would even have that thought, and, coming on the heels of her conversation with John, the sentiment sounded more than crass. It was downright sinful.

"Well…" Tessa wasn't about to start an argument with her mother now, not with her nerves and emotions laid bare by John. "There you go."

Catherine choked. "You don't understand, Tessa."

"No, I can't say that I do." She curled under the sheet and comforter, wishing like hell she hadn't picked up the phone. "What happened to her?"

"Oh, I don't know. Some cancer of something."

How could she be so cavalier about another woman's life? "How old was she?" Tessa asked, a wave of sympathy for Mrs. Donnelly rolling over her. Far more sympathy for the deceased than for the woman who'd slept with *Mr.* Donnelly for almost twenty years.

"Sixty-something," she said. "Oh, God, it hurts, Tessa."

And not, she knew, because of guilt. Catherine had never felt guilt about the affair; she'd only felt remorse that it had ended with her lover's death.

"It hurts?" Tessa couldn't possibly keep the astonishment out of her voice. "How do you think she felt when her husband dropped dead at forty-eight of a heart attack?" Her husband who kept a mistress and an illegitimate child for sixteen years?

"She felt well taken care of," Catherine said bitterly. "She was never a wife to him. Never the way I…" She had the dignity to let her voice trail off. "She got a couple of million dollars in life insurance and I got nothing."

Possibly because *you weren't his wife*? "You got the business," Tessa said.

She snorted bitterly.

"And you got me."

Silence, then a sigh. "I'm sorry to put this on you, Tess. I know how you feel, but I have no one…" Her voice cracked with a sob. "I have no one. There's never been another man for me."

But he wasn't the man for you, either. *He wasn't your husband.*

But Tessa and her mother had had this fight far too many times for her to start it again now. Catherine Galloway had made her choices: She'd loved another woman's husband and she chose work—and time with that man—over being with her daughter.

And now she was all alone.

"When did she die?" Tessa asked.

"A couple of days ago."

"Why didn't you call then?"

She sniffed again. "I guess I didn't care that much. I hate her, have always hated her. She was his wife, always demanding and whining for more of his time."

She was his wife.

"But the funeral was today, and of course I had to go."

"Of course." Because who doesn't love a hypocrite at a funeral?

"And I've been miserable ever since. I thought I was over him, and everything, but I guess not."

Maybe she did feel guilt but didn't recognize it. "Are you sorry, Mom?"

"Sorry?" she spat the word out. "For the best thing that ever happened to me?"

Tessa's heart twisted for multiple reasons, but mainly because she knew she wasn't the best thing that had ever happened to Catherine—Ken was.

"Of course I'm not sorry. I'm wrecked because the place was so packed you couldn't find a seat." Ugly notes of jealousy darkened her voice. "And the eulogies! My God, you'd think they buried Mother Teresa."

Tessa closed her eyes, dark, old emotions swarming. She despised her mother for the way she'd lived, but now all she really felt was sorrow. Nothing but sadness for this bitter, lonely woman.

Good God, how she didn't want to end up that way.

"She has kids and grandkids and ancient-looking sorority sisters and nephews and nieces and neighbors and a bunch of ladies in red hats all wailing over their precious *Mimi*." She dragged out the two syllables like they tasted foul.

Mimi. For a moment, Tessa silently mourned the woman named Mimi who clearly didn't die alone.

"And of course they had to do some ridiculous video montage of every picture ever taken of the woman. Including her…wedding pictures."

She went silent, crying again.

"I know, I know what you're thinking, Tess," she finally said.

Tessa didn't answer, because she'd made her feel-

ings known in many arguments over the last fifteen
years or so.

"But I loved him!" she insisted. "And he loved me."

"If he really loved you, Mom, he wouldn't have spent
his life married to another woman."

But was John much different? His wife might be dead,
but his love for her sure wasn't. Did Tessa even want to
consider being with a man who clearly still loved another
woman? Look what that had done to her mother.

"I better let you get back to sleep, Tessa."

"'Kay. Feel better. I'm sure it won't look so bad in the
morning."

Would it for her? For John?

"Oh, it won't. I have a trial tomorrow and I intend to
kick some insurance-company butt."

Now that sounded like her mother again, a workaholic
with a purpose. No husband, a distant daughter, and no
friends. But a great *job*.

"What about you? How's the farming going?"

"Fine. I intend to kick some sweet-potato butt tomorrow myself."

Her mother laughed softly, her subtle disapproval of
Tessa's "career" always right under the surface. "Okay,
then. G'night."

When she hung up, Tessa walked to the windows and
stared at John's dark and empty bungalow. He was gone,
of course. Running at the first sign of anything *real*.

She snapped the shutters closed, knowing exactly what
she wanted to do first thing in the morning. Well, second.
First, she'd harvest those damn sweets.

* * *

Ian rode. He fired up his bike, took off for the causeway, barreled onto an interstate, found a deserted highway, and kept going into—nothing. The world got so dark his entire focus was on the single lane lit by his headlight, the night closing in like his meager, unacceptable, regrettable decision to confess.

To confess *nothing*. Just enough to realize he should never have opened his mouth. The minute he started talking, he knew he'd said too much. Why didn't he strip her down and silence every emotion with mindless sex, the way he'd done for three years?

Because he'd made the critical and idiotic error of letting this thing go past *mindless*. He'd made the stupid mistake of letting his feelings override his brain.

He swerved around a pothole, forced to slow down as the road narrowed and rutted. The thick smell of brackish water and wet leaves filled his head, doing nothing to clear the self-loathing in there.

And just like that, the road ended. He broke hard, fishtailing and finally coming to a stop by slamming a boot on the ground and letting it drag. Dead ahead was more nothing.

Where the fuck was he?

Blinking into the yellow beam, he peered at murk and mist and a rotted wooden bridge that went out to nowhere. Everything was black and thick and wet.

Good Christ, he'd driven right to the edge of the Everglades. Without thinking, he glanced down, half expecting a gator to chomp off his foot.

Let it. Some giant jaw could gnaw away the pain and misery, bringing it all to an end.

Hitting the kill switch, he silenced the engine and

doused the light. Crickets and night creatures chirped, leaves rustled, and, somewhere out there, something splashed in the black water. He got off the bike and kicked the stand, shaking off the heat and the ride, walking slowly toward the weathered dock that spilled off the end of the road, leading right into a swamp.

He held his breath when one boot hit the wood, ready to fall right into the muck. But it held, and he walked the thirty or forty feet out to the end, the low platform barely above water level. It must be a launch dock for airboats, the only thing that could move through the thick grass of the Everglades.

A mosquito buzzed by and settled on his neck. Ian didn't bother to swat it. *Have a pint, mate. I'm bleeding all over the place tonight.*

Grabbing the splintered rail, he leaned over to look into the water and long reeds that poked through it, sucking in another breath of humid, hot air, tasting a mouthful of regret.

What was he thinking? Why had he given in to that temptation to talk? Now she knew Kate had been murdered. She even had a time frame. How long would it take her to plow through the Internet until she found a clue, a grainy picture, a death notice…the truth?

And then what? A word to her friends, who whisper to a husband, who mention to a coworker, who—

Trapped.

Ian Browning was as trapped as his wife had been in the kitchen the day Luther Vane burst in with murderous intent. Had she screamed? Had she pleaded for her life? Had she lied about the babies to save their lives?

The sob pulled from his throat, doubling him over

in an old and viciously familiar pain. He gave in to it, clutching his belly, growling with the agony. Then he stood straight, lifted his face to the star-spotted sky, and let out a wail that echoed across the Everglades and woke every stinking alligator for miles.

The howl tore at his throat and rattled his ribs and trembled his eyeballs and did absolutely nothing to heal the pain.

Not like Tessa would have.

The realization made him hurt all over again. He ached for the balm of her touch, the soft understanding of her voice. Her nurturing, gentle spirit was exactly what he needed…and the very reason he couldn't drag her into his mess any more than he already had.

Spent, he let his knees buckle and drop to the dock, hitting it hard. He clutched the rough-hewn wood of the rail, bent over and broken. What was he doing out here? Hiding, of course. Running. Escaping.

Would he still be living like this once he got his kids? To a certain extent, but, somehow, he imagined a brighter life, one filled with laughter and love, tucked away on a village in New Zealand or a farm in Australia. Wherever they sent him, he could start over as a single father.

Without Tessa.

Maybe she'd *want* to go to a farm in New Zealand.

He sat straight up at the thought, so loud and clear he almost thought someone else had said it out loud. Maybe he had said it out loud.

Not that the idea was completely new, but the words hadn't really formed in his head before this, taking shape and somehow becoming real. She'd told him about her life with her ex-husband, traveling from country to country, starting organic farms, and how she wanted to settle down and raise a family in one place.

Could he offer her something like that? Who knew when they'd have to uproot again because the wrong information got out or someone found a link to the past or his loose lips sank their ship?

Could he make her love him…for real? Could he get her *to marry him* for real?

Nothing prepared him for the sensation that rocked him at that thought. He actually fell flat on the wood, knocked over by the very idea of *really* marrying her and how much he wanted that.

Motionless on his back, he stared straight up and let the possibility fill him with something so unfamiliar he almost couldn't put a name on it.

Hope. *Hope*. Like a pinprick of light no bigger than one of the stars above him, he saw a glimmer of hope, of happiness, and a chance to love again.

It was the only answer. Well, that or rolling over and letting the beasts eat him. Forget getting Henry to convince some official to bring a "real" certificate of marriage and somehow fooling her into signing. Forget disappearing into Canada and getting an annulment arranged. Forget breaking her heart and being the scum of the earth to get what he needed.

Of course Henry would have to agree. And Tessa would have to leave her home. But if that happened…

Maybe he was as deep into a fantasy as the muck around this old boat ramp. But he folded the new possibility around his heart, tenderly wrapping his wounds. Then he closed his eyes, and slept right on the dock for hours.

He rose before the sun did, got back on the bike, and

rode to Barefoot Bay. When he stepped inside his dimly lit bungalow, the first thing he heard was a rumble in the distance—the steady growl of a tractor.

At dawn? She couldn't sleep, no doubt. What did that mean? His new plan had a snowball's chance?

Time to find out.

The only thing that really surprised him was how much he wanted to hurry the process. Not because they didn't have much time until the fake wedding that he now wanted to be real. But because of how much he wanted to be *with* her.

He washed his face, brushed his teeth, grabbed a pair of jeans, and stuck his feet into sneakers. He was halfway across the gardens before he even bothered to tie them.

He crossed the garden, following the sound of the tractor to the opposite end of the fields, and stopped to stare at the sight. The sun had yet to cross the horizon, but a yellow glow lit the tips of the palm and oak trees along the eastern border of the property, the morning clouds washed gold and pink. Silhouetted against that backdrop, Tessa rolled along on a small tractor, her back ramrod straight, her hair blowing, a look of strength and invincibility visible on her face even from this distance.

Yes, he wanted to be with her. With her, next to her, in her bed, and in her life. The tableau punched him, stealing his breath for a moment. He tried to take another step but couldn't, captivated by the sight of her, the purity of her spare moves as she looked over her shoulder. Behind her, whatever tool she had attached to the tractor plowed up a wake of churning leaves and dirt.

Inside him, more muscles coiled with desire—and affection. It was like she'd crawled right under his skin and taken up residence there. As if she sensed him there, she turned, and the engine hitched in speed like Ian's pulse.

For a long time they just looked at each other across the field. Then he made his way toward her, over dirt and sprays of bright-green vegetable leaves. When he was a few feet away from the tractor, she gave his bare torso a once-over, shaking her head.

"Damn, dude, you don't play fair."

He resisted the urge to tell her everything he'd decided, because he still had to take this idea one baby step at a time. First, he needed to get back to where they were before he fell apart last night.

"Somebody was plowing at five-thirty in the morning. I'm not awake enough for a shirt."

She studied him, no doubt aware that she'd never heard his bike return. "What is that welt on your cheek?"

He touched the bite. "Mosquito. I crashed outside."

"Are you crazy?"

He nodded. "'Fraid so."

She gestured toward the dirt behind her. "So, you too wiped out to help me? I'm running late and once I get these vines torn up, I need to start getting as many potatoes picked and into the storehouse as possible."

"Late? It's barely sunrise. What are you late for?"

"I need to be somewhere at eight," she said vaguely, then glanced at the sunny sky. "And the potatoes can't be in the hot sun once we cut the vines, so anything I cut has to be harvested and put away in the storehouse. Thus, I'm in a hurry."

"I'll help," he said quickly. "Tell me what to do."

She pointed behind her tractor to the plowed row. "Dig up the sweets. As soon as I finish this I'll help, but if we can get one row done, I'll be happy."

"What about the other two rows?"

She glanced toward them, sighing. "I'll get them eventually."

He reached to her, still not ready to gloss over what had transpired. "Tessa, are you all right? With everything I told you last night—"

"I'm fine," she assured him, frowning. "You're the one I'm worried about."

"I'm better than fine. And I want to talk, okay?"

She considered that for a moment, then shook her head. "Not now. I don't want to get distracted. I've put these sweets off for too long. I've put a lot of things off for too long," she added.

What did that mean? But he took her cue and didn't ask; instead went off to find a faded wood bushel basket and carried it to the end of the plowed row, kneeling down to brush dirt off the hefty yams and toss them into the basket. After a while, he looked up, watching her maneuver her tractor.

Funny how he'd mistakenly thought she was a vulnerable woman. She was strong and independent. She could probably handle anything.

Could she handle a life in the government protection program? Raising children who weren't hers? Leaving her friends, who were her whole family?

Doubts pressed like the sun as it rose. When should he tell her if not now?

When she finished plowing, she got another pile of baskets and started at the other end of the row, too far away to really talk intimately until they met in the middle.

"Ever work on a farm before, John?" she called.

Yeah, in the Cotswolds, at his uncle's farm. He could say that. He could start there. *You know, I used to live in England.*

"Now and again," he said when she glanced up at him because he'd taken so long to answer.

"I love farming," she said, the meaningless small talk suddenly taking on much more meaning.

Would she love farming on the other side of the planet—with him? "I noticed."

"Yeah, much to my lawyer mother's dismay. I wandered into it by accident, but it suits me so well. Have you always been passionate about cooking?"

What was she doing? Making conversation or trying to get him to open up? Either way, she was throwing a door wide open for him to walk through.

"Not always," he said. "I like other things."

She looked up from her work. "Like what?"

Finance, stocks and bonds, business, numbers, spreadsheets, and investments. Damn, he'd been good at it, too. "Played a little football when I was young," he said when too much time had passed.

"What position?"

He opened his mouth to say goalie, but shit. She thought he meant American football. He pictured the field and picked a position. Should he say quarterback? That would be another lie. Should he—

She stood up suddenly. "Never mind, John." She gave him a tight smile. "You can throw those in the storehouse for me and leave the tractor here. I really need to be there when the doors open."

"You're shutting me down, aren't you? You don't want to hear about my…my life, do you?"

She backed away. "Another time, okay? I know you understand."

No, he did *not* understand. He'd finally broken the barrier and was ready to trust her and she was off to some appointment? "I want to tell you."

She shook her head. "I don't want to know, John."

"Why not?"

"Because…because I don't want to get close to your heart and know your past and understand your pain and still not…" She stopped, waving her hand.

"Still not what?" He didn't follow where she was going.

"Don't you get it?"

"Get what?"

"I don't *want* to fall in love with you." She tipped her head good-bye and took off across the field, slipping off her gardening gloves and stuffing them into her back pocket.

"But I want to fall in love with you," he whispered but didn't follow her.

He'd have to show her, not tell her, how he felt.

Chapter Twenty-four

Tessa went straight to Lacey's house after her miserable failure at the clinic that morning, aching to cry on her best friend's shoulder. But there was no room on either shoulder; one had a baby, the other a cell phone.

Lacey nearly melted with relief at the sight of Tessa, handing her the baby and mouthing, "It's Willow from the AABC." Her eyes pleaded for help, underscoring how important the call was. "Oh, we can definitely arrange that," Lacey said into the phone, the voice of efficiency as she walked away, leaving Tessa holding the one thing in the world she wasn't sure she could handle right that minute.

"Hey, shrimp," she whispered to the baby as he gave her a slow, toothless smile. Wait, what was that she spied in his gums? "A pearly white, Elijah?" He grinned, as if proud of the first millimeter of tooth he'd grown.

She squeezed the little body, a rock-solid twenty pounds of chunk and charm. Some drool slipped out of the corner of his mouth, and Tessa wandered into the family room, snagging a hand towel from the top of a basket of folded laundry.

As she dabbed his face, she dropped onto the sofa, trying to snuggle, but Elijah only wanted to stand.

"I gotchya, don't worry," she whispered, letting him lock his wobbly baby legs. Standing firm on her thighs with a death-grip on her thumbs, he let out a soft giggle of joy.

Love and longing and no small amount of unfettered envy ripped through her chest. "Enough of that holding stuff, huh? You're Mr. Independent."

His head bobbled a little, along with one leg, but he got his balance and grinned, one huge dimple making her let out a little moan. She couldn't resist pulling him close and nuzzling his neck to sniff that powdery, precious, sweet smell, and got a little dribble on her face.

Really, there ought to be a law against being forced to hold a five-month-old baby an hour after the lady at the fertility clinic—or the infertility clinic, as the case may be—showed you a list of completely unacceptable surrogate options and announced it could be a year or more until the perfect one came along, so would you like your deposit back?

No, damn it. She wanted a baby, not a repayment of her deposit.

"But your eggs are frozen, so what's the rush?" She imitated Maryann's preternaturally bright and cheery voice, tilting her head from one side to the other. The high pitch made Elijah laugh, and she pulled him close again and kissed his cheek, hating the burn behind her eyes.

"I'm tired of waiting, Elijah," she admitted into his rolls of baby neck fat.

A door slammed, making Elijah startle and Tessa turn to the kitchen to see Ashley come in from the garage, earbuds in, backpack sailing toward the kitchen table with a thud.

"Hey, Ash," Tessa said.

But the music must have been too loud, because she didn't look up but let out a little shudder, wiping her eyes.

"Ashley! Are you crying?"

That got her attention, making her whip out the earbuds and blink in surprise. "What are you doing here, Aunt Tess?"

"I stopped by to talk to your mom." When Ashley glanced around, a flash of guilt in her expression, Tessa stood. "She's in her office. What's going on?"

At the sight of his older sister, Elijah let out a soft cry, squirming to get to her.

Ashley shook her head like she didn't want any part of him, then softened at the second cry, reaching out. "Hey, doughnut hole." She gave a shaky smile to Tessa. "That's my secret name for him. Munchkin is too obvious."

She took the baby in a surprisingly natural move, getting close enough for Tessa to confirm she'd been crying, even though she tried to hide her face in the same folds of baby neck Tessa had been snuggling.

"Want to talk?" Tessa asked.

"No. Yes. Oh, Aunt Tess." She squeezed the baby closer. "I'll cry on my brother's shoulder."

"What is it?" Tessa reached for her, a bunch of possibilities jumping through her mind, but she already knew what Ashley was going to say.

"He broke up with me."

She had to fight not to sigh in relief. "Aw, Ash. I'm sorry."

Looking up from her hiding place behind Elijah's head, Ashley's eyes tapered. "Are you?"

"I'm sorry you're hurt."

She glanced toward the hall. "Is she good and involved on the phone or something?"

"Completely involved." Tessa urged her down to the sofa. "Tell me what happened."

She sat, situating the baby on her lap, stroking his little face tenderly as she considered her words. "He dumped me. By text."

"What a jerk."

"No, it's—"

"He's a jerk," Tessa said. "Don't try and defend a text dump."

That made her smile at the same time her eyes filled. "'Kay. It's shitty."

"Utterly. What did he say?"

She screwed up her face. "The usual. I'm too clingy. He's too busy. We want different things from a relationship. He wants freedom but we can be friends with—" She stopped herself and let her forehead lean against Elijah's, looking him in the eye. "You ever offer that to a girl and I'll kill you, little dude. You are not going to be one of those guys."

"Not with you as such a loving sister," Tessa said. "You'll be fine, Ash. Better."

"I know, I know." She swallowed hard. "I should never have…"

Oh, Tessa hated the unfinished sentences. She wanted to ask, but really didn't have the right. "Regret doesn't get you anything," she said.

"You sound like Aunt Jocelyn," she said. "She's got one of those motivational quotes for everything."

"That's 'cause I'm trying not to say what I'm thinking."

Ashley's jade eyes met hers. "You can. I want you to."

"Okay. You were in deep, Ash, and now you're out."

"But being in deep felt so good, Aunt Tess." She let out a dramatic sigh, as only Ashley could do. "It was so nice to have someone focus on me and nothing else."

"You sure it's over, or is this one of those break-up-four-times-before-it's-really-over things?"

"It's over." She handed the baby to Tessa. "I need to eat chocolate. Or potato chips. Or both at the same time."

Tessa laughed softly. "I think you're going to rebound fast, kiddo."

"Hope so. How about you? How's it going with Chef Hottie?"

"About as well," she admitted glumly, bouncing Elijah as he started to fuss. "I think he…what did you say? He wants different things from a relationship."

Ashley nodded knowingly. "Blows. And you have to pretend to marry him." She crinkled her nose. "*Awk*ward," she sang.

"You have no idea."

"Is that you, Ash?" At the sound of Lacey's voice Elijah let out a little wail, squiggling around to find her.

Ashley squeezed Tessa's arm. "Please, not a word. It doesn't make any difference now and I've learned my lesson, believe me."

Tessa lost the fight to keep Elijah once he locked on his mommy-target. He made a cooey, gooey, gummy sound that gave Lacey a huge smile as she practically ran into the room.

"Did you hear that, Ash? He said 'Mama'!"

Without letting Lacey see, Ashley rolled her eyes. "I think he said nyum-nyum-nyum."

Lacey took the baby, eyes bright. "I just talked to Willow from the AABC and nailed down every detail. They are so excited about the wedding."

Another eye roll from Ashley, but Lacey saw this one. "How was school, honey?"

"Fine." She stood. "I'm starved. What's for dinner?"

"Dinner?" Lacey gave a dry laugh. "Tonight's the first walk-through of Tessa's wedding."

Tessa almost fell back on the sofa. "Already?"

"Oh, God, are you still going to use that thing I wrote, Mom?"

Elijah let out a power scream, slapping his little hands on Lacey's shoulder.

"I gotta feed him," she said, turning toward the bedroom. "C'mon, Tess. Did you want to talk to me about something?"

"It's not important," she said, getting a quick "I told you so" secret glance from Ashley before she rounded the counter and headed to the pantry.

"Are you sure?" Lacey said, picking up the vibe. "'Cause I can chat while I feed him."

Tessa shook her head. She'd had enough maternal envy on the heels of infertility disappointments for one day. "I have to get back and finish my sweet potatoes."

"Well, I'll walk out with you." Lacey stayed close until they reached the door, then she glanced over her shoulder. "What were you talking to Ashley about?"

The opportunity was too good to pass up. "Her F in calculus and how drunk she got last weekend."

Lacey almost fell backwards. "Wha—"

"I'm kidding."

"Why?"

"Because you needed the shock treatment."

She frowned, shaking her head in confusion. "What do you mean?"

She may have promised to stay mum about the boyfriend, but she hadn't promised anything about what had caused that small crisis.

"Your daughter misses you," Tessa said softly. "And we've been friends a long time, so I feel like I have a right to remind you that you have two kids, Lace. One who's been your soul mate for a long, long time."

Lacey paled and her shoulders fell. "I know," she whispered, closing her eyes. "Clay said the same thing to me yesterday. There's so much going on."

"There's a lot going on with her, too. Don't let her fall through the cracks."

"I won't." She leaned in to brush Tessa's cheek. "So you came over for advice and I end up getting it."

"I don't need advice," she said. "I need one of these." She pinched Elijah's little toes. "So anytime you want to pass him off and go shopping with your daughter, you know where to find me."

"Oh, God, Tessa. What would I do without you?"

"Be lost." She smiled and pulled Lacey in for a hug. "As I would be without you."

Stepping back, Tessa took a moment to smile and sigh and face the warm sun. She had to remember that she had a family. Right here in Barefoot Bay—kids, sisters, and all the love she needed.

* * *

Tessa walked through the garden to do a quick visual assessment of the sweet-potato rows before changing into work clothes. She kicked off her low-heeled sandals and went barefoot through the leaf-covered path, longing for company to soothe the tear in her heart left by the trip to the clinic. The conversation with Ashley hadn't really done the trick, and Lacey had been up to her eyeballs with her own issues.

On the way, Tessa peered down to the bungalows, seeing the back door to John's place partially open. *He* wasn't the company she needed right now, that was for sure.

Or was he?

She had decisions to make, and maybe it was time for a reset of *how* she got what she wanted in this life. Would an adoption really take years? Would she still be considered a bad risk after a decade of moving around, like she and Billy had been told they were? What should she do?

Dismay welled up as she scanned the horizon for the tractor, bubbling into confusion as she saw—nothing.

Where was her tractor? It wasn't near the sweet potatoes, where she'd left it when she'd run off. Maybe John had driven it back to the equipment house for her. That was thoughtful.

She worked her way through the mustard and collard greens, vaguely noting that they were ready to be picked, too.

But where was the tractor and where—

She had to blink twice at the sweet-potato rows.

Make that the former sweet-potato rows. Every single

yam was dug up and gone. She spun around, scanning the acres of her garden, her greenhouse, the compost bin, the equipment shed, and the storehouse.

The field looked liked she'd been working there all day and had finished everything on her list. Were the potatoes stored?

She made her way to the storehouse, opening the door slowly, squinting into the room kept dark by design. Bushels and bushels of sweets had been picked, dusted, and stored in neat rows.

Except for the potatoes on the floor. She stepped back and stared at the yams in a circle around the storehouse floor. No, not a circle. That was…

A giant heart.

"Oh." She covered her mouth as his message hit directly where he'd aimed, right at her chest, making it swell with something so far past *affection* and *fondness* and *friendship* and *like* that it could only be…

No, it couldn't be that. They were potatoes, and it was a sweet gesture. But not the honest, real, forever kind of thing she wanted. Most likely, that was not much more than a creative invitation to sex.

As if she needed to have him spell out his request in vegetables. She'd practically—no, she *had*—begged last night.

She stepped back, stamping the sight of that sweet-potato heart into her memory forever. Whatever he was trying to tell her, she wanted to know. Backing out of the storehouse, she closed the door, holding tight to the metal handle as if it could keep her grounded. Once she let go, she might bolt across the gardens right to his bungalow.

"Don't get your hopes up, Tess," she whispered to herself. "It's just a damn heart made of potatoes."

But her hopes soared anyway, and she should thank him. Despite the urge to run, she forced herself to walk across the garden to his bungalow. At his patio deck, she took a steadying breath and went to the open door to knock, her hand frozen mid-air when she heard his voice.

"I don't think you get what I'm telling you, Henry." The words, spoken harshly and in that same oddly British-tinged tone. "This isn't a woman I can fuck with."

She flinched, her hand still poised to knock.

"No, damn it. *No!*" He barked the last word. "I *care* about her." He paused long enough for the statement to settle over her, letting it hit her in the same vulnerable place that the potato message had. "I mean, I really, really care about her."

She let her hand press against her lips. *I really, really care about you, too.*

"Well, I'm sorry, too."

She wasn't. She inched closer, refusing to think about standing and listening as an invasion of privacy. He was talking about *her*. This was the answer to her question. This would tell her exactly what he meant with his unconventional message on the storehouse floor.

"Okay, okay. I understand. I understand. I can wait a little while, but not much longer. I want to tell her. I have to tell her."

Tell me what? She fought the urge to call out the words, leaning closer.

"No, you listen to me for a change. I am going to marry this woman in a matter of days. And when I say those vows and put that ring on her finger, it is not going to be some fake charade that we dreamed up."

What? She clutched the wood of the door frame, closing her eyes, swamped by emotions.

"Well, he better be a genuine official and he sure as hell better have a legit marriage certificate, because this is going to be real."

For however long it took for him to listen to the other person, Tessa didn't breathe. She didn't move or think or feel or reason. She let the words cloak her.

This is going to be—

"I didn't expect to fall in…" A second passed. Then another.

Love. *Love. Say it, John!*

But apparently the person on the other end was talking. Tessa waited, eyes closed, willing the words to come her way.

"Of course that hasn't changed," he said, the sound of his footsteps accompanying the statement as he stepped into the kitchen directly into view.

She had to slam her mouth closed to keep from gasping at the sight of him in nothing but a towel, a droplet of water meandering from shower-soaked hair over one granite-carved shoulder.

"…kids mean everything to me, damn it. *Everything*."

Kids do? Had she heard that right?

"She doesn't know that. How could she? I have to tell her, Henry. I have to, but it's…" His voice grew as tight as the air trapped in her lungs. "I've never wanted to before this. I never thought this could happen."

Before he saw her or heard the soft cry aching to get out of her, she dipped back, away from the door. She didn't hear any more—she didn't have to—because of the blood rushing through her ears, pounding in triple time to match her pulse, the deafening sound of—*happiness*.

Yes, he *was* keeping something from her. How he felt about her.

But he couldn't know that she'd overheard his confession. Something told her he wouldn't like it, and she'd be cheated out of the moment he told her directly.

She darted over the deck and across the space that separated their bungalows, reaching her own back door in two seconds flat, already digging into her pocket for the key. She dropped her shoes, turned the lock, and—

"Tessa!"

Damn it. He'd caught her. All the options bounced through her head: Lie. Play dumb. Act as if she'd just arrived home. Or she could…

Drink in every inch of his incredible body as he followed the same path she'd taken, marching toward her bungalow, undeterred by the fact that he wore only a towel. A towel that could fall with any step.

Her whole body melted a little, a blast of heat and desire holding her perfectly still as she appreciated every muscle, every move…and the fact that it was all part of a man who truly cared for her. And the feeling was mutual.

By the time he reached her, her pulse had accelerated, her breathing was rapid, and her breasts and belly ached with the need to be pressed against him.

"Did you hear that conversation?"

"I…I…" Lying to him was impossible. Why would she even consider it? "Yes, I did."

She could have sworn he paled.

"I mean I heard enough."

"Enough?" There was a low-grade panic in that question. "Enough to…what?"

"Enough to ask one question." She reached out to his face, the rough beard he'd yet to shave after his shower tickling her palm. "Why does this terrify you so much?"

He didn't answer, his eyes rich with that same emotion she'd seen the very first night, the one that darkened his expression from time to time.

"You know what I think?" she finally whispered.

He shook his head.

"I think that you're ready to move on and that scares the life out of you. I think you're petrified that loving someone else means you didn't really love the wife that you lost."

His eyes shuttered with the direct hit. "That's part of it."

"And wanting children is also terrifying to you."

"Tessa, listen to me. Listen really carefully." He took a slow, deep breath. "I really do want children."

She smiled. "I know."

"I want two." He sounded so sure of that number.

Her heart rocketed right into her throat, choking her up. "Oh, John. I'd be lucky to have one," she whispered.

"Two, Tessa." He reached for her, putting his hands on her shoulders, the overpowering smell of clean, fresh soap making her dizzy. Or maybe that was the look in his eyes. Or the impact of his words. Or that wave of hope she'd been riding since she saw the potatoes.

"I don't—"

"You could have two," he said, forcefully, coming closer. "Anything could happen, Tess."

Yes, yes anything could. Intoxicated with optimism

and the power of his certainty and his arms, she closed the space between them, rising up to kiss him.

Anything could happen. *Anything could happen.*

Right then, she believed those three words with her heart, soul, and body. The same heart, soul, and body she was about to give to John Brown.

Chapter Twenty-five

Ian could taste her hope and optimism, as savory as wine and sweet as honey. The flavors fired through him, heating his blood and sharpening his nerves, and jolting his cock into a painful erection.

What she'd heard, what she hadn't, what he'd told her, what he hadn't…it all evaporated from his brain as his hands covered her skin and his mouth inhaled her tongue.

They both wanted this. They needed this. They should have this—at least once before he slammed her with everything Henry warned him not to tell her. But his decision was made.

"Anything could happen," she murmured, melting into him as they made their way down the hall.

"I think it's about to."

She flipped off his towel in the hall as he easily unbuttoned and stripped her blouse right outside the bedroom. He unzipped her skirt, helped her step out of it, and had her at the edge of the bed in nothing but a bra and panties in seconds flat.

She clutched his biceps and squeezed, moaning her appreciation as he reached around to unsnap her bra, his palms itching to close over her delicate breasts and lay her down on the bed.

As he did, she fisted his hard-on, pumping the tip until he let out a helpless groan of pleasure. The sensation was so intense it effectively wiped his brain clean.

Should he tell her first? Should he stop this?

No. He couldn't stop. He didn't have control over this, and right that moment, with her hands all over him and her mouth open and kissing and her sweet, sweet body rising and falling and ready for him, he couldn't stop.

After, he'd tell her after. Sweet pillow talk laced with love.

"Tessa," he sighed her name, a pathetic attempt at conversation that might derail this.

"Don't talk." She stroked him harder, desperate, in tune with his thoughts. "Don't…stop."

And, God help him, he didn't. Instead, he trailed kisses down her body, licking her belly, spreading her legs, making her quiver and rise and clutch the sheets helplessly.

Every inch of her was hot and sticky, sweet and feminine, and irresistible. He kissed her hip, licked her taut belly, and softly blew on the pink flesh he wanted to taste.

She let out a cry, her hands digging into his hair, guiding him right there.

He twirled his tongue over her, taking her to the edge of oblivion but refusing to let her fall. He kissed and nibbled his way back up her belly, tenderly suckling her breasts, then her throat, then her ear.

"Inside," he whispered. "Let me inside."

She spread her legs and took another stroke of his erection, leading him there, then stopping to look at him. "Don't we need…"

He lifted up, sweat stinging his eyes, agony and ecstasy ripping through his pulsing erection. "I'm healthy. I have the doctor's signature to prove it."

"I know and I am, too, but…"

He was expecting so much from her—acceptance, understanding, a new life, a new family—all for him. Couldn't he at least reciprocate? Couldn't he give her the one thing she desired most? "Isn't this what you want, Tessa?"

For a long, long time, she stared at him, a million thoughts and feelings crossing in her golden brown eyes, but not one of them readable to him.

"What I want…" She smiled a little. "Is in my arms right now and just a few minutes ago admitted that he wants our fake wedding to be real." Her voice snagged on the last word. When he didn't answer, her brows drew together. "Did I hear right?"

One word. That was all it would take. One simple word. "Yes."

She smiled into a kiss, pulling him against her, shifting enough that his hard-on was right between her legs.

It would take a single stroke of skin against skin, and he'd be inside her. With no barrier at all.

She closed her eyes, and became very, very still.

Long, agonizing seconds dragged by and neither one of them moved. Her eyes stayed closed and he studied each lash, each freckle, each fresh and clean pore of her skin. He memorized her face, letting it wrap around his heart.

Then he closed his eyes, fully expecting to see another woman in his mind's eye.

But there was only Tessa. Only Tessa. Only pretty Tessa.

He entered her slowly, the move making her eyes open to hold his gaze, and they stayed locked on each other as his body joined with hers. Instinct made him want to plunge and pump, but he held back, the moment too exquisite to surrender to sex yet.

Because this wasn't sex. This was a pure, real connection.

It was good. Perfect, sweet, slow, hot, and…

She started to rock, biting her lip, squeezing her legs around his thighs, letting him fill her up and pump all the way into her. "I like that, John," she whispered. "I like you inside me."

He met her stroke for stroke, finally giving up *exquisite* for raw satisfaction, an explosion of pleasure and pain ripping through him as their bodies slapped together loud enough that he could barely hear the incomprehensible words they both muttered and groaned.

"Now, John, now."

He grew bigger inside her, at the point of no return, completely transported. He let go, squeezing his eyes shut and giving out a guttural groan as he spilled and shuddered and completely released himself in her.

As he stilled, she kept rocking, squeezing, panting, and sliding on his erection, letting it hit her right in the sweetest of sweet spots, making her pulse tighter and tighter, deeper and deeper.

He coaxed her with kisses and whispers until she unraveled under him with a long, sweet, sharp orgasm that left her breathless.

"That's my girl," he cooed into her ear. "That's my pretty Tessa."

Pret-ty. Pret-ty.

Oh, had she noticed his accent? Because in the last few minutes, he'd completely forgotten who he was, who he was supposed to be, and who he might become.

He was…hers.

Holding that one identity that finally felt real and right, he kept her very still until they both could breathe steadily again. Then he tried to find the right words to explain who she'd just made love to. The words didn't come, but sleep did.

"Tess."

"Mmmm." She was dreaming about her crocuses. She'd been digging and digging, so certain she'd failed to grow them, and suddenly she found the bulbs deep in the soil. A man was next to her, urging her to dig deeper, while he smoked a pipe like Sherlock Holmes with the aroma of saffron floating up in the air.

"Tess, honey, wake up."

She opened her eyes to see another man, a gorgeous, sexy, blue-eyed god. Between her legs, she felt sore and sticky and so, so satisfied. She blinked at him. "We fell sound asleep."

"Wore ourselves out." He kissed her cheek. "You okay?"

"I'm fine."

He smiled. "You sure are."

Laughing, she reached for him, sliding her hand over

the lines of the blue dragon tattoo that covered his side and rib. "Why do you have all this ink?"

"Boredom."

"What's that one I saw on your hip?" She reached down there, bumping into his erection. "Wow. Again?"

He smiled. "Later. I want to talk to you first."

Something in his voice brought her completely out of her sleepy haze, making her lift her head. "About that conversation I heard?"

"Yes…I…" He frowned for a minute, blinking like a thought had occurred to him. "Did I bring my phone over here?"

She laughed. "Unless you tucked it in a very tight towel, I don't think so."

He sat up, looking around the floor. "I have to have that phone."

The edge in his voice pushed her up as well. "I think you left it at home."

He pushed the covers back, searching, then climbed out of bed, gloriously naked and powerfully erect.

"Is it that important?" she asked.

He didn't answer, lifting the comforter that had fallen to the floor, then some clothes they'd dropped on the way.

"Want me to call it and see if it rings?" she suggested.

He shook his head. "It won't. The ringer's off."

"Are you expecting a call?"

"Always." He spun around, frowning. "I have to find the phone." He bounded out of the hall, head down.

"Hey, you're naked!"

"Bloody hell," he mumbled, scooping up the towel on the floor and wrapped it around him, pounding on the floor until she heard the kitchen door slam.

Bloody hell.

Something started to thrum in her head. A slow, steady barrage of questions, doubts, confusion, half understanding.

Who *had* he been talking to, and why was that phone so important?

Why *did* he slip into a foreign-sounding accent?

Why *was* he struggling with what to tell her and when?

Because in between his declaration of how he wanted this wedding to be real and how kids meant everything to him, she'd heard him in a clear battle with when and how to tell her—something.

What? And why should it be so difficult?

She tried to drown out the question and wallow in her physical satisfaction instead, but the doubts and new resentments prickled against her heart. She smoothed the sheet over her chest as if she could wipe away the annoying sensation.

But the questions and doubts grew louder, so she wrapped her arms around the pillow and inhaled the light, masculine, soapy scent he'd left behind, wanting to smell all that promise and hope and *anything could happen* he'd left behind.

All she could hear was *That's good...so good...Come, sweet girl, come...Pretty Tessa.*

And *Bloody hell.*

She shook her head. She had to get off this kick. So he'd lived in Singapore and picked up a little accent. That didn't mean he was a liar, a cheater, a—

A soft vibration from the hall stopped her thoughts. She pushed out of bed, ignoring her nakedness to follow the sound of the buzz. She stopped, frowning at the linen closet, zeroing in on the vibration.

Opening the door, she spied a thin silver phone on the floor, a green light flashing. He must have dropped it while he was undressing her and one of them had kicked it under the closet door. As she picked it up, she made a face. Wasn't his phone black? She was sure of it.

It vibrated again, a name flashing.

John Brown.

Oh, he must be calling his own phone to find this one. Her finger hovered over the green Speak button, wondering how she should answer. Something sexy? Something meaningful? Playful and fun? How about all her pulse-pounding unanswered questions?

She tapped the green button and put the phone to her ear, opening her mouth to speak, but she was silenced by a man's voice.

"Ian! Ian, listen to me, mate!" The rich English accent stunned her into silence as she clutched the phone. "We got Darius Vane. We got him, damn it. He's under arrest and N1L is officially closed."

Who was this? What the hell was he talking about?

"Ian, do you hear me? You're free. Get whoever it is you found to marry you as soon as humanly possible and stay tuned for instructions. You're going to Canada, Ian Browning. You're going to get your kids. All you need to do is marry someone. Anyone. It doesn't matter who! So if you haven't spilled your bloody guts yet, don't. Okay? Ian? Ian, are you there?"

Her heart pounded so hard Tessa could barely make out the words in her ear. And even if she could hear and understand, nothing, *nothing,* made sense.

"Ian, is that you?"

She stayed perfectly silent, not even breathing.

"Bloody hell." The man clicked off.

"Bloody hell," she repeated in a breathless whisper, staring at the phone as if it had a life of its own.

What had he said? The words rolled around in her head.

You're going to Canada, Ian Browning.

You're going to get your kids.

All you need to do is marry someone…it doesn't matter who.

Her whole body turned to ice-cold nothingness, so chilled that she barely heard the back door open.

"Tessa?" John stepped into the hall. "Tessa, if you find that phone—"

She held it out. "I did." She put it in his hand, close enough to see his stricken expression. "You got a call."

One eyebrow lifted but he made no effort to speak, no attempt to do the one thing he needed to do: Tell the truth.

Bastard.

She turned, now aware of her nakedness and ashamed. Ashamed to be so stupid. Ashamed to be so trusting. Ashamed to have made love with a man whose *name she didn't even know*.

Ian.

"Tessa, let me—"

Rage and pain and an overdose of humiliation rose in her throat, closing up the passageway and stealing her breath. "There was a message with the call," she managed to say.

Both eyebrows shot up now, pure dread in his eyes.

"Some very excited man who wanted Ian Browning to know they found the vein and the N onc something is closed, and they'll send instructions soon."

His eyes widened. "Are you sure?"

"Yes, and he added that you better get someone to marry you so you can get your kids in Canada."

He looked like he might keel over. "Tessa, I have so much to tell you."

"That's too bad, John. Or should I say Ian? Because I don't want to hear it." She walked into the room, slammed the door, locked it with trembling fingers, and let hot, sticky, miserable tears flow.

She did want to hear it. She wanted to hear it all. But right now, she wanted to wallow in the mud of her own trusting, blind, desperate stupidity.

Anything could happen.

Well, it sure as hell had.

Chapter Twenty-six

⌒

Shit. Shit. Bloody hell and *fuck it all*. Ian stared at the phone for one second, wanting to lash out at Henry for calling, at Tessa for answering, at himself for being a fucking idiot and bringing this phone with him.

But it was useless to blame anyone.

He leaned against the door and listened to her soft crying, the sound drowning out the message she'd delivered. Ironic, wasn't it? All these months he'd waited for the news that they'd shut down the deadly gang that held a price on his head, and he couldn't even take a minute to celebrate what that meant.

Because what that meant now is that he would likely lose the first woman he'd cared about in a long time. He had to tell her now, and not because of the call. The need for silence would never go away, no matter who was behind bars. She couldn't talk to her friends about this. She couldn't talk to anyone.

Except him. Would she ever believe the epiphany he'd

had last night, and how he truly wanted her for real? How he'd planned to tell her everything tonight and ask her to leave this life and join him?

She'd never believe him now. She'd never believe another word he said. But he had to make her believe this was still a matter of life and death.

He tried the door, but it was locked, so he slid down the wall and sat on the floor.

"Go away," she called from behind the door.

"Not going to happen."

"I don't want to talk to you." She hiccupped on the last word, gutting him. *Nice going, mate.* Way to fuck up the woman's life.

"Well, you're going to talk to me. Through a door or face-to-face. I have to talk to you and I have to make you understand something."

"I understand enough."

"I'm afraid you don't."

"I understand that everything you've ever said to me has been a lie." He could hear her grind out the words through clenched teeth. "I understand that whoever or whatever you are, you don't trust me enough to tell me the truth."

"It's not that I don't—"

"And I understand that you need to marry someone—anyone, I believe was the way he said it—so that you can get *your kids in Canada*." She said the last three words like they were so utterly agonizing that she couldn't even let them out of her mouth.

He didn't answer.

"Do I understand enough?"

Actually, she did. "But you don't know why."

She let out a soft moan, as if she'd been hoping all that she'd heard was a misunderstanding.

"Okay, why?"

He watched the doorknob, hoping it would move. No such luck.

"I can't tell you why until I elicit a promise from you."

Silence.

"You can't tell anyone."

"Oh no, you don't!" She was close to the door now, inches away. "Don't you dare tell me I can or cannot do anything."

He closed his eyes and bowed his head in resignation, exhaling before speaking. "Tess, unless you want me, two innocent children, and possibly yourself to end up dead, you have to make and keep that promise."

After a long pause, the knob turned. Inch by inch, the door opened, revealing her swollen eyes and blotchy face and a ragged robe around her. She looked down at him, and very slowly dropped to the floor to meet him face-to-face.

"Dead?" She barely whispered the question, her lips quivering as she spoke.

"Dead."

"Has everything been a lie?"

Pain twisted his throat. "Not everything," he said. "I've said plenty that was honest." He reached for her splotchy face. "Starting with…how pretty you are."

She jerked away, spearing him with a look.

"And how much I like you."

One eyebrow rose slightly, pure doubt and disgust in her expression.

"And nothing that happened in that bedroom a few hours ago was a lie."

"Sex?" she spat. "You're going to talk about sex now?" She narrowed her eyes and leaned one inch closer. "Don't…*Ian*."

He sniffed a quick breath of shock, the name sounding so strange coming from anyone but Henry. No one had called him Ian for years. It felt—*so good*.

"I'm going to tell you everything."

She still looked hard at him, her bottle-brown eyes sparking with distrust. "Your version of everything."

"The only version of everything," he said simply. "The whole truth. But I do have to make the stipulation of complete secrecy."

She merely stared at him.

"You can't breathe a word of this to anyone," he insisted. "I mean anyone, Tessa. It is truly a matter of life and death."

Her expression softened. "Are you a spy?"

"Not James Bond, I hate to break it to you."

"Then what…who are you?"

He reached for her hand, but she pulled it back, pressing her fists to her chest protectively. "Answer me," she insisted softly.

He turned away for a second, looking down at the phone that had betrayed him. No, he was grateful Henry had called. He'd wanted to tell her, and he considered starting his story with that truth, but she'd never believe him.

"John, or…" She sighed. "*Whatever.* Please. What is your real name?"

Once more, he gave her a pleading look. "You can't tell Lacey or Zoe or Jocelyn."

"I can't make that promise and you"—she pointed in

his face—"are in no position to ask me to do anything except listen. And I may or may not do that."

He ignored the threat, too focused on what he had to hear her say. "You have to promise me, Tessa. I won't tell you until you do."

"I can't keep a secret from my friends."

"You can't? Two words: your mother."

Her eyes widened at the shot. "You're going to throw things that I shared back in my face, John? *Now?*"

"I'm going to make you understand, which you will when I tell you, that you must give me your word of honor that you will not, under any circumstances, share this with another person. When you know everything, you'll—"

"Everything like your name, country of origin, job, or…or…" Her eyes misted. "Or why in God's name you'd want me to marry you?"

"Because—"

"I'm the first person you found and you needed someone to marry you, quick."

"Yes," he said quietly. "At first, that was my thinking. But everything changed."

"When?"

"Last night."

She coughed a sharp laugh. "Convenient."

He reached for her. "Tessa, make the promise."

She didn't say a word or stop staring at him, hurt and distrust darkening her eyes.

"If you don't," he whispered, "the lives of my two children are at stake. They're only three-and-a-half years old."

"Two," she murmured. "That's what you meant when

you said you wanted two. And you didn't say 'kids' were important, you said *your* kids were important."

He swallowed and nodded. "They are. They're everything to me. And if I ever want to see them again and raise them myself, it seems I need a wife."

Nothing had prepared her for this. Not the bizarre statement of fact, which was both incomprehensible and far too clear, but the look on his face. That was the look she'd been seeing, thinking she'd imagined it. An anguish so profound and real it physically hurt to look at it.

Defeat crushed Tessa like a landslide, burying all her fury and regret and heartache, suffocating her desire to run and tell *everyone* exactly what she'd learned today.

"All right," she managed to say. "I promise."

"You won't tell your friends."

"I will not tell my friends."

He studied her hard, gauging her promise, still wary enough that she knew he hadn't quite accepted it. So she reached out a hand and closed it over his. "I give you my word."

He nodded, satisfied. Then took a shallow inhale and said, "My name is Ian Browning." Then he held up a hand as if to correct that. "My name is Ian Browning," he repeated, this time with a thick, soft English accent.

"From…"

"London. But I haven't lived there, or spoken with my native accent, for years, so I'll stick to what you're familiar with." He hesitated again.

"What are you doing here?" Besides stealing hearts and sanity, she almost added, but there was no room for humor in this quiet hallway. Only honesty.

"I'm in the United Kingdom's version of your witness protection program."

She felt her jaw loosen. "Why?"

"I witnessed a murder. Well, I witnessed the murderer leaving the scene of the crime and identified him, leading to his imprisonment. Ever since then, one of the deadliest, most feared gangs in London, known as the N1L—which stands for No One Lives, if you're curious—has had a hefty price on my head."

Her own head swam, still trying to process this. "And your kids?"

"They're twins, Shiloh and Samuel. Only…they're called Emma and Edward now."

She heard a small intake of breath, only a little surprised that it was her own. He had twins. Her heart did a slow tumble around her chest.

"They're in their own government protection program."

"They saw the murderer, too?"

He shook his head, that cloud cover of agony crossing over his eyes again, leaving him too choked up to answer. "They were in the next room. In their cribs."

Oh, Lord. "And the victim was…your wife?"

"Yes. And her brother."

Tessa put her hand to her mouth, a whimper escaping. "I'm sorry."

"She was stabbed ten times"—he fought not to cry—"and left on the kitchen floor, where I found her, next to her brother, who was the target of the hit."

Both hands to her mouth now, Tessa bit back her own sob. "Oh, no."

It took a moment, but he got his composure, still not looking at her but down at the floor, blowing out slow breaths to keep from losing it.

"The twins," he finally said, "were left alone, thank God. I found them…" He tried so hard to talk, but tears and a closed throat prevented it. "They were not yet six months old."

She let out a soft cry, losing the fight not to let a tear fall. "Why don't you have them?"

"Too easy to find a man living alone with twin children. The government insisted on sending them to…" He shuddered again.

"Canada," she whispered, hearing the word in her head from the phone call.

"They're in Ottawa," he confirmed.

"How long since you've seen them?"

"They were taken two months after my wife was killed."

Everything inside her melted and collapsed with grief for him. "Oh…Ian."

"No." He shook his head sharply. "Don't call me that. Don't let it slip."

"But I thought that man on the phone said…" She tried to piece together exactly what she'd heard. "You can go get them now, right?"

"I don't know. I haven't called him back." He glanced at the phone he'd set on the floor next to him. "Did he know he wasn't talking to me?"

"No, I didn't say anything when the phone rang. It had your name on the ID and I figured you were trying to track the phone down, so I touched the keypad and he started talking. Who is he?"

"Henry Brooker is my government liaison, one of the few people on earth who know who I am and where I am."

This new fact warred for space with all the others, leaving a mess of more questions in her mind. "Where does everyone else think you are? Your family and friends?"

"Dead. I disappeared to Singapore when the kids went to Canada. I lived there under the name Sean Bern. But I got into some trouble and got thrown in jail. The word got out where and who I was." He gave her a harsh look. "I tell you, it's virtually impossible to stay invisible in this world. So, the powers that be at UK Protected Persons pulled some pretty tight strings and Sean Bern was 'killed' in a car accident, hopefully convincing the London gang that their target was now dead."

The words sent another shudder through her and almost—*almost*—explained everything. Every lie. Every evasive answer. Every...

Oh, God, how could she forgive all those lies? How could she have been so trusting and naive and—

"Don't." He put his hand on her arm. "I can see what's going through your mind. Don't blame yourself."

"I don't, but..." She seized a hopeful thought. "He said they're shut down. So it's all over now, right?"

"Not exactly. The thing is this, Tessa: Even if every single member of that gang is caught and put behind bars, I can never, ever take the chance of coming out as Ian Browning or John Brown as long as the leaders are alive. They'll let me have my children, though—maybe. I'll have to go through some pretty tough hoops after three years; the kids have lives now. But, if I get them, I have to…" He tilted his head in apology. "I have to go somewhere and start all over again. Here, people know me and John Brown exists as a single man. But Henry thinks in a place like New Zealand—"

"New Zealand?"

He nodded. "I'd go to the moon to be with them," he said softly.

She drew back, the power of his honesty like a physical force. This had all been for the love of children. She didn't like it, didn't want to accept it, but surely she understood that love. If not, then she was nothing but a hypocrite.

After a second, he gestured to the phone with a soft, ironic snort. "I've been waiting for that call for years, and, what do you know? I miss it."

"But it came, nonetheless."

He nodded. "I'm glad it did. Now I can fully explain to you that one of the hoops of fire I have to go through is to prove I'm in a completely stable situation, and that means I have a wife."

At first that sounded preposterous, then she remembered the adoption hoops she and Billy had researched. So that was why he wanted the pretend marriage. "And that's why you were going to try and convince me to marry you for real."

"It's more complicated than that. At first, the plan was to have you sign a document that would be legitimate, at least that's what Henry wanted to do. But then I decided, I wanted…"

"…the wedding to be real. I heard you say that." She tamped down the disappointment that came with the fact that what she'd heard and what he'd meant were two different things. "How were you going to do that?"

He reached for her. "I really *do* want it to be real."

What did that mean? That he wanted to marry her or that he wanted to tell her the truth or…What did it matter? Tessa had fallen for it. She glanced behind her toward the bed, still tussled from their bodies, from a woman so willing to believe that anything could happen.

Humiliation burned in her chest, rising up, making her dizzy.

"Hey." He took her chin and forced her to look at him. "I'd have told you if there was any possible way. I swear that's true. I wouldn't ever want to risk anyone else's life, let alone mine or the kids'."

She tried to turn but it was too late. He saw the tears. "I'm sorry, Tess."

"There's nothing to be sorry for," she said, her voice gruff.

But he gave her a look that said he wasn't quite that dumb. "You saw right through me."

"Not exactly, but I knew you were hiding something."

"How did you know that?"

Reaching to his face, she touched his skin, shameless in how much she still loved the feel of it. "I hate to tell you, but your eyes are a dead giveaway. They have so much pain sometimes."

He closed them, as if he could hide that pain. "I was very happy with Kate before the…before."

Another sting hit her chest. *Kate.*

"I was content," he continued, unaware that she felt anything, as he should be when he was the one confessing his personal hell.

"I can't imagine how horrible that must have been," she said.

He barely nodded. "As horrible as it is to find the woman you love murdered, the fact that they took Shi and Sam away from me is worse." He hissed in a breath, more angry than hurt. "I've completely missed their first three years. Just…gone. I'll never get them back. First steps, first words, first…everything."

"But now you can get them," she said, her head throbbing a little as she imagined how much worse it would be to have the child and lose it—two of them!—than never to have had one at all. "You have to get them, John."

He looked at her, expectation and a question in his eyes.

"You guys!"

They both whipped around to find Zoe standing in the hall entrance, hands on hips, scowl on her face. "The ceremony rehearsal started fifteen minutes ago. Everyone is on the beach waiting for you two."

They both stared at her, equally stunned by the intrusion.

Zoe's gaze slid over Tessa in her robe and John's shirtless chest, then behind both of them to the bedroom. She fought a smile and rolled her eyes. "I suppose it would be sheer hypocrisy for a pregnant and engaged woman to remind you that you're supposed to have the honeymoon after the wedding."

John started to slowly push up. "We were talking."

Zoe snorted softly. "Well, you better shut up and get down to the beach."

"I know the rehearsal started," Tessa said, holding up a hand. "But we—"

"No buts, baby, because we even got the mayor here for the walk-through and he won't stay long." Zoe marched closer, as if she planned to yank them both into action. Instead she snapped her fingers like a drill sergeant. "Dress, you two. Stat." She looked from one to the other, maybe taking in Tessa's tear stains. John looked pretty ravaged, too.

"Um, if you can't come to the rehearsal," she said slowly, "I can stand in for you."

"Give us a few minutes," John said.

Zoe nodded and left.

When they were alone, John stood and reached his hand down to Tessa. "You don't have to do this, Tess," he said.

"I have to go through with a wedding for the consultants who are visiting," she said, letting him pull her up. "I promised Lacey."

"But it doesn't have to be a real wedding."

She wished she knew the answer, but she didn't.

"I'll meet you down there," she said softly, going into her room and closing the door.

Alone, she leaned back against the cool wood and searched her heart for the answer. Should she marry a man under false pretenses to help him have the very thing she couldn't have? A family? A man who'd planned to annul the wedding and disappear to New Zealand under a different name?

What kind of woman would that make her?

Stupid? Crazy? Desperate?

No, it would make her sleep better at night. Alone, but better.

Chapter Twenty-seven

The chaos on the beach matched the turmoil in Tessa's heart. Only with more players, noise, and a postcard-worthy sunset. All over the sands of Barefoot Bay, resort staff zipped around, shouting questions and walking off space for seats and makeshift aisles on the sand. In the midst, Lacey had a clipboard in one hand, a phone to her ear, and about five conversations going at once. Jocelyn had rallied the spa staff as stand-in guests who milled about, and Zoe had marked off an area where a pilot would launch a hot-air-balloon ride for the bride and groom.

Tessa scanned the scene, looking for one man in the crowd, and found him almost instantly. John stood at the water's edge, deep in conversation with Mayor Lennox, both of them barefoot like everyone else. In the span of a heartbeat, he found her, too, holding her gaze despite the people and space between them.

John...whose name was Ian Browning. Who hid his

life and still managed to melt her heart right down to her toes. Who—

"Have you been crying?" Jocelyn cut into Tessa's view and pitiful thoughts.

"Out in the garden too long?" Lacey was on the other side in a flash, clipboard abandoned for a close inspection.

"She's been busy breaking test tubes." Zoe's hands landed on Tessa's shoulders with an affectionate squeeze. "And testing the real deal for a change."

Tessa dipped out of her touch. "I'm fine, and Zoe has an overactive imagination."

Zoe held out a hand. "Hah. You owe me twenty bucks."

Tessa slapped it. "Let's get this thing over with. I've got a lot to do."

"Sounds like it," Jocelyn teased.

Tessa looked down at her toes curling into the sand. "Please stop."

Instantly, the humor evaporated, replaced by three concerned faces, the genuine look of love filling Tessa's already tender heart.

How could she *not* tell them? The secret about her mother gave her enough guilt, and now this? But she'd promised, and that was enough for her.

"This isn't easy," Tessa finally said, letting *this* cover a multitude of possibilities.

"Oh, hon." Lacey immediately went into mama nurturer mode, reaching out to Tessa. "You don't have to do this." She gestured toward the crowd and the mayor—and the man.

Didn't she? If she didn't marry John—for real—then he couldn't get his kids.

"I can stand in for you," Jocelyn said. "If you want to go back and regroup."

Behind Jocelyn, Tessa could see John's silhouette moving in her direction, his large, muscular form outlined against the setting sun. "I don't want to regroup," she said. "I only want…" *To figure this out.*

John came up to the group, instantly stealing the light and air and any sensible answers. He looked worried enough that Tessa knew he thought she might be spilling his secrets right then and there.

Her chest tightened at the thought. She'd never betray him, but he didn't know that. She'd have to prove it to him somehow.

He reached out a hand to Tessa. "I've been talking to Mayor Lennox, Tess. Have you met him?"

The other women stepped aside, making room for him to take Tessa's hand.

"Oh, wait," Lacey said, lifting a paper on her clipboard. "I have the vows."

"Vows?" Tessa asked.

"It is a wedding rehearsal," Lacey answered. "I've tried to think of everything, but God knows, I'm not a wedding planner." She produced two index cards with handwriting. "Ashley wrote them."

"Ashley?" Tessa practically choked.

"I know, right?" Lacey grinned. "She had to do it for her psych class. They're really nice thoughts. You'd think the girl understood a thing or two about love."

Or what she thought was love. So maybe Ashley's vows were perfect—pretend vows for pretend love in a pretend marriage for all the wrong reasons.

"C'mon, Tess," John said. "We can practice while they iron all this out."

He closed his fingers around her hand, warm and secure, tugging her away from her friends. Was that because he wanted her to himself or away from the temptation to tell?

"Watch your step," he said as they reached a small reef of shells left from the last high tide. She was looking down to avoid any broken edges when she spied a brown-and-white spiral tip jutting up. Habit and hope made her bend down to check it out.

The instant she touched the shell, she knew. "A junonia," she whispered, an actual thrill shooting through her.

"You found one?" John asked, coming closer. "Let me see."

She brushed the sand off the smooth shell with a little cry. "It's perfect," she exclaimed. "A perfect, unchipped junonia." She ran her finger over the flawless spindled edge, finally tearing her eyes from the prize to look at him, holding it up proudly. "Behold, the mother of all shells."

Literally.

"You found one," he said, his whole face lit like hers must have been. "Congratulations."

"To both of you!" Mayor Lennox sidled up next to them. "I know there's a lot to rehearse, but I'm afraid I've got a town council meeting in less than half an hour. Can we do our run-through right now?"

"Of course," John said, putting his arm on Tessa's shoulder and leaning close. "You hold on to that shell for luck, okay?"

But it wasn't for luck. It was for dreams. Her dreams. The dream.

The junonia wasn't a symbol of her dreams coming true. It was…meaningless. Just like this marriage.

"It's only...a shell." Holding the shell loosely, she walked with the two men to the very edge of the foamy Gulf water.

There, Mayor Lennox held up his hand. "Okay, dearly beloved, blah blah blah. I'll read some stuff, ask you a few questions, and then you'll say those vows. John, you'll go first."

"Okay." He held up the card. "My dearest Tes—"

"You don't have to read them now," she said.

"But I want to." He looked at the mayor. "Indulge me, will you?"

Mayor Lennox angled his head as if it say "Whatever," and John turned right to Tessa, taking one of her hands. Behind them, everyone quieted.

John cleared his throat and Tessa looked down at their joined hands, her gaze locked on the shell that she'd once thought would be a sign she would have a baby.

"My dearest Tessa," he said again. "I stand before you a simple man with a simple need."

Not so simple, it seemed.

"I need you."

"Awww." That was Zoe, of course.

"I *need* you," he said again, softer this time, forcing her to look up.

And there was the agony in his eyes one more time. The look of a man who knew pain so deep and indescribable that it had etched misery on his heart.

All he wanted was his children. Yes, she was hurt and mad and embarrassed. Worse yet, she was still feeling things for him that would probably make her more hurt and mad and embarrassed when this all ended.

As it would have to.

"And I promise—"

She held up her hand to his lips. "No."

"No?" His eyes flashed deep, dark, and afraid.

All he wanted was his children. If she didn't understand that, then who did? "No…you don't have to do this now. Let's save it, John." She touched his face, vaguely aware of the shell in her palm. "Save it for the real wedding. The *real* one."

She felt the breath from his sigh of relief. "The real one," he repeated. Reaching out, he pulled her into his arms and squeezed, his heart pounding so fast and furious she could feel it through his muscles. His heart that deserved to be healed.

She wrapped her arms around him, heard the ooohs and ahhs of the crowd, and laid her head on his chest.

"Thank you, Tessa," he whispered into her ear.

Behind him, she opened her hand and let the shell fall to the sand, knowing the next wave would wash it away.

That was fine. Someone else would find it. Someone should have their dreams come true. It just wasn't going to be her.

Ian paced his little bungalow long after dark, something he couldn't name gnawing at his gut and doing a damn good job of devouring him. Urges ravaged, and he tried—and failed—to walk them off.

He wanted to march over to Tessa's place and…no, she wouldn't want that.

So maybe he should jump on his bike and ride, but that would merely be running from his problems.

And, of course, there was always the bottom of a bottle of booze. But he hadn't had more than a glass or two of wine in weeks, and not even scotch held its usual appeal.

He wandered into his kitchen, restless, one eye out the window, and caught the glimmer of a flashlight being carried through the garden. It was all he needed to see. He stepped out to his patio, checked Tessa's very dark bungalow, then followed the light, staying a good distance behind.

It only took a few minutes to confirm that he was following Tessa, who moved like a ghost through the garden in a long, sheer dress that might have been a nightgown or a swimsuit cover-up.

Where was she going? To work in the garden? Not at two in the morning. To sit alone and cry? His chest squeezed at the thought of her shedding one more tear. Maybe to Lacey's house for some girl talk? Some *honest* girl talk.

He wiped that possibility out of his head. She'd given him her word that she wouldn't tell anyone his story, and that was good enough for him. At the edge of the Rockrose property, she turned and headed toward the beach. He followed, part of him curious, another part wanting to protect her in the dark.

But the biggest part wanted to be with her. The need ate at him, forcing him to slow his step and keep from running, calling, tackling, and kissing her until she couldn't breathe.

No such need seemed to consume Tessa, who walked slowly along the beach, staying away from the water, flashlight pointed down, bending over occasionally.

She was shell hunting. Hadn't she found her prize hours ago?

When she stopped and crouched down for a minute, he nearly caught up with her. The beach was black and bleak, and he needed to call her name so he didn't scare the life out of her. But he took the time to watch her shadow, his mind whirring with possibilities.

He'd never told her about the epiphany he'd had in the Everglades. Because it seemed so wrong now to think she'd ever leave for him. After the way she'd discovered the truth, she probably wouldn't believe him if he…

Her shoulders shook with a sob. Bloody hell, she was crying. "Tessa!"

She spun so fast she toppled right onto her backside with a soft gasp.

"I didn't mean to scare you," he said, slowing as he came closer.

"What are you doing out here?"

"I followed you," he admitted. Good God, honesty felt great. That was what had ahold of him. Not only the need to be with her, but the chance to finally be honest about everything with her.

"Why?"

He didn't answer right away, closing the space and slowly dropping down next to her. "I thought you found your special shell today."

"I threw it in the water."

He drew back. "Why?"

"Because I'm dumb. And now I'm trying to find it again, since the tide's come and gone."

"Why did you throw it in the water, Tess?"

"Because it…" She swiped her eyes and pushed her

hair back, revealing her whole face in the ambient beam of the flashlight. "You want the truth?"

He laughed softly. "Honey, from this moment on, the truth is all we want. Can we make that one promise? Nothing but the truth, on any subject, with no wavering. Deal?"

She nodded. "I threw it away because it was a lie."

He frowned, shaking his head. "How can a shell be a lie?"

"The dream it represented," she said. "The fantasy, the possibility, the stupid game I'd played all these months telling myself if I found the right shell, then everything I've ever wanted would fall into my arms and I would be happy forever and ever, amen." She gave a bitter laugh. "I was holding on to a lie."

"So, why are you out here looking for it now?"

"'Cause I still want to find one, but now I want it for the right reasons."

"To get your picture in the paper?"

She smiled. "You really do listen to me."

"Every word." He reached his hand to hers, but she gave him a wary look, and then put the flashlight in his open palm. "What are the right reasons?"

"Because…it's rare. It's special. It's like…love."

"And that doesn't represent your dreams anymore, Tess?" He could barely stand to ask the question, because if he'd stolen that hope from her, he'd never forgive himself.

She pushed up and shook sand from the gauzy dress. "In case I'm wrong and it does represent dreams."

"So you still have hope."

"Eternally. Flash the light on that ridge, please."

He did, watching her for a moment, then saw the tide-driven crest of about a zillion shells. "How can you find anything in all those broken shells?"

"Takes a keen eye," she told him.

They walked for a while in silence, stopping now and again when she saw something that caught her eye. Finally, he asked, "Why were you crying?"

"Frustration. Confusion. Longing."

He knew them all so well. "About this situation?" he asked, even though he knew the answer.

She paused from her searching, clearly struggling with an answer. "Not exactly."

No? "Hey." He tipped her chin and forced her face toward his. "We made a deal about the truth."

"Speak in your regular accent," she answered softly.

The request threw him. "Excuse me?"

"In English."

"You mean British."

"Whatever. I want to hear it."

"I'm so trained not to, I don't think I can."

She wasn't buying it, narrowing her eyes at him. "You didn't have any problem when you were talking to Henry."

"Okay." He glanced around as if someone might be lurking in the shadows or surf. "What do you want me to say?" He still didn't break into British.

"My name."

He nodded. "Tessa Galloway."

"Sounds almost the same." She seemed disappointed.

He took a slow breath. "Don't be sad, pretty Tessa." He infused the words with the clipped sound of his native accent, reaching to slide his hand around her neck and into her hair. "I will never, ever lie to you again."

"Nevah, evah?" she repeated with a slow smile.

"Nevah." He exaggerated the sound, then his own smile faltered as he looked at her. "Oh, Tess." He closed his eyes and pulled her closer. "I'm sorry. I'm so, so sorry."

She relaxed a little, letting their bodies touch in a move that felt orchestrated by mother nature. Like they belonged together. "I know you are."

"Do you?" he asked. "Do you know how very sorry I am? How much I care about you? God, *I* didn't even know how much I cared about you."

"Mmm." She wrapped an arm around his waist and laid her head against his shoulder. "I like that."

"How much I care about you?"

"No, that sexy accent."

He chuckled into her hair. "Then I'll whisper it in your ear all night." Tipping her face up, he kissed her forehead, her nose, then brushed her lips. "Do you forgive me, Tessa?"

"God, no. But you can keep talking like that and you have a chance."

Warmed by the humor, he clicked off the flashlight and let the dark descend over them. "Let's walk in the water," he said, guiding her to the surf. "Unless you don't want your dress to get wet."

"I don't care. It's made for the beach."

Like her, he was barefoot, and he doubted they'd go in deep enough to get his cargo shorts wet. Arm in arm, they walked toward the swells and foam of low tide, the sand cool between Ian's toes, the first knots of his restlessness starting to untangle in his gut.

"I talked to Henry," he finally said.

"And?"

"He's pissed but not much he can do. I assured him you were trustworthy and he seemed satisfied enough when I told him…" He hesitated as they reached the water, letting the first splash of cold chill his nerves about how to phrase the rest of his sentence. "You'd agreed to sign the paperwork."

She didn't answer immediately, using one hand to lift her dress from the next wave. "Sounds so romantic when you put it that way."

"I guess because it's not romantic." But it could be. If only…

"I know, you're right. I'm still not sure how I'm going to handle things."

"*Things*." He dragged the word out. "We're not lying anymore, Tessa, so—"

"*I* never lied," she shot back, almost slipping out of his arm, but he held on too tight. "And I'm not lying or using euphemisms now." She stopped fighting his hold and pressed against his side again. "There are a lot of things to consider. Like…" She swallowed and looked up at him. "What happens when you leave?"

Nothing. Everything. The end. "I can't contact you after that. We'll have to work out something to tell people."

She considered that. "If you mean my friends and all the people who work here, there's nothing to tell. They think I'm doing a pretend ceremony for the benefit of the wedding planners. Mayor Lennox doesn't know that; we'll get a real marriage license to sign and then you'll take it…" She blew out a breath and shook her head. "Where will you be?"

"I don't know. And you can't either…" *Unless you*

come with me. He tamped down the plea. "It might be embarrassing with your friends, Tessa, if I disappear."

"Don't worry, I'm not going to tell them the truth."

He slowed his step and turned her to face him. "I'm not. I'm worried about how you'll feel."

"How I'll feel?" She looked up at him, the cloud-covered moonlight casting a soft blue glow on her face. "I'll feel like a woman who did the right thing. I'll feel like a hero, a volunteer, a savior of one little family."

His heart swelled. "And I'll never forget that."

She put her fingers on his lips to quiet him. "I'll also feel…" Her throat hitched and caught. "Like I had that damn shell in the palm of my hand and threw it away."

"Oh, Tess." He yanked her into him, hope swamping him. "You don't have to throw it away."

She inched back, a moment's hesitation and even a glimmer of light in her eyes. Then it disappeared and she shook her head quickly. "I can't, John. I can't."

Of course she couldn't, and he had no bloody right to ask. "It's a hard life," he agreed. "Lonely and scary and not normal in the least."

Misty-eyed, she nodded.

He stroked her hair, cupping her cheek. "You have no idea how much I would like to offer you something else."

"There isn't anything else, is there?"

"I'm afraid not."

She closed her eyes, but it didn't hide the hurt.

"You don't want to live that way," Ian said, mustering a truth he didn't want to say. Then he couldn't stop himself from adding, "Do you?"

For a long, long moment, she stood still and silent. In

that time, the gnawing and angst in his gut dissolved completely, transforming into—hope.

Then she dropped her head against him. "How can I?"

Easily. Happily. In his arms and in his life forever. "You can't," he said. "I could never ask you to." Except that in his heart, he had asked a hundred times. And every time, the answer was the same.

She looked up at him. "We have a little time left."

"A week or two. How do you want to spend it?"

She smiled slowly. "Naked."

"That can be arranged."

"With you speaking in an accent."

"Quite feasible," he said with a pronounced British clip.

"And when we're alone and you're…inside me?"

He waited, not breathing, knowing what she wanted. With each passing second, he was more certain. She wanted a baby. And, good Lord, he would give her that.

"Tessa," he finally said. "I can't stand to have another child in the world that I don't know. But if you really—"

She silenced him again with her hand. "I don't want a baby, Ian."

"Now, I know that's a lie."

"I don't. That's what I realized with the shell. I thought a baby would solve everything, but that's not what I want at all."

"Then what do you want?" he asked.

She smiled and let out the softest sigh. "The same thing you do…a family."

His jaw loosened. "Then—"

Shaking her head, she put her fingers over his lips. "I can't do that. I can't live a lie or in secret. But I do want one other thing from you."

"Anything."

"When we're alone, in bed, in…each other, I need to call you by your real name."

He exhaled softly, unable even to think of the stupid amount of happiness that gave him. Instead, he kissed her pretty mouth and fell a little deeper in love with a woman he could have, but never keep.

Chapter Twenty-eight

⟋⟍

She couldn't avoid them forever. After several days and nights of lame excuses, Tessa finally accepted the invitation to meet her best friends for a quick drink at the Toasted Pelican. She arrived on her own, a little late, and headed straight to their favorite booth in the back.

The three of them were already deep in conversation with drinks, though only Jocelyn had anything with kick in it. The tension of their first real long talk had Tessa's stomach in a knot of nausea. She couldn't slip, not one little bit, not one word, not one hint.

Even though every night since she'd known the truth about Ian—John, *John*—she'd been wrapped in his arms, in his bed, in his real world as he'd opened up and shared everything. Each tidbit was a gold mine of discovery— he'd gone to Cambridge!—tarnished by the fact that she could never share this with her three closest friends. Every kiss, every night, and every morning she felt closer to him, all overshadowed by the fact that in a short amount of time he'd not only disappear from sight, but his very existence would be wiped away.

But she knew enough about how that man felt about his children to accept that fate.

"Well, look who crawled out of the sack for some girl time." Zoe slid over and made room for her. "We were just talking about you."

"Don't you have anything better to do than gossip about my love life?"

"Actually we were talking about your wedding," Lacey corrected. "And wondering if maybe we'll be having a real one sometime soon?"

Yeah, they would. In a few days, as a matter of fact. "Not likely," she said, looking around for a waitress.

"I don't know," Jocelyn said playfully. "I saw you two kissing good-bye the other afternoon outside the restaurant."

"And you didn't answer the door when I knocked this morning at seven-thirty," Zoe said.

A good defense was her only offense. "Since when have you ever been up at seven-thirty in your life?" she demanded.

"I had a sunrise balloon ride to see off," Zoe said. "And since I can't go up until Junior is born, I had nothing to do and you were the only human I know guaranteed to be awake. Alas, no answer. I didn't knock on John's door."

At seven-thirty? They'd been awake. Wide awake and making love. "I was in the garden." Might as well start the lies now, even though that made her belly flutter. "Is there a waitress around? I need a drink."

"She'll be here," Jocelyn assured her. "And you don't have to lie, sweetie."

As a matter of fact, she did.

"We've all been there," Lacey said, a tad patronizing. "The first few weeks are the best."

Zoe gave a loud tsk. "Speak for yourself, Lace. Oliver and I still have the glow and I'm knocked up."

Tessa looked up to the ceiling. "Give me strength. And a drink."

"All right, we'll lay off." Jocelyn turned a legal pad around so Tessa could read the twenty-seven line items on a classic Jocelyn Bloom To-Do list. "We have work to do."

Thank God. "I don't see any check marks or cross-offs, Joss."

"Let's get on that, then."

Tessa agreed, grateful to read the list and follow the conversation to ideas for how to entertain the VIPs with spa treatments, balloon rides, and every luxury amenity they could dream up.

But all she could think about was Ian. The depth of his kiss this morning. The laughter in the shower together. The tender way he—

"You'll need some kind of father-daughter moment."

Tessa yanked herself back to the table. "What?"

"I went over the checklist on the AABC site," Jocelyn said, pointing at item number nine on the list. "You know, to be sure we cover everything these consultants want to see in a destination wedding. Apparently, the father-daughter dance is huge to them."

She felt the color rise and almost pumped a fist in relief when she saw the waitress and waved her over.

"Obviously your mother isn't going to be here," Lacey said, "but do you have some music we can play that reminds you of your dad?"

Your Cheating Heart? Me and Mrs. Jones?

"No." She looked up at the waitress, head buzzing along with a roll of unexpected queasiness. All this lying was actually making her sick. "Just…an ice water," she said.

"Nothing at all?" Jocelyn prodded.

"Water's fine."

"I meant with your father."

"I don't. I don't…" *Even have a father.* "I can't…"

"Honey, what is it?" Lacey asked, reaching across the table. "You are pale as a sheet and, oh my God, you're shaking. What's wrong?"

Her throat closed as she looked from one to another. "I've been lying to you." The words actually felt good on her tongue, but, holy hell, now what?

They continued to stare, all of them waiting—for the truth.

"Well, that's not like you," Jocelyn said after a long, awkward moment. "Want to come clean?"

She did, but she couldn't. "Um…I would, but I can't."

"You can't." Zoe leaned closer. "But you will."

This was all it took? Fifteen minutes in the Toasted Pelican with her three best friends and she was ready to spill the beans? What kind of promise had she made? How flimsy was her loyalty to Ian? How could she expect to withstand the pressure when he disappeared and they demanded to know what happened?

"Tess." Lacey squeezed her hand. "You know we're here for you, no matter what."

She nodded, grabbing hold of that absolute unassailable fact.

"We always have been and always will be," Jocelyn

added. "We love you, so no matter what you want to tell us, it's okay."

Tessa waited for the classic Zoe zinger but only got a heartfelt smile. "We're your family, baby girl. And we don't pass judgment on each other."

It all welled up, erupting like a little emotional Vesuvius. "I have a secret," she admitted with a catch in her throat. "And I don't know how to tell you guys."

Zoe moved closer. "You simply tell us. The same way we do everything."

They were her family. They were the one real, true, forever family, these three beautiful, honest, trustworthy women and, by extension, their loved ones. They were all she needed, which was good, because they might be all she ever had.

But she could not betray her trust to Ian.

"I lied about my parents," she finally said. "And I've been carrying around this secret since we met in college."

They exchanged a look of surprise and all three, whether they realized it or not, closed in a little like a tight circle of support.

As Tessa looked around and chose her first words to finally tell them the secret she'd kept about her mother all these years, the only thing she could think was just how lost she'd be without these three women.

Tessa didn't open her eyes but stayed suspended in that magic pre-dawn bliss when sleep fades but reality doesn't quite crash. Ian's arm braced her against his body, one hand flattened possessively against her bare breast. His morning erection nestled into her backside, his thigh pressed against hers, his breathing soft against the top of her head.

She could stay like this forever.

Except that she couldn't.

Opening her eyes, she guessed sunrise about a half hour away based on the pale blue light sneaking between the cracks of the shutters. Without moving at all, she let her gaze drift down to the powerful forearm that locked her in place, studying each individual golden hair and the deep purple tattoo that swirled over his skin.

He'd teared up when he'd told her about all those nights in Singapore, when his personal hell drove him to drink and ink, as he called it. Even his lilting British accent hadn't masked the torture he'd been through.

Life in a witness protection program was no picnic.

And yet...

Her heart climbed up its familiar path into her throat, as it did every time even the whisper of the possibility blew through her mind. He'd never really asked her to go with him—not like on-one-knee kind of asking—but she knew what Ian wanted. If she said yes, then...

She'd give up her life. She'd give up her gorgeous gardens and fabulous friends. Just thinking about the three women she considered "sisters" made that lump in her throat even bigger. When she'd told them the real story about her parents, it had been nothing but anticlimactic. True to character, Jocelyn was fascinated, Lacey was sympathetic, and Zoe called Ken Donnelly an asshat.

And that made it even more devastating to even think about leaving. How could she do it? Explain before she left? Write a note? Disappear? They'd move heaven and earth looking for her, and that was exactly what Ian didn't want to have happen.

Their story was worked out, more or less. When Henry gave Ian the word—which could be any day now—he'd take off for Canada and Tessa would miss her lover, but blame his departure on wanderlust and her heartbreak on a bad choice of men. Quietly, the UK government protection people would have the secret marriage annulled and no one would be the wiser. The girls wouldn't know the wedding hadn't been "fake" because they'd sign the certificate away from everyone, with only the mayor as witness.

Then, Ian would go—*somewhere*—with his beloved Shi and Sam, and Tessa would...

"You're upset."

The words startled her, spoken by a man she'd have sworn was sleeping. "How could you know that?"

"Heart rate goes up." He gave her left breast a soft squeeze; she'd forgotten he had his hand there. "Muscles tighten." He rocked into her thighs. "And, of course, that heavy sigh was a dead giveaway."

Had she sighed?

His hand traveled up her chest, over her throat, and rested on her cheek, stroking under her eyes. "At least you're not crying."

"Why would I cry?"

"Because you're getting married tomorrow and the whole thing is a—"

She whipped around, not able to bear him calling it a sham or charade or fake-out one more time. "That's not why I'm upset," she said. "I know what we're doing and why."

He searched her face. That gentle, appreciative light in his blue eyes always made her feel like he was seeing her for the first time. And he liked what he saw. "Then what has you all tense?"

Did he really have to ask? A few safe answers to the question floated around, but they were drowned out by their solemn promise to never, under any circumstances, lie to each other for the rest of the time they were together.

"Losing you," she admitted.

His eyes closed like she'd shot him.

"Ian." The name was still precious on her lips, spoken only when they were like this. The problem was, they'd spent so much time like this, she thought of him as Ian now. "It's okay."

"It's not okay." His voice was gruff, his eyes still closed. "I don't want to lose you, either."

She drifted closer, not that they could get too much deeper under each other's skin. He responded instantly, wrapping his leg around her, tunneling his fingers in her hair, his hard-on pressed against her belly.

Sparks flared over her, mini–lightning bolts between her legs and fireworks deep inside her body. She let out a soft moan, already moving against him, wanting that pressure in the pleasure point he always found.

"Every time," he murmured, dipping his head to kiss her throat.

"Every time what?"

"Every time I touch you, I get hard."

"You woke up hard."

"I touched you all night." He caressed her breast, leaning her back into the pillow to get on top of her. "Anyway, every time I think about you, I get hard."

They started to move in perfect rhythm, going to the place they'd both found exciting and comfortable—and the perfect escape when the conversation moved from their past and present to the future.

But the future loomed and the call from Henry would come very, very soon.

Tessa closed her eyes and erased the thought, instead letting feelings win this round. The pressure of his big, hard body over hers. The pleasure of his strong hands stroking her. The delicious, tickling, fluttery sensation that traveled from her toes to her eyelids when they started to make love.

This was when he whispered with his accent, when all the walls were completely torn down, when all the secrets and lies and history were silenced by their strangled breaths and precious moans of delight.

This was also when he reached to the drawer, sheathed himself, and entered her.

"Spread your legs, pretty Tessa," he urged, his fingers already working to make her weak and wet.

She did, of course, bracing for him to lift off her, but he slid his tip right in the spot where his finger had been, making her gasp a little and open her eyes in question.

"What are you doing?" she asked.

He lifted a brow.

"Get a condom." Except for the first time, they'd never made love without one.

"I don't want to."

Her heart did a roll and dip, landing low in her stomach. "Ian, we talked about this."

"You want—"

She gripped his shoulders. "Forget what I want. We've

already got the most screwed-up, impossible, complicated, unreal relationship in the history of love. We're already going to long for what we'll never have, wonder about the missing person in our lives..." Her voice cracked. "I don't want that."

"You do," he insisted, but didn't go any deeper. "You want a baby. Could you get pregnant now?"

She almost laughed. "I'm pretty sure I can't get pregnant at all, but if I were normal and functioning, yeah, I could. So, don't."

"Let me give this to you. Tessa. You're doing everything for me."

"I'm going through the motions of a wedding and letting you leave without a fight. Hardly everything."

He crushed her with a little more weight. "It's everything to me."

"This." She gestured between them. "Is not a sacrifice for me. I've had a few weeks of the most fun, the best sex, and the sweetest guy I've ever known. It's not a sacrifice, trust me."

"But if you had my baby, you'd never be alone."

Tears welled up that he knew her weak spots so well. No one had ever known that about her. Not Billy, not even her friends. Only this man.

"It would be worse," she whispered. "If I had your baby, I'd never forget you. He'd have blue eyes and a sweet smile and"—she fought the physical pain of it—"he could calculate Pi to twenty digits without a calculator."

"See?"

See what? She didn't see anything but a tear-blurred beautiful man that she—"No."

"That first night, you were looking for a sperm donor. If I'd have said yes, you could be pregnant now."

"I was looking for one to go in a test tube."

He moved ever so slightly, a centimeter deeper into her. "Screw the test tube."

"Ian!" She inched away. "Don't you know I'd writhe in absolute agony if I couldn't tell you about your child? Not to mention that I already have to lie to my friends and act like I'm a little bit brokenhearted because I'd fallen for a man with wanderlust who was bound to disappear."

Pain crossed his face—that same misery she used to see before she knew his true story. "But you'd have a baby."

Probably not. "But I wouldn't have you."

"You'd have a piece of me."

"I don't want a piece." She wanted it all. The whole of him, his heart, his life, his world, his children. She stroked his face, wishing she didn't deeply love and hate the idea at the same time. "And how would you feel, knowing that you have yet another child in the world you can't see?"

"I'd feel…" He shook his head. "This isn't about how I feel."

"This isn't how I wanted it to be, Ian," she finally whispered. "The baby isn't supposed to make me hurt because I love his father, the baby—"

"You love me." There was nothing but awe in the statement.

For a second, her mouth hung open. Had she said that?

"Well, I…" She closed her eyes, caught by her words and her promise not to lie. "Yes, I—"

He cut her off with a kiss, hard and deep and soul-rocking. Clutching her, he nearly broke her in half, devouring her mouth and sliding right back inside her, even deeper.

"Ian, I—"

He finally lifted his head, his eyes moist and sparking with emotion. "I love you, Tessa."

She swallowed her own admission, letting his wash over her.

"I love you so much." He covered the crack in his voice by smashing his face into her neck and hair. "I never thought I could love anyone or anything again, but I love you, Tessa Galloway. I love you."

All the heat of the kiss disappeared, replaced by a wholly different sensation. An ecstasy she couldn't quite grasp, like soaring down a rollercoaster with all her breath stolen and a scream trapped in her throat.

When he looked at her, all she could do was nod. Words simply wouldn't form.

She'd take that piece of him; it wasn't such a big risk. She couldn't get pregnant.

"Yes?" he asked.

"Yes."

He slid into her all the way, filling her, thrilling her, loving her. Slowly at first, looking into each other's eyes, lost in love, they rocked in perfect timing. Her body floated and rolled, each thrust twisting pangs of pleasure deeper into her, his manhood swelling and pulsing as far into her as he could get. His skin was on fire, his body taut, his face transformed by the moment.

Every stroke took her closer to release, but she fought it off, wanting to be a hundred percent in the moment when he lost control. Grasping his shoulders, she forced him in deeper, watching for the moment when he cringed and cried and exploded into her.

"Tessa. Tessa." His body froze for a second, his breath caught, almost as if he were waiting for permission.

"I love you, Ian," she whispered. "And I'll never, ever forget you."

He closed his eyes, bowed his back, and plunged all the way, giving in to a long, powerful orgasm and filling her with his seed. She rolled against him but let her own pleasure subside.

"Don't you want to?" he asked.

She didn't. She wanted to hold him. That was satisfaction enough. "I'm fine," she whispered.

"You sure are," he replied, his very first pickup line sounding so different now.

He stayed in her a long time, quiet and close, as connected as two people could be. Tomorrow they'd be married and, soon after, parted forever. But right this moment, this frozen dawn-dusted moment, Tessa loved and was loved. And whatever might come out of that would be loved, too.

Across the room, under a pile of clothes they'd stripped off the night before, a soft vibration hummed.

The Henry phone.

"I'm not getting that."

"You have to."

He shook his head. "He can bloody well suck it."

"Ian." She pushed him up. "This could be the call you've been waiting for. You could get your kids."

"What if I didn't?"

Her eyes widened, horrified. "You have to. You can't live without them, not if there's any chance you can."

"I know, I know." He backed away, shooting a glance at the noise. "I want you both."

And the only way he could have that was if she gave up everything and everyone and went with him.

He slipped out of her, rolled out of bed, and bounded to the phone, stabbing it. "What?"

Tessa pulled the sheet higher, staring at Ian's naked torso backlit by fingers of golden sunlight slipping through the shutters. She'd always remember him this way. The sex-god from the bar who stole her heart and gave her hope.

Because she couldn't help but hope that—

"Seriously?"

The note in his voice grabbed her attention, forcing her gaze at his face to try and interpret the response.

"Monday? Okay, Monday." He nodded, turning sideways as if he couldn't even look at her. "I'll be there Monday."

And all that hope withered inside her like a flower that had been denied even a single drop of water.

Chapter Twenty-nine

⟨⟩

That might be the cutest thing I've ever seen." Lacey glided into the spa massage room that, in the last few hours, had been transformed into a makeshift bridal dressing room, her eyes on her cell phone.

"What is?" Tessa asked, pulling away from the mascara wand Zoe held to her eyes.

"The guys as groomsmen." Lacey clicked and grinned. "I got a picture of the three of them with John. Look."

They butted heads trying to see the tiny screen, peering together at a posed shot of the four men.

"Oh, look at Oliver," Zoe exclaimed. "I could eat him alive. Again."

"Wow, Will looks hot in a suit." Jocelyn pointed to the phone. "And I thought that baseball uniform did him justice."

"How about Clay?" Lacey gave a nudge. "That boy is sexy."

They all looked expectantly at Tessa, who managed to pull her gaze from the dizzying sight of Ian Browning—groom.

"Well?" Zoe asked. "Boyfriend assessment?"

"He's not my…" She straightened and slid the mascara wand from Zoe's hand. "I'll finish this."

But they all continued to stare at her with twinkles in their collective eyes. Oh, this would all get worse on Monday when she had to tell them that John took off, too, freaked out by the speed of their romance, and they'd split up. Then the happy eyes would turn to pity hugs.

At least she wouldn't have to fake a broken heart.

"What?" she finally said. "I'm telling you, this is a fun fling with a hot guy. I can already tell he's getting itchy to fly. Don't be surprised if we're looking for a new chef soon."

"Why are you doing this?" Jocelyn demanded.

"Why am I being realistic?" she fired back, irritation making her stomach burn. Although she'd pretty much felt like throwing up since she'd gotten up this morning and remembered it was her wedding day. You know, the day before her "husband" disappeared forever.

"Why are you being fatalistic?" Jocelyn replied. "It's like you won't even give the guy a chance."

"I know him better than you." Much better. "I know the signs of a man who won't settle down and, honestly, I'm fine with that." She leaned back from the mirror and checked out her makeup. "I look a little—"

"Gorgeous," Lacey said. "You look gorgeous."

Actually, she was going to say pale and suggest more blush, but she went with Lacey's assessment. "Guess it's time for the dress, huh?"

Three loud knocks at the door cut into the reaction. "Tessa, you in there?"

At the woman's voice, they all shared a quick, slightly panicked look. Lacey held up a finger to hush them. "One second, Willow." She leaned closer to the girls. "I haven't heard a peep from them since last night, have you?"

"They loved the spa treatments," Jocelyn mouthed.

"I saw them on the beach this morning," Zoe said. "They seem really happy."

"And they were walking around the wedding setup when I came in here, so"—Lacey held up two sets of crossed fingers—"let's keep up the good work."

She walked to the door and opened it, letting in all three of their VIP guests to fill the tiny room with a whole lot of female squealing and laughter and jokes.

Tessa, terrified she'd say one wrong thing about the fake-wedding-that-wasn't-really-fake, played the subdued bride.

"Where's the gown?" Gussie had short blue hair this weekend, and wore it quite well. "You know that's my specialty?"

"It's not exactly a gown." Tessa opened the closet door where the dress she'd picked in Naples hung. An onslaught of oohs and aah ensued.

"So, not your first time, huh?" Gussie asked, fingering some pearls. "That's usually why the blush color."

"Not my first time," Tessa confirmed. "That's why the whole event is so low-key."

That and the fact that we pulled it together in two weeks for your benefit.

She could practically hear Lacey, Joss, and Zoe's shared thoughts.

"I like low-key weddings," Arielle said, crossing her arms and leaning against the counter. "As a set specialist in charge of all the logistics, I can tell you it's the over-the-top events that give me consulting headaches. This place is tailor-made for small and intimate, which is very much in keeping with the economy and mind-set of a lot of brides."

Lacey couldn't hold back the smile. "So you guys like what you've seen so far?"

It was the wedding consultants' turn to share a look, one that had its own secret language that Tessa and her friends couldn't quite read.

"So what shoes?" Gussie asked, breaking the awkward silence.

"No shoes for the ceremony," Tessa said. "Because of the sand."

"It is Barefoot Bay," Zoe added. "And our motto is 'Kick off your shoes and fall in love.'"

The women laughed and exchanged another impossible-to-read look.

"Great motto," Gussie said. "For a great place."

"I'm really intrigued by how you built this resort from nothing," Willow commented. "What was here before?"

"My grandparents had most of the property and I bought the neighboring lots," Lacey told her. "But, trust me, it's been a group effort."

"We've never been anywhere quite like it," Willow said.

"It's like a little oasis in the middle of nowhere," Gussie added.

Well, that was damning with faint praise. Did they like the place or not?

Lacey was obviously thinking the same thing. "Not going to lie," she said. "We'd really love it if Casa Blanca made your recommendations list."

Willow gave a quick smile, a little too noncommittal for any of them to breathe a sigh of relief.

"Is there anything you think we could do to attract more destination-wedding business?" Jocelyn asked.

Once again they shared a look, and Tessa felt that same sensation of sickness roll around inside her. Something was up with these three. Did they know the wedding was a charade? Did they hate the resort?

"A better dressing room for the bride," Gussie said, gesturing to the surroundings. "This is a massage room."

"We could create a dressing area," Jocelyn said quickly. "The spa's always in flux."

"And I had my baby in this room," Lacey added with a smile. "So we think it has good vibes."

The other three women gave the unexpected dropped jaw.

"My fiancée delivered it," Zoe added.

"And my husband proposed while the baby was being born," Jocelyn finished.

Gussie gave a hearty laugh. "Sounds like you guys have stories."

Once again the three guests gave each other a look no one could decipher.

"Well, we gotta hear these stories," Arielle said, pushing up from the chair she'd taken. "But you better get your wedding on, ladies."

"Good luck today, Tessa," Gussie said. "What's your ONBB?"

Tessa gave her a confused look. "My...what?"

"Old, new, borrowed, blue," Willow explained. "It can take brides weeks to figure that out."

Not this bride—a real one. Was this a test? Did they know that the whole thing was a farce?

"Oh, we're covered there," Lacey said quickly. "I was about to give her my grandmother's earrings for something old."

"And the dress is new," Jocelyn added.

The all looked at Zoe expectantly. She lifted her foot gingerly, a bright-blue shell ankle bracelet dangling. "Borrowed and blue," she assured them, slipping it off. "We have every angle of a wedding covered."

Willow gave a wave and Gussie blew a kiss. "You'll be a beautiful barefoot bride," she called out as she left.

Right before the door closed, Willow exclaimed, "Barefoot bride! Clever, Gus. We could work with that."

The remaining four women stood stone still until the others were out of earshot. Then Lacey collapsed in a chair and Zoe let out a grunt of frustration and Jocelyn shook her head.

"That was kind of a weird vibe, wasn't it?" Tessa asked.

"What does 'We could work with that' mean?" Jocelyn mused.

"I can't tell if they love this place or not." Lacey dropped her head back and closed her eyes. "I hope this whole thing isn't a complete waste of time and money."

"It's not," Tessa assured her, reaching for the dress hanger. It was the perfect way to get Ian a legitimate marriage certificate without anyone the wiser.

"They did seem a little underwhelmed," Jocelyn said,

gnawing on her lower lip. "I wonder what we've done wrong."

"Nothing," Zoe insisted, fluttering the anklet in front of Tessa. "Put this on. And don't anyone fall into a worry spiral. Let's get this show on the road."

With little urging, Tessa stepped into the dress and the silk sighed over her skin at the same time her three best friends circled her with a chorus of appreciation.

Tessa turned to the mirror and stared, a little light-headed at how pretty she looked.

"Wow," she whispered.

"He's going to love that," Lacey said.

That was the problem: He already did.

But Tessa smiled and took the steadying hands offered by her friends. "You guys, I…" She blinked, hating that the tears welled. She was an emotional wreck lately. "I have to tell you something."

Not the truth, but something close to it.

"What?" they asked in unison.

"I don't think you three know how much I love you." Because if she didn't, she'd probably leave on Monday and never look back.

"Oh!" They embraced in a group hug that lasted long enough for Tessa to remember why she had to stay.

Because this was her *real* family.

When Tessa appeared across the beach in a pale pink dress and bare feet, her hair blowing in the late afternoon breeze, her three closest friends hovering like mother hens, Ian forgot everything.

He forgot that he'd somehow orchestrated this surreal event.

He forgot that he wasn't truly marrying the woman he deeply loved.

And, best of all, he forgot that he'd done this once before, a long time ago.

He flat-out forgot everything but how beautiful Tessa was and how insanely nervous he'd become.

A slow smile pulled at his lips as she walked over the sand toward him, her gaze down like she was still looking for that damn junonia shell. Didn't she know she could buy one in any tourist shell shop in Fort Myers?

She finally looked up and caught his eye, and it felt like someone took a mallet to his chest and cracked it wide open, exposing the raw reality of what was happening.

He was using her to get what he wanted. "I can't do this," he murmured.

Instantly, the mayor's hand was on his arm. "Sure you can, son. Cold feet are natural, but that there is a lovely young woman. She'll make you happy and give you babies."

Exactly. That was exactly what she should do. For some deserving man who didn't have the devil on his back and a price on his head. He had no right to do this to her, this selfish act that was purely for his convenience. No matter that it was on paper only; he was about to take vows and sign that paper, just so he could have a life on the run and in hiding with Shiloh and Sam.

It was such a stinking ugly betrayal of love. But…

"Who do I love more?" he muttered.

"Exactly," the mayor said. "No one. That's the woman

you love and if your feet are cold, son"—he gave a squeeze and looked down at the hard, wet sand and their bare feet—"it's natural."

But was what he was doing natural? Dragging her into this, using her, and leaving her? Yes, he wanted to be with Shiloh and Sam, but he also wanted Tessa. Why, good God, *why* couldn't he have both?

Maybe he could. He hadn't really asked her, and she hadn't offered. Maybe now was the time to ask—in front of everyone. Without anyone but Tessa knowing. How could he do that?

How could he not?

"Here's your bride," the mayor said under his breath.

As she reached him, the small crowd hushed and a wave splashed and off in the distance a seagull squawked his own wedding song. Without thinking, Ian reached out his hand, only a little stunned that it trembled, and Tessa did the same.

A little electric shock jolted when they touched.

"Dearly beloved…" Mayor Lennox's words were loud, but they sounded like Ian's head was underwater and he…couldn't…breathe. The mayor went on about lifelong commitments and joined hands, but Ian didn't listen.

He looked at the woman he loved and loved her even more for what she was doing for him.

Tessa looked as pale as he felt, her chin quivering a little, her palm damp against his hand. Every cell in his body wanted to scream his love for her and howl that leaving her was the number-one biggest mistake he'd ever made.

"I have the copies of your vows." The mayor pulled

two cards from his pocket, leaning in to whisper, "I've yet to meet a couple who remembered them even when they swore to memorize."

"I don't need that," Ian said, waving off the card, his gaze locked on Tessa. "I know what I want to say." The certainty of that pressed on him, and the weight felt good.

"I'll take the card," Tessa said softly. "I don't think I could remember my name right now."

The guests in the front laughed softly, but Ian didn't. "I can't remember mine, either." Because John Brown seemed…right.

"John?" The mayor said. "Can you state your vows to Tessa?"

"Yes." He cleared his throat, and took both her hands, lifting them a little, clutching them too tightly. "Tessa Galloway, I want to marry you."

The mayor let out a soft laugh, but Tessa frowned at the words, a question in her eyes. He could read that question. *Was this real?*

"For real and forever," he added.

Her mouth opened in an "O" shape, so he squeezed her hands again to underscore how serious he was.

"I don't want to live even a day without you." Another squeeze. "I don't ever want anyone or anything or any…*circumstance* to come between us. Not time or *space*. I love you and I want you to be my wife and partner and mother of…" He swallowed. "*Our* children."

Would she understand what he was asking her to do?

A few of her friends "aahed" audibly but the color continued to drain from Tessa's cheeks as if she did understand.

He stood silent, not at all certain what else to say. That

was it, right? After an awkward beat, he added, "Okay?" and got another laugh from the mayor.

"Very much okay," Mayor Lennox said. "Heartfelt. Tessa?"

She stared at him, glancing down at her card, then back up as she let it flutter to the sand. "John Brown, I want to make you happy and whole and help you find the things you've been looking for all this time."

His children. That was what she meant, but he wanted—her.

"I'm vowing to do whatever it takes even if, some-times, I don't…understand." He heard the soft undercur-rent of surprise from the people close by and felt the mayor bristle, but Ian knew what she was saying. She'd do anything—even give him up—so that he would be happy.

Would she give up everything?

"Is that all?" the mayor asked after a beat.

"Yes. No! I also want to say publicly and officially that"—she glanced to the crowd—"no matter what hap-pens I think you are the finest man I've ever met…" The words caught, but she swallowed again and finished. "And I love you."

He lifted her hands to his mouth and kissed her fingers, closing his eyes to fight his own tears.

"Do you have a ring?"

Tessa's eyes widened. "I never thought of that."

The mayor looked at him. "Do you?"

"Um, sort of."

"You do?" Tessa looked stunned and almost scared.

"Not exactly a ring," he said, reaching into his pocket to close his hand over the seashell. He'd planned to give it to her as a parting gift when he'd left, but nothing about this day or weekend was going as planned. "I have this."

She gasped softly, her jaw unhinged. He slipped the junonia into her palm and closed her fingers over it. "It means your every dream will come true."

For a long minute they looked at each other, both hands clasped over the shell, the connection as real and powerful as when they made love.

"Well, then, that's unconventional," the mayor joked. "But good enough for me to pronounce you husband and wife. You may kiss your bride, sir."

They both waited a second, then leaned into each other, angling their heads, meeting their mouths, and finally breaking their clasped hands to put their arms around each other.

"Don't throw that shell away," he whispered in her ear.

"Not this time," she promised.

The cheer went up over the beach, but the crowd really didn't know what they were cheering for. A life found, that was what.

Ian threw an arm around Tessa and walked through the small gathering, nodding to a few people he recognized from the resort and restaurant, holding his wife tight to his side. As they got through the crowd and reached the sea grass, he stopped.

"We're going over to Rockrose to sign the papers," she said. "That's where we're supposed to meet the mayor."

He shook his head.

"No?"

"Yes, but not yet." Taking her shoulders, he pulled her closer. "Tessa, listen to me. This is important. I made a—"

"John Brown?"

He whipped around, ready to jump down the throat of whoever felt it was necessary to congratulate him now. Then he just froze and stared at the very last person he ever dreamed he'd see here. Bloody hell.

Sharp-eyed, bearded, and leaning in to lower his voice, Henry Brooker always had impeccable timing. "You need to come with me. Now."

Instinctively Ian stepped in front of Tessa, wanting to protect her from this part of his life, this dark, broken, abnormal life of his. "Why?" he demanded.

"It's now or never if you want any chance of getting Shiloh or Sam. Things have changed. Drastically."

Yes, they had.

"What's going on?" Tessa asked, her face china white now, her eyes wide with horror.

"Nothing." Damn it, he wouldn't let Henry toss him around like a rudderless boat on whitewater. He had to have a life, and Tessa was his—

"Ms. Galloway," Henry said softly. "John is going to leave now. You have about one minute to say good-bye."

"What?"

"One minute," he said gruffly.

She put her hand on her chest, and, right in front of him, Tessa collapsed in the sand.

Chapter Thirty

Sign the paper. *Sign the paper.* Tessa had to sign the paper before that man took John—

"Tessa? Honey, wake up."

John. No, no, that was…"Ian."

"Shhh, wake up, sweetheart."

Using every ounce of strength, she managed to open her eyes, the face in front of her a blur before the features crystallized into…"Ian."

He put light fingers over her lips, his eyes flashing enough so she got the message.

"Is she awake?"

"Is she okay?"

"Tess, you fainted."

She managed to tear her gaze away long enough to focus on Lacey. And Jocelyn. And Zoe. All of them and at least a dozen others peered at her over Ian's shoulder. Not Ian. John. She had to call him John.

And she had to say good-bye to him. *One minute.*

"Tess?" He stroked her face. "You still with us, honey?"

She nodded and opened her eyes, pushing herself up, feeling sand under her elbows and backside. God, she was lying on the sand surrounded by wedding guests. "This is a nightmare," she whispered, trying to laugh but, honestly, nothing was funny.

"Brides faint. I've seen it a lot." The comment came from the back of the group—the girl with blue hair.

Oh, Lord, the wedding planners. The fake wedding was a complete failure—unless she signed that paper. At least John could get his kids.

She grabbed his hand and tugged him closer. "We have to sign the papers before you go."

He shook his head, using her hand to help her up. "You have to get steady on your feet."

"In Rockrose," she insisted. "Take me into the villa." That was where the marriage certificate waited to be signed and witnessed. "Where's the mayor?"

"Right here, dear." White-haired Mayor Lennox stepped through the circle of people.

"I'm fine," she said, standing now and still holding John's hand. "Where's…" She tried to speak silently through her eyes. "That man?"

Ian barely nodded in acknowledgment, taking her a step forward.

"Is he gone?" she asked in a soft whisper.

"Come with me, Tess." He gestured to move her friends back. "Let me take Tessa into Rockrose for a few minutes."

"We'll come with you," Lacey said, already on her other side.

"No." Tessa gave her a firm look. "I need to be alone with John."

Confusion and maybe a flash of hurt passed over her expression, but Lacey was a friend for life, and she got the message. "Okay. I'll take care of...everyone."

"I'm sorry," Tessa said quickly. "I think the wedding is a bust."

Lacey almost smiled. "Vows felt real enough. And you dropped this." She put the junonia in Tessa's hand. "Go rest a few minutes and we'll take it from there."

Tessa squeezed the shell, grateful. Behind Lacey, in the distance, the hot-air balloon waited for the sunset wedding flight that was supposed to be the showstopper for the consultants.

"Zoe, c'mere," Tessa said, reaching for her other friend. "Can your pilot take the VIPs up instead of us? It would be a good way to deflect some of this mess."

"We can do that," she said. "I'll talk to them."

That would buy some time. Enough to sign the papers and...say good-bye. The thought almost made her dizzy again, damn it. Taking a slow, deep breath, Tessa looked up at John.

She would not be that woman. She would not be weak, helpless, faint, or pathetic. He needed her help for the most important thing in his life and she'd give it; somehow, explanations would follow.

"Let's go," she said when he hesitated. "We're not done...yet."

The crowd backed off enough for them to walk to the closest villa near the beach, with Mayor Lennox offering to meet them in a few minutes so Tessa had a chance to recover. But they weren't alone when they stepped inside the living room, and Tessa wasn't the least bit surprised about that.

"How are you feeling?" Henry Brooker's British accent was thicker than John's, she noticed, and maybe that was why the question didn't feel exactly sincere. Or maybe it was his tense demeanor, like he was ready to bolt any second.

And take John with him.

"You better have a damn good reason for this, Brooker." John guided Tessa to one of the dining chairs, pulling it out for her. "Your timing sucks."

Henry angled his head, silent.

"Don't be coy, either," John said, standing behind her and placing solid, protective hands on her shoulders. "Tessa knows everything there is to know. Say what you have to say and be prepared to leave. I'm not ruining this day any more than we already have."

Drawing back with a little surprise, Henry crossed his arms and scowled. "This is not my timing," he said quietly. "This timing was dictated by your son."

John's grip tightened. "What?"

"Edward is sick."

"Sam," John said softly, coming around the table as if the news somehow drew him closer to Henry. "His name is Samuel. What's wrong with him?"

"They don't know. He'd developed a strange infection and he's been hospitalized overnight. To be blunt, it's touch and go and you need to get there, fast."

"Good Lord."

At John's pained whisper, Tessa stood, her own light-headedness forgotten and replaced by his. She put her hand on his back. "You better go."

He gave Henry a questioning look, then nodded solemnly.

Tessa barely breathed and John turned to her, his anger at Henry replaced by something else even more intense. Raw, rugged determination and the same certainty she had seen on the beach.

"Come with me."

The words stunned her.

"John, I—"

"Tess, please. Please. Come with me. We're married now. Stay with me, be with me, don't ever leave me."

She stood paralyzed by the invitation and sincerity in his eyes.

Henry stepped closer, practically between them. "If you get the children in your custody, we'd still strongly recommend you start over with a new name in a new location." He looked hard at Tessa. "You'd have no contact with anyone."

"Come with me," he repeated as if Henry weren't even there. He grabbed her shoulders and pulled her closer. "I meant every bloody word I said out there, woman. I love you. I love you. Come with me, live with me, be my reason."

"Your reason."

He squeezed and practically shook her, his eyes on fire. "For living. For breathing. For everything."

Blood pulsed so loudly she couldn't hear herself think. And she needed to. She needed to think hard and straight. "You want me to leave and go into the program with you?"

"Yes. It's wrong. It's selfish." He squeezed his eyes shut. "But I love you. Tessa, I love you so much, but I love my kids, too."

And now one of them was sick. When push came to shove, that was the family he'd choose—as he should. Just like…

She closed her eyes as the image of her mother popped so unexpectedly into her head. Her mother who gave up everything for a man who wouldn't give up a damn thing for her. And look how she'd ended up. Alone.

She'd promised to help him, but did that mean she would give up everything so he could have—everything?

"Does he still have to prove he's married?" she asked Henry.

"It's going to help the process, yes. All I know is I was sent here to fly you up there immediately because of the situation with your son. Beyond that, I can't say what will happen, but I'm confident that you'll be taking a new identity and so would your…" He gestured to Tessa.

"She's my wife," he said simply.

Three words that nearly buckled her knees again. Then the front door opened and Mayor Lennox walked in.

Henry didn't wait or bother with introductions. "I'll be outside," he said. "I have a car waiting."

"You two going somewhere?" The mayor asked as Henry brushed by him and left.

They didn't answer but looked at each other, John's stare so hard that prickles of heat stung Tessa's neck, her pulse thrumming every vein in her body.

She's my wife.

Not quite yet.

"Here's the certificate of marriage." Mayor Lennox flipped open a manila envelope and pulled out a sheet of paper, taking it to the table. "Most people have a photographer here for this part."

"We're not most people," John said.

He chuckled. "I got that impression during the ceremony."

"In fact, we'd like to be alone."

The mayor's white brow shot up. "I need to witness the signatures."

John gestured around the room. "You see anyone else?"

"Like I said, unconventional." But he took out a pen, set it on the table, and gave a nod. "Have at it, kids."

Neither of them moved, even after the door clicked shut and they were alone. For a long moment, they looked at each other, both taking slow, uneven, slightly terrified breaths.

"Are you going to sign that?" she finally asked.

"Are you going to come with me?"

"How can I do that?" she asked, wishing he really had an answer but knowing he didn't. "How can I walk out of here and get in a car and disappear from the people who love me most in the whole world? They'd never stop looking for me."

"They'd never find you."

And that hurt. "I love them too much to put them through that."

He closed his eyes and nodded. "I understand that, but I want you to know something, too." He reached for her hands, pulling her closer. "I meant every word I said during that wedding. I really did. I've been given a second chance and a second life, so I wanted to—"

She put her hand over his mouth, not sure she could take this confession. It would hurt too much on lonely nights to remember these words and how close they came to happiness.

"You've been given a second chance with your children. Love—our love—is great and glorious. But *that* love? The parent love? That is *it*, Ian. That is what counts the most. And, honestly?" She smiled as the real truth descended. "I would make the same choice, if I only could."

He bit his lip, eyes filling, pulling her into an embrace so tight she couldn't breathe. "I know you would."

"Go to them, Ian," she whispered. "I could never love a man who wouldn't, and I could never forgive myself if I went with you."

Sighing in agreement, he kissed her head. "I will never forget you, Tessa. I'll never forget you."

She pinched her eyes shut and fought the tears, nudging him away. "One more thing," she said, her voice hoarse. She picked up the pen. "We're not quite married yet."

"You don't have to sign that," he said. "I understand if you don't want to."

"I want to." She scratched *Tessa Galloway* above her typed name. "Here."

He took the pen, looking miserable, unable to do anything but stare at the document.

"You said Henry will arrange the annulment," she reminded him. "This is a formality."

He squeezed the pen in a death grip, staring at the certificate. "It's not a bloody formality to me."

"It's a way to get your children, and that's all that matters."

"Is it, Tessa?" He didn't look up from the paper, but his jaw clenched tight and a vein in his neck throbbed at about the same rate as her heart. "Because I think it's a fucking lie." He tossed the pen on the table and took a step back. "And we made a promise never to lie to each other."

"You're not lying to me," she said softly.

He turned to her, eyes blazing. "I'm making a mockery of marriage and of us. I won't do that. When I sign that, it's forever and it's real. I won't do that for some stupid board who thinks they know what's right for me and for my family."

She fisted her hands, fighting another wave of emotion and dizziness. "Your family consists of two little children, one of whom is sick. I am not part of this decision."

"That's where you're wrong."

An impatient tap on the door made Ian step back and look around the room.

"I need a piece of paper," he said. He scanned the living room, seeing none. "Damn it." He took the marriage certificate and ripped a corner off, then grabbed the pen to write on the scrap. "This is Henry's secure, private, and totally trustworthy number. If you ever need anything, absolutely *anything*, or if you want to get a message to me, call Henry."

He stuffed the paper into her hand, then grabbed her fingers and pulled her into him, wrapping his arms around her. Tessa closed her eyes and nodded into his chest, his heart hammering against her, yet not loud enough to drown out her thoughts.

Go with him, you idiot! Go!

But she simply couldn't move.

He slipped out of her arms, brushed her hair back one last time, and gave her a smile. "I don't blame you, Tess. Not at all."

"Okay. Bye." She closed her eyes and turned away, incapable of watching him walk out the door. When she finally opened her eyes, she focused on the scene out the window in front of her.

The hot-air balloon was lifting off, surrounded by the people she loved, all cheering and waving and wishing them well. Everyone was too immersed in the excitement to notice the groom walking across the path, on his way to a car that would take him away forever.

Forevah and evah.

She squeezed the shell so hard she thought she heard it crack. But it didn't. The seashell was stronger than that. Only her heart was broken.

Chapter Thirty-one

The verdict's in. Meet at my house. Now!

Lacey's text went to all three of her best friends and business partners simultaneously. Instantly, Tessa dropped the composting fork and pulled off her gloves, throwing them on a work table as she headed out of the gardens toward Lacey's backyard.

It had been two weeks since the wedding planners left Barefoot Bay; and, of course, two weeks, one day, and fourteen hours since John had left.

Stop counting, Tess.

Her friends had surprised her by accepting the "family emergency" explanation—though she'd caught their looks of worry and pity when they thought she wasn't paying attention. However, Willow, Arielle, and Gussie hadn't been quite so understanding and, with the groom gone, the reception fizzled. And so, they feared, had their chances of being a "recommended resort" at the next meeting of the American Association of Bridal Consultants.

Willow said she'd be calling Lacey today to deliver the final news, and they'd all agreed they wanted to be together for the announcement. Tessa'd done a masterful job of avoiding her friends for the better part of the past two weeks, even begging off as sick for the Thanksgiving feast Lacey had hosted. That hadn't been a lie; heartache had wrecked her physically and emotionally, and her friends had read her cues perfectly. But that couldn't last too much longer.

Especially if the AABC said they thought the wedding had been a bust. Then there'd probably be some serious questions sent Tessa's way. She'd stick to her story: The wedding wasn't real and she'd never expected a drifter like John Brown to stick around long. His inexplicable "personal emergency" was the excuse he needed to disappear from any emotional entanglements.

And, honestly, none of that was a lie. It just wasn't the whole truth.

"Hey, Aunt Tess."

She stopped at the urgent but soft cry, peering into the shade of a live oak tree at the edge of Lacey's property. "Ashley?"

She stepped into the light and gave a frantic wave for Tessa to come closer. "I need to talk to you."

Tessa didn't hesitate but headed right toward Ashley, whose ruddy cheeks and mascara smudges told of tears. "Boy troubles again, hon?"

Ashley shook her head, taking Tessa's hand to pull her around to the other side of the tree. "Worse troubles. I'm late."

"For what?"

Ashley let out a dry, uncomfortable laugh. "I'm *late*." She pointed to her stomach.

Realization dawned and Tessa nearly swayed as she reached out for Ashley. "How late?"

"I don't know, I never tracked it very well, but…" She balled up her fists in front of her mouth as if the words horrified her. "I haven't had a period for a long time, Aunt Tess."

Oh, good God. "How long?"

"Long." Her voice was tight with terror as she cupped her face in dismay. "My mom's gonna kill me."

"Your mom…" *Has been there.* "Is never going to hurt you and will always love you."

"I know, but"—she closed her eyes—"I can't believe it happened after one time."

What was the name of that book on her shelf? *Every Drunken Cheerleader…Why Not Me?* Except Ashley wasn't a drunken cheerleader; she was the closest thing to a daughter Tessa would likely ever have, and this wasn't funny.

This was real, and the implications were huge. "Have you taken a test?"

Ashley held up a white plastic bag from the pharmacy. "I had to drive to the mainland to get one. I couldn't exactly pop into the Super Min or Charity would be on the phone with my mom before I got out of the parking lot."

"But you haven't taken the pregnancy test yet?" Then there was still hope this was a false alarm.

"I don't think I have to. Lately I've been feeling so icky. Like I was sick all the time, but not sick, you know? And dizzy. Every time I stand up I feel like I smoked something, and, trust me, I didn't."

"That could be anything."

"I Googled it and those are definite signs."

"They're also symptoms of your allergies," she said, grabbing at desperation straws. "Pollen's bad right now."

"The only thing I'm allergic to is Marcus Lowell."

Who'd quit the day after John left. "Have you told him?"

"He booked, Aunt Tess. No one's seen or heard from him for weeks." She rolled her eyes. "Man, can we pick 'em or what?"

Except John hadn't *booked*. He'd gone to his children and back into hiding. "He might have had a good reason for leaving, Ash."

She got a "Get real" look in response. "I don't care about him. I have to know."

"And so does your mother," Tessa said.

She dropped her head back and closed her eyes. "She's going to be so disappointed in me."

"For a minute." But not much more. Tessa remembered so, so well the day Lacey had returned to Gainesville after she'd gone home to deliver this same news to her parents. Lacey wouldn't make her daughter feel like the world's biggest disappointment, like her own mother had. "But you have to tell her. Now."

"Will you break it to her?"

The question hit hard. Tessa knew, or had at least suspected, that Ashley was doing more than kissing her short-term boyfriend. And she hadn't told Lacey.

"I'm the one she's going to be disappointed in," Tessa said on a sigh. "I should have stepped in and done something." But she'd been too busy with her own romantic interludes.

"No, Aunt Tess, you did what I asked you. I won't let her be mad at you for that. Anyway, if she hadn't been so wrapped up in the baby and the resort—"

Tessa stopped her. "Don't, Ash. Don't blame other people for your mistakes. Own them." She pulled the girl a little closer, the full weight of what this news could mean actually hitting her. Another baby, another life, and Ashley's whole future suddenly turned on its head.

But before they could worry about that, they needed to tell Lacey. And get confirmation.

"Tessa!" Zoe's voice came from the lanai, excited and high-pitched. "What's taking you so long?"

Ashley and Tessa shared a look.

"Come on, kiddo. You better hope the wedding consultants give good news."

Holding hands, they crossed the grass to the open screen door where Zoe waited, bouncing on her toes. "They're on the phone in Lacey's office right now. She's got the door closed." Zoe grabbed both their hands. "What are you guys doing out there?"

"Talking," Tessa said, stepping in front of Ashley to save her from Zoe's prying "Have you been crying?" questions. "Is Joss here?"

"She's changing Elijah. Come, come." Zoe led them around the pool deck to the open sliding doors leading to the family room, where Jocelyn was settling down on the rocker with the baby. "Door's still closed," Joss reported. "Anyone have a working boob?"

Ashley spun around and headed for the kitchen. "I'll get a bottle for him. She has some pumped in the fridge now that he has a tooth."

"Good girl," Jocelyn said. "What an awesome mother you'll make."

Tessa didn't dare look at Ashley. Oh, *Lord*. They weren't ready for this. She covered up the awkward silence by cooing over the baby.

"Hey, little boy blue." She stroked his cheek and was rewarded with a huge baby grin as the office door popped open. They all froze, waiting for Lacey, who took her sweet time coming down the hall. That couldn't be good.

Even Elijah was quiet, as if he knew the importance of the moment.

Zoe leaned forward on the sofa, her hands in a classic prayer position. Ashley came in holding the bottle. Tessa reached to hold Jocelyn's hand.

"Are you all sitting down?" Lacey called as she walked in.

"Sitting down and *dying*," Zoe said.

"Well." Lacey put her hands on her hips and made a tight face, shaking her head. "They're not going to recommend us to the AABC."

"What?"

"Why?"

"That's BS!"

Lacey didn't say a word during the outburst, but quietly took the bottle Ashley was holding and thanked her with a quick, gentle touch on the shoulder. While Zoe spewed near obscenities and Jocelyn and Tessa grumbled under their breath, Lacey scooped up her son, gave him a kiss, and settled on the sofa next to Zoe, still silent.

"You're pretty zen about this," Jocelyn observed.

"Because you all didn't let me finish."

That quieted them.

Lacey positioned the baby to take the bottle, humming softly as she got him settled in and comfortable. "Have you seen his little tooth?" she finally asked.

"Lacey!" All four of them shouted loud enough to startle Elijah.

Finally, Lacey's smile widened. "They aren't recommending us because it would be a conflict of interest."

Another shower of questions rained, but she waited until they were quiet.

"It would be a conflict of interest because..." Her eyes danced as her smile widened. "They are banding their three consulting businesses together, starting one super amazing wedding-planning organization, and they are moving here to hold the weddings at Casa Blanca."

"*What?*" They all screamed that question, too.

"Can you believe it?" Lacey leaned forward, beaming over her baby. "They didn't like Barefoot Bay, they *loved* it. They adored Casa Blanca, but they don't think we know anything about how to put on a great wedding."

"We don't," Zoe said. "We need professional planners on staff."

"Exactly. Remember all the strange looks and weird vibes we got? They'd been planning this from the minute they got here and, seeing how many times we slipped up, they were certain it was the right move."

"So they're going to work for us?" Jocelyn asked.

"Not on staff, but I think we're going to figure out a way to give them office space here. Between the three of them with existing destination-wedding clients lined up for years, they'll have Casa Blanca booked for at least two weddings a month for the next year, maybe more. We

don't need to be recommended to the AABC!" She nearly
hoisted Elijah with joy. "The word will get out all on its
own. And wait until you hear the name of their new company."

They all waited breathlessly.

"Barefoot Brides!"

"Oh, I love it!"

"Perfection!"

"All brides should be barefoot."

Ignoring the outburst, Lacey looked around, a frown
pulling. "Where did Ashley go? Did she even hear this
news? Ash?"

Tessa's gut twisted. It was time. Good news about to
be followed by—*no*. No one could think a baby was bad
news.

"I'll get her," she said, pushing up. "Ashley?"

She headed down the hall to take the back stairs up
to Ashley's room, but as she passed the master, Ashley's
arm reached out and grabbed her.

"Aunt Tess! C'mere!" Her eyes bright, she pulled
Tessa into the dimly lit room and stuffed the plastic bag
into Tessa's hand. "Don't need this!" She practically sang
the words. "I just got my period!" She threw her arms
around Tessa. "Could I be any happier?"

She couldn't answer as an old twist of envy spiraled
through her. What must it be like to be happy to get your
period?

"Are you sure?"

"Absolutely! That's why I ran out of the room, but
judging by the screaming we got the recommendation."

"Actually, we didn't, but it's even better news. Come
on, let's—"

"What's going on, you two?" Lacey stood in the doorway, still holding Elijah. "Ashley, are you okay?"

"I'm great, Mom!"

"Ashley." Tessa turned and gave her a harsh look. "You can't do this anymore."

"Do what?" Lacey asked.

Ashley pushed her hair off her face, looking hard at her mother. "I thought I had a problem, Mom, but I don't so you don't even have to—"

"Ashley!" Tessa held up the bag. "You have to tell her everything."

For a whole lot of heartbeats, Ashley stared at her mother, then nodded slowly. "The whole truth," Tessa said.

"And nothing but," she promised.

Lacey frowned, moving into the room. "I'm not liking the sound of this. What's going on, honey?"

Ashley covered her mouth. "I really screwed up, Mom, but it's okay. Honest, it's okay."

"Why don't I take the baby," Tessa offered. "Then you two can talk alone."

"No, Aunt Tess. Stay."

But Lacey handed over the baby anyway, dividing her attention between Tessa and Ashley. "I need to know what's going on." Ashley took a slow breath, glancing at Tessa, who just shook her head. "Um, Mom, I kind of had a pregnancy scare."

Lacey's jaw dropped and Tessa tightened her grip on the baby, so glad she'd taken him as Lacey's reaction shook her. "*What?*"

"I had, you know, some symptoms."

"And it sounds like you had, you know, some *sex*." Lacey whipped around to Tessa. "Did you know this?"

"I knew that—"

"No, Mom. She did not know anything except I was dating…someone." At Tessa's look, she rolled her eyes. "Okay, Marcus. I was seeing Marcus. But I didn't tell Aunt Tess I was…I swear I didn't tell her. And she kept the secret about us because I begged her to."

Lacey dragged her hand through her hair. "What made you think you were pregnant?"

"Hey! Where are you guys?" Zoe's voice traveled in from the family room.

Lacey gave Tessa a gentle nudge. "Go, we'll talk later."

"Do you hate me?"

She angled her head and puffed out a breath. "As if. Let me talk to Ashley."

Tessa patted the baby's back and headed into the hall, cuddling Elijah as she paused to lean against the wall and let a wave of warm relief roll over her.

In the bedroom, she heard Ashley's soft voice. "…couldn't remember my last period and I was sick all the time, but not sick. And dizzy. Like, every time I stood up I got light-headed."

Another wave hit, this one hard and hot and so, so stunning.

She knew those symptoms. She was living those symptoms *right now*.

"Oh my God," she whispered, pressing her lips against Elijah's peach fuzz. Her head felt like it was going to pop, and her whole body suddenly felt heavy and weak and *dizzy*.

She'd been light-headed for weeks—blaming the heartbreak, the sun, the sleepless nights of crying. Blaming everything but…

A baby.

She held tight to the one in her arms, her fingers still clutching the plastic bag Ashley had given her. Taking one steadying breath, she marched into the family room and handed Elijah to Jocelyn.

"I have to go."

"Where? Why? We need to celebrate."

Not quite yet. She had to be sure.

"I have to go," she repeated. "Tell Lacey I'll call her later." She turned and tried not to run, gripping the bag, and barely hearing the questions in her wake.

Chapter Thirty-two

‿

December in Ottawa was a hell of a lot different from December in Barefoot Bay. Icy wind whipped down asphalt corridors, and barren trees rose naked from the snow-covered ground. To Ian, the world seemed colorless after the emeralds and turquoises of the Gulf Coast.

The only green was the oxidized copper roofs topping the government buildings, and the only blue was the bruise all over Ian's heart.

For a while he'd been able to ignore that hollow feeling in his chest. He'd filled any emptiness by spending hours next to a hospital bed holding the tiny hand of a young man who was clearly born with a fighter's spirit.

Witnessing Eddie—he didn't even answer to Sam, so Ian gave up trying to call him that—survive his mysterious infection went a long way toward healing Ian's own wounds. The little man not only charmed every nurse, doctor, and visitor in the process, he completely threaded his way right into the fabric of Ian's heart. And his twin sister, far quieter and a little more terrified of life's un-expected curveballs, had insisted on staying in the room with a menagerie of stuffed animals she kept in a small suitcase with the name Emma embroidered on it.

By the end of the hospital stay, Ian had given all the animals different talking voices and accents, learning quickly that wee Emma was far more at ease with a stuffed pig than a human being.

She barely spoke to the couple who'd had the children for the last year, which only confirmed Ian's decision. They greatly favored Eddie, but his illness had taken its toll, and the couple—the third family the children had been placed with—had asked that Emma be sent on to yet another home.

Ian would die first, and that was why Henry had taken the extraordinary step of flying to Florida to reunite the family. The twins would never be separated, and they only had one more home to go to—Ian's.

Assuming he made it through one last hoop this after-noon: the final Protected Persons review board stamp of approval. Three nameless faces were given the responsi-bility of granting Ian's request for one more identity and supporting one more move to obscurity.

While that meeting dragged on in a basement office of Ottawa's sprawling government complex, Ian leaned against a stone wall high over the city, but the expansive metropolitan view was lost on him. Every two minutes he turned to look at the door where Henry had disappeared nearly an hour ago.

With each sigh, a cloud of cold air puffed in front of his face, making him stuff his frozen hands deeper into his jacket pockets. What was taking so long?

Wasn't this a technicality, a rubber stamp that blessed his new name, new location, and new life story? The N1L gang members that represented any real threat were behind bars, though as long as they were alive, Ian had to watch his back and keep his story a secret.

He would do that. He'd do anything to keep his children and make sure they were together. Anything—even leave the woman who made him feel whole, happy, and healed.

Another sigh escaped at the thought, interrupted by the vibration of his phone, which was wrapped in his chilled fingers. He yanked it out and stabbed the green button. "Yeah?"

"We have a problem, mate."

Damn it. "What is it?"

"The answer's no."

A bright white light exploded in his heart. "No…what? Why?"

Henry sighed. "There's a woman on the board."

Like that explained it. "So?"

Henry paused long enough for Ian to sense that he wasn't going to like the answer. "She's transferred here from the Singapore operation."

Was everything he did in Singapore going to haunt him? "Really."

"Yeah, not a fan of yours. I tried, but the best we could do was let them agree that you could live somewhere in Canada, probably on the other side of the country, and visit."

Visit? Fuck that. "I'm coming in."

Before Henry could answer, Ian marched toward the door. Also, fuck the security and their trumped-up rules about review boards not having direct contact with program members. If some prejudiced, small-minded, idiot woman who read a negative report thought she could ruin his life, she was going to answer to *him*.

He shoved the heavy door open, instantly blasted by hot air and a scowl from a guard. Undeterred by the protective glass, metal detector, or the gun on the guy's hip, Ian powered toward him.

"I need to see—"

"Me!" Henry barreled around the corner, still holding his phone. "I'll clear him through," he called to the guard.

Ian sailed through the metal detector and met Henry on the other side. "Don't even try to stop me."

"I warned them this might happen. She seemed to relish the opportunity to meet you." Henry gestured for him to head down a flight of stairs into the chilly bowels of the building. "Last door on the left."

"What's her problem? The fact that I got in a fight in Singapore?"

"She's hung up on stability. I told you it would have been better to wave a marriage certificate."

Ian gave a derisive snort. That was one decision he did not regret in the least. "A fake, meaningless piece of paper that's going to be annulled before this board convenes again? Why bother?"

"It makes them feel better," Henry said, hustling to keep up with Ian's long and furious strides. "They're bureaucrats and you need to appeal to their love of red tape." They stopped at a closed door. "Her name is Sarah Banks and she's got an agenda. I don't have any idea what it is."

"Well, fuck Sarah Banks and—" Ian's words halted when the door opened. "Oh. I already have."

Bloody hell. It was only a matter of time until one of those many, many one-night stands would come back to bite him in the ass.

Sandy hair, blue eyes, and a smile he'd pronounced "pretty" the night he'd met her in Singapore. She'd probably been a government plant to see if he could stick to his story. And now she'd been promoted to a position in Canada.

He didn't bother averting his eyes, but held her cold gaze as Henry made a brief round of introductions around a long conference table. He didn't bother to listen to the names of the two men; they weren't why he was in this room.

Oh, bollocks. Sarah. It all came back to him now. She'd approached him in a dive in Geylang and he'd been drunk enough to believe she was a British tourist who'd ended up in the wrong part of Singapore. Her accent had sounded like home and her hair reminded him of...

"We've met," she said icily. "Unless you don't remember."

He ignored the comment, narrowing his eyes to remind her that even though she'd been a plant sent to test his ability to keep his identity secret, she'd also been a willing and eager sex partner. No doubt that wasn't in her job description.

"I want my children," he said softly. "And I'm here to find out exactly what I need to do to get them short of taking them, which I will do if forced."

One of the men leaned forward. "We take threats like that very seriously."

You ought to, Ian said with his glare.

"Your unstable lifestyle concerns me," Sarah said,

turning a page in a file he assumed was a blow-by-blow description of his many instabilities. "We have no issue how you choose to live in your government-granted identity when you are on your own, Mr. Browning, but bringing children into the mix is an entirely different equation."

"Henry gave us the impression you were settling down, even marrying," the other man said. "That would go a long way to assuaging our issues."

He practically curled his lip and fought the urge to make a fist to *assuage* his *issues*. "You expect me to marry someone and not tell them my life story?"

Sarah shrugged. "It's been done, and, frankly, we think that encourages you to fully embrace your identity, forcing you to become the new person we say you are."

He managed not to spit or leap over the table and throttle her skinny neck, but only thanks to a superhuman effort. "I'll never be the person you say I am."

"Then you can't have your children." She leveled him with a look that sent his blood pressure soaring. "Unless and until you prove your stability."

He closed his eyes, drawing in a slow breath, mining every drop of composure he had. "I assume you don't have children, Ms. Banks."

"My life is not on the table."

"My life"—he clenched his jaw and leaned closer—"isn't a life. Do you have any idea what it's like to live in the personal hell you condemn people to every day?"

She launched one well-drawn brow. "You'd perhaps prefer a slow death at the hands of some London gang member?"

Just his bloody luck to have his fate in the hands of a woman he'd screwed every way possible. "I'd perhaps prefer to live exactly as I did before some maniac murdered my wife, left my children screaming, and stole any semblance of normalcy I've ever had."

"It's that semblance of normalcy we're looking for, Mr. Browning. Get it and we'll see what we can do about your kids. But you'll have to hurry. They turn four in a few months."

Next to him, Henry's phone hummed and he checked it, pushed back his chair, and left.

After a moment, Ian pinned her with a long look. "What exactly do you want from me?"

"We need to believe those children will live in a secure and stable environment," one of the men said.

"My children are on the third family in as many years," he fired back. "They're about to be separated after my son was hospitalized. What is stable and secure about that?"

It was the other man's turn as Sarah flipped through the file without looking at him. "We need to see a record that shows you are prepared to raise and rear those children."

"They're mine. I was prepared to raise and rear them the day they were born. Before."

Sarah fluttered the file. "Until we know you are completely safe, the children stay in Canada, in two different families. As you know, when they are four, you can no longer move them, so—"

He launched toward the table, ripped the file out of her hand, and stuck his face right in front of hers, eliciting a soft cry as she pushed backward.

"How many times do I have to die for you people to be satisfied?" He ground out the words. "Because I died in London, I died in Singapore, I died in Florida, and I'm dying here." He balled the papers in fisted hands. "I want to live. I finally want to live so, for God's sake, lady, let me do that."

She closed her eyes and shook her head.

The door popped open, startling all of them. Henry held his phone, his eyes sparking as he seized the shoulder of Ian's jacket and pulled him off the table. "Save your breath, mate. The game changed. This meeting's over."

Tessa gingerly set the plastic stick on the bathroom counter, washed her hands, and closed the door as she walked out.

A watched test never reveals two lines.

Exhaling softly, she went into the living room, paced from one side to the other, then closed her eyes. Time for the same prayer she'd said every single time she'd gone through this exercise in fertility-futility, as Billy once called her obsessive test-taking when her period was about four minutes late.

"Please, God, let this be the—No…" She shook her head, letting her voice trail off.

That wasn't the plea she wanted to make. Deep inside, Tessa wanted to pray for something else. This time, the negative result was for the better.

Stunned, she unfolded her prayer-hands and pressed them to her burning cheeks.

Was it possible she was *hoping* for a negative test? How could that be?

Of course she wanted to be pregnant! That desire was as much a part of her as gardening or breathing. She'd wanted a baby for as long as she could remember. In front of the bookcase, she crouched down to her secret infertility shelf, remembering how John had discovered the books and pulled one out.

Five Hundred Ways to Get Pregnant. She could still hear the humor in his voice. *Who knew there were more than one?* She'd died a little that moment. Because he was funny and sweet and honest and—

Not *honest*.

She straightened. She'd forgiven him the lies in the beginning because during their last days and nights together, she'd shared more with him than she ever had with Billy. And he'd told her every minute detail of his life, his childhood, his education, his marriage, his hopes and dreams.

And with each revelation, she'd fallen deeper and deeper in love. In love enough that she didn't want John's baby…not without John. Where was the joy in that? What did that leave her for a future?

She wanted a family, not a baby. A child didn't make a family; love did.

For one thing, she'd merely ache for him for the rest of her life. And what would she tell her child? The same pack of lies her mother had told her? She'd have no hope of being honest with her child and her life would be like her mother's—buried in secrets and lies, all motivated and rationalized and carried on generation after generation.

The overpowering realization of that made her head spin.

No, something else made her head spin. How could she have ignored that dizziness all these weeks?

Because the sensation wasn't distinct or long-lasting enough to make her stop and think about it, but now she realized that at least once or twice a day she'd been feeling a distant humming in her brain, the sense that, for one flash of a second, her head wasn't quite connected to the rest of her.

Truth was, she'd thought she was lovesick until Ashley described her symptoms. But Ashley had been wrong about being pregnant, and Tessa might be, too.

She squeezed her hands and started another prayer. "Please, God. Not this time. Not this time. *Not this time.*"

The whispered words were like a mantra, relieving her and calming her and reassuring her that this was nothing but a false alarm, like she'd had other times in her life. Still, they didn't erase the irony of how much she didn't want to be pregnant.

But it was time to find out. On a slow breath, she walked into the bathroom and closed her eyes, letting her pulse hammer a good five or six beats before she dared to look.

And there were the hard cold facts that couldn't be denied.

She grabbed the counter and let the impact wash over her, her fingers brushing the bright pink box and knocking it to the floor. Another test slipped out, still sealed in its pouch.

The backup, she used to call it. Should she? It wouldn't be the first time she refused to believe the results. Once she'd taken five tests because her period was ten days late.

Because all she wanted was a child of her own.

Wrong. She wanted a *family.* And there was a difference, at least to her. She didn't want a child of her own, and that was probably why she'd been dragging her heels on adopting or surrogacy or even foster parenting. She wanted the whole package: a father, a mother, kids.

Everything she'd never had. Everything she'd never get.

She turned her back on the extra test, certain this one was accurate enough, slowly sinking to the floor with burning eyelids and a heavy heart.

Why had she let him go? John was what she wanted, John was the man who could give her a family and a life. But she'd let him go. Stubborn, unwilling to lie and leave, now she'd live without him.

Why hadn't she run after him like in the movies? Why couldn't she profess her love and jump into that car and whisk off to a fairy-tale ending? Because her fairy tale included the people she'd have to give up forever. Without her friends—her family—there was no happy ending.

But without him, there was no happy beginning.

If you ever need anything, absolutely anything, or if you want to get a message to me, call Henry.

She did want to get a message to him. She had to tell him: *I know what I want now. Not a baby, but you. You and your family, our family, any family. All I want is you.*

Leaning against the wall, she pulled out her phone with a shaky hand. She carefully dialed the extra-long number, including an international code. Taking a breath, she pressed the phone to her ear and imagined Henry's face as he looked at the screen and realized his job just got more complicated.

The first ring startled her, it was so loud. The second one seemed to last forever. The third one matched the flutter of her heart as she slowly sank to the floor.

In the middle of the seventeenth ring, she hung up and stared at the two pink lines. They weren't nearly as beautiful as she'd always dreamed they'd be.

Chapter Thirty-three

The Red Russian was more than ready to harvest. Tessa kneeled before the long row, examining the largest leaves, the red veins like lifeblood to the brilliant green.

"Best kale yet," she whispered, breaking the best leaf close to the stem to enjoy a good sniff of the gorgeous smell of earth and vegetable. After the kale, she'd tackle the citrus crop, since those trees were heavy with fruit.

She started to pick the kale, kneeling, humming, letting the sun warm her head and air clear her thoughts. Every day had gotten a little easier. With the farming and friends to occupy her mind and a tiny life inside her to occupy her body, she hardly thought about the man who'd left four weeks ago. And five days. And seventeen hours.

The cell phone she now carried everywhere—just in case—vibrated with a welcome message. Yanking off a gardening glove, Tessa pulled the phone from the pocket of her cargo shorts, tapping the screen and trying not to let Zoe's name give her a punch of disappointment. Maybe another week and she'd stop hoping. Another month, surely. She squinted at the message.

Visitors on the way to garden. Brace yourself for cuteness overload.

Cuteness overload? With Zoe that could mean a hot guy or a sweet baby or some starry-eyed honeymooners on their way to tour the gardens. All her friends were being overly protective of Tessa's wild emotional swings these days.

No need. She was fine.

You sure are.

She snapped a few more leaves and heard his voice. The American voice that made her laugh. The British voice that made her sigh. And now silence just made her cry. She'd never tried that number again, certain he must have not wanted her to find him. Of course, it was safer this way.

But that didn't stop her from wondering where Ian was right now. Hopefully setting up his new life in New Zealand, kids by his side. Sighing, she crawled deeper into the bed of greens and cracked off kale leaves with a crisp, spare movement, getting a whole row finished before a childlike giggle floated over the fields, making Tessa look up.

By the rockrose hedges, she saw two children snagging blooms. So the cute overload was kids. Shielding the sun with one hand, she peered toward them, sizing up the guests. Usually garden tours were for the organic moms interested in growing all their food in their own backyards. But there were no adults in sight, only two tots plucking at the irresistibly bright flowers.

Tessa pushed up. Any minute a young mother would appear to limit the rockrose theft, so she wanted to assure them they could take all they wanted. The blooms were plentiful, doubling sometimes overnight, and the pink flowers made lovely little hair decorations for the girls.

But no mother came around from the villa side, so Tessa set down her basket and took off one gardening glove, using her bare hand to brush the dirt from her knees as she eyed the tiny tourists. Very tiny, if she could tell from this distance. Mere toddlers, scampering around, snagging more flowers, the music of their high-pitched voices ringing across the open fields.

She took a few steps, waiting until she got closer to call out to them, careful not to startle them.

As she got about twenty feet away, she could see they were not even five, a boy and a girl whispering as they picked the lower half of one hedge completely clean of fuchsia flowers.

"We have about five million!" the little boy called out. "Is that enough?"

Tessa laughed softly. "That's probably enough."

The girl turned then, her eyes widening as Tessa approached. Suddenly, she shook her head ferociously and grabbed the boy's arm, turning him so he could see Tessa.

"It's all right, honey," Tessa assured her, holding up her hand in greeting. "I'm the gardener and you can take some flowers."

They both stared at her.

"Is your mommy here?"

The girl's eyes widened and the boy shook his head.

"Daddy?"

Another shake.

Tessa reached them, taking in their porcelain white skin, free of a single freckle. Snowbird babies, she thought, on a winter Florida vacation.

"Are you with a grown-up?" she asked gently.

The little girl turned to the other boy, clearly a brother, and whispered in his ear. He nodded, listening before meeting Tessa's gaze. "Can she have the flowers?"

Tessa's heart folded a little. "Of course."

The girl shook her head, blue eyes flashing, and then whispered again, clutching his arm.

"Okay," he said, calming her. Looking at Tessa, he said, "She wants you to know they're a gift."

"For your mom?" she asked.

"For you." The man's voice, soft and low, came from behind the hedge, startling her and making the children turn.

"Is this our lady, Ian?" the boy called out.

The words jumbled for a moment, not making any sense.

Had he said…Tessa put a hand over her chest, as if that could contain her heart and catch her breath. *Ian?*

"I believe it is our lady." He stepped out from behind the thick hedge, slowly enough so the sunshine poured over him and highlighted his tentative smile. His hair was cut much shorter, his face shaved clean, but his eyes were as blue as—as the two sets staring at her.

"Oh, yeah. This is most definitely our lady."

She was dreaming. Dizzy, dazed, and dumbstruck.

The boy elbowed the girl. "Em! Now, like we practiced?"

She took a slow step forward, lifting a fistful of flowers, her creamy cheeks deepening with color as she
looked right at the ground.

"Hello, pretty Tessa." Her voice was little more than
a breath of sweet air, but it was enough to practically do
Tessa in.

"Oh…" With shaking hands, Tessa reached for the
offering with her ungloved hand, all blood and reason
draining from her head. "Hello."

The boy got next to her. "She's Emma. I'm Edward."

And I'm speechless. Tessa blinked and finally let her
gaze settle on the man, who walked up behind them,
putting his hands on their shoulders.

"I'm Ian Browning," he said softly, the British accent
as mesmerizing as the smile on his lips.

She couldn't speak. Her mouth opened, but nothing
would come out.

The little girl leaned over to whisper to her brother again.

"She wants to pick those yellow flowers," he said,
pointing at a row of hibiscus.

"Of course," Tessa said.

The kids took off, each one taking a different path
around her as they tore to the trees.

She took a slow breath and stared at the man in front
of her. "I don't understand this."

"Neither do I." He took a step closer, nothing but
warmth and love in his eyes.

"But…" All the questions welled up inside her. Why
was he here? With his children? Openly calling himself
Ian Browning and speaking in his native accent? But she
couldn't form a single question, because he was so close
all she could do was look. And when he reached for her

gloved hand, all she could do was let him take it and when he leaned close, all she could do was close her eyes and brace for impact.

"I don't understand how I could even imagine a life without you." He breathed the words into her ear. "And now I don't have to."

"John…"

He inched back. "Ian."

"How is that possible?"

A high-pitched squeal came from the kids, making them both turn to see them running wild around a lemon tree, Emma's curls flying and Eddie's legs whirring.

Ian pulled her closer as he looked from the kids to her. "They're mine."

She laughed. "I assumed as much."

He shook his head. "No, I mean they're *really* mine. To keep and raise out in the open."

Joy flooded her, like warm rain from her head to toes. "I'm so happy for you."

He brushed her hair off her face with one hand, still holding her other. "Bloody hell, I missed you, woman."

More joy cascaded. No, not joy. Love. A straight-out, full-on, explosion of true love. "How is it that you are out here in the open air, being…you? What happened?"

He sighed. "Lightning struck twice."

She shook her head, confused.

"The Vane brothers were killed in a prison riot," he explained. "They're dead, the gang's finished, and no one on this sweet earth is trying to hunt me down."

She took a moment to let that sink in, but it would take longer. Maybe a year. Maybe a lifetime. "Except me. I called Henry," she admitted.

"You did?"

"There was no answer."

"Probably because he was with me and thought it was a—why did you call?"

"Just to tell you…" Childish laughter rang again and she couldn't help but turn and look at them. "They're beautiful."

He just smiled. "I know. And you're going to love them."

She already did. But, deep inside, she fought the sensation, terrified to get too hopeful. "How could everything change that easily?"

"Nothing was easy," he assured her. "I had Henry on my side, though, and we fought, cajoled, begged, convinced, and finally charmed our way into getting me this far." He kissed her forehead. "I wasn't going to live without you. Or them."

"Ian, look! Lemons!" The boy's voice rose with excitement. "Can I pick one?"

"Of course," Tessa called back. "He's all better?"

"Completely." Ian beamed at them. "They're a little confused by the whole thing, but think I'm a new foster parent. I'm calling them the names they've grown up with and hoping to ease them into the truth as they get older. But now? I just want to love them."

"Of course." She stole another look, her heart swelling. "How could you do anything but?"

"Emma's having a hard time adjusting. She's shy and won't talk to anyone but Edward and a few stuffed animals."

Sympathy swamped her. "She needs—"

"A mother." He took one step closer and put his hands

on her shoulders. "They both do. A sweet, nurturing, tender mother who can teach them about potatoes and flowers and seashells and love."

Oh. She closed her eyes, full of a sensation she'd never, ever known before. Now this…this was the way she always imagined she'd feel the day she found out she was going to have a baby. Utterly at peace and in love.

"They need to love you the way I do," he whispered. "The way I will for the rest of my life." He tightened his grip. "That's why we're here," he said. "To get you."

Oh, God. "And go…somewhere?"

"A few places, but no more hiding," he assured her. "First, we're going to find that white-haired mayor."

"Lennox?"

He nodded. "We have a—no, sorry, *I* have a piece of paper to sign."

The marriage certificate. "You still need that?"

"I still want that. Don't you?"

More than anything. She nodded.

"Then we're going to fly by Ottawa to finalize some custody paperwork which will ensure that Emma and Eddie are ours."

Ours. Her heart squeezed. "And then?"

"A trip to London, I think."

"London?"

"My parents want to meet you and, of course, see the kids. I have a few other things I'd like to do there, but mostly see the people I left behind."

"And then…where?" New Zealand? Timbuktu? What did it matter if they were—

"Right here, of course. A resort in paradise, which

happens to be the closest thing to heaven on earth I can imagine."

"Here?" She put her hands to her mouth, the earthen smell on the glove invading her head, making her dizzy with joy. "You'll live here in Barefoot Bay?"

"We'll live here." He lifted her gloved hand and very slowly pulled it off, one finger at a time. She thought he would kiss her knuckles as he had the first time they stood in this garden together, but he reached into his pocket instead.

"To beginnings, pretty Tessa."

She laughed. "I've heard this the last time you stripped my glove off and started courting me."

"Not this." In his other hand, he held a blindingly bright diamond ring, the stone catching the sun and stealing her breath. "You haven't heard this."

"No," she managed to say. "I don't think I have."

He slipped the ring on her finger and closed his hand around hers. "This is real, Tessa. Real life. Real love. Marry me and let's be a real family of four."

"Actually..." She looked at the ring, then him, everything blurred by joy and hope and a sense of completion as palpable as the budding life around her. Stepping back, she took his hand and placed it on her stomach. "There are five of us now."

He drew back, his eyes wide, his lower lip quivering in disbelief. "Tessa." He barely whispered her name. "Are you sure?"

She reached up and touched his cheek, the diamond on her hand as lovely as the tears in his eyes. "I've never been so sure of anything in my whole life."

"Well...how are you? Is everything good? Are you okay...I mean, is everything..."

"I'm fine." She laughed at the stuttering of a stunned new father. "I'm perfect."

He folded her into his arms, lifting her off the ground for a kiss. "You sure are, pretty Tessa. You are perfect."

And so, it seemed, was her life.

Epi*blogue*

⁓

The Vixen of Vacation Vows

Blog Post—August 12

The maid of honor was a dead woman.

The bouquet was a squirming baby.

And the place was so littered with eye-candy, a girl could get whiplash from checking out the groomsmen.

But I'm getting ahead of myself. Let me back up, loyal followers, and explain why I chose to blog about the wedding I just attended in the most dreamy spot called Barefoot Bay.

Do you remember almost a year ago when I visited a Moroccan-inspired resort on the Gulf Coast of Florida? I had been invited for what was, admittedly, a "soft" opening, as they say. Soft? This was more like the squishy underbelly of a fat cow. Gooey like the dozen eggs I dropped in the grocery store parking lot. Limp like that guy I...never mind, you get the idea. They made some beginner's blunders and I let them have it, V3-style. (Slice and dice with a dash of vitriol and sarcasm.) I left the Casa Blanca resort quite underwhelmed, despite the lovely ladies who run the place and their high, high hopes.

Well, what a difference a little time makes!

It wasn't easy to get me to go back (there are thirteen thousand destination-wedding resorts in the world and only one Vixen to critique them for you, kittehs!) but some quite influential friends plied me with...er, twisted my arm. The lovely folks at AABC (that's the American Association of Bridal Consultants, not the a-alphabet) convinced me to attend a wedding as a VIP guest and what an affair it was! I must share all I experienced that day for it was a wedding like no other. Well, it was like many others. Two people got married. They seemed frightfully in love. The sandy stage was draped with pearls and lace and all manner of white stuff.

But it wasn't the wedding setting that did me in...it was the people who peppered that place that I can't forget.

Casa Blanca is one of the few mom and pop resorts left on this earth...and let me warn you, I don't mean Ma and Pa Kettle. Owner Lacey is a gorgeous ginger who not only handles a teenager and a toddler, she has a smokin' hot "pop" who was the architect for the place. Yikes. Can you say Matthew McConaughey with a wicked drafting pencil? And the Moroccan design was a result of their mutual love of the movie Casablanca. *Awww. I know, gives me a cavity, this sweetness. These two are a powerhouse couple and I see great success in their future. (The teenager's a handful, though. Good luck with that one.)*

The owner has an executive staff made up of her BFFs who—get this—have all been gal pals since college. Do you love it, ladies? Jocelyn is the spa manager and former life coach (and Olympic-quality list maker) who is all spit and polish and perfection. She's married to a carpenter who, I must say, could nail me anytime. (Oh, I crack myself up.) When they're not organizing and laying, um, carpet, then they are taking care of her doddering ol' dad who offered to knit me a scarf. A scarf? In Florida? He knit me two. Forgot about the first one, dear thing.

And here's something they have that I don't recall seeing at any other destination wedding resort—a hot air balloon so the bride and groom can literally fly off into the sunset. This pristine beach is stunning from any view, but from three thousand feet in the air with the one you just "I do'd"...best photo op ever.

Coincidentally, the wedding I attended was for the woman who owns and flies the balloon, Zoe, who could give any airhead a good name. Can you spell eccentric? Neither can I, so I'll describe. Our blonde bride carried her newborn baby in place of a bouquet (I told you this one never met a tradition she couldn't trample) but thankfully did not toss little Maya to any eligible bachelorettes.

While her three besties were bridesmaids, natch, the place of the maid-of-honor was held by a photograph of her great-aunt who went to be with the angels over a year ago. Honestly, the creativity of some people! Am totes stealing that idea if I ever scare up a husband. If I do, I pray he's tall, dark, loaded, and looks at me like I hung the moon...which, I should tell you, is exactly the doctor *this bride married. I might have to hate her. Oh, and the ring bearer was the doctor's son, a future rocket scientist named Evan who brought his dog and stole the show.*

And did I mention the food? I certainly did last year. The kitchen was definitely where the place fell short on my previous visit, but now they have a chef de cuisine (with a to-die-for English accent—tally ho, my lord!) who is married to the organic gardener, offering the all-important "farm to table" experience for the healthy elitists among you. (I know there are plenty!!)

Can I please coo about these two for a moment? Madly in love and running after a matched set of totally adorbs five-year-olds and growing another in their personal garden of Eden. They divide and conquer with the wee boy following Daddy about in the kitchen, nattering about tomahtoes and potahtoes (he's picked up his old man's pronunciations). The girlie hangs with her mom, riding shotgun on a tractor and making it look like so much fun, I almost wanted to go all country and redneck and shit.

Then that passed.

So, am I recommending Casa Blanca at Barefoot Bay for your destination wedding? Only if you want perfection on a platter. The atmosphere is elegant, but not ostentatious. The location is tropical, but not tasteless. The food is fantastic, the villas are romantic, the people are precious, and love is in the air.

And here's the best part—there's now an on-site wedding planning company called "Barefoot Brides." Clever girls! And these aren't your plain vanilla planners, friends. These ladies are former board members of AABC, so they know their business and their business is getting a bride down the aisle in style.

Arielle handles decor, Gussie will dress you fine, and

Willow feeds the hungry guests. I know you'll love them.

Full disclosure: these planners are (drinking) buddies of mine. I've followed them around the country as they visited resorts to recommend to their colleagues and I know a little bit about how they work. Their standards are as high as the bar tab when I'm in tow. So high that I understand they've made some kind of pact to never get married. You know what they say—always a wedding planner, never a bride.

What? They don't say that? Well, let's see what happens next in Barefoot Bay, hmm? I understand you can't help but kick off your shoes and fall in love. (Oh, shut up. They paid me to slip in the slogan.)

Vow to be happy!

Vix

When a hurricane roars through Lacey Armstrong's home on the coast of Barefoot Bay, she decides all that remains in the rubble is opportunity.

And nothing, especially not a hot, *younger* architect, is going to distract Lacey from finally making her dreams a reality...

Please turn this page for an excerpt from the first Barefoot Bay novel,

Barefoot in the Sand.

Chapter 1

♥

The kitchen windows shot out like cannons, one right after another, followed by the ear-splitting crash of the antique breakfront nose-diving to the tile floor.

Shit. Granny Dot's entire Old Country Rose service for twelve was in there.

Lacey pressed against the closet door, eyes closed, body braced, mind reeling. This was it. Everything she owned—a meager baking business, a fifty-year-old hand-me-down house, and a few antiques she'd collected over the years—was about to be destroyed, demolished, and dumped into Barefoot Bay by the hand of Hurricane Damien.

She stole a glance over her shoulder. Everything she owned, but not everything she had. No matter what happened to the house, she had to save her daughter.

"We need to get in the bathtub and under a mattress!" Lacey screamed over the train-like howl of one-hundred-and-ten-mile-per-hour winds.

Ashley cowered deeper into the corner of the closet, a stuffed unicorn clutched in one hand, her cell phone in the other. "I told you we should have evacuated!"

Only a fourteen-year-old would argue at a moment like this. "I can't get the mattress into the bathroom alone."

The storm was inside now, tearing the chandelier out of the dining room ceiling, clattering crystal everywhere. Pictures ripped off their hooks with vicious thuds and furniture skated across the oak floor. Overhead, half-century-old roof trusses moaned in a last-ditch effort to cling to the eaves.

They had minutes left.

"We have to hurry, Ash. On the count of—"

"I'm not leaving here," Ashley cried. "I'm too scared. I'm not going out there."

Lacey corralled every last shred of control. "We are. Together."

"We'll die out there, Mom!"

"No, but we'll die in here." At Ashley's wail, Lacey kneeled in front of her, sacrificing precious seconds. "Honey, I've lived on this island my whole life and this isn't the first hurricane." Just the worst. "We have to get in the tub and under the mattress. Now."

Taking a firm grip, she pulled Ashley to her feet, the cell-phone screen spotlighting a tear-stained face. God, Lacey wanted to tumble into Ashley's nest of hastily grabbed treasures and cry with her daughter.

But then she'd die with her daughter.

Ashley bunched the unicorn under her chin. "How could those weather people be so wrong?"

Good damn question. All day long, and into the night, the storm had been headed north to the Panhandle, not expected to do more than bring heavy rain and wind to the west coast of Florida. Until a few hours ago, when Hurricane Damien had jumped from a cat-three to a cat-four and veered to the east, making a much closer pass to the barrier island of Mimosa Key.

In the space of hours, ten thousand residents, including Lacey and Ashley, had been forced to make a rapid run-or-hide decision. A few tourists managed to haul butt over the causeway to the mainland, but most of the hurricane-experienced islanders were looking for mattress cover and porcelain protection about now. And praying. Hard.

Lacey cupped her hands on Ashley's cheeks. "We have to do this, Ashley. We can't panic, okay?"

Ashley nodded over and over again. "Okay, Mom. Okay."

"On the count of three. One, two—"

Three was drowned out by the gut-wrenching sound of the carport roof tearing away.

Lacey pushed open the closet door. Her bedroom was pitch black, but she moved on instinct, grateful the storm hadn't breached these walls yet.

"Get around to the other side of the bed," she ordered, already throwing back the comforter, searching wildly for a grip. "I'll pull, you push."

Ashley rallied and obeyed, sending a jolt of love and appreciation through Lacey. "Atta girl. A little more."

Right then the freight train of wind roared down the back hall, hurtling an antique mirror and shattering it against the bedroom door.

"It's coming!" Ashley screamed, freezing in fear.

Yes, it was. Like a monster, the storm would tear these old walls right down to the foundation Lacey's grandfather had laid when he'd arrived on Mimosa Key in the 1940s.

"Push the damn mattress, Ashley!"

Ashley gave it all she had and the mattress slid enough for Lacey to get a good grip. Grunting, she got the whole thing off the bed and dragged it toward the bathroom. They struggled to shove it through the door just as the wind knocked out one of the bedroom windows, showering glass and wood behind them.

"Oh my God, Mom. This is it!"

"No, this isn't it," Lacey hissed, trying to heave the mattress. "Get in!" She pushed Ashley toward the thousand-pound cast-iron claw-foot tub that had just transformed from last year's lavish expenditure into their sole means of survival.

In the shadows Lacey could see Ashley scramble into the tub, but the mattress was stuck on something in the door. She turned to maneuver the beast when the other window ruptured with a stunning crash.

Ducking from the flying debris, Lacey saw what had the mattress jammed.

Ashley's unicorn.

Window blinds came sailing in behind her. No time. No time for unicorns.

"Hurry, Mom!"

With a Herculean thrust, she freed the mattress, the force propelling her toward the tub, but in her mind all she could see was the goddamn unicorn.

The one Zoe brought to the hospital when Ashley was born and Ashley slept with every night until she was almost ten. In minutes Aunt Zoe's uni would be a memory, like everything else they owned.

From inside the tub Ashley reached up and pulled at Lacey's arm. "Get in!"

This time Lacey froze, the mattress pressing down with the full weight of what they were losing. Everything. Every picture, every gift, every book, every Christmas ornament, every—

"Mom!"

The bathroom door slammed shut behind her, caught in a crosswind, making the room eerily quiet for a second.

In that instant of suspended time, Lacey dove for the unicorn, scooping it up with one hand while managing to brace the mattress with the other.

"What are you doing?" Ashley hollered.

"Saving something." She leaped into the tub on top of her shrieking daughter, dropping the stuffed animal so she could hoist the mattress over and seal them in a new kind of darkness.

The door shot back open, the little window over the toilet gave way, and tornado-strength winds whipped through the room. Under her, Lacey could hear her daughter sobbing, feel her quivering with fright, her coltish legs squeezing for dear life.

And life was dear. Troubled, stressful, messy, not everything she dreamed it would be, but dear. Lacey Armstrong was not about to give it up to Mother Nature's temper tantrum.

"Reach around me and help me hold this thing down," Lacey demanded, her fingernails breaking as she dug into the quilted tufts, desperate for a grip.

Her arms screaming with the effort, she clung to the mattress, closed her eyes, and listened to the sounds of that dear life literally falling apart around her.

It wasn't much, this old house she'd inherited from her grandparents, built with big dreams and little money, but it was all she had.

No, it wasn't, she reminded herself again. All she had was quivering and crying underneath her. Everything else was just stuff. Wet, ruined, storm-tattered stuff. They were alive and they had each other and their wits and dreams and hopes.

"This is a nightmare, Mom." Ashley's sob silenced Lacey's inner litany of life-support platitudes.

"Just hold on, Ash. We'll make it. I've been through worse." Hadn't she?

Wasn't it worse to return to Mimosa Key a pregnant college dropout, facing her mother's bitter and brutal disappointment? Wasn't it worse to stare into David Fox's dreamy, distant eyes and say "I'm going to keep this baby," only for him to announce he was on his way to a sheep farm in Patagonia?

Pata-frickin'-gonia. It still ticked her off, fourteen years later.

She was not going to die, damn it. And neither was Ashley. She stole a look over her shoulder, meeting her daughter's petrified gaze.

"Listen to me," Lacey demanded through gritted teeth. "I'm not going to let anything happen to you."

Ashley managed a nod.

They just had to hang on and… pray. Because most people would be cutting some sweet deals with God at a time like this. But Lacey wasn't most people, and she didn't make deals with anybody. She made plans. Lots of plans that never—

A strong gust lifted the mattress, pulling a scream from

her throat as rain and wind and debris whipped over them, and then part of the ceiling thudded down on the mattress. With the weight of saturated drywall and insulation holding their makeshift roof in place, Lacey could let go of the mattress. Relieved, she worked a space on the edge where the tub curved down to give them some air and finally let her body squeeze in next to Ashley.

Now Lacey could think of something else besides survival.

After survival, comes… what? Facing the stark truth that everything was gone. What was she going to do with no home, no clothes, no struggling cake-baking business, and maybe no customers remaining on Mimosa Key to buy her cookies and cupcakes?

The answer was the thunderous roar of the rest of the second floor being ripped away as if an imaginary giant had plucked a weed from his garden. Instantly rain dumped on them.

Once the roof was gone the vacuum dissipated, and, except for the drumbeat of rain on the mattress, it was almost quiet.

"Is this the eye of the storm?" Ashley asked.

Lacey adjusted her position again to curl around Ashley's slender frame. "I don't know, honey. Hey, look what I brought you."

She fished out the unicorn from behind her and laid it on Ashley's chest. Even in the darkness she could see Ashley smile, her eyes bright with tears.

"Aunt Zoe's uni. Thank you, Mommy."

Mommy just about folded her heart in half.

"Shhh." She stroked Ashley's hair, trying to be grateful for the rare moment when her daughter didn't roll her eyes or whip out her cell phone to text a friend. "We're gonna be fine, angel. I promise."

But could she keep that promise? When the storm passed, the home her grandfather had christened Blue Horizon House would be little more than a memory sitting on a stretch of pristine beach known as Barefoot Bay.

But Mimosa Key would still be here. Nothing could wipe away this barrier island or the people who called this strip of land home. Like Lacey, most of the residents were the children and grandchildren of the first group of twentieth-century pioneers who'd built a rickety wooden causeway to take them to an island haven in the Gulf of Mexico.

And nothing could rid Mimosa Key of its natural resources, like magical Barefoot Bay with its peach-toned sunsets or the fluffy red flowers that exploded like fireworks every spring, giving the island its name. Nothing could stop the reliable blue moon that sparkled like diamonds on the black velvet Gulf every night.

If Mimosa Key survived, so would Lacey.

And there is such a thing as insurance, a pragmatic voice insisted.

Insurance would cover the value of the house, and she owned the land, so Lacey could rebuild. Maybe this was her chance to finally turn the big old beach cottage into a B and B, a dream she'd nurtured for years, one she'd promised both her grandparents she'd pursue when they'd left her the house and all the land around it.

But life had gotten in the way of that promise. And now she had nothing.

Instead of wallowing in that reality, she let the B and B idea settle over her heart once again, the idea of finally,

finally seeing one of her dreams come true carrying her through the rest of the storm while Ashley drifted off into a fitful sleep.

By the time the howling had softened to a low moan and the rain had slowed to a steady drizzle, the first silver threads of dawn were weaving through the air space she'd made. It was time to face the aftermath of the storm. Using all the strength she had left, Lacey managed to push the soaked mattress to the floor.

"Oh my God." Ashley's voice cracked with whispered disbelief as she emerged. "It's all gone."

Yes, it was. A dilapidated old house that was more trouble than it was ever worth had been washed away by Hurricane Damien's clean-up campaign. Lacey's heart was oddly light in the face of the devastation. Buoyed, in fact, with possibilities.

"Don't worry," she said, gingerly navigating the debris, peering into the early morning light. "It's not the end of the world." It was the beginning.

"How can you say that, Mom? There's nothing left!"

A few drops of warm tropical rain splattered her face, but Lacey wiped the water from her cheek and stepped over broken wall studs wrapped in shredded, sopping-wet attic insulation.

"We have insurance, Ashley."

"Mom! Our house is gone!"

"No, the building's gone. The beach is here. The sun will shine. The palm fronds will grow back."

Her imagination stirred again, nudged alive by the reality of what she saw around her. She could do this. This land—and the insurance money—could be used to make a dream come true.

Beside her Ashley sniffed, wiping a fresh set of tears. "How can you talk about palm fronds? We don't even have a—oh!" She dropped to her knees to retrieve a muddy video-game remote. "My Wii!"

"Ashley." Lacey reached for her, pulling her up to hold her close. "Baby, we have each other. We're alive, which is pretty much a miracle."

Ashley just squeezed her eyes shut and nodded, working so hard to be strong and brave.

"I know it hurts, Ashley, but this"—she took the broken remote and pitched it—"is just stuff. We'll get more, better stuff. What matters is that we've made it through and, you know, I'm starting to think this hurricane was the best thing that ever happened to us."

Ashley eyes popped open with an incredulous look. "Are you nuts?"

Maybe she was, but insane optimism was all she had right now.

"Think about it, Ash. We can do anything with this property now. We don't have to pay to remodel a sixty-year-old house; we can start from scratch and make it amazing." Her voice rose as the idea sprouted to life and took hold of her heart. "You know I've always dreamed of opening an inn or B and B, something all mine that would be an oasis, a destination."

Ashley just closed her eyes as if she couldn't even compute an oasis right then. "But if you couldn't figure out a way to make it happen when you had an actual house, how can you now?"

The truth stung, but Lacey ignored the pain. This time she wouldn't make excuses, that was how. She wouldn't be scared of not finishing what she started and she wouldn't let anyone's disapproval make her doubt herself. Not anymore.

"Old Mother Nature just handed us a 'get out of jail free' pass, kiddo," she said, giving Ashley's shoulder a squeeze. "And you know what? We're taking it."

THE DISH

Where Authors Give You the Inside Scoop

♥ ♥ ♥ ♥ ♥ ♥ ♥ ♥ ♥ ♥ ♥ ♥ ♥ ♥ ♥

From the desk of Roxanne St. Claire

Dear Reader,

Years ago, I picked up a romance novel about a contemporary "marriage of convenience" and I recall being quite skeptical that the idea could work in anything but a historical novel. How wrong I was! I not only enjoyed the book, but *Separate Beds* by LaVyrle Spencer became one of my top ten favorite books of all time. (Do yourself a favor and dig up this classic if you haven't read it!) Since then, I've always wanted to put my own spin on a story about two people who are in a situation where they need to marry for reasons other than love, knowing that their faux marriage is doomed.

I finally found the perfect characters and setup for a marriage of convenience story when I returned to Barefoot Bay to write BAREFOOT BY THE SEA, my most recent release in the series set on an idyllic Gulf Coast island in Florida. I knew that sparks would fly and tears might flow when I paired Tessa Galloway, earth mother longing for a baby, with Ian Browning, a grieving widower in the witness protection program. I suspected that it would be a terrific conflict to give the woman who despises secrets a man who has to keep one in order to stay alive, with the added complication of a situation that can only be resolved with a fake, arranged marriage. However, I never dreamed just how much I would love writing that marriage of convenience! I should have known, since I adored the first one I'd ever read.

Throughout most of BAREFOOT BY THE SEA, hero Ian is forced to hide who he really is and why he's in Barefoot Bay. And that gave me another story twist I love to explore: the build-up to the inevitable revelation of a character's true identity and just how devastating that is for everyone (including the reader!). I had a blast being in Ian's head when he fought off his demons and past to fall hard into Tessa's arms and life. And I ached and grew with Tessa as the truth became crystal clear and shattered her fragile heart.

The best part, for me, was folding that marriage of convenience into a story about a woman who wants a child of her own but has to give up that hope to help, and ultimately lose, a man who needs her in order to be reunited with his own children. If she marries him, he gets what he needs... but he can't give her the one thing she wants most. Will Tessa surrender her lifelong dream to help a man who lost his? She can if she loves him enough, right? Maybe.

Ironically, when the actual marriage of convenience finally took place on the page, that ceremony felt more real than any of the many weddings I've ever written. I hope readers agree. And speaking of weddings, stay tuned for more of them in Barefoot Bay when the Barefoot Brides trilogy launches next year! Nothing like an opportunity to kick off your shoes and fall in love, which is never convenient but always fun!

Happy reading!

Roxanne St. Claire

♥ ♥ ♥ ♥ ♥ ♥ ♥ ♥ ♥ ♥ ♥ ♥ ♥ ♥ ♥

From the desk of Kristen Ashley

Dear Reader,

As it happens when I start a book and the action plays out in my head, characters pop up out of nowhere.

See, I don't plot, or outline. An idea will come to me and *Wham!* My brain just flows with it. Or a character will come to me and all the pieces of his or her puzzle start tumbling quickly into place and the story moves from there. Either way, this all plays in my mind's eye like a movie and I sit at my keyboard doing my darnedest to get it all down as it goes along.

In my Dream Man series, I started it with *Mystery Man* because Hawk and Gwen came to me and I was desperate to get their story out. I'm not even sure that I expected it to be a series. I just *needed* to tell their story.

Very quickly I was introduced to Kane "Tack" Allen and Detective Mitch Lawson. When I met them through Gwen, I knew instantly—with all the hotness that was them—that they both needed their own book. So this one idea I had of Hawk and Gwen finding their happily ever after became a series.

Brock "Slim" Lucas showed up later in *Mystery Man* but when he did, he certainly intrigued me. Most specifically the lengths he'd go to do his job. I wondered why that fire was in his belly. And suddenly I couldn't wait to find out.

In the meantime, my aunt Barb, who reads every one of my books when they come out, mentioned in passing she'd like to see one of my couples *not* struggle before they capitulated to the attraction and emotion swirling around them. Instead, she wanted to see the relationship build and grow, not the hero and heroine fighting it.

This intrigued me, too, especially when it came to Brock, who had seen a lot and done a lot in his mission as a DEA agent. I didn't want him to have another fight on his hands, not like that. But also, I'd never done this, not in all the books I'd written.

I'm a girl who likes a challenge.

But could I weave a tale that was about a man and a woman in love, recognizing and embracing that love relatively early in the story, and then focus the story on how they learn to live with each other, deal with each other's histories, family, and all that life throws at them on a normal basis? Would this even be interesting?

Luckily, life *is* interesting, sometimes in good ways, sometimes not-so-good.

Throwing Elvira and Martha into the mix, along with Tess's hideous ex-husband and Brock's odious ex-wife, and adding children and family, life for Brock and Tess, as well as their story, was indeed interesting (and fun) to write—when I didn't want to wring Olivia's neck, that is.

And I found there's great beauty in telling a tale that isn't about fighting attraction because of past issues or history (or the like) and besting that to find love; instead delving into what makes a man and a woman, and allowing them to let their loved one get close, at the same time learning how to depend on each other to make it through.

I should thank my aunt Barb. Because she had a great idea that led to a beautiful love story.

Kristen Ashley

♥ ♥ ♥ ♥ ♥ ♥ ♥ ♥ ♥ ♥ ♥ ♥ ♥ ♥ ♥

From the desk of Eileen Dreyer

Dear Reader,

The last thing I ever thought I would do was write a series. I thought I was brave putting together a trilogy. Well, as usual, my characters outsmarted me, and I now find myself in the middle of a nine-story series about Drake's Rakes, my handsome gentleman spies. But I don't wait well as a reader myself. How do I ask my own readers to wait nine books for any resolution?

I just couldn't do it. So I've divided up the Rakes into three trilogies based on the heroines. The first was The Three Graces. This one I'm calling Last Chance Academy, where the heroines went to school. I introduced them all in my short e-novel *It Begins With A Kiss*, and continue in ONCE A RAKE with Sarah Clarke, who has to save Scotsman Colonel Ian Ferguson from gunshot, assassin, and the charges of treason.

I love Sarah. A woman with an unfortunate beginning, she is just trying to save the only home she's ever really had from penury, an estate so small and isolated that her best friend is a six-hundred-pound pig. Enter Ian. Suddenly she's facing off with smugglers, spies, assassins, and possible eviction. I call my Drake's Rakes series Romantic Historical Adventure, and I think there is plenty of each in ONCE A RAKE. Let me know at www .eileendreyer.com, my Facebook page (Eileen Dreyer), or on Twitter @EileenDreyer. Now I need to get back. I have five more Rakes to threaten.

Eileen Dreyer

♥ ♥ ♥ ♥ ♥ ♥ ♥ ♥ ♥ ♥ ♥ ♥ ♥ ♥ ♥

From the desk of Anne Barton

Dear Reader,

Regrets. We all have them. Incidents from our distant (or not-so-distant) pasts that we'd like to forget. Photos we'd like to burn, boyfriends we never should have dated, a night or two of partying that got slightly out of control. Ahem.

In short, there are some stories we'd rather our siblings didn't tell in front of Grandma at Thanksgiving dinner.

Luckily for me, I grew up in the pre-Internet era. Back then, a faux pas wasn't instantly posted or tweeted for the world to see. Instead, it was recounted in a note that was ruthlessly passed through a network of tables in the cafeteria—a highly effective means of humiliation, but not nearly as permanent as the digital equivalent, thank goodness.

Even so, I distinctly remember the sinking feeling, the dread of knowing that my deep dark secret could be exposed at any moment. If you've ever had a little indiscretion that you just can't seem to outrun (and who hasn't?), you know how it weighs on you. It can be almost paralyzing.

In ONCE SHE WAS TEMPTED, Miss Daphne Honeycote has such a secret. Actually, she has two of them—a pair of scandalous portraits. She posed for them when she was poor and in dire need of money for her sick mother. But after her mother recovers and Daphne's circumstances improve considerably, the shocking portraits come back to haunt her, threatening to ruin her reputation, her friendships, and her family's good name.

Much to Daphne's horror, Benjamin Elliott, the Earl of Foxburn, possesses one of the paintings—and therefore, the power to destroy her. But he also has the means to help her discover the whereabouts of the second portrait before its unscrupulous owner can make it public. Daphne must decide whether to trust the brooding earl. But even if she does, he can't fully protect her—it's ultimately up to Daphne to come to terms with her scandalous past. Just as we all eventually must.

In the meantime, I suggest seating your siblings on the opposite end of the Thanksgiving table from Grandma.

Happy reading,

Anne Barton

♥   ♥

From the desk of Mimi Jean Pamfiloff

Dear Reader,

After living a life filled with nothing but bizarre, Emma Keane just wants normal. Husband, picket fence, vegetable garden, and a voice-free head. Normal. And Mr. Voice happens to agree. He'd like nothing more than to be free from the stubborn, spiteful, spoiled girl he's spent the last twenty-two years listening to day and night. Unfortunately for him, however, escaping his only companion in the universe won't be so easy. You see, there's a damned good reason Emma is the only one who can hear him—though he's not spilling the beans just yet—and there's a damned bad reason he can't leave Emma: He's imprisoned. And to be set free, Mr. Voice is going to have to convince Emma to travel from New York City to the darkest corner of Mexico's most dangerous jungle.

But not only will the perilous journey help Emma become the brave woman she's destined to be, it will also be the single most trying challenge Mr. Voice has ever had to face. In his seventy thousand years, he's never met a mortal he can't live without. Until now. Too bad she's going to die helping him. What's an ancient god to do?

Mimi